Julius Hutchinson, Charles Harding Firth, Lucy Apsley Hutchinson

Memoirs of the Life of Colonel Hutchinson

Governor of Nottingham. Vol. 2

Julius Hutchinson, Charles Harding Firth, Lucy Apsley Hutchinson

Memoirs of the Life of Colonel Hutchinson
Governor of Nottingham. Vol. 2

ISBN/EAN: 9783337166618

Printed in Europe, USA, Canada, Australia, Japan

Cover: Foto ©Raphael Reischuk / pixelio.de

More available books at **www.hansebooks.com**

MEMOIRS OF THE LIFE

OF

COLONEL HUTCHINSON

GOVERNOR OF NOTTINGHAM

By his Widow LUCY

EDITED FROM THE ORIGINAL MANUSCRIPT
By the REV. JULIUS HUTCHINSON

*TO WHICH ARE ADDED THE LETTERS OF COLONEL HUTCHINSON
AND OTHER PAPERS*

REVISED WITH ADDITIONAL NOTES
By C. H. FIRTH, M.A.

With Ten Etched Portraits of Eminent Personages

IN TWO VOLUMES
VOL. II.

LONDON
JOHN C. NIMMO
14, KING WILLIAM STREET, STRAND, W.C.
1885

PUBLISHER'S NOTE.

Three hundred copies of this book printed for England, and two hundred, with an American Imprint, for sale in that country. No more will be printed.

LIST OF ETCHED PORTRAITS.

VOL. II.

MEMOIRS

COLONEL HUTCHINSON.

To return to Nottingham : after the prince had
marched away out of the country, the enemy without was still designing against the garrison, and
the governor's enemies within were still perplexing
all his affairs.   Upon the eleventh of May, a letter
was found by a wench in the night-time, dropped
in the shoemakers' booths ; which letter was directed
to Sir Richard Biron, informing him that "the
business between them went on with good success,
and that the time drawing on, it behoved him to be
very diligent, and desiring him to burn the letter ; "
which was subscribed, " Your careful servant,
A. C. ; " and a postscript written, " Fail nothing by
any means, and there shall be no neglect in me."
The governor took all courses that could be imagined
to discover this person, but could never find him

VOL. II.   A

out.[1] About this time some troopers·going by a
house, where one Henry Wandall, a debauched
malignant apothecary, had lived (but the house was
now empty, and he had the key of it), they perceived a smoke to come out of it, and went in and
found some kindled sticks, laid in a potsherd, just
by a rotten post, under the staircase, with hurds[2]
and other combustible things about it, which it was
evident were put there to fire the house, but for
what reason, or by whom, was not discovered.

The governor hearing of some troops of the
enemy in the Vale, had a design to go thither, and
acquainted the committee with it; telling them he
would take out all the horse, and himself march
with the body, and leave a foot company and thirty
horse behind him at the bridges, so as by that
time he was ·marched by Wiverton, which would
give Shelford the alarm, the thirty horse, which
were more than Shelford had to send out, should
face the house on that side next Nottingham, and

---

[1] "The governor charged the wench to say nothing of
it, and the next day had all the Covenant rolls searched,
to see if he could own the hand, but could find none to do
it.   Then, the sabbath·day, after sermon was ended in the
afternoon, he called the whole town together, and read
the letter to them, and offered £50 to whomsoever could
either discover the hand, or anything of the plot, but he
could never hear more of it."—Note-Book.

[2] Hurds or hards—coarse flax, the refuse of flax or
hemp.—Halliwell.

the foot should march a private way through the
closings;[1] so that if Shelford's horse or foot should
come forth against those thirty horse, the foot might
get between them and home, or take any advantage
that was offered. All this the committee very well
approved, and so it was resolved to put it in execution the next night after, because it would take
some time to provide horses for the musketeers.
The governor coming out of the committee, met
Captain White upon the parade in the castle-yard,
and acquainted him with the design, who, with a
dejected countenance and a faint voice, pretended
to approve it, but desired the thirty horse who
were to stay some hours behind, might be of his
troop; to which the governor assented to gratify
his desire, though he told him, he was very loath
to spare any of that troop, who were old soldiers
and well acquainted with the country;[2] but he desired him the rest might not fail to be ready. The
captain promised they should, and so departed.
When the governor had made ready all the horse
and dragoons, and was himself just ready to march
out with them, being at Colonel Thornhagh's house,

---

[1] Closings, closes, fields, vulg. Notts. *closen.*—J. H.
[2] The Note-Book calls this troop "the best armed and
fullest in the garrison, for it consisted of fourscore or
thereabouts." The whole of this incident is related at
much greater length in the Note-Book. Whitelocke, who
mentions the skirmish, makes the date of it June 1644.

White came in; the governor, not doubting of his intention to go, asked him if his troop were ready? He replied, "They are out upon service; thirty," said he, "are gone by your consent, and the rest went to fetch in a malignant at Ekering; some few odd ones remain, which you may have if you will." The governor desired him to go himself and assist him; the captain desired to be excused, for "to what purpose should he go when his troop was not there?" The governor went from thence to his own lodgings, and meeting the committee, acquainted them how White had served him, who seemed to resent it very ill at that time; and while they were discoursing of it, White's officer came up with warrants to be signed for hay for the quarters, which being offered the governor, he tore, and said he would sign no warrants for such a disorderly troop, as would do no service but what they list, whose officers knew neither how to give nor obey commands.

Notwithstanding this discouragement, to want eighty of his best men, the governor went out with the rest, and when he had drawn them into the Trent Lanes, one of his spies came in with intelligence that at a town in the Vale, called Sierston, and at another next it, called Elston, there were two hundred horse quartered, who being come in weary and secure, might easily be surprised that night. The governor, calling the captains together,[1] imparted the intelligence, and they were all forward to go on in the design, except Captain Pendock, who persuaded much against it; but while they were discoursing another intelligencer came in, to second the former; whereupon the governor told the captains, that if they would go, he was resolved to do something that night, and because Captain Pendock was best acquainted with that side of the country, he appointed him to lead on the forlorn hope, which accordingly he did, but with such sloth and muttering, that in two or three miles' riding, the governor was forced to send up some officers to him, to hasten him on. Neither was this from cowardice, but only humour and faction, for the man was stout enough when he had a mind to it, but now he rid along, muttering that it was to no purpose, and when he came to Saxondale Gorse, purposely lost himself and his forlorn hope; which the governor missing, was much troubled, fearing that by some misadventure they might have been enclosed and cut off between the enemies' garrisons; but when they came to Saxondale Lane, Pendock and his forlorn hope were found safe in the rear of the body. The governor perceiving Pendock's backwardness, had sent out some parties,[2] one troop under Captain-lieutenant

---

[1] "The governor called Captain Palmer, Captain-lieutenant Palmer, and the rest of the officers together."—Note-Book.

[2] "The governor then sent Captain-lieutenant Palmer

Palmer, and another party with Cornet Peirson, to
some near towns, to execute some of the committee's warrants, in fetching in delinquents; when the
cornet came back with an alarum that two or three
hundred horse were quartered at Elston and Sierston,
which he must either fight with or retreat. Captain
Pendock was again wonderful unwilling to go on,
and said it would be day before they should come
there; but the governer bade those that would,
follow him, for he would go; and accordingly he
went, and when he came to the town, drew up his
men at the town's end in a body, from which he
sent in some parties, to fall into the town, himself
staying with the body between them and Newark,
to defend them from any of the enemies that might
have come upon them: so they brought out two
captain-lieutenants,[1] some cornets, and other gentlemen of quality, thirty troopers, and many more
horses and arms; Captain Thimbleby, absolutely

with his troop to fetch in one Shipman of Scarrington,
and having before, when he perceived Pendock's backwardness, sent Cornet Peirson with a party of men, in to
Carcolston, to receive further intelligence, and bring in
some malignants, according to the committee's warrants,
said he must go to fetch in a party he had sent out, and
came to Carcolston, where, as soon as he came, the alarum
was brought to him, that two or three hundred horse were
quartered at Sierston."—Note-Book.

[1] Captain - lieutenants Herne and Cartwright. — Note-
Book.

refusing quarter, was killed. The governor sent into the town to command all his men immediately away; but a lieutenant and cornet making not haste to obey,[1] while they stayed for some drink, were surprised by a party that came from Newark, before the corporal, the governor had sent to fetch them off, was well out of the town; but with those he had taken, and all the booty, and many horses and beasts fetched from malignants in the enemies' quarters, the governor came safe home, to the great discontent of Captain White, who was something out of countenance at it. This may .serve, instead of many more, to show how hard a task he had to carry on the service, with such refractory, malicious persons under him.

About this time it happened, that the engineer being by, Captain Pendock took occasion to rail at the town-works, and Hooper making answers which drew on replies, Pendock struck him, whereupon the man, angry, laid his hand upon his sword and half drew it out, but thrust it in again. The maid ran affrighted into the kitchen, where was one Henry Wandall, who presently called some musketeers, disarmed Mr. Hooper, and sent him prisoner to the governor; who, asking him upon what account he came so, he told him he had no reason to accuse himself; if those that sent him had any-

---

[1] Lieutenant Smith and Cornet Peirson.—Note-Book.

thing against him he was ready to answer it. After
the governor had expected till about midnight and
nothing came, he sent for Wandall, and inquiring
why and by whose authority he committed Mr.
Hooper prisoner? He answered, "for drawing
his sword, he, as an officer of the garrison, had
sent him up." The governor asked who made him
an officer? and taking it upon him, why he did
not send up both parties, but only one in a quarrel?
and he being able to give no answer, but such as
showed it was done out of malice, the governor
committed him for his insolency, who being but a
common soldier, presumed to make an officer.
prisoner, without rendering an account to the
governor, and let the other engaged in the quarrel
go free. The next day after this, Plumptre
came to the Trent bridges, where, being stopped,
he sent up a pass which he had procured from my
lord general, to come and stay in the town during
his own pleasure; which, when the governor saw
he sent him word, that in regard of my lord
general's pass he might stay at his own house, but
bade him take heed, as he would answer it, that he
meddled not to make any mutiny or commotion in
the garrison; to which he sent an insolent reply,
that he was glad the governor was taught manners;
he was come to town for some business, and when
he had occasion he would repair to the committee.
The committee, hearing this, were very sensible of

his insolent carriage, and drew up articles against
him, which were signed by six of their hands, and
sent up to Mr. Millington to be preferred against
him in the house of parliament, and to be showed
to my lord general, as the lieutenant-colonel should
see occasion ; whom the governor sent immediately
to the general, to acquaint him with the reason why
Dr. Plumptre had been forced to procure his pass
for his protection.   The governor took this occasion
to send to the general about his cannoniers, whom
some days before he had been forced to confine as
prisoners to their chamber till the general's pleasure
could be known concerning them ; for, at the insti-
gation of Captain Palmer, all the ministers in town,[1]
and, to make the cry the louder, certain loose
malignant priests, which they had gotten to join
with them, had most violently urged, in a petition
to the committee, that these men might be turned
out of the town for being separatists ; so that the
governor was forced, against his will, to confine
them to prevent mutiny, though they were otherwise honest, obedient, and peaceful.   After the
lieutenant-colonel was gone, with letters concerning
these matters, to the general, Plumptre behaved
himself most insolently and mutinously, and he and
Mason entering into a confederacy, had contrived
some articles against the governor for committing

---

[1] " Except Mr. Huet."—Note-Book.

Wandall;[1] but when they tried and found they could
do no good with them, Mason came to the governor
and was most saucily importunate for his release,
which, by reason of the insolent manner of seeking it, the governor would not grant.

The general, upon the governor's letters, sent
down a letter to Plumptre, to discharge him the
garrison, and another to the governor to release
the cannoniers; which he accordingly did, to the
satisfaction of his own conscience, which was not
satisfied in keeping men prisoners for their consciences, so long as they lived honestly and in-
offensively. But it caused a great mutiny in the
priests against him, and they blew up as many of
their people as they could, to join in faction against
the governor, not caring now what men they entered
into confederacy with, nor how disaffected to the
cause, so they were but bitter enough against the
separatists; which the cunning malignants perceiving, they now all became zealots, and laughed

---

[1] " Plumptre was very seditious and active in the meantime against the governor, and Captain Dolphin being in
the town, was called by him into a room at Widow
Millington's, where he was questioned whether he remembered some passages concerning his imprisonment, which
he answering he had almost forgot, Plumptre bade him
call them to memory, for he should be questioned upon
oath concerning them; Mason also was in the room, and
they were contriving some articles against the governor
for committing Wandall."—Note-Book.

in secret to see how they wrought these men to
ruin their own cause and champions.

Plumptre not taking notice of the general's
letters, the governor sent him word he expected he
should obey them and depart. Plumptre replied,
his business was done, and he would go ; but in
spite of his teeth he would have a guard. The
lieutenant-colonel would have put in the articles
into the parliament, which the committee had sent
up against Plumptre, but Mr. Millington pretending
all kindness and service to the governor, would
needs undertake it, and desired the lieutenant-
colonel to trouble none of the governor's friends in
any business he had to do, but to leave it in his
hands, who would employ all his powers, and serve
him with all vigilance and faithfulness, against all
persons whatsoever; and whereas he heard the
governor had some thoughts of coming to London,
he wished him not to trouble himself, but to charge
him with anything he had to do. Notwithstanding
all this, the governor went to London, having some
occasions thither. A little before his going, he
and the rest of the committee had required Mr.
Salusbury, their treasurer, to give in his accounts,
which he being either unwilling or unable to do,
he bent his utmost endeavours to raise a high
mutiny and faction against the governor ; and
Captain White was never backward in any mischief; these, with Plumptre and Mason, made a

close confederacy, and called home Chadwick to
their assistance, having engaged the persecuting
priests and all their idolaters, upon an insinuation
of the governor's favour to separatists. During
Colonel Thornhagh's sickness, the governor undertook the command of his horse regiment, while it
was quartered in the garrison; and made the men
live orderly, and march out upon designs more
frequently than they used to do when their colonel
was well, upon whose easiness they prevailed to
do what they list; and some of them, who were
great plunderers, were connived at, which the
governor would by no means suffer. Wherefore
these men were, by the insinuations of their officers
and the wicked part of the committee, drawn into
the faction, which was working in secret awhile,
and at last broke into open prosecutions. They
had determined that as soon as the governor was
gone, White, the devil's exquisite solicitor, should
also follow to London, but knew not what to do for
a pretence to send him upon the public purse;
when wickedness, which never long wants the
opportunity it waits for, found one soon out, for
the committee of both kingdoms had sent a command for all the horse in Nottingham to repair to
Sir John Meldrum in Lancashire; the town was
put upon a hasty petition that their horse might
not go, and Captain White must carry it, who
pretended to have known nothing of it half an hour

before, yet he was ready, and Dr. Plumptre, too, prepared to make good his brags, and go with his convoy. Presently after he was gone, the engine of mischief, comes to town, Colonel Chadwick, whom Mr. Salusbury receives with great joy and exultance, boasting, to use his own words, that they would now mump the governor. At the mayor of the town's house he was entertained with much wine, whereof Mr. Ayscough, a committee man, having taken a pretty large proportion, coming that night to supper to the castle, told the lieutenant-colonel and the governor's wife, that he would advise them to acquaint the governor there was mischief hatching against him, and that Chadwick was come to town on purpose to effect it, which though the fellow discovered in his drink, was true enough, and he himself was one of the conspiring wicked ones.

To fortify their party, in all haste they endeavoured to raise a new troop of dragoons, under one Will Hall, a debauched malignant fellow, and therefore one of the governor's mortal enemies; but some of the honester townsmen perceiving the design, and not yet being seduced, would not raise him any horse, so at that season the troop was not formed.

And now Captain White came home, when it was observed that after his return he would not allow the governor that name, but only called him

Colonel Hutchinson, and when any one else termed
him governor, would decline the acknowledgment
of that name ; then cajoling his fellow horse-officers
and the troopers, they, through his insinuations,
everywhere began to detract from the governor, and
to magnify Captain White, and not only to derogate
from the governor, but from all persons that were
well-affected to him.   Now was there a petition drawn up to be presented to the committee
of both kingdoms, desiring that Mr. Millington
might be sent down to compose the differences
which were in the garrison.   The lieutenant-
colonel and some others refusing to sign it, Captain
White told them it was a pretence, which Mr. Millington desired the favour of them that they would
make, to obtain leave for him to come down and
visit his wife and children, whom he had a longing
desire to see, and knew not any other way to bring
it about.   The gentlemen, to gratify Mr. Millington, signed it ; and he himself at London, with the
same pretext, obtained the governor's hand to it,
while the governor, deceived by his high and fair
professions of service and kindness to him, never
entertained any suspicion of his integrity ; and
this was the greatest of the governor's defects,
through the candidness and sincerity of his own
nature he was more unsuspicious of others, and
more credulous of fair pretenders, than suited with
so great a prudence as he testified in all things

else. Nothing awakened jealousy in him but
gross flattery, which, when he saw any one so
servile as to make, he believed the soul that could
descend to that baseness might be capable of falsehood ; but those who were cunning attempted him
not that way, but put on a face of fair, honest,
plain friendship, with which he was a few times,
but not often in his life, betrayed. At Mr. Millington's entreaty the governor released Wandall, but
would have prosecuted the committee's petition
against Plumptre, which Mr. Millington most earnestly persuaded him not to do, but desired that ·
he would permit him to come and live quietly in
his own house, upon engagement that he should
not raise nor foment any mutiny nor faction in
the garrison, or intermeddle with any of the affairs
thereof. The governor was easily wrought to
assent to this also, but Plumptre refused to enter
into such an engagement for quiet behaviour, and
so for that time came not to town. There was
again a new design against the garrison by the
enemy discovered, and a spy taken, who owned
a soldier in the major's company had enlisted
himself on purpose to effect this mischief; but
through careless custody the spy escaped the day
that the garrison were celebrating their joy for the
great victory at York. Meanwhile the governor,
supposing Mr. Millington to be, as he professed
himself, highly his friend and his protector, com-

plained to him of the mutinous carriage of the horse, and his disturbance and discouragement in the public service thereby, and desired him to get a resolution in the thing, whereby his power and their duty might be defined, that he might know wherein he was to command them in his garrison, and they to obey him. Mr. Millington advised him to write a letter to him concerning this, setting down his own apprehensions, what he was to exact from them, and they to render him ; which accordingly the governor did, and left it with Millington, and returned to his garrison. Mr. Millington told him, that he had showed the letter to the committee of both kingdoms, who had given their opinion of it, that he required no more of them than he ought to have. Soon after the governor, Mr. Millington came down to Nottingham, with instructions from the committee of both kingdoms, to hear and, if he could, compose the differences at Nottingham; if not, to report them to the committee of both kingdoms. Mr. Millington, coming down with these, brought Plumptre as far as Leicester with him, and begged of the governor to permit him to return to his house, engaging himself that he should not meddle with anything belonging to the garrison, nor come near the castle nor any of the forts: which engagement the governor received, and suffered the man to come home ; and Millington, lest the governor should suspect his great concern in Dr. Plumptre, made strong professions to him, that he desired his re-admission into the town for nothing but to be a snare to him : for he knew the turbulency and pride of his spirit such, that he would never be quiet; but if, after this indulgence, he should, as he believed he would, return to his former courses, he would be inexcusable in the eyes of all men. Then Mr. Millington desired the governor to draw up some heads, wherein he conceived his power to consist, which he did, reducing almost all the words of his commission into eight propositions ; which, when he showed first to Mr. Millington, before the committee saw them, Mr. Millington seemed very well to approve of them, and protested again to the governor, the faithfulness of his heart to him, excusing his intimacy with his enemies, upon a zeal he had to do him service, by discovering their designs against him, and called himself therein, Sir Politic Wouldbe :[1] but the governor disliking this double dealing, though it had been with his enemies, desired him

---

[1] Sir Politic Wouldbe is a character in Jonson's Volpone. Explaining his own character, Sir Politic Wouldbe says :—

> " I do love
> To note and to observe : though I live out,
> Free from the active torrent, yet I'd mark
> The currents and the passages of things,
> For mine own private use ; and know the ebbs
> And flows of state."

rather to declare himself ingenuously as his conscience led him, though it should be against him,
and told him freely he liked not this fair carriage
to both. When the governor put in his propositions to the committee, they desired each of them
might have a copy of them, and all a week's time
to consider them; at the end of which, when the
governor pressed their answer, whether they
assented to them, or could object any thing against
them; they, with false flattering apologies to the
governor, that if such command were due to any
man, they should rather the governor should employ it than any person whatsoever, by reason
of his unquestioned merits; but they conceived
that such a power given to a governor, would not
consist with that which belonged to a committee,
whereupon they produced a tedious impertinent
paper, in answer to the governor's propositions,
which, when the governor read over, he flung by,
saying it was a ridiculous senseless piece of stuff.
Some of them taking exceptions, that he should so
contemn the committee's paper; he replied, he
knew not yet whose it was, not being signed by
any one; if any of them would own it, he desired
them to subscribe it, and then he should know
what to say. Thereupon, the next day, it was
again brought out, signed by Mr. Millington,
Chadwick, Salusbury, White, and the mayor of the
town. The sum of the paper not containing any

exceptions against the governor himself, but against his power, and wholly denying that my Lord Fairfax had power to make a governor, or confer any such power on him, as his commission imported ; the governor told them, it no further concerned him, but only to acquaint my Lord Fairfax, with whom he should leave it, to justify his own commission, and his authority to give one.   But forasmuch as my lord was concerned in it, the gentlemen who had more respect for him disowned it, and these were the governor, the lieutenant-colonel, Mr. Pigott, Colonel Thornhagh, Major Ireton, Major Widmerpoole,[1] Captain Lomax, and Alderman James.   Then the governor told them, how he had been informed that this paper was of Chadwick's contrivance, and that when Mr. Millington saw it, he hugged Chadwick in his arms, with such congratulation, as is not to be imagined they could give to a fellow of whom they had justly entertained so vile an opinion ; and then before his face he declared all their thoughts of indignation and contempt, which they had formerly expressed of Colonel Chadwick, whom he asked, with what face he could question my lord's authority to make him governor, when he had formerly used such

---

[1] In the Note-Book Major Widmerpoole's name comes last. " Major Widmerpoole then being of the doubtful gender."

surreptitious cheats to obtain it for himself, by the
same authority? And he asked the committee,
how it came to pass, they now believed my Lord
Fairfax had not authority to make him governor,
when they themselves at first writ to him for the
commission? And to Mr. Millington he said, that
he had dealt very unfaithfully to those that entrusted
him to compose differences, which he had rather
made than found; and very treacherously with
him, making himself a party and the chief of his
adversaries, when he pretended only to be a re-
conciler. Having at full laid them open one to
another, and declared all their treachery, malice,
pride, and knavery, to their faces, he went away,
smiling at the confusion he had left them in, who
had not virtue enough in their shame to bring
them back to repentance, but having begun to
persecute him, with their spite and malice, were
resolved to carry on their wicked design; wherein
they had now a double encouragement to animate
them, Mr. Millington's sheltering them in the
parliament house, and obstructing all redress the
governor should there seek for, and the hopes of
profit and advantage they might upon the change of
things expect by the garrison, if they could wrest
it out of the governor's hands, either by wearying
him with unjust vexations, or by watching some
advantage against him, to procure the discharge
of his office by the parliament; for they, knowing

him to be impatient of affronts, and of a high spirit, thought to provoke him to passion, wherein something might fall out to give them advantages; but he, perceiving their drift, showed them that he governed his anger, and suffered it not to master him, and that he could make use of it to curb their insolency, and yet avoid all excursions that might prejudice himself. When the governor undertook this employment, the parliament's interest in those parts was so low, and the hazard so desperate, that these pitiful wretches, as well as the other faithful-hearted to the public cause, courted him to accept and keep the place; and though their foul spirits hated the daylight of his more virtuous conversation, yet were they willing enough to let him bear the brunt of all the hazard and toil of their defence, willinger to be secured by his indefatigable industry and courage, than to render him the just acknowledgment of his good deserts. This ingratitude did not at all abate his zeal for the public service, for as he sought not praise, so he was well enough satisfied in doing well; yet through their envious eyes, they took in a general good esteem of him, and sinned against their own consciences in persecuting him, whereof he had after acknowledgments and testimonies from many of them. All the while of this contest, he was borne up by a good and honourable party of the committee, and greater in number and value than the wicked ones, whom Mr. Millington's power in the house only countenanced and animated to pursue their mischiefs. What it was that drew Mr. Millington into their confederacy was afterwards apparent; they hired him with a subscription of losses, for which they gave him public credit double to what he really had lost;[1] and they offered him a share of the governor's spoils, if he would help them to make him a prey, which would have been good booty to his mean family: for although the governor had hitherto got nothing but desperate hazard and vast expense, yet now, this garrison began to be in a more hopeful condition, by the late success in the north. After York was taken, the Earl of Manchester marched into our parts, upon whose coming Bolsover and Tickhill castles were delivered up to him, and Welbeck, the Earl of Newcastle's house, which was given into Colonel Thornhagh's command, and much of the enemy's wealth, by that means, brought into Nottingham: Wingfield Manor, a strong garrison in Derbyshire, was taken upon composition, and by this means a rich and large side of the country was laid open to help to maintain the garrison at Not-

---

[1] Of this custom of applying to the parliament for reparation or compensation, and of its being granted generally at the expense of delinquents or cavaliers, there appear many instances in Whitelocke—no doubt many abuses crept in. In Walker's Hist. of Indepen., p. 81, Mr. Millington is declared to have received in this manner £2000.—J. H.

tingham,[1] and more hoped for by these gentlemen,
who were now as greedy to catch at the rewards of
another's labours, as unable to merit anything
themselves.   But when the hopes of the harvest of
the whole country had tempted them to begin their
wicked plots, God, seeming angry at their ill use of
mercy, caused the Earl of Manchester to be called
back into the south, when he was going to have
besieged Newark, and so that town, with the petty
garrisons at Wiverton, Shelford, and Belvoir, were

---

[1] On the Earl of Manchester's movements after the
capture of York the documents contained in the volume
published by the Camden Society, entitled "Manchester's
Quarrel with Cromwell," give detailed information.
  York surrendered on July 16, 1644, and Manchester
marched south on the 20th (Rushworth, III. ii. 641).
Tickhill was taken by a detachment under Lieutenant-
colonel John Lilburne on 26th July. Then, sending a strong
force under Crawford to besiege Sheffield, Manchester
marched to Welbeck, which surrendered on August 2d
(Rushworth and Manchester's letter of August 6th in the
Camden Society's volume). After the surrender of Welbeck
Manchester established himself at Lincoln, and quartered
his troops near Gainsborough. Crawford took Sheffield
(August 10), Stavely House (August 12), and Bolsover
Castle (August 14), and then joined Gell, before Wingfield
Manor, which surrendered on August 21st. Why the
remaining royalist fortresses in the district were not taken
is explained in Cromwell's charge against Manchester
("Manchester's Quarrel with Cromwell," p. 81). A few
weeks earlier, Gell, aided by Grey, had taken Wilney Ferry

still left for further exercise to Nottingham. Yet
the hopes these would in time be gained, made
these gentlemen prosecute their design against
the governor, whose party they endeavoured with
all subtleties to weaken: and first attempted
Colonel Thornhagh, who having by his signalised
valour arrived to a great reputation, they thought
if they could gain him, he would be their best lever
to heave out the governor, and that prop once
removed they despaired not to make him contribute

(July 18, Rushworth, III. ii. 769; Vicars, "Parliamentary
Chronicle," iii. 287). A vigorous attack on Newark would
have put an end to the war in Nottinghamshire, but
Manchester delayed until he was summoned to take part
in the second battle of Newbury.

The Note-Book, after mentioning the surrender of
Welbeck, adds—"There came great benefit to this garrison
thereby, for there were found in the house of Mrs. Markham's
and other malignants goods to the value of —— thousand
pounds, besides much money that was gathered out of that
side of the country, and brought into the treasury at Nottingham, amongst which Lieutenant-colonel Hutchinson's
troop went to a malignant's house, and brought in almost
six hundred pounds in gold." Welbeck, however, did not
long remain in the possession of the parliament. It was
surprised on July 16, 1645, by Major Jammot and a party
from Newark ("Mercurius Belgicus," "Diary of Richard
Symonds," p. 224). It was finally disgarrisoned by agreement in Nov. 1645, the parliamentarians at the same time
disgarrisoning Wingfield (Letter-Book of the Committee
of both Kingdoms, Nov. 11–13, 1645).

to his own ruin; for they had discovered in him a
facility of nature, apt to be deluded by fair pretences, and more prone to suspect the kind plain
dealing of his friends, than the flattery of his
enemies: but the governor, after they had displayed themselves, by his vigilancy prevented many
of their malicious designs, and among the rest those
they had upon this gentleman. During his sickness the governor took care of his regiment, and
employed the troops that quartered in the garrison:
but through the wicked instigations of Captain
White, being very refractory, and the regiment
often called out on field-service, the governor sent
for a commission, and raised a troop of horse,
which the lieutenant-colonel commanded, and a
troop of dragoons for the peculiar service of the
garrison. These cunning sowers of sedition
wrought, upon this occasion, Colonel Thornhagh
into a jealous belief, that Colonel Hutchinson was
taking the advantage of his sickness to work himself into his command. Colonel Thornhagh was
grieved at it, but said nothing; but the governor
discovering the thing, notwithstanding his silence,
when the lieutenant-colonel went to London, procured a commission for Colonel Thornhagh to be,
next under Sir Thomas Fairfax, commander-in-chief
of all the parliament's horse in Nottinghamshire, at
all times; which being brought to Colonel Thornhagh, when he knew nothing of it, cleared him of

that suspicion. And now, although they were more inclined to delude than openly to oppose Colonel Thornhagh, yet they, having no exceptions against the governor in his own person, but only against his authority, were forced to deny Colonel Thornhagh's command as well as the governor's, they being both derived from the same power. The horse-captains, who were allured by fair colours of preferment, and indulged in their plunder, which they hoped to do with more freedom if Captain White prevailed, were more obedient to Captain White and their own ambition, than to their colonel or the laws and customs of war. The committee hoped, by thus disputing the colonel's powers, under a face of parliament authority, to wear them out, and make them cast up their commissions, when they had, by Mr. Millington, blocked up the way of their complaint, so that they feared not being turned out of the committee for the abuse of that trust: and perhaps they had succeeded but that the governor scorned to give up a good cause, either particular or public, for want of courage to defend it amidst many difficulties; and then, although he had many enemies, he had more friends, whom if he should desert, would be left to be crushed by these malicious persons; and more than all this, the country would be abandoned into the hands of persons who would only make a prey of it, and not endeavour its protection, liberty, or real advantage, which had been his chief aim in all his undertakings.[1]

The conspirators, as I may more justly term them, than the committee, had sent Captain White to York, to my Lord Fairfax, to get the governor's power defined; which the governor understanding, the next day went thither himself, and Mr. Pigott, who from the beginning to the ending showed himself a most real and generous friend to the governor, and as cordial to his country and the great cause, went along with him, arriving a day after Captain White. When my lord gave them a hearing together, he asked whether the governor had · done anything of consequence without consulting

---

[1] Just before the account of White's mission to York, the Note-Book gives the following relation :—" After Wingfield Manor was taken, there was a design against Wiverton House, on which the governor intended to go himself, and command the party; and, just as he was marching forth, there was a paper given him where Captain White, who thought he had an excellent faculty that way, had drawn in the name of the committee a summons to summon them to deliver the house to the committee, which summons the committee had signed. The governor put the summons in his pocket, and told them he could do it without them."

In the siege of Wingfield here alluded to, some of the Nottingham forces also took part. According to Gell's "True Account," Colonel Thornhagh sent his major and several troops of horse, whilst Colonel Hutchinson sent two hundred foot.

the committee, which White could not say he had;
then he asked White if he had any other mis-
government to accuse him of, which when White
could not allege against him, the governor before
his face told my lord all the business, whereupon
White was dismissed with reproof and laughter, and
letters were written to the committee, to justify the
governor's power, and to entreat them to forbear dis-
turbing him in his command,[1] and to Mr. Millington,
to desire him to come over to York to my lord, both
which the governor delivered, but Mr. Millington
would not go over, but, on the contrary, continued to
foment and raise up the factions in the town against
the governor, and by his countenance the committee
every day meditated and practised new provocations,
to stir up the governor to rage, or at least to weary
him in his employment.   The horse, without his
knowledge, they frequently sent abroad; protections,
tickets, and passes, they gave out; and, encroaching
upon his office in all things whatsoever, wrought
such a confusion in the garrison, that while all men
were distracted and amazed, in doubt whose orders
to obey, and who were their commanders, they
obeyed none, but every man did what he listed;
and by that means the public service was in all
things obstructed and prejudiced.   The governor,

---

[1] A letter from Lord Fairfax to the committee of both
kingdoms on this subject is given in the Appendix.

while the injury was only to himself, bore it, but
when it extended almost to the destruction of the
garrison, he was forced to endeavour a remedy.
For about this time it happened that Salusbury,
being treasurer, had given base terms and wilful
delays to the soldiers who were assigned their pay,
when the money was ready for them in the treasury;
and when this base carriage of his had provoked
them to a mutiny, the governor was sent for to
appease it, which he did; but coming to the committee, told them he would no longer endure this
usage of theirs, to have all things of power, honour,
and command, wrested out of his hands, and all
things of difficulty and danger put upon him; while
they purposely stirred up occasions of rigour and
punishment, and then expected he should be the
executioner of it, by which he perceived they did
these things only with design to render him contemptible and odious to all persons. Not long
after a command came for all the horse that could
be spared in the garrison to go to Sir John
Meldrum, to the relief of Montgomery Castle.[1]   The

---

[1] Montgomery Castle was surrendered to Sir Thomas
Middleton by Lord Herbert of Cherbury on September
4, 1644. The Shrewsbury cavaliers under Sir Michael
Earnley made a determined effort to retake the castle,
and besieged Colonel Mytton in it. Middleton marched
to relieve Mytton, joined by the Lancashire forces under
Sir John Meldrum, those of Cheshire under Sir William

governor went to the committee to consult what troops should march, and they voted *none*. The governor told them, he conceived when a command was given, they were to obey without dispute, and that he came to advise with them what troops should be sent forth, not whether any or no ; therefore although they voted disobedience of the command, that would not discharge him, especially the service being of great consequence, and the troops lying here without employment : wherefore at night he summoned a council of war, and there almost all the captains, having no mind to march, so far from home, declared they conceived themselves to be under the command of the committee, and would only obey their orders. Upon this the governor went to the committee and desired them that, in regard unanswerable things were done, the public service neglected, and all the transactions of the garrison confused, they would unite with him in a petition to the parliament to define their several powers ; and in the meantime, either quietly to let him execute his duty, or else to take all upon them and discharge him. They presently made a motion,

---

Brereton, 'and a Yorkshire regiment under Sir William Fairfax. The besiegers also had been reinforced by Lord Biron. In the battle which took place beneath the walls of the castle (September 18), the royalists were defeated with the loss of one thousand prisoners."—Rushworth, III. ii. 746 ; Phillips, " Civil War in Wales," 247–251.

that he would call a muster, and put it to all the
soldiers, whether they would be governed by the
committee or the governor. The governor told
them his command was not elective, but of right
belonged to him, and this way was only the next
occasion to cause a mutiny, which he could not
consent to.   But they persisting in their course, he
came again to them and desired they would at length
surcease these affronts in his command, and their
underminings, whereby they endeavoured to alienate
men's hearts from him, and to raise a faction against
him by close unworthy practices.   So after much
debate it was on all hands agreed, that they should
not at all intermeddle with anything belonging to
the soldiery, nor interrupt the governor in his command, till the house of parliament should decide it,
and that the governor and Captain White should
both go to London, to procure a speedy determination of the powers in a fair and open way.   This
they all faithfully promised the governor, and made
many hypocritical professions to him, some of them
with tears ; whereupon he, who was of the most
reconcilable nature in the world, accepted their fair
pretences, and went to drink friendly with them in
token of kindness.   Yet was all this but hypocrisy
and falsehood, for even at that very time they
wearied many of the governor's officers out of the
garrison, by the continued malice wherewith they
persecuted all that had any respect for him.

Among these was Mr. Hooper the engineer, a man
very faithful to the cause, and very honest, but
withal rough, who having to do with hateful businesses, was made odious to the common people, the
priests too having a particular spite at him, as one
they esteemed a leader of the separatists; yet he
was very ingenious and industrious in his office,
and most faithful as well to the governor himself as
to the public service. The committee, to insinuate
themselves with the common people, regarded him
with an evil eye, and so discouraged him, that being
offered much better preferment, and invited by
Colonel Cromwell into other parts, he acquainted
the governor with it, offering withal that, if he might
yet be protected from affronts in his employment,
he would stay and serve the governor for half the
salary offered elsewhere. But the governor, although he was very sorry to part with him, and the
service would much miss him, yet being so much
injured himself, could not undertake the protection
of any of his officers, and therefore would not hinder
his preferment, but suffered him to go to Cromwell.
Such was the envy of the committee to him, that,
just as he was going, that very day, they not willing
to let him depart in peace, although they knew he
had justly expended all the money he had received
of them, yet they called for an account, from the
beginning of his employment, which they had often
seen in parcels; but believing he could not so

readily give it them altogether, they then demanded it. He immediately brought it forth, and got by it twelve shillings due to him upon the foot thereof, which he intended not to have asked them, but receiving it upon the exhibition of his account, went away smiling at their malice ; which yet would not let him go so, for then Henry Wandall came with a petition to the governor, that he would vindicate the honour of the Earl of Essex against Mr. Hooper, whom he accused of having spoken words against him, and done actions to his dishonour. The governor knowing this was but malice, accepted security for him, which was offered by Mr. Pigott and Major Watson, that he should answer what could be objected against him at any council of war he should be called to.[1]

Wednesday, September the 25th, 1644, Captain White went to London, to solicit the committee's business against the governor, for they were intended to put it upon a fair debate, as was pro-

---

[1] This Mr. Hooper was undoubtedly a person of singular abilities. Mr. Sprigge, in his Anglia Rediviva, mentions him as serving Sir Thomas Fairfax at the siege of Oxford and other places as engineer extraordinary, and greatly expediting all his enterprises, the rapidity and number of which were surprising : he was at the siege of Ragland Castle, the last garrison that surrendered ; he came again to Nottingham during Colonel Hutchinson's government, and, by the list of the garrison in Deering's Nottingham, appears to have continued with Captain Poulton.

mised. The next day the governor commanded Captain Barrett's troop to convoy him towards London; but just as he was going to horse, the committee, contrary to their engagements not to meddle with any military affairs, commanded them another way, and so he was forced to go without a convoy, although the captain was afforded a whole troop to wait on him.

Two or three days before the governor went, Chadwick came privately to the governor's brother, and told him that his conscience would not suffer him to conceal the malicious designs, and that treachery, which he now discovered to be in these men's oppositions of the governor; and with many insinuations, told him they were framing articles against the ,governor, whereof he gave him a copy, which the governor carried to London with him, and showed the lieutenant-colonel the originals in Mason's and Plumptre's own handwritings. Three days after the governor, Colonel Thornhagh went to London. That day the governor went, one of the presbyterian ministers, whose name was Goodall, preached the lecture at the great church, with many invectives against governors and arbitrary power, so plainly hinting at the governor, that all the church well understood it; but for the committee, he glozed with them, and told them he had nothing to say to them, but to go on in the good way they went. Some months after, this

poor man, preaching at a living the committee had
put him into, was taken by the enemy, and much
dejected at it, because he could not hope the governor would exchange him, after his unworthy pulpit
railings at him ; but the governor, who hated poor
revenges, when his enemy and one of his friends
were both in the same prison, and he had but one
exchange ready, first procured the minister's release,
and let his own officer stay for the next exchange.
Whereupon the man coming home, was struck with
remorse, and begged the governor's pardon, with
real acknowledgments both to himself and others ·
of his sin, in supporting faction against the governor; who was told that on his death-bed, for
he died before the garrison was dissolved, he expressed to some of the governor's friends his trouble
for having been his enemy.   But not only to him,
but to many others of his enemies, the governor
upon sundry occasions, when they fell into his
power to have requited their mischiefs, instead of
vengeance rendered them benefits ; so that at last
his own friends would tell him, if they could in
justice and conscience forsake him, they would
become his adversaries, for that was the next way
to engage him to obligations.   But although his
friends, who had greater animosities against his
unjust persecutors than he himself, would say these
things in anger at his clemency, his nature was as
full of kind gratitude to his friends as free from

base revenges upon enemies, who either fell down
to him by their own just remorse, or were cast
under his power by God's just providence.

As soon as the governor was gone, the committee
took all power upon them, and had the impudence
to command the lieutenant-colonel, who was deputy-
governor, and absolute in his brother's absence,
to draw out his troop: he went to them and told
them he was sorry they broke their agreement, but
he could not break his trust of his brother's authority to obey them.   Then they feigned a pretence
and turned out the governor's quarter-master,[1]
who by the governor's appointment had quartered
soldiers at an ale-house Mr. Millington had given
a protection to, that they should quarter none, upon
the account of some relation they had to him, who
married one of the daughters of the place.   This
occasioning some dispute, Cooke the quarter-master
had uttered some words, for which they sent for
him and cast out great threats, how they would

---

[1] Adrian Cooke.   " Cooke had quartered some soldiers
at the house of a malignant fellow, kinsman to Mr. Millington and of his name, to whom Millington had given a
protection that he should quarter none ; but the governor
bade Cooke quarter them there.   The man telling Cooke
that he would quarter none, for he was a soldier, Cooke
told him he was mistaken, for at the best he was but a
watchman ; for this he was discharged his place by the
committee, and by them also Colishaw was the next day
appointed quartermaster."—Note-Book.

punish him; which frighted his wife, big with child,
in that manner, that her child died within her, and
her own life was in great hazard.   The committee
then called a hall, and caused the townsmen to bring
in horses for dragoons, whereof they voted a regiment to be raised, Chadwick to be the colonel, and
Hall and Selby to be captains under him.   They
took upon them to command the soldiers, and made
horrible confusion, by which they often put the
garrison in great danger, if the enemy had known
their advantage.[1]   Among the rest, one night after
the guards were set, the captain of the guard, missing the deputy-governor to receive the word from ·
him, gave them the same word they had before, till
he had found out the governor to receive a new

---

[1] The Note-Book gives this amongst other instances.
"Wednesday there was an alarum, the lieutenant-colonel
went down and appointed the men to their places, but
riding with the major to the guards, he found almost no
men left, whereupon inquiring of the soldiers what were
become of the men, he was answered they were gone forth
with Colonel Chadwick, so they stayed till his return, who
soon after came home with the soldiers, himself having no
weapons either of offence or defence, but a cudgel cut out
of the crabtree (his own stock).   The lieutenant-colonel
told him he was an early man : he said he went out to
have done service and redeemed the poor people's cattle,
but that he came too late.   The major told him he had
no order to draw out the men : he said he had as much to
do to command them as any man in the garrison, and he
would command them."

one. Mr. Millington coming by, half flustered, would have had the captain take a word from him, which when the captain refused, he being angry, commanded Captain Mason's drums to beat, and set a double guard. The lieutenant - colonel hearing the drums, and having no notice of this command, sent to Mason to command him to forbear drawing any men to the guard, but Mason would not obey him. Besides this, they did a thousand such like things, to provoke him to give them some colour of complaint, or some advantage against him and his brother, for the carrying on of a wicked design, which they were secretly managing to destroy them; but God, by a wonderful providence, brought it to light.

Their conspiracy was to accuse the colonel and his brother, as persons that had betrayed the town and castle, and were ready to surrender them to the enemy, which they would pretend to have discovered, and to have prevented their treachery, by a surprise of the lieutenant-colonel, the castle and the bridges, and all the officers that were faithful to the governor and his friends. Because they had not force in town who would act this villany, they sent to Sir John Gell, in whom they had a great interest, and a man likely enough to promote their wickedness, had they even acquainted him with it, as black as it was in the cursed forge of their own hearts: but to carry their business closely, they sent to tell him they had cause of suspicion that the lieutenant-colonel was false to his trust, and would deliver the castle to the enemy, to prevent which they desired him to assist them with some men and ammunition ; which ammunition was very secretly conveyed into the town, and the men were ready to march, and quarters taken up for them in Nottingham.   The lieutenant-colonel dreamed nothing of the mischief that was hatching against him, when, just at the very time of the execution, there came into Nottingham two gentlemen, whom the parliament employed to carry intelligences between the north and the south, and who used to meet at this town.

Mr. Fleetwood, who came from the south, came. immediately up to the castle, and there was familiarly and kindly treated, as he used to be, by the lieutenant-colonel.   This was upon a Saturday night, in the month of October.   Mr. Marsh, his correspondent, that came from the north, passing through Derby, was cautioned so by Sir John Gell, that he durst not come up to the castle, but on the Lord's day sent for Mr. Fleetwood to meet him in the town ; who coming to him, he told him what information he had received from Sir John Gell, and for that reason durst not trust himself in the castle. Mr. Fleetwood undertaking for his safety, brought him up to the lieutenant-colonel, and finding the untruth of their forgeries, told the lieutenant-colonel all the machinations against him ; whereupon, on the Monday morning, he went away to London,

and sent Mr. Millington word, that having understood the suspicion they had of him, he was gone
to London, where, if they had anything to accuse
him of, they might send after him, and he should
be ready to answer it, and in his absence had left
Captain Lomax governor of the garrison.   The
committee, very much confounded that their wickedness was come to light, resolved to outface the
thing, and denied that they had sent to Derby for
any men.   They said indeed it was true, that
having formerly lent Sir John Gell some powder,
they had sent for that back ; but this was not all,
for they had also persuaded the master of the
magazine that was in the castle to convey, unknown
to the lieutenant-colonel, two barrels of powder,
with match and bullet suitable, to such place as
Chadwick should direct.   This he, not dreaming of
their evil intention, had condescended to do, and
sent them to Salusbury's house ; but as soon as the
lieutenant-colonel was gone, they took what care
they could to shuffle up this business, and presently
despatched Captain Palmer to London and Lieutenant Chadwick to Derby, where he so wrought
with Sir John Gell, that he brought back a counterfeit letter, pretended to have been all that was sent
from the committee of Nottingham to him, and
another of Sir John Gell's writing, wherein he disowned all that Mr. Marsh had related of his information.   But God, who would not let them be hid,

had so ordered that while matters were thus hudd-
ling up at Derby, Sir John Gell's brother came by
chance to Nottingham, and affirmed that the committee of Nottingham had sent to his brother for
three hundred men, to surprise Nottingham Castle;
which, when the committee heard, they sent Captain
Pendock after him the next day to charm him, that
he might no more discover the truth in that particular.   Also that very day that these intentions of
theirs were thus providentially brought to light, one
of Sir John Gell's captains was known to be in
town, whom Sir John had sent to discover the state
of things, and the new quartermaster had been all ·
that day taking billet for soldiers in several houses
in the town.[1]

When the governor came to London, the committee of both kingdoms had appointed a sub-
committee to hear his business, whereof young
Sir Henry Vane had the chair, Mr. William
Pierrepont, Mr. Solicitor St. John, Mr. Recorder,
and two of the Scotch commissioners, were nominated for the committee; before whom the governor's
propositions and the committee's answers had been
read, and when their solicitor, Captain White, saw
they were likely to be cast out as frivolous, he pro-

---

[1] The Letter Book of the Derby House Committee contained an order sent to Sir John Gell to send up at once any
evidence against Colonel Hutchinson.   The order is dated
October 19, 1644.

duced some articles, which they had formed against the governor, lieutenant-colonel, and Mr. Pigott; but they proved as frivolous as the other, and the gentlemen answered them so clearly, that they appeared to be forged out of malice and envy, only to cause delays, there being scarcely anything of moment in them if they had been true, whereas they were all false. And now after they had trod down the fence of shame, and impudently began with articles, there was not the least ridiculous impertinency that passed at Nottingham, but they put it into a scrip of paper and presented it as an additional article to the committee; to each of whom particularly Mr. Millington had written letters, and given them such false impressions of the governor, and so prepossessed them against him, that was a stranger to them all, that they looked upon him very coldly and slightly, when he made particular addresses to them. But he that scorned to be discouraged with any man's disregard, from whom he had more reason to have expected all caresses and thankful acknowledgments of his unwearied fidelity and good services, resolved to pursue his own vindication through all their frowns and cold repulses: these he met with more from Mr. William Pierrepont than from any of the rest, till Mr. Pierrepont perceived the injustice of their prosecution, and then there was no person in the world that could demean himself with more justice,

honour, and kindness than he did to the governor,
whose injuries became first apparent to him, when
the lieutenant-colonel came and told his brother
what combinations had been discovered against him
at Nottingham, which the governor resenting with
great indignation, complained of it to the committee. The Solicitor White impudently denied
the whole matter, or that ever the committee at
Nottingham had had the least suspicion of the
governor or his brother, or the least ground of any.
When this had been with stiffness and impudence
enough outfaced before the committee, Mr. Pierrepont, then fully convinced of their devilish malice, ·
pulled a letter out of his pocket, wherein Mr. Millington made this suggestion to him against the
governor and his brother, and desired that he might
be armed with power to prevent and suppress
them. This would have made others ashamed, but
their solicitor was notwithstanding impudent and
rudely pressing upon the committee, who though
they were persons of honour, and after they discovered the governor's innocence, not forward to
oppress him, yet as they were statesmen, so they
were not so ready to relieve him as they ought to
have been, because they could not do it without a
high reflection upon one of their own members,
who encouraged all those little men in their wicked
persecution of him. They were such exquisite
rogues, that all the while some of them betrayed

one another to the governor, and told him, under pretence of honesty and conscience, the bottom of their whole designs, showed the foul original drafts of their articles, in the men's own hands that contrived them; and told him how, not so much dislike of him, as covetousness and ambition to advance themselves upon his ruins, engaged them thus against him, and made them contrive that villany to accuse him and his brother of treachery, and to have seized their garrisons, under that pretence, and gotten them to be made prisoners; and then Mr. Millington undertook to have lodged their petitions so in the parliament, that they should never have been heard and relieved.[1] Colonel Thornhagh too was to have been wrought out of his command, and they had divided the spoil before they caught the lions.   Millington's son was designed to be governor of the castle; the ten pounds a week allowed for the governor's table, so many of the committee-men were to share by forty shillings a man; Chadwick was to be colonel of the town regiment, and Mason major; White colonel of the horse regiment, and Palmer, the priest, his major; and all the governor's friends to be turned out, and their places disposed to creatures of their

---

[1] It is averred in the History of Independency, " that the active speaking men pack committees who carry all the business of the house as they please, and when the matter is too bad, smother it with artificial delays."—J. H.

own, who drawn on with these hopes, were very active to work the governor and his party out of the opinion of all men. They forgot the public interest in this private quarrel, taking in all the malignant and debauched people that would join with them, to destroy the governor, whom they hated for his unmoved fidelity to his trust, and his severe restriction of lewdness and vice. But because he protected and favoured godly men that were sober, although they separated from the public assemblies, this opened wide the mouths of all the priests and all their idolaters, and they were willing enough to let the children of hell cry out with them to make the louder noise ; and as we have since seen the whole cause and party ruined by the same practice, so at that time the zealots for God and the parliament turned all the hate they had to the enemies of both, and called on them to assist in executing their malice upon the faithful servant and generous champion of the Lord's and his country's just cause. And now the name of cavalier was no more remembered, Castilian [1] being the term of reproach with which they branded all the governor's friends ; and lamentable it was to behold how those wretched men fell away under this temptation, not only from public spiritedness,

---

[1] Castilian became a term of reproach, according to Nares, after the defeat of the Spanish Armada. It was also used to signify a delicate courtier, and is used in that sense by Marston.

but from sobriety and honest, moral conversation;
not only conniving at and permitting the wickedness of others, but themselves conversing in taverns
and brothels, till at last Millington and White were
so ensnared that they married a couple of alehouse
wenches, to their open shame and the conviction of
the whole country of the vain lives they led, and
some reflection on the parliament itself, as much as
the miscarriage of a member could cast on it, when
Millington, a man of sixty, professing religion, and
having but lately buried a religious matronly gentlewoman, should go to an alehouse to take a flirtish
girl of sixteen; yet by these noble alliances, they
much strengthened their faction with all the vain,
drunken rogues in the town against the governor.
Now their first plot had, by God's providence,
been detected, they fell upon others, and set on
instruments every where, to insinuate all the lies
they could, that might render the governor odious
to the town and to the horse of the garrison, whom
they desired to stir up to petition against him, but
could not find any considerable number that would
freely do it; therefore they used all the strong
motives they could, and told them that the governor
sought to exercise an arbitrary power over them,
and to have all their booties at his own dispose,
and other such like things, by which at length they
prevailed with many of Col. Thornhagh's regiment
to subscribe a petition that they might be under

the command of the committee, and not of any other person in the garrison. This petition was sent up by Captain Palmer, and he meeting Mr. Pigott at Westminster Hall, Mr. Pigott, in private discourse with him, began to bewail the scandalous conversation of certain persons of the committee, hoping that he, being familiar with them, might be a means to persuade them to reformation.

After this the governor, Colonel Thornhagh, Mr. Pigott, and some other, being in a tavern at Westminster, where they dined, Captain Palmer came to the door, and they bade him come in. Upon discourse, the governor pulled out of his pocket the articles which the committee had put in against him, showed them to Captain Palmer, and asked him whether he thought it possible that he should, after all his toils and services, have been articled against for such things. Palmer, who had been from the beginning with the governor, and knew the falsehood of these accusations, professed he was amazed at them, and that he had not till then heard anything of them. Continuing in further discourse, the governor mentioned an unchristian-like sermon, which Mr. Goodall had preached with invectives against him, in his absence. Palmer undertook the justification of it with such saucy provocations, that the governor told him if it had not been more in respect to his black coat than his grey, he would have beaten him out of the room, which

for his own safety he advised him to leave; so he
went out very angry, and going to Captain White,
told him how Mr. Pigott called him a whoremaster,
Mr. Millington a drunkard, and Chadwick a knave.
White, meeting Mr. Pigott in the hall, challenged
him of these scandals.   Mr. Pigott, seeing Palmer
not far off, led White to him, and told him he
knew that person had been his informer, repeating
all he had said to him, and added, that it was in a
desire for their reformation, but he would maintain
that all the things he spoke were true.   Palmer
further, in his rage, puts into the committee a paper
of reasons why he desired to be exempted from
being under the governor; whereof one was, that
he had cowardly and unhandsomely behaved himself on an occasion when Palmer's troop marched
out with him to Elston.   The governor sent a copy
of this paper down to Palmer's own troop, and the
lieutenant, cornet, and all the troopers sent up a
certificate, under their hands, of the falsehood of
their captain's accusation.   After this, Palmer came
into the garrison, and made a grievous exclamation
all over the town against the governor and Mr.
Pigott for traducing the ministers, Mr. Millington,
and the committee; adding a false report, that the
governor had thrown a trencher at his head; and
abusing the pulpit to persuade the people to
vindicate them.   Among other things, he misap-
plied a place in Nehemiah, where Nehemiah says,

" I ate not the governor's bread, because the fear
of the Lord was upon me," to the governor; that
his accepting a public table, was a mark of the
want of the fear of God; and many other such
malicious wrestings of scripture did he and his
fellow priests at that time practise. The committee
of Nottingham, on their side, taking this occasion,
called a public hall in the town, where two orations
were made by Mr. Millington and Colonel Chadwick. Millington began with a large enumeration
of Chadwick's worthy actions (known to no man),
whereby he merited honour of all men, especially,
of this town; and then mentioning his own good
services for the town, told them how ungratefully
they were repaid by Mr. Pigott, with the scandalous
aspersion of being drunkards and knaves; and that
their singular affections and endeavours for the good
of the town had exposed them to this calumny,
wherefore they desired the town to join in their
justification. Chadwick made just such another
speech, and both of them seemed to pass by their
own particular, and only to desire the other's justification; Chadwick, in his speech, saying that Mr.
Pigott's abuse of Mr. Millington did not only asperse
the committee, but even the parliament itself. Captain Lomax, then deputy-governor of the garrison,
after they had spoken, stood up, and advised the
townsmen that they should forbear to entangle
themselves in things they understood not, adding

that Mr. Pigott, and the gentlemen at London, were persons of such honour and prudence, that they would maintain whatever they had spoken of any man.   Hereupon Captain Mason, and two malignant townsmen his soldiers, began to mutiny with high insolence, and to lay violent hands on him to thrust him out of the hall, giving him most reproachful terms; but the man, being very stout, quieted them, and would not depart till the hall broke up.   After this, without acquainting the deputy-governor, they summoned another hall; but Lomax, seeing their inclination to mutiny, forbade it.   Then, at ten o'clock at night, they got a common council together, at Mr. Salusbury his house, and there Mr. Millington again desired they would join in the vindication of himself, the ministers, and the committee, and got about eight of them to subscribe a blank paper.   Then the committee, with certain instruments of theirs, appointed rounds to walk the town, persuading some, and threatening others, to set their hands to a petition, which none of them that subscribed knew what it was, but they told them it was for the good of the town.

All this while these petty committee fellows had carried themselves as absolute governors, and Plumptre was now their intimate favourite, and began to vapour that he would have the castle pulled down to re-erect the church, and the fort at the bridges thrown down, and all the arms and soldiers brought into the town.

But at London, the governor being grown into acquaintance with the gentlemen of the sub-committee that were to hear his business; and they perceiving with how much wicked malice he was prosecuted, Sir Henry Vane was so honourable as to give him advice to put his business in such a way, as might take away all colour from his enemies. Whereupon he put in some propositions to the committee of both kingdoms, for the composure of these differences, wherein he was willing to decline all things of his own right, which might be done without prejudice to the public service, and to pass by all the injuries that had been done him; which condescension gave such satisfaction, that forthwith the whole business was determined at the committee of both kingdoms, and the governor sent back to his charge, with instructions drawn up for all parties, and letters written to the officers and soldiers, both of horse and foot, to be obedient; and likewise letters to the mayor of the town and the committee. The governor returning, word was brought to Nottingham, that on Friday night he lay at Leicester, whereupon the committee, who had heard the determination of things above, got them ready to be gone, but the soldiers having notice thereof, went to the deputy-governor and entreated him to stop the treasurer; whereupon he and the major of the regiment went to them, and entreated them to stay till the governor came, but to see what instruc-

tions he brought with him from the powers above;
but when they would not be persuaded fairly, then
the deputy peremptorily forbade the treasurer, as
he would answer it, not to go. But he refusing to
obey, the deputy told him he should pass on his
sword's point if he went, and accordingly went
down to set guards at the Trent bridges; which
being told them, they made haste and fled out at
the other end of the town. Millington, Chadwick,
Ayscough, Salusbury, and Mason (whom they had
gotten added to the committee to increase their faction), were the committee-men, who took with them
their new marshal and another of their created
officers, Palmer, two more priests, and a town captain.[1] The governor was met on his way homewards
by some of his officers, and told with what joy his
garrison and regiment were preparing to entertain
him, in all expressions they could possibly make,
by volleys of cannon and muskets, and ringing of
bells, and all such declarations as used to be made
in a public and universal rejoicing; but the governor, fearing his enemies might not bear such
testimonies of love to him without grief, sent into
the town to desire them to forbear their kind intentions of giving him so loud a welcome. When he
was now near the town, another messenger came

---

[1] A list of names is given in the Note-Book. Besides
those in the text it mentions Goodal, Upton, Martin, Rily,
and Smith.

to acquaint him, that all those who would have been grieved at his joyful entertainment were fled, and that those who remained would be much grieved if he should not be pleased to give them leave to receive him with such demonstrations of their joy as they could make. He now permitted them to do what they pleased; which leave being obtained, every one strove to declare his gladness with all imaginable expressions of love and honour, and with all the solemnities the time and place would afford. The governor on his side received them with a cheerful obliging courtesy to all, and a large bounty to his loving soldiers, who made that day as great a festival as if themselves and their families had been redeemed from captivity. The mayor of the town, with his brethren in their scarlets, met him, and told him if he had been guilty of anything prejudicial to him, he was exceedingly sorry for it, for he infinitely honoured him, and all his errors had been through ignorance or misinformation, which he should be most ready to repair. That evening White came home pining with spite and envy at the governor and the gentlemen that joined with him, viz. Colonel Thornhagh, Mr. Pigott, Lieutenant-colonel Hutchinson, Major Widmerpoole, Captain Lomax, and Alderman James; for as to the mayor of the town, notwithstanding his fair professions publicly to the governor, White had the same night again turned about that weathercock.

The next day the governor and the committee
with him sent a command to all the horse in town
to march to the assistance of Derby and Leicester,
to fortify a house called Coleorton;[1] which not being
taken notice of, the governor and Colonel Thornhagh summoned all the horse officers, and declared
to them the orders of the committee of both kingdoms, to which they cheerfully promised obedience ;
but White being sent for among them, insolently
refused to come up to the castle, and bade the
governor come down to him to the committee's
chamber ; yet upon second thoughts he came up,
and the governor took no notice for that time.
Monday the governor sent to the mayor to call a
hall, but the mayor intreated him to forbear till
they saw whether the committee-men that ran
away would come back, and that he might go
with Captain White to persuade them ; both which
the governor assented to ; but the men would not
return, but went from Derby to London.   Then
the governor called a general muster, and read to

---

[1] This appears to have taken place in November 1644.
Sir John Gell says that he had just before established a
garrison at Barton Park to block up Tutbury.   " Leicestershire committee seeing this sent to Colonel Gell for his
assistance to set up a garrison at Coleorton, within a mile,
and opposite to Ashby de la Zouch.   Thereupon he sent
them all the horse and dragoons he could well spare; and
so continued there all the month of November 1644 till
it was perfected."—A True Relation, &c.

them the instructions he had brought from the committee of both kingdoms, with which all men were exceeding well pleased. But Captain White all this while would not deliver the letters he had for the committee and the mayor of Nottingham.

Some few days after word was brought the governor that the new dragoons were come for ammunition, to march out upon some design he was not acquainted with, whereupon he sent to the guards at the bridges not to suffer them to pass without his ticket. Immediately afterwards, White came along with them, and being denied to pass, gave the guards such provocative language that they were forced to send for the governor. He came down and found White in high rage, who gave him all the vile terms and opprobrious language he could invent, to provoke him to some anger upon which he might have taken his advantage; but the governor only laughed at his fogue,[1] and would not let him go till he showed a warrant from the council of war at London, and then he permitted him, after White had told him that he would not be commanded by him, and a thousand such mutinous speeches. As he went towards London he met the horse coming home from Coleorton, to whom he told such lies of the governor's usage of him, that they were frighted from coming into the garrison, but that

---

[1] French—*Fougue*, fury or passion.—J. H.

Colonel Thornhagh prevailed with them to take his engagement, that the governor should give them no ill usage. So they came back, and that week their colonel charged the enemy's quarters with them and took eighty horse, two horse colours, a major and some other officers.[1] The bridge troop also met with Colonel Stanhope, governor of Shelford, who

---

[1] Colonel Rossiter gained a similar success about November 18th, when, according to "The True Informer," he drew forth a party of horse from Lincoln, and surprised the cavaliers about two miles from Newark, capturing about two hundred men and several officers. The exploits mentioned in the text are described in a letter from Nottingham in the "London Post," No. 16, December 17, 1644. "After our governor's return from London, Colonel Thorney gave a great blow to a party of Sir John Girlington's horse at Muskham Bridge, whereof no doubt you have received intelligence before this time. On Tuesday last the cavaliers were gathering in their contributions and assessments in the country, whom a small party of Lieutenant-colonel Hutchinson's horse encountered, in which skirmish it happened that twenty of our men charged thirty of the enemy and took them prisoners, with their horses and arms, and with them a colonel of great repute, who is uncle to the governor of Shelford. The prisoners were all sent hither unto Nottingham, being conveyed with a small party of our men, which a fresh party of the enemy's having notice of, they charged the convoy, and the other party of our men opportunely coming in, we took of them there also seven more prisoners and ten horses. . . . We have since taken three more cavaliers, who say they believe that the devil is in us roundheads, and that at last we will fetch them all away, though by twos and by threes."

had two parties, each as many as they; his, where himself was, they routed, and he ran away, while the other party charged them in the rear, upon whom they turned, routed, and chased them out of the field, took Lieutenant-colonel Stanhope and his ensign, and many other prisoners, with many horse and arms. In the absence of the governor and his brother, the committee had done all they could to discourage and dissipate this troop, and would neither give them money nor provisions; yet, upon hopes of their captain's return, they kept themselves together, and when the governor came home he recruited them.[1]

The committee of both kingdoms had sent down at this time an order for all the horse of Nottingham and Derbyshire to join with three regiments of Yorkshire, and quarter about Newark, to straiten the enemy there; and accordingly they rendezvoused at Mansfield, and from thence marched to Thurgarton, where Sir Roger Cooper had fortified his

---

[1] The Note-Book supplies this amongst other instances :—
"The committee in the absence of the governor had pressed some men, which by special warrant were appointed to be pressed for the completing of his regiment, which were listed under Hall and Selby, wherefore at his return the governor demanded his men, but because Selby was thought a man that might be useful for the garrison, the governor was content to let him have the men, but those which Hall had he took away and put into the foot companies."

house, and lined the hedges with musketeers, who, as the troops passed by, shot and killed one Captain Heywood. Hereupon Colonel Thornhagh sent to the governor, and desired to borrow some foot to take the house. The governor accordingly lent him three companies, who took the house, and Sir Roger Cooper and his brother, and forty men in it, who were sent prisoners to Nottingham;[1] where, although Sir Roger Cooper was in great dread of being put into the governor's hands, whom he had provoked before upon a private occasion, yet he received such a civil treatment from him, that he seemed to be much moved and melted with it. The foot had done all the service, and run all the hazard, in taking the house, yet the booty was all given to the horse; this they had very just reason to resent, but notwithstanding, they marched along with them to Southwell, and there were most sadly neglected, and put upon keeping outguards for the horse, and had no provisions, so that the governor was forced

---

[1] The Note-Book gives a fuller account of the capture of Thurgarton. "Then the governor sent him, the major's, Captain Poulton's and Captain Wright's companies, under the command of Captain Poulton, who, as soon as they came, were commanded to fall on, yet no provision made of anything fit to make the breach; however, the men went up to the church and took it, entering at the windows, and then Captain Poulton's men took the stables, and soon after the house was yielded."

to send them some out of his garrison, or else they had been left to horrible distress. Hereupon they sent to the governor to desire they might come home, but upon Colonel Thornhagh's entreaty and engagement that they should be better used, the governor was content to let them stay a little longer, till more horse came up, which were sent for out of Yorkshire. In the meantime, those who were there already did nothing but harass the poor country ; and the horse officers were so negligent of their own duty, and so remiss in the government of their soldiers, that the service was infinitely prejudiced, and the poor country miserably distressed. The Nottingham horse, being in their own country, and having their families in and about Nottingham, were more guilty of straggling than any of the rest; and Capt. White's whole troop having presumed to be away one night when they should have been upon the guard, the Newarkers beat up our quarters, and took almost two whole troops of that regiment.[1]

---

[1] The Nottingham horse were so disorderly, that "out of six hundred, there seldom were above six score at Southwell."—Note-Book. The surprise referred to in the text is described in "Mercurius Aulicus" for January 6, 1645. It states that on December 22d, the garrison of Newark, "having intelligence of two troops of the rebels quartered at Upton, Colonel Eyre went out with some Newark horse, fetched a compass round about the rebels' headquarter, and broke down a bridge ; then gallantly charged the

White's lieutenant, without any leave from the colonel, thereupon posted up to London, and contrived a complaint against the governor, to make him appear guilty of this disorder; but soon after Newark gave them another alarum, and the parliament horse made so slender an appearance that the officers, thereupon consulting in a council of war, concluded that the design was not to be prosecuted without more force, and for the present broke up their quarters.

The committee-men that ran away when the governor returned had taken the treasurer away with them, and left neither any money, nor so much as the rent-rolls whereby the governor could be instructed where to fetch in any;[1] but by the prudence and interest of himself and his friends, he procured a month's pay for the foot, and twenty shillings a man for the horse,[2] as soon as he came

---

rebels, who instantly fled towards that bridge, which being broken, made four of them drown themselves for haste; the rest, two whole troops, both officers and soldiers, were taken to a man, who, with their colours, horses, and arms, were brought prisoners to Newark, Since which time the rebels are all driven from the parts about Newark, as you shall hear in the next." The Note-Book states that the two troops were those of Captains Barrett and Samson.

[1] Rent-rolls of sequestrated or forfeited estates.

[2] One out of many instances of Colonel Hutchinson's generous devotion to the cause, which brought on him that load of debt, so oppressive to him in the reverse of affairs.

home; and recruited all the stores, which the committee had purposely wasted in his absence, and fetched in a small stock of powder they had laid in at Salusbury's house.[1]   While he was thus indus-

---

In p. 623 and 624, of Rushworth, Thornhagh's Nottinghamshire horse state that they had served five years, and received barely six shillings a week in all; and that there was £40,000 due to them.   Judge, from these two corps, Colonel Hutchinson's being twelve hundred infantry, and two or three troops of dragoons, Thornhagh's about six hundred horse, what was the general state of the army as to pay!   Mr. Sprigge might well say of the troops as he does, "it was not their pay that pacified them, for had they not had more civility than money, things had not been so fairly managed."—J. H.

   [1] "When the governor came home, he scarce found a fortnight's provision in the garrison, whereupon he acquainted the committee with it, who ordered that all those countrymen who were behind of their rents and assessments should have their corn stopped at the market and brought into the castle, whereby there was about a hundred quarter of corn brought into the store.   Mr. Salusbury had laid up the three barrels of powder that came from Derby, and one he had out of the magazine, with match and bullet answerable, into his own house, which the governor sent for two or three times, but Mrs. Salusbury denied it; and being asked what she would do with it, answered, she kept it for the good of the town. Then the governor sent a warrant for it, but she absolutely refused, so it being night the governor sent Captain Poulton with a squadron of men to watch it all night, and the next morning he broke open the door where it was and brought it away."—Note-Book.

triously setting the things in order which they had confounded, they at London were as maliciously active to make more confusion. They contrived many false and frivolous articles and petitions against him, and proceeded to that degree of impudence in desiring alterations, and casting reflections upon the sub-committee itself, that they grew weary of them. Mr. Pierrepont and Sir H. Vane being now taken notice of as leaders of the independent faction, when those gentlemen out of mere justice and honour discountenanced their envy and malice, they applied themselves to the presbyterian faction, and insinuating to them that the justice of those gentlemen was partiality to the governor, because he was a protector of the now hated separatists, they prevailed to have Sir Philip Stapleton and Sir Gilbert Garrett,[1] two fierce presbyterians, added to the sub-committee, to balance the other faction, and found this wicked invention not a little advantageous to them: yet Mr. Hollis, who was a person of honour, did not comply with their factious spirits, but gave the governor all just assistance against their malice which lay in his power.[2] But they quitting all modesty, and pressing the committee with false affirmations and

[1] Sir Gilbert Gerrard.
[2] Mrs. Hutchinson, who in other places speaks with much disapprobation of Mr. Hollis, here most candidly gives him his due.—J. H.

forgeries, that all men would lay down their arms
if the governor were not removed, at length they
prevailed, that he was the second time sent for
to London to justify himself against them.   In
that blank, to which they had by fraud and threats
procured so many hands, they writ a petition,
alleging that the governor was so generally detested,
that if he were not removed all men would fling
down their arms ; and the subscriptions they thus
abused were those they procured to vindicate Mr.
Millington.   Salusbury and one Silvester had, for
their own profit, gotten a commission to set on
foot the excise in the county, and joined with them
one Sherwin.   These two were such pragmatical
knaves, that they justly became odious to all men ;
and although necessity might excuse the tax in
other places, yet here it was such a burden that
no man of any honesty or conscience could have
acted in it.   For when plundering troops killed all
the poor countrymen's sheep and swine, and other
provisions, whereby many honest families were
ruined and beggared, these unmerciful people would
force excise out of them for those very goods which
the others had robbed them of; insomuch that the
religious soldiers said they would starve before they
would be employed in forcing it, or take any of it
for their pay.   The governor, being inclined in
conscience to assist the poor country, was very
active in his endeavours to relieve them from this

oppression, which his enemies highly urged in their articles against him.   These excisemen came very pressingly to urge the governor to enforce the payment of it in the town; he told them before he would use compulsion he would try fair means, and call a hall to see whether the townsmen would be persuaded, which accordingly he did : but when the day came the excisemen came to the governor and advised him to take a strong guard with him, telling him that the butchers had been whetting their knives, and intended mischief, and had cast out many words intimating a dangerous design. The governor told them he should not augment his usual guard, and could fear nothing, having no intent to do anything that might provoke them to mutiny.   They went again to the men and told them the governor intended to come with many armed men, to compel them to pay it : whereupon when he came to the hall he found but a very slender appearance, yet those who were there were all fully resolved not to pay it; but the governor wrought with them to represent their reasons, in a humble manner, to the committee of both kingdoms, and that there should be a fuller meeting for that purpose the next week, and that in the meantime both parties should forbear any private addresses in this matter.   To this the excisemen agreed; yet, notwithstanding, the governor took a whole packet of their letters going to London, which when

he discovered, he also wrote to his friends in London
on behalf of the garrison. The next week at a full
meeting, a petition was signed, which the governor
offered the town to have carried, being himself to
go up, but they in a compliment refused to give him
the trouble, pitching upon Captain Coates and the
town-clerk to go up with it. They accordingly
went, about the time that, after seven weeks' stay
in the garrison, the governor was called again up
to London to justify himself against the malicious
clamours of his adversaries. When Captain Coates
and the other came to London they applied themselves to Mr. Millington, who, perceiving that the
governor stood for the ease of the garrison, put them
into a way to frustrate their own designs, and so
they returned home ; and at the sessions, rendering
the town an account of their negotiations, they told
them they found it an impossible thing to get the
excise taken off. Yet the governor knew a way
how to ease them, but they feared he would be discouraged in it, because at his coming up he had
found their disaffections expressed against him in a
petition to cast him out of his command, " which,"
said the clerk, " you cannot do, for he still is and
must be governor ; therefore, if any of you have
been cheated of your hands, contrary to your intentions and desires, you would do well to testify your
honesty, by disclaiming what goes under your
name." Soon after, these malignants stirred up the

soldiers to mutiny, and there being no governor in
the garrison that could tell how to order them
otherwise, they were appeased with money; [1] upon
which occasion a general muster being called, the
major told the soldiers how they were injured at
London by a petition, preferred in the name of the
whole garrison, to cast the governor out of his
command, which, if it were not their desire, he
wished them to certify to the contrary. They all
with one voice cried, they desired no other governor;
whereupon a certificate to that purpose was drawn
up; but when it came to be subscribed, certain of
the committee faction went up and down persuading
the companies not to subscribe; [2] and when they
found how little they prevailed, they foamed for
anger, and such malicious railing, that one of the
governor's soldiers, not able to bear them longer,

---

[1] "The next day the major's and Captain Poulton's
soldiers refused to watch, because they had not a fortnight's
pay more than the other soldiers in recompense of their
hard duty at Southwell; the major's were persuaded to
'their watch and Poulton's likewise were willing to watch
till somebody in the mutiny persuaded them from it, so
that they did not watch that night, therefore the day after
a general master was called," &c.—Note-Book.

[2] "When it came to be subscribed, Hall and Wandall
so stirred up Mason's and Martin's companies that they
refused, and Rily and the old marshal went with them
from one company to another persuading against the
governor."—Note-Book.

cried out, "Why do we suffer these fellows to vapour thus? let us clout them out of the field:" but the major hearing it, committed him; and the next morning the certificate went up, subscribed with seven hundred townsmen's hands. After all was done, the major gave some small sum to the soldiers to drink, and the malicious faction, when they saw they could not hinder this certificate, made another false one of their own, that the major had with crowns a-piece hired all these subscriptions, with other such like lies, which when they could not make good, it is said they retracted their certificate at London.[1]

The committee at London could never finish the business by reason of the impertinent clamours of the governor's enemies, therefore at length, wearied with the continual endless papers they had daily brought in, they made an order, wherein they assigned a certain day for the determination of the power, and in the meantime commanded all matter of crimination on both sides should be forborne. At the day they both appeared, but Mr. Millington presented a petition of a most insolent nature, and fresh articles against the governor, which gave the committee much distaste. The petition was, that whereas the committee had kept them ten weeks at

---

[1] With this incident the narrative contained in Mrs. Hutchinson's Note-Book ends.

great charges, they desired a speedy despatch now, according to their propositions. The committee were much offended at this, and told them they did them much injury to lay their stay upon them, who five weeks before desired them to return, and only leave a solicitor for each, and then they refused it ; that they had broken their first orders, and given no satisfaction for it, and now also their last, in bringing in articles against the governor. They took it very ill that they, who were plaintiffs, should prescribe to them, who were judges, how to determine the business ; wherefore they ordered that the governor should return and pursue his first instructions, till he received new ones, and that the business should be reported to the house. The governor sent his brother down to take care of the garrison, and stayed himself to receive the final determination of the house, where Mr. Millington, through his interest, kept off the report, by several tricks and unjust delays, for about three or four months.[1]

When the lieutenant-colonel came down, the captains were wonderful obedient, and all things pretty quiet, but the governor's officers were discouraged at the countenance which was given to his enemies, and the impunity of all the crimes of that faction. He having a certain spirit of government, in an extraordinary manner, which was not

---

[1] The report of the Committee is given in the Appendix.

given to others, carrying an awe in his presence that
his enemies could not withstand, the garrison was
much disordered by his absence, and in daily peril ;
although the lieutenant-colonel was as faithful and
industrious in managing that charge as any person
could be, and as excellent a person, but in a
different way from his brother. Firmness and zeal
to the cause, and personal valour he had equally,
but that vigour of soul which made him invincible
against all assaults, and overcame all difficulties he
met in his way, was proper to himself alone. The
lieutenant-colonel was a man of the kindest heart and
the most humble familiar deportment in the world,
and lived with all his soldiers as if they had been
his brothers ; dispensing with that reverence which
was due to him, and living cheerful and merry, and
familiar with them, in such a manner that they
celebrated him, and professed the highest love for
him in the world, and would magnify his humility
and kindness, and him for it, in a high degree
above his brother. But with all this they grew so
presumptuous that, when any obedience was exacted
beyond their humours or apprehensions, they would
often dare to fail in their duty ; whereas the
governor, still keeping a greater distance, though
with no more pride, preserved an awe that made
him to be equally feared and loved, and though
they secretly repined at their subjection, yet durst
they not refuse it ; and, when they came to render

it on great occasions, they found such wisdom and
such advantage in all his dictates that, their reason
being convinced of the benefit of his government,
they delighted in it, and accounted it a happiness
to be under his command, when any public necessity superseded the mutiny of those private lusts,
whereby all men naturally, but especially vulgar
spirits, would cast off their bridle, and be their
own only rulers.[1]

As the governor's absence was the occasion of
many neglects in the government, not by his
brother's fault, but the soldiers', who wanting of
their pay (which, while the committee should have
been providing, they were spending it in vexatious prosecutions of the governor), and therefore
discontented, and through that, careless of their
duty ; so, on the other side, the cavaliers, who were
not ignorant of the dissensions in the garrison, took
the advantage, and surprised the lieutenant-colonel's
fort at the Trent bridges, while he was employed
in keeping the castle.   His soldiers in his absence
lying out of their quarters, had not left above thirty
men upon the guard, who were most of them killed,
the ensign fighting it out very stoutly, after their

---

[1] In the delineation of characters Mrs. Hutchinson remarkably excels.   Nothing can be more amiable than that
which she here draws of Mr. George Hutchinson, and this
character he will be found to sustain with increased esteem
to the end of the history.—J. H.

entrance, till he died. The lieutenant-colonel was exceedingly afflicted with this loss, but presently applied himself to secure what remained. The whole town was in a sad uproar, and this happening upon a Lord's day in the morning, in May, 1645, all the people were in such a consternation that they could keep no sabbath that day.[1] Then the lieutenant-colonel had an experiment of vulgar spirits, for even his own soldiers, who were guilty of the loss of the place by being out of their quarters, began to exclaim against him for a thousand causeless things ; and although he laboured amongst them with as much courage and vigour as any man could use, to settle their spirits and regain the place, yet they slighted him most unjustly, and all cried out now to have the governor sent for, as if he himself had been their castle.

Immediately after the unhappy surprise of the bridges, the lieutenant-colonel sent away to his brother a post, who by some of the lower fords got over the water, and carried his sad news to London. A trumpet was sent to the bridges, and obtained the dead bodies of the soldiers who were slain at

---

[1] Mrs. Hutchinson is mistaken in the date. The surprise of the bridges occurred on April 20th, as the Journals of the House of Commons for Tuesday, April 22d, prove. On this incident see the note in the Appendix, on the quarrel between Colonel Hutchinson and the committee.

the surprise, and they were brought up to the town
in carts and buried.   There was about twenty of
them, very good and stout men, though it availed
them not in their last need, when a multitude had
seized them unawares.   All that day a body of
the enemy faced the town, which, through terrors
without and discouragements and discontents within,
was in a very sad posture.   The malignant faction
against the governor improved even this occasion,
and suggested to the town that the castle would
be the cause of their ruin; that the governor and
his soldiers would secure themselves there, and
leave the town undefended; and because the lieutenant-colonel was very strict that none of the
castle-soldiers should lie out of their quarters,
lest that place might be surprised as well as the
other, the townsmen renewed their railings against
the castle, and their malice to all that were in it;
but the lieutenant-colonel, regarding none of their
unjust railings, by God's blessing upon his vigilance,
kept the town and castle till his brother's return.

As soon as the news came to the governor at
London, he thought it time to throw off that patience
with which he had hitherto waited at great expense,
and went to the parliament-house before the house
sat, and there acquainted the Speaker what was
befallen at Nottingham, desiring he might be called
to make a relation of it in the open house, or else
he told the Speaker, though he died for it, he would

press in and let them know how much the cause
suffered by the indirect practices, which were par-
tially connived at by some of their members.   The
Speaker seeing him so resolved, procured him, when
the house was set, to be called in : and there he
told them how their fort was lost, and, for aught
he knew, the garrison, by that time ; which was no
more than what he had long expected, through the
countenance that was, by one of their members,
given to a malignant faction, that obstructed all the
public service, disturbed all the honest soldiers and
officers in their duty, and spent the public treasury,
to carry on their private malice.   He further told
them, how dishonourable, as well as destructive to
their cause, it was, that their members should be
protected in such unjust prosecutions, and should
make the privilege of the house their shelter, to
oppress the most active and faithful of their servants.   This and many other things he told them,
with such boldness, that many of the guilty members
had a mind to have committed him, but he spoke
with such truth and convincing reason, that all those
of more generous spirits were much moved by it,
and angry that he had been so injuriously treated,
and desired him to take post down and to use all
means to regain the place, and gave him full orders
to execute his charge without disturbance.   From
that time Mr. Millington so lost his credit, that he
never recovered the esteem he formerly had among

them; and after that time, the govenor's enemies perceiving they were not able to mate [1] him, made no more public attempts, though they continued that private malice, which was the natural product of that antipathy there was between his virtues and their vices.   Neither was it his case alone; almost all the parliament-garrisons were infested and disturbed with like factious little people, insomuch that many worthy gentlemen were wearied out of their commands, and oppressed by a certain mean sort of people in the house, whom to distinguish from the more honourable gentlemen, they called *Worsted-stocking Men.*[2]   Some as violently curbed their committees, as the committees factiously molested

---

[1] Mate, conquer; Fr. mater, an expression taken from the game of chess.—J. H.

[2] At a time when sumptuary laws were hardly obsolete, an expression signifying a difference in dress might well be used to express difference in rank.   Whitelock, in describing the approval with which the army viewed Cromwell's expulsion of the Rump, uses a similar figure of speech.   One of the soldiers, he says, "did not stick to say to the father (he being a parliament man, and the son a captain in the army), that this business was nothing but to pull down the father and to set up the son; and no more but for the father to wear worsted and the son silk stockings."—Whitelock Memorials, ed. 1853, vol. iv. p. 6.

Cleveland also, in his "Character of a Country Committee-Man," describes amongst the members of the committee "a new blue-stockinged justice, lately made of a good basket-hilted yeoman."

them. Nor was the faction only in particular garrisons, but the parliament house itself began to fall into the two great oppositions of Presbytery and Independency : and, as if discord had infected the whole English air with an epidemical heart-burning and dissension in all places, even the king's councils and garrisons were as factiously divided. The king's commissioners and the governor at Newark fell into such high discontents, that Sir Richard Biron, the governor, was changed, and Sir Richard Willis put into his place.[1] This accident of the bridges put an end to that vexatious persecution wherewith the governor had had many sore exercises of his wisdom, patience, and courage, and many experiences of God's mercy and goodness, supporting him in all his trials, and bearing him up against all discouragements, not only to stand without the least dejection himself, but to be able to hold up many others, who were ready to sink under the burthen of unrighteousness and oppression, where they expected just thanks and rewards. It cost the governor above three hundred pounds to defend himself against their calumnies, renewed forgeries, and scandals, laid upon him ; but God was with him in all in a wonderful manner, bringing truth to

---

[1] An important letter relating to this change is given in Warburton's " Prince Rupert," vol. iii. p. 48 : Joseph Rhodes to Prince Rupert, January 10, 1645.

light through all the clouds of envy that sought to obscure it, and making his innocence and upright-ness to shine forth as the noon-day, justifying him even in the eyes of his enemies, and covering them with shame and confusion of face. They maintained their prosecution of him out of the public stock, and were not called to account for so mis-spending it. Mr. Millington perceiving how much he had lost himself by it, applied himself to seek a reconcilia-tion by flattering letters, and professions of convic-tion and repentance of his unjust siding with those men. The governor, who was of a most reconcile-able nature, forgave him, and ever after lived in good friendship with him.[1] Others of them also afterwards, when they saw the governor out of their power, some through fear, and others over-come with his goodness, submitted to him, who lived to see the end of them all ; part of them dying before any disgrace or great sorrows overtook him, and those who survived, renouncing and apostatising from their most glorious engagements, and becom-ing guilty of those crimes for which they falsely accused him, while he remained firm, and dying

---

[1] As Mr. Millington will figure no more in this history, the reader is here informed that he finished his career, after becoming one of the judges who sentenced Charles the First, by coming in upon proclamation, making a pitiful recantation, and being sentenced to perpetual imprisonment.—J. H.

sealed up the profession of his life ; in all the future difficulties of which, he was still borne up with the experience of God's goodness and manifold protections.

The governor being dismissed from the parliament, immediately took post, and coming through Northampton, met his old engineer, Hooper, and brought him with him to Nottingham, where, by God's mercy, he arrived safe about three days after the loss of the bridges, and was welcomed as if safety and victory, and all desirable blessings, had come in his train. His presence reinforced the · drooping garrison, and he immediately consulted how to go about regaining the fort. To this purpose, and to hinder the enemy from having an inlet into the town by the bridges, he made a little fort on the next bridge, and put a lieutenant and thirty men into it, thereby enclosing those in the fort the enemy had surprised, whom he resolved to assault on the town side, having thus provided that their friends should not come from the other side[1] to help them. But those of Newark understanding this, came as strong as they could one morning, and assaulted the little new fort, where the lieu-

---

[1] To understand this rightly it is necessary to be informed, that in approaching Nottingham from the south there is a very wide valley, through which the Trent and the Lene run in several branches, over which are bridges united by a causeway.—J. H.

tenant, Hall, failing of that courage which he had professed when he begged the honour of keeping it, gave it up, which the governor seeing from the other side, was exceedingly vexed at, and marched up to the bridge to assault them in that fort; but he found that they had only stormed the other little fort to make their own way to be gone, and that they had made shift to get to their friends upon the ribs of two broken arches, which, when they had served to help their passage, they pulled up, to hinder pursuit after them: and thus in a month's space God restored to the governor the fort which was lost in his absence; and he new fortified the place and repaired the bridges, whereby the great market out of the vale was again brought into the town, to their exceeding joy and benefit.

This summer there was another kind of progress made in the war than had been before, and the new parliament army prosecuting it so much in earnest, that they made a show to block up the king in his main garrison at Oxford, he breaks out, and joining Prince Rupert's horse, came, after several attempts otherwhere, to Leicester, which he took by storm.[1]   The loss of this town was a great affliction and terror to all the neighbouring garrisons and counties, whereupon Fairfax closely attended the king's motions, came within a few days and

---

[1] Leicester was taken on May 29th, 1645.

fought with the king, and overcame him in that
memorable battle at Naseby, where his coach and
cabinet of letters were taken ; which letters being
carried to London were printed,[1] and manifested his
falsehood, when, contrary to his professions, he had
endeavoured to bring in Danes and Lorrainers,
and Irish rebels, to subdue the good people here,
and had given himself up to be governed by the
queen in all affairs both of state and religion.
After this fight Fairfax took again the town of
Leicester, and went into the West, relieved Taunton,
took Bristol, and many other garrisons. West .
Chester also and other places were taken that
way. Meanwhile, the king, having coasted about
the countries, came at last to Newark, and there
his commanders falling out among themselves, he
changed the governor, and put the Lord Bellasis
into the place, and went himself to Oxford, where
he was at last blocked up.[2]

---

[1] In the pamplet entitled " The King's Cabinet Opened,"
which is to be found amongst other places in the seventh
volume of the Harleian Miscellany.

But the parliament merely printed a selection from the
letters taken, thirty-nine letters and papers out of about
fifty-seven. Of those which they omitted, several were
discovered by the Royal Commission on Historical Manuscripts, and printed in their first report in 1870.

[2] The battle of Naseby took place on June 14th. The
king came twice to Newark ; he was there on August 21st,
and again from October 14th to November 3d. The

When Sir Thomas Fairfax was made chief general, Poyntz was made major-general of the northern counties, and a committee of war was set up at York, whereof Colonel Pierrepont, by his brother's procurement, was appointed one, and pretty well satisfied, as thinking himself again set above Colonel Hutchinson, because all the northern garrisons were to receive orders from that committee : but the governor heeding not other men's exaltations or depressions, only attended to his own duty. About the latter end of this summer, Poyntz came to Nottingham with all the horse that could be gathered in the neighbouring counties. He had before marched with them and the Nottingham regiment into Cheshire,[1] and brought several gentle-

---

events referred to, took place during the second visit. *Vide* Clarendon, " History of the Rebellion " ix. 121–132.

[1] The battle of Rowton Heath, near Chester, took place on September 24th, 1645, in which the king's attempt to raise the siege of Chester was defeated with the loss of 1300 men. The following letter is from "Perfect Occurrences " for October 9 :—" We have been indebted to the Nottingham horse for their good service in the last routing of the king near Chester, as you may see by Colonel Thornhagh's letter, part of which, it being too long to print all, followeth :—

" ' SIR,—In pursuit of the king so far I pursued, that retreat I could not, fight I must ; commending myself and soldiers to God's protection, I resolved to charge them with my regiment. The enemy came down to us, and in a career charged ; we stood and moved not till they had

men prisoners into the garrison of Nottingham, who had been taken in divers encounters. When he marched out, Palmer the Priest, not daring to venture himself in the field, laid down his commission, when he saw that there was now no connivance to be found at disobeying commands.

By reason of the rout at Naseby, and the surrender of Carlisle to the Scots and several other garrisons, the broken forces of the cavaliers had all repaired to Newark, and that was now become the strongest and best fortified garrison the king had ; and Poyntz was ordered to quarter his horse about it, till the Scots should come on the other side and besiege it. At that time also the king himself was there.[1]   The governor having informed Poyntz how prejudicial it would be to his design to suffer those little garrisons in the Vale at Shelford and Wiverton to remain, it was agreed that all the forces should take them in their way.   But the governor having

---

fired, which made Gerrard swear (God damn him), the rogues will not stir.' Upon those words we clapped spurs to our horses, and gave him such a charge as I daresay was the accomplishment of the victory, for we routed him and pursued him, and made him fly to Holt Castle, over a river in the night, with six men of a thousand which before were with him."—Francis Thornhagh, September 30.

[1] Having come hither from Wales with a body of three thousand men ; he stayed till, fearing to be besieged by the Scots, who were approaching, he went away by night to Oxford, November 6, 1645.—J. H.

obtained permission of Poyntz, through a respect
he had to the family, sent to Colonel Philip Stanhope, governor of Shelford, a letter to persuade
him to surrender the place he could not hold, and
to offer him to obtain honourable terms for him, if
he would hearken to propositions. Stanhope returned a very scornful, huffing reply, in which one
of his expressions was, that he should lay Nottingham castle as flat as a pancake, and such other
bravadoes, which had been less amiss if he had
done anything to make them good. Hereupon the
whole force marched against the place, and the
several posts were assigned to the several colonels.
The governor, according to his own desire, had
that which seemed most difficult assigned to him,
and his quarters that night appointed in Shelford
town. When he came thither, a few of Shelford
soldiers were gotten into the steeple of the church,
and from thence so played upon the governor's men
that they could not quietly take up their quarters.
There was a trap door that went into the belfry, and
they had made it fast, and drawn up the ladder
and the bell-ropes, and regarded not the governor's
threatening them to have no quarter if they came
not down, so that he was forced to send for straw
and fire it, and smother them out. Hereupon they
came down, and among them there was a boy who
had marched out with the governor's company, when
he went first against Newark, and carried himself

so stoutly, that Captain Wray begged him for a
foot-boy, and when his troop was once taken by
the enemy, this boy, being taken among them, became one of their soldiers.[1] The governor making
him believe he should be hanged immediately for
changing his party, and for holding out to their
disturbance, where he could not hope for relief,
the boy begged he might be spared, and offered to
lead them on to a place where only they could enter,
where the palisade was unfinished. The governor,
without trusting to him, considered the probability
of his information, kept him under guard, and set him
in the front of his men, and he accordingly proved
to have told them the truth in all that he had said,
and did excellent good service, behaving himself
most stoutly. The governor being armed, and ready
to begin the assault, when the rest were also ready,
Captain White came to him, and, notwithstanding all
his former malicious prosecutions, now pretended
the most tender care and love that could be declared,
with all imaginable flattery; and persuaded the
governor not to hazard himself in so dangerous an
attempt, but to consider his wife and children, and
stand by among the horse, but by no means to storm

---

[1] This surprise of Captain Wray's troop occurred in
May 1643, near Grantham ("Mercurius Aulicus," May 11),
so that the boy had been more than two years with the
royalists.

the place in his own person.   Notwithstanding all his
false insinuations, the governor perceived his envy
at that honour which his valour was ready to reap
in this encounter, was exceedingly angry with him,
and went on upon the place.   This being seated on
a flat, was encompassed with a very strong bulwark,
and a great ditch without, in most places wet at the
bottom, so that they within were very confident,
there being no cannon brought against them, to
hold it out ; because also a broken regiment of the
queen's, who were all papists, were come in to their
assistance.   A regiment of Londoners was appointed
to storm on the other side, and the governor at the
same time began the assault at his post.   His men
found many more difficulties than they expected,
for after they had filled up the ditches with faggots
and pitched the scaling-ladders, they were twenty
staves too short, and the enemy, from the top of
the works, threw down logs of wood, which would
sweep off a whole ladderful of men at once : the
lieutenant-colonel himself was once or twice so
beaten down.   The governor had ordered other
musketeers to beat off those men that stood upon
the top of the works, which they failed of by
shooting without good aim ; but the governor
directed them better, and the Nottingham horse
dismounting, and assailing with their pistols and
headpieces, helped the foot to beat them down from
the top of the works, all except one stout man, who

stood alone, and did wonders in beating down the assailants, which the governor being angry at, fetched two of his own musketeers and made them shoot, and he immediately fell, to the great discouragement of his fellows. Then the governor himself first entered, and the rest of his men came in as fast as they could. But while his regiment was entering on this side, the Londoners were beaten off on the other side, and the main force of the garrison turned upon him. The cavaliers had half moons within, which were as good a defence to them as their first works ; into these the soldiers · that were of the queen's regiment were gotten, and they in the house shot out of all the windows. The governor's men, as soon as they got in, had taken the stables and all their horses, but the governor himself was fighting with the captain of the papists and some others, who, by advantage of the half moon and the house, might have prevailed to cut off him and those that were with him, which were not many. The enemy being strengthened by the addition of those who had beaten off the assailants on the other side, were now trying their utmost to vanquish those that were within. The lieutenant-colonel, seeing his brother in hazard, made haste to open the drawbridge, that Poyntz might come in with his horse ; which he did, but not before the governor had killed that gentleman who was fighting with him, at whose fall his men gave way. Poyntz seeing them shoot from the house, and apprehending the king might come to their relief, when he came in, ordered that no quarter should be given. And here the governor was in greater danger than before, for the strangers hearing him called governor, were advancing to have killed him, but that the lieutenant-colonel, who was very watchful to preserve him all that day, came in to his rescue, and scarcely could persuade them that it was the governor of Nottingham; because he, at the beginning of the storm, had put off a very good suit of armour that he had, which being musket-proof, was so heavy that it heated him, and so would not be persuaded by his friends to wear any thing but his buff coat. The governor's men, eager to complete their victory, were forcing their entrance into the house : meanwhile Rossiter's men came and took away all their horses, which they had taken when they first entered the works and won the stables, and left in the guard of two or three, while they were pursuing their work. The governor of Shelford, after all his bravadoes, came but meanly off; it is said he sat in his chamber, wrapt up in his cloak, and came not forth that day; but that availed him not, for how, or by whom, it is not known, but he was wounded and stripped, and flung upon a dunghill. The lieutenant-colonel, after the house was mastered, seeing the disorder by which our men were ready to murder one another, upon the command Poyntz had issued to give no quarter, desired Poyntz to cause the slaughter to cease, which was presently obeyed, and about sevenscore prisoners saved. While he was thus busied, inquiring what was become of the governor, he was shown him naked upon the dung-hill; whereupon the lieutenant-colonel called for his own cloak and cast it over him, and sent him to a bed in his own quarters, and procured him a surgeon. Upon his desire he had a little priest, who had been his father's chaplain, and was one of the committee faction; but the man was such a pitiful comforter, that the governor, who was come to visit him, was forced to undertake that office: but though he had all the supplies they could all ways give him, he died the next day.[1] The house

---

[1] Thoroton, in his "History of Nottinghamshire," says, "Shelford House was a garrison for the king, and commanded by Colonel Philip Stanhope, son of the first Earl of Chesterfield, which being taken by a storm, he and many of his soldiers were therein slain, and the house afterwards burned; his brother Ferdinando Stanhope was slain sometime before by a parliament soldier at Bridgford." This last happened in that skirmish with the bridge soldiers recited in page 56, where he is·said only to have been made prisoner. Lady Catherine Hutchinson, who attested the remark to Colonel Hutchinson her son-in-law's disadvantage, vol. i. p. 249, was the sister of the Earl of Chesterfield, and of course aunt of Colonel Stanhope, and as she takes no exception to it, we may safely give credit

which belonged to his father, the Earl of Chesterfield, was that night burned, none certainly knowing by what means, whether by accident or on purpose; but there was most ground to believe that the country people, who had been sorely infested by that garrison, to prevent the keeping it by those who had taken it, purposely set it on fire. If the queen's regiment had mounted their horses and stood ready upon them when our men entered, they had undoubtedly cut them all off; but they standing to the works, it pleased God to lead them into that path he had ordained for their destruction, who being papists, would not receive quarter, nor were they much offered it, being killed in the heat of the contest, so that not a man of them escaped.

The next day our party went to Wiverton, a house of the Lord Chaworth's, which, terrified with the example of the other, yielded upon terms, and was by order pulled down and rendered incapable of being any more a garrison.

Poyntz now quartered all his horse in the towns about Newark, and in regard he had no peculiar

---

to this story of the storming of Shelford with all its circumstances.—J. H.

In spite of the fact that Lady Catherine Hutchinson let the story pass, it is difficult to believe this account of Colonel Stanhope's cowardice. In the two letters relating the storming of Shelford, given in the Appendix, no misconduct on the part of the governor is even hinted at.

regiment of his own, the governor's regiment served him for his guards. The Scots also came and quartered on the other side of the town towards the north.[1]

All that winter the governor lay at the leaguer, and about Christmas time writs were sent down for new elections to fill up the parliament.[2] There being a burgess-ship void at Nottingham, the town would needs, in a compliment, make the governor free, in order to make an election of him for the parliament. Mr. Francis Pierrepont hearing this, writ to the governor to desire that he would rather come into his father's place in the county, and give him his assistance in

---

[1] The Sutherland Clarendon, in the Bodleian Library, contains two maps showing the positions of the besiegers of Newark. The letters and orders of the Derby House Committee, in the Public Record Office, give the fullest information relative to the composition of the besieging forces.

[2] A new writ for Nottingham town for the election of a burgess, in place of Mr. William Stanhope disabled, was ordered on 12th November 1645. The following entry in the Corporation Records shows the powerful interest exerted for Mr. Pierrepont :—"22d December 1645. The letter sent from the committee at York concerning Mr. Pierrepont to be burgess of the parliament for this town, was read this day, and an answer thereunto agreed upon and subscribed by the aldermen."—Bailey, "Annals of Nottingham-shire," p. 749. The writ for the election of two knights for the county was ordered February 10, 1646.

this, as he should engage his own and all his
friends' interest for him in the county.   The
governor, who was ever ready to requite injuries
with benefits, employed his interest in the town to
satisfy the gentleman's desire, and having very
many in his regiment that had voices, he sent for
them all home the night before the day of election ;
which had like to have been a very sad one, but
that by the mercy of God, and the courage of
Poyntz and the lieutenant-colonel and Captain
Poulton, it had not so bad event.   The Newarkers,
hearing that so many of the regiment were away,
fell upon their quarters, and most of the men being
surprised, were rather endeavouring flight than
resistance ; when the lieutenant-colonel and Captain Poulton rallied all they could find, lined some
pales with musketeers, and beat the enemy again
out of their quarters, and Poyntz, mounting with as
many horse as were about him, which was very
few, followed them in the night up to the very
works of Newark.   Some loss there was in the
quarters, but nothing considerable; some soldiers
ran away home, and brought the governor word
they were all cut off, but his brother sent a messenger to acquaint him with the contrary.   Hereupon, immediately after the election, he returned
back again with his men.   Not long after, the elections were made for the county, who all pitched
upon the governor, in his father's room.   White,

whose envy never died, used all the endeavours he
could to have hindered it; but when he saw he
could do no harm, with a sad heart, under a false
face, he came and took his part of a noble dinner
the new knights had provided for the gentlemen of
the country. Without any competition Mr. Hutchinson had the first voice in the room of his father,
and Mr. Pigott the second, in the room of Mr.
Sutton, now a commissioner at Newark. About
the same time Colonel Thornhagh was chosen
burgess for the town of Retford; but none of them
went up to their places in parliament till the siege .
of Newark was finished.

Poyntz drew a line about the town, and made a
very regular entrenchment and approaches, in such
a soldier-like manner as none of them who had
attempted the place before had done. Most of that
winter they lay in the field, and the governor,
carried on by the vigour and greatness of his mind,
felt no distemper then by that service, which all his
captains and the soldiers themselves endured worse
than he. Besides daily and hourly providences,
by which they were preserved from the enemy's
cannons and sallies, there were some remarkable
ones, by which God kept the governor's life in this
leaguer. Once as Poyntz and he, and another
captain, were riding to view some quarter of the
town, a cannon bullet came whizzing by them, as
they were riding all abreast, and the captain, with-

out any touch of it, said he was killed; Poyntz
bid him get off, but he was then sliding down from
his horse, slain by the wind of the bullet; they
held him up till they got off from the place, but the
man immediately turned black all over. Another
time the governor was in his tent, and by chance
called out; when he was scarce out of it, a cannon
bullet came and tore up the whole tent, and killed
the sentinel at the door. But the greatest peril
wherein all on the English side were, was the
treachery of the Scots, which they had very good
reason to apprehend might have been the cutting
off of all that force. Sir Thomas Fairfax had now
besieged Oxford, and the king was stolen out of the
town and gone in disguise, no man knew whither,
but at the length he came into the Scots' army.[1] They
had before behaved themselves very oddly to the
English, and been taking sundry occasions to pick
quarrels, when at the last certain news was brought
to the English quarters, that the king was come to
the Scots, and by them received at Southwell. The
English could then expect nothing but that the
Scots, joining with those that were in Newark,
would fall upon them, who were far inferior in
number to the other, and therefore they all prepared

---

[1] The king left Oxford on April 27, 1646, and came to
Southwell on May 5th. See Dr. Hudson's account of
the king's escape, Gutch's "Collectanea Curiosa," vol. ii.
p. 452.

themselves as well as they could, to defend themselves in their trenches. The governor had then very fine horses at the leaguer, which he sent home to the garrison ; but while they were in expectation of being thus fallen upon, the king had more mind to be gone ; and because the Scots knew not how to break up their quarters while the town was not taken, the king sent to my Lord Bellasis, the governor of Newark, to surrender up the place immediately, which he did upon pretty handsome terms, but much discontented that the king should have no more regard to them who had been so constant to his service.[1] The governor with his regiment was appointed to receive the town and the arms, and to quarter in it ; where he now went and had the greatest danger of all, for the town was all over sadly infected with the plague ; yet it so pleased God that neither he nor any of the fresh men caught the infection, which was so raging there that it almost desolated the place.

Whether the king's ill council or his destiny led him, he was very failing in this action ; for had he gone straight up to the parliament and cast himself upon them, as he did upon the Scots, he had in all probability ruined them, who were highly divided

---

[1] Among the names of those who signed the capitulation on the part of the parliament (as it appears in Rushworth) are those of Colonel Hutchinson and Colonel Twissleton.

between the presbyterian and independent factions ;
but in putting himself into the hands of the mercenary Scotch army, rather than the parliament of
England, he showed such an embittered hate to the
English nation, that it turned many hearts against
him.   The Scots in this business were very false
both to the parliament and to the king.   For them
to receive and carry away the king's person with
them, when they were but a hired army, without
either the consent or knowledge of the parliament,
was a very false carriage of them ; but besides that,
we had *certain evidences* that they were prepared,
and had an intent to have cut off the English army
who beleaguered Newark,[1] but that God changed
their counsels and made them take another course,
which was to carry the king to Newcastle, where
they again sold him to the parliament for a sum of
money.

The country being now cleared of all the enemy's
garrisons, Colonel Hutchinson went up to London
to attend his duty there, and to serve his country
as faithfully, in the capacity of a senator, as he had
before in that of a soldier.   When he came there
he found a very bitter spirit of discord and envy
raging, and the presbyterian faction (of which were

---

[1] What the "certain evidences" mentioned may have
been must remain uncertain ; but though the relations of
the two armies were strained, this is a gross exaggeration.

most of those lords and others that had been laid
aside by the self-denying ordinance), endeavouring
a violent persecution, upon the account of conscience, against those who had in so short a time
accomplished, by God's blessing, that victory which
he was not pleased to bestow on them. Their
directory of worship was at length sent forth for a
three years' trial, and such as could not conform to
it, marked out with an evil eye, hated and persecuted under the name of Separatist.[1]　Colonel
Hutchinson, who abhorred that malicious zeal and
imposing spirit which appeared in them, was soon
taken notice of for one of the independent faction[2]
[whose heads were accounted Pierrepont, Vane,
　　　St. John and some few other grandees,
being men that excelled in wisdom and utterance,
and the rest believed to adhere to them only out
of faction, as if those who did not vain-gloriously
lay out themselves, without necessity, but chose
rather to hear and vote, had had no understanding
of right and wrong but from the dictates of these
great oracles].　Though, to speak the truth, they

---

[1] The position of affairs at this moment, and the progress of the struggle between the Independents and the
Presbyterians, is admirably described by Masson. " Life
of Milton," vol. iii., book iii., chap. ii.

[2] All that is contained between these two brackets had
lines struck through it in the manuscript, and one of the
names defaced.—J. H.

very little knew Colonel Hutchinson that could say
he was of any faction ; for he had a strength of
judgment able to consider things himself and propound them to his conscience, which was so upright
that the veneration of no man's person alive, nor the
love of the dearest friend in the world, could make
him do the least thing, without a full persuasion
that it was his duty so to act. He very well
understood men's gifts and abilities, and honoured
those most whom he believed to manage them
with most uprightness of soul, for God's glory and
the good of his country, and was so far from envying the just renown any man acquired that he
rejoiced in it. He never was any man's sectary,
either in religious or civil matters, farther than he
apprehended them to follow the rules of religion,
honour, and virtue ; nor any man's antagonist,
but as he opposed that which appeared to him
just and equal. If the greatest enemy he had in
the world had propounded anything profitable to
the public, he would promote it ; whereas some
others were to blame in that particular, and chiefly
those of the presbyterian faction, who would
obstruct any good, rather than that those they
envied and hated should have the glory of procur-
ing it ; the sad effects of which pride grew at length
to be the ruin of the most glorious cause that ever
was contended for. At the first, many gentlemen,
eminent in gifts and acquirements, were as eminent

in zealous improvement of them, for the advantage of God's and their country's interests, whereby they obtained just glory and admiration among all good men ; but while the creature was so magnified, God, who was the principal author, was not looked upon, and gave them therefore up to become their own and others' idols, and so to fall.

And now it grew to a sad wonder, that the most zealous promoters of the cause were more spitefully carried against their own faithful armies, by whom God had perfected their victory over their enemies, than against the vanquished foe, whose restitution they henceforth secretly endeavoured, by all the arts of treacherous, dissembling policy, in order that they might throw down those whom God had exalted in glory and power to resist their tyrannical impositions.   At that time, and long after, they prevailed not, till that pious people too began to admire themselves, for what God had done by them, and to set up themselves above their brethren, and then the Lord humbled them again beneath their conquered vassals.

So long as the army only resisted unjust impositions, and remained firm to their first pious engagement, Mr. Hutchinson adhered to that party which protected them in the parliament house.   His attendance there, changing his custom of life, into a sedentary employment, less suitable to his active spirit, and more prejudicial to his health, he fell into a long and painful sickness, which many times brought him near the grave, and was not perfectly cured in four years. The doctors could not find a name for it; but at the length resolved upon the running gout, and a cure, proper for that disease, being practised on him, took effect.

The truth is, his great mind so far surmounted the frailty of his flesh, that it would never yield to the tenderness of his constitution, nor suffer him to feel those inconveniences of martial toils, which often cast down his captains, men of more able bodies and healthful complexions, while the business was in hand; but when that was finished, he found, what he had not leisure to consider before, that his body's strength was far unequal to the vigour of his soul.

After the surrender of Newark, Nottingham town and castle was continued a garrison for some time: between this and his greater employment at London, the governor divided himself. Meanwhile, upon the 15th day of July, 1646, propositions [1] were sent to the king, then with the Scots at Newcastle, little higher than those which had been made him at Uxbridge; but he wove out delays, and would not assent to them, hoping a greater advantage by

---

[1] The Nineteen Propositions. The king refused to give a positive or immediate answer, but offered to come to London, on certain guarantees, to treat personally.

the difference betweeen the two nations, and the factions in the city and parliament, which both he and all his party employed their utmost industry to cherish and augment. Both parliaments perceiving this, and not yet senseless of approaching destruction from the common enemy, began to be cemented by the king's averseness to peace, and to consider how to settle the kingdom without him ; and when they had agreed that the Scots should deliver up the English garrisons for a certain sum of money, it fell into debate how to dispose of the king's person ; where the debate was, not who should, but who should not have him. At the length, about January of the same year, two hundred thousand pounds was carried down by part of the army to Newcastle ; and upon the payment of it, the Scots delivered their garrisons to the soldiers, and the king to certain commissioners of both houses of parliament, who conducted him honourably to his own manor of Holmeby, in Northamptonshire.

During this time Sir Thomas Fairfax himself lay at Nottingham, and the governor was sick in the castle.[1] The general's lady was come along with him, having followed his camp to the siege of Oxford, and lain at his quarters all the while he

---

[1] The king passed through Nottingham on the way to Holmby, February 11, 1647. Fairfax writes from Nottingham on February 18. (Fairfax Correspondence, "Memorials of the Civil Wars," i, 332.)

abode there.   She was exceeding kind to her husband's chaplains, independent ministers, till the
army returned to be nearer London, and then the
presbyterian ministers quite changed the lady into
such a bitter aversion against them, that they could
not endure to come into the general's presence
while she was there; and the general had an
unquiet, unpleasant life with her, who drove away
from him many of those friends, in whose conversation he had found such sweetness.   At Nottingham
they had gotten a very able minister into the great
church, but a bitter presbyterian; him and his
brethren my Lady Fairfax caressed with so much
kindness, that they grew impudent to preach up
their faction openly in the pulpit, and to revile the
others, and at length would not suffer any of the
army chaplains to preach in the town.[1]   They then

---

[1] In Whitelock's Memorials there is the following entry
under the date of December 10, 1651 :—" Letters that
two troops of Colonel Whaley's regiment, quartered at
Nottingham, had meetings twice a week, where their
officers or some of the soldiers did preach and pray; for
which they were hated and cursed by the presbyterians
and their preachers, who say they are the greatest plague
that ever did befall a town."   The soldiers were equally
intolerant.   "From Newark 'tis certified lately," says
"Mercurius Elencticus" of November 21, 1647, "that a
party of Colonel Thornhagh's men endeavoured lately (*vi et
armis*), to hinder the reading of the Common Prayer-book;
but the resolute and religious dames of the town fell upon

coming to the governor and complaining of their
unkind usage, he invited them to come and preach
in his house, which when it was known they did, a
great concourse of people came thither to them ;
and the presbyterians, when they heard of it, were
mad with rage, not only against them, but against
the governor, who accidentally gave them another
occasion about the same time, a little before the
general came.   When formerly the presbyterian
ministers had forced him, for quietness' sake, to go
and break up a private meeting in the cannonier's
chamber, there were found some notes concerning
pædobaptism, which were brought into the governor's
lodgings ; and his wife having then more leisure to
read than he, having perused them and compared
them with the Scriptures, found not what to say
against the truths they asserted, concerning the
misapplication of that ordinance to infants ; but
being then young and modest, she thought it a kind
of virtue to submit to the judgment and practice of
most churches, rather than to defend a singular
opinion of her own, she not being then enlightened
in that great mistake of the national churches.   But
in this year she, happening to be with child, communicated her doubts to her husband, and desired

---

them (*manibus tantum expansis*), beat them forth of the
church, and afterwards performed their devotions in despite
of the cowards.   A fair testimony to the perseverance of
that loyal town in their obedience and loyalty."

him to endeavour her satisfaction; which while he did, he himself became as unsatisfied, or rather satisfied against it.   First, therefore, he diligently searched the Scriptures alone, and could find in them no ground at all for that practice; then he bought and read all the eminent treatises on both sides, which at that time came thick from the presses, and still was cleared in of the error of the pædobaptists.   After this, his wife being brought to bed, that he might, if possible, give the religious party no offence, he invited all the ministers to dinner, and propounded his doubt, and the ground thereof to them.   None of them could defend their practice with any satisfactory reason, but the tradition of the church, from the primitive times, and their main buckler of federal holiness, which Tombs and Denne had excellently overthrown.   He and his wife then, professing themselves unsatisfied in the practice, desired their opinions, what they ought to do.   Most answered, to conform to the general practice of other Christians, how dark soever it were to themselves; but Mr. Foxcraft, one of the assembly, said, that except they were convinced of the warrant of that practice from the word, they sinned in doing it : whereupon that infant was not baptized.[1]   And now the governor and his wife,

---

[1] John Tombes, 1603–1676, one of the leaders of the Baptists (*vide* Wood, "Athenae Oxonienses," vol. ii., and

notwithstanding that they forsook not their assemblies, nor retracted their benevolences and civilities
from them, yet were they reviled by them, called
fanatics and anabaptists, and often glanced at in
their public sermons.   And not only the ministers,
but all their zealous sectaries, conceived implacable
malice against them upon this account; which was
carried on with a spirit of envy and persecution to
the last, though he, on his side, might well have
said to them, as his Master said to the old Pharisees:
" Many good works have I done among you; for
which of these do you hate me ? "   Yet the generality, even of that people, had a secret conviction
upon them, that he had been faithful to them, and
deserved their love; and in spite of their own
bitter zeal, could not but have a reverent esteem

Calamy's "Nonconformists' Memorial," ed. by Palmer, 1802,
vol. ii. p. 293).   He published in 1645 two treatises on
infant baptism, and in 1647 held a great disputation on it
with Baxter.   " All scholars then and there present," says
Wood, " who knew the way of disputing and managing
arguments, did conclude that Tombes got the better of
Baxter by far."

Henry Denn was another Baptist champion, and in 1657
held a public deputation on the subject with Dr. Gunning
at the Church of St. Clement Danes (Wood, ii. 766).
Some account of him is given by Vicars, " Gangraena," pt. i.
pp. 49 and 76.   John Foxcraft, minister of Gotham, was
one of the representatives of Nottinghamshire in the
Westminster Assembly (*vide* Wood, " Fasti " 1617).

for him, whom they often railed at, for not thinking and speaking according to their opinions.[1]

This year Sir Allen Apsley, governor of Barnstaple for the king, after the surrender of that garrison,[2] came and retired to the governor's house, till his composition with the parliament was completed, the governor's wife being his sister, and the governor's brother having married the other sister; and this was another occasion of opening the mouths of the malignants, who were ready to seize on any one to his prejudice. Sir Allen Apsley had not his articles punctually performed, by which he suffered great expense and intolerable vexation; and the governor, no less concerned in the injustice done to him than if he had suffered it himself, endeavoured to protect him only in that which was just,

---

[1] Mr. Matthew Arnold makes some amusing comments on this story, as illustrating social intercourse amongst the Puritans (Mixed Essays, "Equality," p. 81).

[2] Barnstaple surrendered April 13, 1646, Sprigge, "Anglia Rediviva," pt. iv. chap. vi. A letter from Sir Thomas Fairfax's quarters, published at the time, says, under the date of March 30th—"It is generally believed that Sir Allen Apsley is willing to surrender the town, fort, and castle, but that his desperate brother swears he will cut him to pieces if he offer to surrender the castle." This brother was probably Colonel James Apsley, who in 1651 made an attempt to assassinate St. John, then ambassador of the Commonwealth in Holland (see "Mercurius Politicus," 1651, p. 728). This attempt at assassination is sometimes erroneously attributed to Sir Allen.

and for this was called a cavalier, and said to have
changed his party, and a thousand more injuries;
in which none were so forward as those who had
all the while been disaffected to the whole parliament party; but after they were conquered, burying
their spite against the cause in their own bosoms,
suffered that secret fire to rise up in a black smoke
against the most faithful assertors of it.

When the commissioners went down to fetch up
the king from the Scots, one of the lords coming
to visit the governor, and finding him at that time
very sick, persuaded him to make use of one of the
king's physicians that was with them, that was
called Dr. Wilson, and was a very able physician;
but mistook the method of his cure, and made
issues in both his arms, which rather wasted his
strength than his disease, and when he was cured
were stopped up.   That spring, growing a little
better for the present, he went to London, and
having ineffectually tried several physicians, Sir Allen
Apsley persuaded him to make use of Dr. Frazier,
with whom he began a course of physic, in the
midst of which the doctor came and acquainted him
that he was likely to be imprisoned upon suspicion
of carrying on designs against the parliament under-
hand, for now the Scots were threatening invasion
and open war.   He professed his innocency with
many protestations, and desired Mr. Hutchinson to
oblige him so far as to engage for him that he

managed no design but his calling; which the
colonel believing, undertook for him to the committee of Derby-house.   When the false Scot having
thus abused him, left a letter of lame excuse to
him, and stole away out of England to the princes,
then beyond the seas, leaving a blot upon Mr.
Hutchinson for having undertaken for him; [1] but
he, acknowledging his error in having been so
abused, was thereby warned from credulity of any
of that false nation any more.   That summer he
attended to the service of the house, being freed
for a while from his distemper during the summer,
till the fall of the leaf that it returned again.   In
the meantime jealousies were sown between the
parliament, the city of London, and the army.   The
presbyterian faction were earnest to have the army
disbanded; the army resented the injury, and, being
taught to value their own merit, petitioned the
general that they might be satisfied, not only in
things relating to themselves particularly as an
army, but the general concernments and liberties of
the good people of the nation which they had fought
for.   The presbyterians were highly offended at
this, and declared it with such violence as gave
the army cause to increase their jealousies.   The
soldiers, led on to it by one Cornet Joyce, took

---

[1] This Dr. Frazier was afterwards employed by Charles
the Second to negotiate with the Scots.—J. H.

the king from Holmeby out of the parliament commissioners' hands, and carried him about with them.
The parliament voted that the king should come to
Richmond, attended by the same persons that
attended him at Holmeby ; but the army, instead
of obeying, impeached eleven members of the house
of commons of high treason, and petitioned that
those impeached members might be secluded the
house, till they had brought in their answer to the
charge ; which being violently debated, they made
a voluntary secession for six months. The general
also entreated that the king might not be brought
nearer to London than they would suffer the army
to quarter. So he was carried with them to Roy-
ston, Hatfield, Reading, and at last to Owborne,[1] till
about July, 1647, when London grew into a tumult,
and made a very rude violation upon the parliament
house, which caused them to adjourn ; when, understanding the fury of the citizens, the greatest part
of the members, with the Speaker, withdrew and
went to the army, among whom was Colonel
Hutchinson.[2] The presbyterian members who
stayed behind chose new Speakers, and made many
new votes, and vigorously began to levy forces to

---

[1] Owborne, *i.e.* Woburn. The king removed from
Caversham to Woburn on July 22 (Rushworth, iv. i. 639).

[2] As did fourteen peers and one hundred commoners.
—J. H.

resist the army, which were conducted by Massie
and Poyntz. The parliament that was with the
army made an order against the proceedings of the
members at London, and advanced with the general ;
which, when the city heard of, their stomachs would
not serve them to stand it out, but they sent commissioners, and, by the consent of the members with
the general, obtained a pacification, upon condition
that the city should disband all their new forces,
deliver up their Tower and their forts to the general,
and desert the members now sitting. They daring
to deny nothing, the general came triumphantly to
Westminster, and brought back both the Speakers
and the members, and put them again in their seats.
The general had solemn thanks from both houses,
and then, with all his chief officers, marched through
the city, from the western parts of it to the Tower,
where many commands were changed, the presbyterian party depressed, and their generals, Poyntz
and Massie, with all the remaining officers of that
faction, forced to retire ; who most of them then
changed their party, and never more appeared on
the parliament side. Yet there was still a presbyterian faction left in the house, of such as were
moderate, and who were not by the bitterness of
their zeal carried out to break their covenant with
God and men, and renew a league with the popish
interest, to destroy that godly interest which they
had at first so gloriously asserted. After this tumult

at London was quieted, about August of that year the king was brought to one of his stately palaces at Hampton Court, near London, and the army removed to quarters about the city, their head-quarters being at Putney. The king, by reason of his daily converse with the officers, began to be trinkling[1] with them, not only then but before, and had drawn in some of them to engage to corrupt others to fall in with him ; but to speak the truth of all, Cromwell was at that time so incorruptibly faithful to his trust and to the people's interest, that he could not be drawn in practise even his own usual and natural dissimulations on this occasion. His son-in-law Ireton, that was as faithful as he, was not so fully of the opinion (till he had tried it and found to the contrary) but that the king might have been managed to comply with the public good of his people, after he could no longer uphold his own violent will ; but, upon some discourses with him, the king uttering these words to him, " I shall play my game as well as I can," Ireton replied, " If your majesty have a *game* to play, you must give us also the liberty to play ours." Colonel Hutchinson privately discoursing with his cousin about the communications he had had with the king, Ireton's expressions were these : " He gave us words, and we paid him in his own coin, when we found he had no real intention to the

---

[1] Trinkling, *i.e.* tampering with.

people's good, but to prevail by our factions, to regain by art what he had lost in fight."

The king lived at Hampton Court rather in the condition of a guarded and attended prince, than as a conquered and purchased captive; all his old servants had free recourse to him; all sorts of people were admitted to come to kiss his hands and do him obeisance as a sovereign. Ashburnham and Berkley, by the parliament voted delinquents, came to him from beyond the seas, and others by permission of the army, who had hoped they might be useful to incline him to wholesome counsels;[1] but he, on the other side, interpreting this freedom wherein he was permitted to live, not to the gentleness and reconcilableness of his parliament, who, after all his injuries, yet desired his restitution, so far as it might be without the ruin of the good people of the land, but rather believing it to proceed from their apprehension of their own declining and his re-advancing in the hearts of the people, made use of this advantage to corrupt many of their

---

[1] Amongst the persons employed in this negotiation was Sir Allen Apsley. Berkley came back from France in the autumn of 1647, and met Apsley, who had been at one time Lieutenant-governor of Exeter under him, on his way to London. "He told me that he was going to me from Cromwell, and some other officers of the army with letters, and a cypher, and instructions" ("Memoirs of Sir John Berkley," Masere's "Select Tracts," part i. 356–63). Ludlow copies Berkley.

officers to revolt from them and betray them ;
which some time after they did, and paid the forfeiture with their lives. When the king was at
Hampton Court, the lords who were formerly of his
privy council at Oxford also repaired to him, to be
as a council attending him, but this was so much
disgusted at London that they retreated again ; but
the Scotch lords and commissioners having free
access to him, he drew that nation into the design
of the second war ; which brake out furiously the
next summer, and was one of the highest provocations which, after the second victory, brought
him to the scaffold. But I shall respite that, to
return to his affairs whom I principally trace.

After the parliament was by the general restored
to their seats, Colonel Hutchinson came down
to the garrison at Nottingham, which, the war
being ended, was reduced only to the castle, the
works at the town and the bridges slighted, the
companies of the governor's regiment, all but two,
disbanded, and he thinking, now in a time when
there was no opposition, the command not worthy
of himself or his brother, gave it over to his kinsman, Captain Poulton.[1] With the assistance of his
fellow parliament men he procured an order from the

---

[1] March 1, 1647. It was ordered that the works of the
town should be slighted, and the castle be garrisoned with
one hundred foot. On March 17 Captain Poulton was
appointed governor.

parliament for five thousand pounds, that had been
levied for the Scotch army, but which they, depart-
ing with too much haste, had not received, to be
distributed among the officers and soldiers of his
regiment that were at this time disbanded, in part
of their arrears; and, that it might go the farther
amongst them, himself had none of it. The garrison
at Nottingham being reduced, Colonel Hutchinson
removed his family back to his own house at
Owthorpe, but found that, having stood uninhabited,
and been robbed of everything which the neighbouring garrison of Shelford and Wiverton could
carry from it, it was so ruinated that it could not be
repaired, to make a convenient habitation, without
as much charge as would almost build another.
By reason of the debt his public employment had
run him into, not being able to do this at present
while all his arrears were unpaid, he made a bad
shift with it for that year. At this time his distemper of rheum was very sore upon him, and he
was so afflicted with pains in his head, which fell
down also with violent torture upon all his joints,
that he was not able to go for many weeks out of
his chamber; and here we had a notable example
of the victorious power of his soul over his body.
One day, as he was in the saddest torture of his
disease, certain horse came, somewhat insolently
and injuriously, exacting quarters or monies in the
town; whom he sent for, and telling them he

would not suffer such wrong to be done to his
tenants, they seeing him in so weak a condition,
would not be persuaded to forbear violent and
unjust actions, but told him his government was
expired, and they no more under his command ;
with which, and some other saucy language, being
provoked to be heartily angry, he felt not that he
was sick, but started out of his chair and beat them
out of the house and town, and returned again
laughing at the wretched fellows and at himself,
wondering what was become of his pain, and thinking how strangely his feebleness was cured in a
moment.   But while he and those about him were
in this amazement, half an hour it was not before,
as his spirits cooled, that heat and vigour they had
lent his members retired again to their noble palace,
his heart ; those efforts, wherein they had violently
employed his limbs, made them more weak than
before, and his pain returned with such redoubled
violence, that we thought he would have died in
this fit.

While he was thus distempered at home, Major-
general Ireton sent him a letter, with a new commission in it, for the resuming his government of
Nottingham Castle, which the principal officers of the
army, foreseeing an approaching storm, desired to
have in the same hand, wherein it had before been
so prosperously and faithfully preserved : but the
colonel sent them word, that as he should not have.

put his kinsman into the place, but that he was assured of his fidelity, so he would never join with those who were so forgetful of the merits of men that had behaved themselves well, as to discourage them without a cause. Hereupon they suffered Captain Poulton to remain in his command; but while the house was highly busy in faction, they took no care of any of the garrisons, especially of such as were likely to continue firm to the cause; the presbyterian faction having a design to weaken or corrupt them all, that they might be prepared for the great revolt from the parliament, which was now working in all countries. In Nottinghamshire, a brother of Lord Biron's, Colonel Gilbert Biron, meeting Captain Poulton, began to insinuate into him, and tempt him to betray Nottingham Castle; [1] which proposition, when he heard, he thought not

---

[1] Lord Biron, in a letter to the Earl of Lanerick, dated March 10, 1648, writes :—" Since my coming into the parliament parts, I have negotiated with some eminent persons, formerly of the adverse party, with so good success, that I doubt not upon the first entrance of your army in England, the greatest part of Lancashire, Cheshire, and North Wales will declare for the king, and that the principal places of strength in these countries will be secured for his service. I have likewise laid a design for the surprise of Nottingham Castle and the city of Oxford at the same time, and had I but a reasonable sum of money I should not doubt to make all sure."—Hamilton Papers, p. 167, Camden Society.

fit utterly to reject, lest the castle being then in a
weak condition, and the soldiers discontented, some
of his under officers might be more ready to
embrace it and betray both the place and him.
He therefore took a little time to consider of it, and
came to Colonel Hutchinson and acquainted him
with it.   He advised to hold his cousin Biron on
in the treaty, till he himself could go to London
and provide for the better securing of the place,
which his distemper of health a little abating, he
did : and when the place was well provided, Captain
Poulton, who was too gentle-hearted to cut off Mr.
Biron under a pretence of assenting to him, sent to
him to shift for himself, which Mr. Biron accordingly did ; and now the insurrection began everywhere to break out.

In the meantime, some months before, when the
king had laid the design of the second war with
the Scots, and had employed all his art to bring
the English presbyters to a revolt, and was now
full of hopes to bring about *his game*, and conquer
those who had conquered him, while he was amusing
the parliament with expectations of a treaty, he
privily stole away from Hampton Court, by the
assistance of Ashburnham and Berkley, no man
knew whither; but these wise men had so ordered
their business, that instead of going beyond seas,
which was his first intent, he was forced to give
himself up to Hammond, governor of the Isle of

Wight, who immediately gave notice to the parliament, and they sent him thanks for his fidelity, and ordered that the king should be honourably attended and guarded there in Carisbrook Castle. The parliament were again sending him propositions there, when they received a letter from him, urging that he might come to a personal treaty at London. Hereupon the two houses agreed on four propositions to be sent him, to pass as bills; upon the passing of which, they were content he should come to a personal treaty for the rest. The four propositions were, 1st. That a bill should pass for the settling the militia of the kingdom. 2ndly. That all oaths, declarations, &c., against the parliament and their adherents should be called in. 3rdly. That the lords made by the great seal at Oxford, should not be capable of sitting in the house of peers thereby. 4thly. That the parliament may have power to adjourn, as the two houses think fit. The Scotch commissioners opposed the sending these bills to the king, and urged his coming to a personal treaty at London. The king, understanding their mind and the factions in London, absolutely refused to sign them. Wherefore the houses, debating upon the king's denial, at length these votes were passed by both houses, on the 17th day of January :—That they would make no more addresses nor applications to the king. That no person whatsoever should make address or applica-

tion to him.   That whoever should break this order,
should incur the penalty of high treason.   That
they would receive no more messages from the king,
and that no person should presume to bring any
to either house, or any other person.   Upon these
votes the army put forth a declaration, promising
to stand by the houses in them, which was signed
by the general and all his officers, at Windsor,
January 19th, 1647.   But in May following, first
tumults began in London; then the Surrey men
came with a very insolent petition, and behaved
themselves so arrogantly to the parliament, killing
and wounding some of the guards, that a troop of
horse was fetched from the Mews, and was forced
to kill some of them before they could quiet them.[1]
After this, the parliament were informed of another
insurrection in Kent, coming under the face of a
petition, and sent out General Fairfax with seven
regiments to suppress them, who pursued them to
Rochester.   A great company of these Kentish men
were gotten together about Gravesend, with fifteen
knights, and many commanders of the king's army
to head them; who, although they were more in
number than Fairfax his men, yet durst not bide his
coming.   Some of them went to Dover Castle and

---

[1] The account given of the second civil war is mainly
based on May's "Breviary of the History of the Parliament of England."

besieged it, but the general sent out Sir Michael
Livesey, who happily relieved that place and raised
the siege; others went to Maidstone, and a few
kept together about Rochester.   The general himself went to Maidstone, where two thousand of them
were gotten into the town, and resolved to keep it;
whom the general assaulted, and with difficulty
entered the town, and fought for every street, which
were barricaded against him and defended with
cannon.   Yet at length he killed two hundred, and
took fourteen hundred prisoners.   Four hundred
horse broke away to an army of their friends,
bigger than Fairfax's, who saw the town taken, yet
had not the courage to engage against the general
for the relief of it, but after they saw his victory
dispersed.   The Lord Goring then having rallied
about two thousand of these Kentish men, led them
to Greenwich, from whence he sent to try the affections of the Londoners; but while he stayed there
expecting their answer, some troops of the army
came, upon the sight of whom, he and his men fled,
the Kentish men, most of them to their own houses;
himself, with about five hundred horse, getting boat,
crossed the Thames into Essex, where the Lord
Capel with forces out of Hertfordshire, and Sir
Charles Lucas with a body of horse at Chelmsford,
joined him; to whom, in a short time, divers that
had been the king's soldiers, with many Londoners,
and other malignants flocked in.   General Fairfax,

with part of his forces crossed the Thames at
Gravesend, and sending for all the rest out of Kent
and London, pursued the enemies, and drove them
into Colchester, where he besieged them, and lay
before them three months.   At last, hearing of the
defeat of Duke Hamilton and the Scots, and others
of the king's partisans, and being reduced to eating
horse-flesh, without hopes of relief, they yielded to
mercy.   The general shot Sir Charles Lucas and
Sir George Lisle to death upon the place, and
reserved Goring, Capel, and others, to abide the
doom of the parliament.   While Fairfax was thus
employed in Kent and Essex, Langhorne, Powell,
and Poyer, celebrated commanders of the parliament
side, revolted with the places in their command,
and got a body of eight thousand Welshmen, whom
Colonel Horton, with three thousand, encountered,
vanquished, routed, and took as many prisoners as
he had soldiers ; but Langhorne and Powell escaped
to Poyer, and shut up themselves with him in
Pembroke Castle, a place so strong that they refused all treaty ; and thereupon were besieged by
Lieutenant-general Cromwell, to whom at length,
after some months' siege, it was surrendered at the
conqueror's mercy.[1]   In divers other countries, at

---

[1] Poyer commenced the revolt in the beginning of
March ; Langhorne and Powell followed his example a
few days later.   The battle of St. Fagan's took place on

the same time, there were several insurrections and revolts; but those of the parliament party, as if they had lost courage and conscience at once, could no more behave themselves with that valour, which had before renowned them; and were slain or taken, losing the places they had betrayed to their old companions, whose fidelity was crowned with success everywhere. Among the rest, Colonel Gilbert Biron was risen, with other gentlemen of Nottinghamshire and Lincolnshire, and had gotten together about five hundred horse; wherewith, after he failed of his hopes of corrupting, the governor of Nottingham,[1] they intended to go and join themselves with others that were up in other countries; and this was so suddenly and secretly done, that they were upon their march before the rising was suspected. The governor of Nottingham had not time enough to send a messenger to be before them with Colonel Hutchinson at his house, and therefore shot off a piece of cannon; which Colonel Hutchinson hearing as he sat at dinner, and believing some extra-

---

May 8th; on May 24th Cromwell commenced the siege of Pembroke, and its surrender took place on July 11th.

[1] According to Rushworth (IV. ii. 1149), a report was made in the House of Commons on June 13th, "of the endeavouring to surprise Nottingham castle; and how the faithful governor thereof, Captain Poulton, surprised the complotters and took them all prisoners." See the Appendix.

ordinary thing to be in it, commanded horses to be made ready, and went to Nottingham ; but met the messenger who came to give him notice of the enemies' approach. The news being sent home in haste, his arms and writings, and other things of value, were put in a cart and sent away ; which was not long gone before the enemy marched by the house, and keeping their body on a hill at the town's end, only sent a party to the house to fetch them what provisions of meat and drink they found there ; besides which, they took nothing but a groom with two horses, who having ridden out to air them, fell into their mouths, because he could not be readily found when the rest of the horses were sent away. The reason why no more mischief was done by the cavaliers to his family, at that time, was, partly because Colonel Gilbert Biron had commanded not to disturb them, if he were not there, and partly because they were so closely pursued by the Lincolnshire troops, that they could not stay to take, nor would burden themselves with plunder, now they saw it unlikely to get off without fighting. This they did the next day at Willoughby within three miles of Owthorpe, and were there totally routed, killed, and taken by a party under Colonel Rossiter's command, by whom Colonel Biron was carried prisoner to Belvoir Castle.[1]

---

[1] This battle took place on July 5th, 1648. On July 8th

There being in distress, although he was an enemy, and had dealt unhandsomely with Colonel Hutchinson, in endeavouring to corrupt one for whom he was engaged, yet the colonel sent him a sum of money for his present relief, and after procured him a release and composition with the parliament. The greatest of all these dangers seemed now to be in the north, where Duke Hamilton's faction being prevalent in Scotland, he had raised an army, and was marched into England. Sir Marmaduke Langdale and Glenham having already raised some men in those parts, whom Lambert, with the assistance of some Lincolnshire forces, joined to his Yorkshire brigade, kept in play ; but they reserved themselves to join with Hamilton. Argyle and others of the · Kirk party protested against him, and many of the ministers cursed his attempt, but were silenced for

---

the Commons Journals contain this entry :—"A letter from Colonel Edward Rossiter of the 6th of July 1648, giving notice of the great victory it has pleased God to bestow upon the forces under his command against the Pontefract forces under the command of Sir Philip Mouncton, general, on the 5th of July 1648, in Willoughby fields."

The House then ordered that Colonel Rossiter should be paid £2000 on account out of the sequestrations, and that Captain Norwood, who brought the news, should receive £100. Norwood was commanded to write an account of the battle and have it printed. See the Appendix.

it, although God heard them. The presbyterians in London secretly prayed for his success, and hardly could the house of lords be brought to join with the house of commons in voting all the English traitors, that should join with the Scots, which yet at the last they did.

Colonel Hutchinson having been about this time at London, and wanting a minister for the place where he lived, and for which he had procured an augmentation, repaired to some eminent ministers in London, to recommend a worthy person to him for the place. They, with a great testimonial, preferred a Scotchman to him, whom the colonel brought down; but having occasion to be with the committee at Nottingham, to take order for the security of the county in these dangerous times, while he was out the man made strange prayers in the family, which were couched in the dark expressions; but Mrs. Hutchinson, understanding them to be intended for the prosperous success of those who were risen against the parliament, and of his nation that were coming to invade ours, told her husband at his return, that she could not bear with nor join in his prayers. The next day, being the Lord's day, the colonel heard his sermon, which was so spiritless and so lamentable, that he was very much vexed the ministers should have put such a man to him; withal he publicly made the same prayers he uttered in the family for the success of the Scots; where-

upon, after dinner, the colonel took him aside, and
told him that he had done very sinfully to undertake an office to which he was so ill gifted, and
desired him to depart in peace again the next day,
and to forbear any further employment in his
house.   The man at first was very high, and told
the colonel he was there by authority of the parliament, and would not depart ; the colonel then dealt
high with him, and told him he would declare to
them the expressions of his prayers, and so confounded the man, that he besought him to have
pity, and confessed that he was fled from his own
country for having been of Montrose's party ; and
that covetousness, against his conscience, had
drawn him to dissemble himself to be of the parliament's principles, but that God had judged him for
his hypocrisy, and withdrawn his Spirit from him,
since he practised it ; and submitted himself to
go quietly and silently away, begging it as a
favour of the colonel, that he would permit him so
to do.   He did it with such a counterfeit sorrow
and conviction, that the colonel being of a most
placable nature, freely forgave him, and sent him
not away empty, for he had fifteen pounds for only
a fortnight's service ; yet this rogue, before he went
out of the country, went to the presbyters at
Nottingham, and told them his conscience would not
permit him to stay in the colonel's house, because
he and his wife were such violent sectaries, that

no orthodox man could live comfortably with them ;
and this scandal those charitable priests were ready
to receive and more largely spread it.   They themselves, with divers of their zealous disciples, whom
they had perverted, among whom were Colonel
Francis Pierrepont, Captains Rosse, White, Chadwick, and many others, were watching opportunity
to break their covenant and rise against that parliament, under which they had served and sworn to
assist, till all delinquents, as well greater as less,
were brought to condign punishment.

At London things were in a very sad posture,
the two factions of presbytery and independency
being so engaged to suppress each other, that they
both left off to regard the public interest ; insomuch,
that at that time a certain sort of public-spirited
men stood up in the parliament and the army,
declaring against these factions and the ambition of
the grandees of both, and the partiality that was in
these days practised, by which great men were
privileged to do those things which meaner men
were punished for, and the injustice and other
crimes of particular members of parliament, rather
covered than punished, to the scandal of the
whole house.   Many got shelter in the house and
army against their debts, by which others were
defrauded and undone.   The lords, as if it were
the chief interest of nobility to be licensed in vice,
claimed many prerogatives, which set them out of

the reach of common justice, which these good-hearted people would have equally to belong to the poorest as well as to the mighty; and for this and such other honest declarations, they were nicknamed Levellers. Indeed, as all virtues are mediums, and have their extremes, there rose up afterwards with that name a people, who endeavoured the levelling of all estates and qualities; which these sober Levellers were never guilty of desiring, but were men of just and sober principles, of honest and religious ends, and therefore hated by all the designing self-interested men of both factions. Colonel Hutchinson had a great intimacy with many of these; and so far as they acted according to the just, pious, and public spirit which they professed, owned them and protected them as far as he had power. These were they who first began to discover the ambition of Lieutenant-general Cromwell and his idolaters, and to suspect and dislike it. About this time, he was sent down, after his victory in Wales, to encounter Hamilton in the north. When he went down, the chief of these levellers following him out of the town, to take their leaves of him, received such professions from him, of a spirit bent to pursue the same just and honest things that they desired, as they went away with great satisfaction, till they heard that a coachful of presbyterian priests coming after them, went away no less pleased; by which it was apparent he dissembled with one or the other, and by so doing lost his credit with both.

When he came to Nottingham,[1] Colonel Hutchinson went to see him, whom he embraced with all the expressions of kindness that one friend could make to another, and then retiring with him, pressed him to tell him what thought his friends, the Levellers,[2] had of him. The colonel,

---

[1] Pembroke surrendered on July 11th. Cromwell arrived at Nottingham on August 3d. His cavalry, thirty troops in number, was sent on to join Lambert, which was effected at Baynards Castle on July 27th. Cromwell himself remained about a week at Nottingham, resting his infantry, and collecting the forces of Leicestershire, Nottinghamshire, and Derbyshire. On the 13th of August he was at Otley, and on the 17th attacked the Scots at Preston. He left in Nottingham castle Langhorne, Poyer, and seven other important prisoners whom he had brought with him from Wales.—Rushworth, IV. ii. 1211–8.

[2] The information Mrs. Hutchinson gives us on this subject is curious and valuable, but differs from the tradition generally received respecting the Levellers; it is, however, well supported by Walker in his "History of Independency." He begins with describing two Juntos of Grandees, and calls the rest the common people of the house; the former only feigned opposition, but played into one another's hands, the latter were sincere and earnest in it : he speaks of the *honest middlemen*, the same as Mrs. Hutchinson calls by that name, and likewise *Levellers;* he declares Levellers and asserters of liberty to be synonymous terms : in a variety of places they are treated as the only sincere patriots and opposers of the selfish schemes of the

who was the freest man in the world from concealing truth from his friend, especially when it
was required of him in love and plainness, not
only told him what others thought of him, but
what he himself conceived; and how much it
would darken all his glories, if he should become
a slave to his own ambition, and be guilty of what
he gave the world just cause to suspect, and therefore he begged of him to wear his heart in his
face, and to scorn to delude his enemies, but to
make use of his noble courage to maintain what
he believed just, against all great opposers. Cromwell made mighty professions of a sincere heart
to him, but it is certain that for this and such like
plain dealing with him, he dreaded the colonel, and
made it his particular business to keep him out of
the army; but the colonel never desiring command

Grandees of both parties, peculiarly the independents, and
above all, of Cromwell; and the engrossers and mono-
polisers of oligarchy, desiring to make themselves a corporation of tyrants, are said chiefly to dread the opposition
of these Levellers; but the most remarkable passage is in
p. 194. "Reader, let me admonish thee that the Levellers,
for so they are miscalled, only for endeavouring to level
the exorbitant usurpations of the council of state and
council of officers, are much abused by some books lately
printed and published in their names, much differing from
their declared principles, tenets, and practices, but forged
by Cromwell and others to make the sheep (the people)
betray the dogs that faithfully guard them."—J. H.

to serve himself but his country, would not use that art he detested in others, to procure himself any advantage.

At this time Colonel Thornhagh marched with Cromwell, and at his parting with Colonel Hutchinson, took such a kind leave of him, with such dear expressions of love, such brotherly embraces, and such regret for any rash jealousies he had been wrought into, that it took great impression in the colonel's kind heart, and might have been a presage to him that they should meet no more, when they parted with such extraordinary melting love; but that Colonel Hutchinson's cheerful and constant spirit never anticipated any evil with fear. His prudence wanted not foresight that it might come, yet his faith and courage entertained his hope, that God would either prevent, or help him to bear it.

This summer the revolt was not greater at land than at sea. Many of the great ships set the vice-admiral on shore, and sailed towards Holland to Prince Charles: to whom the Duke of York was come, having, by his father's advice, privately stolen away from London, where the parliament had received and treated him like a prince, ever since the surrender of Oxford. To reduce these revolted ships, and preserve the rest of the navy from the like, the Earl of Warwick was made lord high admiral of England. But at the same time

his brother, the Earl of Holland, who had floated
up and down with the tide of the times, rose also
against the parliament, and appeared in arms, with
the young Duke of Buckingham and Lord Francis
Villars, his brother, and others, making about five
hundred horse, at Kingston-upon-Thames.   Here
some of the parliament troops, assailing them
before they had time to grow, they were totally
routed and dispersed.   The Lord Francis Villars
was slain; the Earl of Holland, flying with those
he could rally, was fought with at St. Neots,
Dalbier and others of his associates slain, and
himself taken prisoner and carried to Warwick
Castle.   Buckingham fled, and at last got beyond
seas, with a blot of base ingratitude and treachery,
which began then to appear, and hath since marked
out all his life.   For these two lords being pupils,
and under the king's tuition, were carried with
him to Oxford, where they remained till the rendition of the place; and then coming to London, in
regard they were under age, had all their father
and mother's great estates, freely, without any
sequestration or composition; and while they
enjoyed them, their secret intentions of rising
being discovered to the parliament, the parliament
would not secure them, as some advised, but only
sent a civil warning to the duke, minding him how
unhandsome it would be, if the information should
prove true.   Whereupon the duke protested he

had no such intention, but utterly detested it,
making all the expressions of just gratitude to
them that could be; and yet, within very few
days after, openly showed himself in arms, to tell
the world how perfidious a hypocrite he was; for
which the parliament exempted him from pardon,
and ever after detested his name, as one that rose
only to fall into contempt and obloquy.

And now was Cromwell advanced into Lancashire, where Lambert, retreating from the invading
Scots, joined with him and made up an army of
about ten thousand; which were but few to
encounter five-and-twenty thousand, led by Hamilton, Langdale, and other English joined with them.
Yet near Preston, in Lancashire, they fought, and
Cromwell gained an entire victory, about the end
of August, and had the chase of them for twenty
miles, wherein many fell, and many were taken
prisoners. Hamilton himself, with a good party
of horse, fled to Uttoxeter, and was there taken
by the Lord Grey. But, in the beginning of this
battle, the valiant Colonel Thornhagh was wounded
to death. Being at the beginning of the charge
on a horse as courageous as became such a master,
he made such furious speed to set upon a company
of Scotch lancers, that he was singly engaged and
mortally wounded, before it was possible for his
regiment, though as brave men as ever drew sword,
and too affectionate to their colonel to be slack in

following him, to come time enough to break the fury of that body, which shamed [1] not to unite all their force against one man : who yet fell not among them, but being faint and all covered with blood, of his enemies as well as his own, was carried off by some of his own men, while the rest, enraged for the loss of their dear colonel, fought not that day like men of human race ; but deaf to the cries of every coward that asked mercy, they killed all, and would not a captive should live to see their colonel die ; but said the whole kingdom of Scotland was too mean a sacrifice for that brave man.[2]   His soul was hovering to take

---

[1] Shamed not, used neutrally, instead of were not ashamed, blushed not.

[2] " I ordered Colonel Thornhagh," writes Cromwell to the speaker, " to command two or three regiments of horse to follow the enemy, if it were possible to make him stand till we could bring up the army. The enemy marched away seven or eight thousand foot, and about four thousand horse ; we followed him with about three thousand foot, and two thousand five hundred horse and dragoons ; and, in the prosecution, that worthy gentleman, Colonel Thornhagh, pressing too boldly, was slain, being run into the body and thigh and head by the enemy's lancers. And give me leave to say, he was a man as faithful and gallant in your service as any ; and who often heretofore lost blood in your quarrel, and now his last. He hath left some behind him to inherit a father's honour ; and a sad widow ; both now the interest of the Commonwealth."

The House of Commons responded to Cromwell's appeal

her flight out of his body, but that an eager desire to know the success of that battle kept it within till the end of the day, when the news being brought him, he cleared his dying countenance, and said, "I now rejoice to die, since God hath let me see the overthrow of this perfidious enemy; I could not lose my life in a better cause, and I have the favour from God to see my blood avenged."[1] So he died, with a large testimony of love to his soldiers, but more to the cause, and was by mercy removed, that the temptations of future times might not prevail to corrupt his pure soul. A man of greater courage and integrity fell not, nor fought not, in this glorious cause; he had also an excellent good nature, but easy to be wrought upon by flatterers, yet as flexible to the admonitions of his friends; and this virtue he had, that if sometimes a cunning insinuation prevailed upon his easy faith, when his error was made known to him, notwithstanding all his great cour-

---

by an order, "that it be referred to the committee of the Northern Association to consider and present some way of satisfaction to be given to the wife and children of Colonel Thornhagh." (August 23d.)

[1] Ludlow states that Colonel Thornhagh, "perceiving by the wasting of his spirits" that he was mortally wounded, "to express his affection to his country, and joy for the defeat of the enemy, desired his men to open to the right and left, that he might have the satisfaction to see them run before he died" (Memoirs, p. 101).

age, he was readier to acknowledge and repair, than to pursue his mistake. Colonel Thornhagh's regiment, in the reducing of the garrison forces, had one Major Saunders (a Derbyshire man, who was a very godly, honest, country gentleman, but had not many things requisite to a great soldier) assigned them for their major, and with him he brought in about a troop of Derbyshire horse; but the Nottinghamshire horse, who certainly were as brave men as any that drew swords in the army, had been animated in all their service by the dear love they had to their colonel, and the glory they took in him, and their generous spirits could not take satisfaction in serving under a less man, which they all esteemed their major to be. But remembering their successes under Colonel Hutchinson, and several other things that moved them to pitch their thoughts upon him, the captains addressed themselves to Cromwell, and acquainted him with the discouragement and sorrow they had by the death of their colonel, for whom nothing could comfort them, but a successor equal to himself; which they could not hope to find so as they might in the person of Colonel Hutchinson, with whose worth and courage they were well acquainted, and he was now out of employment. The only difficulty was, whether he would accept the command, which they hoped to prevail in, if he would oblige them by sending to Lord Fairfax, to stop

all other ways that might be thought of for dis-
posing it, till they could know whether Colonel
Hutchinson would accept it, for which they had
prepared a messenger to send to his house. Cromwell, with all the assentation imaginable, seemed
to rejoice they had made so worthy a choice, and
promised them to take care the regiment should not
be disposed of till they received Colonel Hutchinson's answer; whereupon the captains severally
wrote to Colonel Hutchinson, with most earnest
entreaties, that he would give them leave to procure a commission for him to conduct them, which
the lieutenant-general had already promised to send
for, if he pleased to accept it.

The colonel, though he had more inclination at
that time, by reason of the indisposition of his
health, to rest, yet not knowing whether the earnest
desires of his countrymen were not from a higher
call, writ them word that he preferred the satisfaction of their desires before his own, and if the
commission came to him to be their leader, he
would not refuse it, though he should not do anything himself to seek any command. Meanwhile
Cromwell, as soon as the Nottinghamshire men had
imparted their desires to him, sent for Saunders,
and cajoling him, told him none was so fit as himself to command the regiment; but that the regiment thought not all of them so, but were designing
to procure themselves another colonel, which he

advised him to prevent, by sending speedily to the
general, to whom Cromwell also writ to further the
request, and before the messenger came back from
Owthorpe procured the commission for Saunders.
When it came, he used all his art to persuade the
captains to submit to it, and to excuse himself from
having any hand in it; but they perceived his
dissimulation, and the troops were so displeased
with it, that they thought to have flung down their
arms; but their captains persuaded them to rest
contented till the present expedition was over. But
they had not only this cheat and disappointment by
Cromwell, but all the Nottingham captains were
passed over, and a less deserving man made major
of the regiment. The new colonel and major made
it their business to discountenance and affront all
that had showed any desire of Colonel Hutchinson,
and to weary them out, that they might fill up their
rooms with Derbyshire men; but as soon as they
got to London, all that could otherwise dispose of
themselves, went voluntarily off; and the rest that
were forced to abide, hated their commanders, and
lived discontentedly under them. The reasons that
induced Cromwell to this, were two : first, he found
that Colonel Hutchinson understood him, and was
too generous either to fear or flatter him; and he
carried, though under a false face of friendship, a
deep resentment of the colonel's plain dealing with
him at Nottingham. He had besides a design, by

insinuating himself into Colonel Saunders, to flatter
him into the sale of a town of his called Ireton,
which Cromwell earnestly desired to buy for Major-
general Ireton, who had married his daughter; and
when at last he could not obtain it, in process of
time, he took the regiment away from him again.[1]
Colonel Hutchinson was not at all displeased that
the regiment was not given to him, but highly
resented it that the men were ill used for their
affections to him; and was sorry that this particular
carriage of Cromwell's gave him such a proof of
other things suspected of him, so destructive to the
whole cause and party, as it afterwards fell out.

Sir Marmaduke Langdale, after the rout of
Hamilton, came with two or three other officers to
a little alehouse which was upon Colonel Hutchinson's land, and there was so circumspect, that

---

[1] This gentleman is mentioned in Granger's Biography;
and there is a print of him in the hands of some curious
collectors, peculiarly of John Townely, Esq. He is said to
be of Ireton, in Derbyshire; but Ireton is believed to be
in the Vale of Belvoir.—J. H.

Cromwell writes on 17th June 1648 to Major Thomas
Saunders, ordering him to siege Sir Trevor Williams,
(Letter LX.), and Saunders also served under Cromwell
in Scotland. In the Appendix to the third volume of
Harris's Lives, is a paper said to be written by Colonel
Saunders, setting forth the demands of the army in 1647.
In a letter from Titus to Sir E. Hyde (24th October 1656),
it is stated that Cromwell had recently cashiered Saunders
"for not complying."—Clarendon State Papers, III. 309.

some country fellows, who saw them by chance, suspecting they were no ordinary travellers, acquainted
Mr. Widmerpoole, who lived within two or three
miles, and had been major to the colonel in the first
war: whereupon he came forth, with some few
others, and sent down to the colonel to acquaint
him that some suspicious persons were at the lodge.
The colonel, hearing of it, took his servants out,
and was approached near the house, when Major
Widmerpoole, being beforehand in the house, had
given Langdale some jealousy that he might be
surprised; therefore one of his company went out
to fetch out his horses, which were stopped for the
present, and they seeing the colonel coming up
towards them, rendered themselves prisoners to
Major Widmerpoole, and were sent to Nottingham
Castle, where they continued some months, till at
last Langdale finding an opportunity, corrupted one
of the guard, who furnished him with a soldier's
disguise, and ran away with him. The major, who
had been baffled by these persons, if the colonel
had not come in, had all the booty, which the
colonel never took share of anywhere: but the major
thinking the best of his spoils justly due to him,
presented him with a case or two of very fine
pistols, which he accepted.[1]

---

[1] Compare the account given in Captain Poulton's
letter, in which Colonel Hutchinson is made to play a
much less important part.

About this time, the gentlemen that were commissioners for the king at Newark, fell into disputes
one with another; nor only so, but suits were commenced in the chancery upon this occasion.   One
Atkins, and several other rich men at Newark,
when that garrison began to be fortified for the
king, lent certain sums of money, for the carrying
on of that work, to the commissioners of array,
for which those gentlemen became bound to the
Newarkers.   After the taking of that town by the
parliament, they, with other persons, coming in
within the set time, were admitted to composition:
Having been so cunning as to put out their money
in other names, they ventured to leave out these
sums, believing they were put into such sure hands,
that it would never be discovered.   Mr. Sutton,
Sir Thomas Williamson, Sir John Digby, Sir Gervase
Eyre, the Lord Chaworth, Sir Thomas Blackwell,
Sir Roger Cowper, Sir Richard Biron, and others,
had given bond for this money, which Mr. Sutton,
presenting to the king, as a sum that *he* had raised
to signalize his loyalty, the king, to reward him,
made him a baron.   The whole sum thus taken up
for the king's service, was eight or ten thousand
pounds; fifteen hundred of it, that was lent by
Atkinson, being demanded, would have been paid,
but they would not take the principal without the
interest.   Sir Thomas Williamson was openly
arrested for it in Westminster Hall; upon which

Mr. Sutton and he, being madded, put in a bill in chancery against Atkinson and others, praying that they might set forth to what ends and uses this money was lent to the said gentlemen, &c., &c.[1]

The parliament had made a law, that all estates of delinquents, concealed and uncompounded for, should be forfeited, one half to the state, and the other half to the discoverer, if he had any arrears due to him from the parliament, in payment of them. There were clerks and solicitors, who in those days made a trade of hunting out such discoveries, and making them known to such as had any arrears due to them. Colonel Hutchinson at that time had received no pay at all. One of the clerks of that committee, which was appointed for such discoveries, sent him word that two officers of the army were upon this chancery bill, endeavouring to make a discovery of certain concealed moneys in Nottinghamshire, which being his own country, he thought might be more proper for him. Colonel Hutchinson, who had never any mind to disadvantage any of the gentlemen of the country, demurred upon this information, and did nothing in it, till some came to him, intimating a desire of my Lord Lexington's, that the colonel would pitch upon that for the pay-

---

[1] According to Mr. Cornelius Brown, the Atkins or Atkinson referred to was probably Thomas Atkinson, Mayor of Newark in 1641, *vide* Brown's "Annals of Newark," pp. 181–8.

ment of his arrears, that so they might fall into
the hands of a neighbour, who would use them
civilly, rather than of a stranger.   After that the
colonel was thus invited by the gentlemen themselves, to pitch upon this money, he waived all the
rest, and only entered as his discovery that money
which these townsmen of Newark had lent, and
upon full search and hearing at the committee, the
money was found to be forfeited money, and the
debtors were ordered to pay it into the committee,
and Colonel Hutchinson had also an order to receive
his arrear from that committee of Haberdashers'
Hall.   Hereupon Sir Thomas Williamson and Lord
Lexington, who being the men of the best estates,
were principally looked upon for the debt, applied
themselves to Colonel Hutchinson, begging as a
favour that he would undertake the management of
the order of sequestration given out upon their
estates; and would also oblige them, by bringing
in several other gentlemen, that were bound to bear
proportionable shares.   The colonel, to gratify them,
got the order of sequestration,[1] and brought them to
an accommodation, wherein every man, according

---

[1] On April 25, 1649, it was ordered by the House of
Commons "that the arrears of Colonel Hutchinson, a
member of this House, being stated, and debentures given
him for the same, he be paid out of such concealed
delinquents' monies as he hath already, or shall hereafter,
discover to Haberdashers' Hall."

to his ability, agreed upon an equal proportion; and
the gentlemen, especially Mr. Sutton, acknowledged
a very great obligation to the colonel, who had
brought it to so equal a composition among them;
and then, upon their own desires, the order of
sequestration was laid upon their estates, but managed by one of their own bailiffs, only to free them
from inconveniences that otherwise would have
come upon them. Some of them made use of it to
get in arrears of rent, which they knew not how else
any way to have gotten, and for which at that time
they pretended the greatest sense of gratitude and
obligation imaginable. The colonel also procured
them days of payment, so that whereas it should
have been paid this Michaelmas, 1648, it was not
paid till a year after; and for these, and many
other favours on this occasion, he was then courted
as their patron, though afterwards this civility had
like to have been his ruin. And now, about
Michaelmas, 1648, he went to attend his duty at the
parliament, carrying his whole family with him,
because his house had been so ruined by the war
that he could no longer live in it, till it were either
repaired or new built. On coming to London, he
himself fell into his old distemper of rheumatism
with more violence than ever, and being weary of
those physicians he had so long, with so little
success, employed, he was recommended to a young
doctor, son to old Dr. Rudgely, whose excellence

in his art was everywhere known; and this son
being a very ingenious person, and considering
himself, and consulting with his father, believed
that all the other physicians who had dealt with him
had mistaken his disease; which he finding more
truly out, in a short space perfectly cured him of
the gout, and restored him, by God's blessing on
his endeavours, to such a condition of health as he
had not enjoyed for two years before. When he
was well again to attend the house, he found the
presbyterian party so prevalent there, that the
victories obtained by the army displeased them;
and so hot they grew in the zeal of their faction,
that they from thenceforth resolved and endeavoured
to close with the common enemy, that they might
thereby compass the destruction of their independent
brethren. To this end, and to strengthen their
faction, they got in again the late suspended
members; whereof it was said, and by the consequence appeared true, that Mr. Hollis, during his
secession, had been in France, and there meeting
with the queen, had pieced up an ungodly accommodation with her; although he were the man that
when at the beginning, some of the soberer men,
who foresaw the sad issues of war and victory
on either side, were labouring an accommodation,
openly in the house said, "he abhorred that
word accommodation." After these were gotten in
again, and encouraged by the presbyterian ministers

and the people in the city, they procured a revocation of the votes formerly made, with such convincing reasons publicly declared for the same, why they had resolved of no more addresses to be made to the king. And now nothing was agitated with more violence than a new personal treaty, with honour and freedom; and even his coming to the city, before any security given, was laboured for, but that prevailed not. Such were the heats of the two parties, that Mr. Hollis challenged Ireton, even in the house; out of which they both went to fight, but that one who sat near them overheard the wicked whisper, and prevented the execution of it.[1]

Amidst these things, at last a treaty was sent to the king, by commissioners, who went from both houses, to the Isle of Wight; and although there were some honourable persons in this commission, yet it cannot be denied, but that they were carried away by the others, and concluded, upon most dangerous terms, an agreement with the king. He would not give up bishops, but only lease out their

---

[1] According to Clarendon, "Ireton told Hollis his conscience would not suffer him to fight, upon which Hollis in choler pulled him by the nose; telling him, if his conscience would keep him from giving men satisfaction, it should keep him from provoking them" ("Rebellion," x. 107). Ludlow, however, who was probably present ,confirms Mrs. Hutchinson's story.

revenues; and upon the whole, such were the terms upon which the king was to be restored, that the whole cause was evidently given up to him. Only one thing he assented to, to acknowledge himself guilty of the blood spilt in the late war, with this proviso, that if the agreement were not ratified by the house, then this concession should be of no force against him. The commissioners that treated with him had been cajoled and biassed with the promises of great honours and offices to every one of them, and so they brought back their treaty to be confirmed by the houses; where there was a very high dispute about them, and they sat up most part of the night: when at length it was voted to accept his concessions, the dissenting party being fewer than the other that were carried on in the faction. Colonel Hutchinson was that night among them, and being convinced in his conscience that both the cause, and all those who with an upright honest heart asserted and maintained it, were betrayed and sold for nothing, he addressed himself to those commissioners he had most honourable thoughts of, and urged his reasons and apprehensions to them, and told them that the king, after having been exasperated, vanquished, and captived, would be restored to that power which was inconsistent with the liberty of the people, who, for all their blood, treasure, and misery, would reap no fruit, but a confirmation

of bondage; and that it had been a thousand
times better never to have struck one stroke in the
quarrel, than, after victory, to yield up a righteous
cause; whereby they should not only betray the
interest of their country and the trust reposed in
them, and those zealous friends who had engaged
to the death for them, but be false to the covenant
of their God, which was to *extirpate prelacy*, not to
lease it.[1] They acknowledged to him that the
conditions were not so secure as they ought to
be; but in regard of the growing power and insolence of the army, it was best to accept them.
They further said, that they enjoying those trusts
and places, which they had secured for themselves and other honest men, should be able to
curb the king's exorbitances; and such other things
they said, wherewith the colonel, dissatisfied,
opposed their proceedings as much as he could.
When the vote was passed, he, telling some men of
understanding, that he was not satisfied in conscience to be included with the major part in this
vote, which was contrary to their former engagements to God, but thought it fit to testify their
public dissent, he and four more entered into the
house-book a protestation against that night's votes

---

[1] There is, among Clarendon's State Papers, a letter from
the queen to the king, assuring him that those with whom he
had to deal were too penetrating to be duped by this artifice;
if they were, or pretended to be, the queen was not.—J. H.

and proceedings.   Whether it yet remains there, or whether some other of them got it out, he knew not, but he much wondered, after the change and scrutiny into all these things, that he never heard the least mention of it.[1]

By this violent proceeding of the presbyterians they finished the destruction of him in whose restitution they were now so fiercely engaged, for this gave heart to the vanquished cavaliers, and such courage to the captive king that it hardened him and them to their ruin.   On the other side, it so frightened all the honest people, that it made them as violent in their zeal to pull down, as the

---

[1] The debates mentioned took place on the 4th and 5th of December 1648.   It was decided by one hundred and twenty-nine to eighty-three, "that the answers of the king to the propositions of both Houses are a ground for the House to proceed upon for the settlement of the peace of the kingdom."   "At which," says Ludlow, "some of us expressing our dissatisfaction, desired that our protestation might be entered ; but that being denied as against the orders of the House, I contented myself to declare publicly that being convinced that they had deserted the common cause and interest of the nation, I could no longer join with them ; the rest of those who dissented also expressing themselves much to the same purpose" (Memoirs, p. 104). The question whether the members of the minority of the House of Commons possessed the right to protest, had been conclusively settled in the negative, in Mr. Palmer's case, during the debates on the Grand Remonstrance.   If Colonel Hutchinson actually entered a protest, it must have been immediately erased.

others were in their madness to restore, this kingly
idol; and the army, who were principally levelled
and marked out for the sacrifice and peace-offering
of this ungodly reconciliation, had some colour to
pursue their late arrogant usurpations upon that
authority which it was their duty rather to have
obeyed than interrupted; but the debates of that
night, which produced such destructive votes to them
and all their friends, being reported to them, they
the next morning came and seized about [1]   of
the members as they were going to the house, and
carried them to a house hard by, where they were
for the present kept prisoners.   Most of the presbyterian faction, distasted at this insolence, would no
more come to their seats in the house; but the
gentlemen who were of the other faction, or of none
at all, but looked upon themselves as called out to
manage a public trust for their country, forsook
not their seats while they were permitted to sit in
the house.[2]   Colonel Hutchinson was one of these,
who infinitely disliked the action of the army, and

---

[1] Forty-one members were seized and kept prisoners on
December 6th, further arrests were made the next day, and
many others were excluded but not put under any other
restraint.   "Altogether the number of the arrested was
forty-seven, and that of the excluded ninety-six."—Masson,
Life of Milton, iii. 697.

[2] Whitelocke, who was exactly in the same predicament,
acted in the same manner, and gives the same reasons
for it.—J. H.

had once before been instrumental in preventing such another rash attempt, which some of the discerning and honest members having a jealousy of, sent him down to discover.   When he came, going first to commissary Ireton's quarters, he found him and some of the more sober officers of the army in great discontent, for that the *lieutenant-general* had given order for a sudden advance of the army to London, upon the intelligence they had had of the violent proceedings of the other party, whereupon Cromwell was then in the mind to have come and broken them up ; but Colonel Hutchinson, with others, at that time persuaded him that, notwithstanding the prevalency of the presbyterian faction, yet there were many who had upright and honest hearts to the public interest, who had not deserved to be so used by them, and who could not join with them in any such irregular ways, although in all just and equitable things they would be their protectors.   Whereupon at that time he was stayed;[1]

---

[1] Mrs. Hutchinson does Ireton that justice which Whitelocke refuses him, who seems to consider him in the light of an *instigator ;* but this is clearly decided by Ludlow, who declares that "he himself, being sensible that the presbyterian party were determined to sacrifice the common cause to the pleasure of triumphing over the independents and the army, by agreeing with the king, or by any means, went down to apprise Fairfax and Ireton, then at the siege of Colchester, of this design, and to court the interposition of the army.   Fairfax readily agreed,

but having now drawn the army nearer London, they put this insolent force upon the house. Those who were suffered to remain, not at all approving thereof, sent out their mace to demand their members, but the soldiers would not obey. Yet the parliament thought it better to sit still and go on in their duty than give up all, in so distempered a time, into the hands of the soldiery; especially there having been so specious a pretext of the necessity of securing the whole interest and party from the treachery of those men, who contended so earnestly to give up the victors into the hands of their vanquished enemies. Many petitions had been brought to the parliament from thousands of the well-affected of the city of London and Westminster and borough of Southwark, and from several counties in England, and from the several regiments of the army, whereof Colonel Ingoldsby's was one of the first, all urging them to perform their covenant, and bring delinquents, without partiality,

---

but Ireton demurred to interfering till the king and presbyterians should have actually agreed, and the body of the nation been convinced of the iniquity of their coalition." Additional provocations and imperious circumstances afterwards constrained him, but he acted no conspicuous part in the business. In this difference of opinion respecting the interference of the army we may see the source of the dissension which more openly took place afterwards between Colonel Hutchinson and Ludlow, and caused the latter to calumniate Colonel Hutchinson as he did.—J. H.

to justice and condign punishment, and to make
inquiry for the guilt of the blood that had been
shed in the land in both wars, and to execute
justice ; lest the not improving the mercies of God
should bring judgments in their room.

Then also a declaration to the same purpose was
presented to the house from the Lord General
Fairfax and his council of officers, and strange it is
how men who could afterwards pretend such reluc-
tancy and abhorrence of those things that were done,
should forget they were the effective answer of their
petitions.[1]

After the purgation of the house, upon new
debate of the treaty at the Isle of Wight, it was
concluded dangerous to the realm and destructive
to the better interest, and the trial of the king
was determined.   He was sent for to Westminster,
and a commission given forth to a court of high
justice, whereof Bradshaw, serjeant-at-law, was
president, and divers honourable persons of the
parliament, city, and army, nominated commissioners.   Among them Colonel Hutchinson was
one who, very much against his own will, was put

---

[1] On January 26th, 1649, "the petition of the well-
affected people in the county of Nottingham, and in the
town of Nottingham," was ordered to be read the next day.
It was read on the 30th, and Hutchinson and Millington
ordered to thank the petitioners.   A petition was also
presented from the garrison.

in ; but looking upon himself as called hereunto, durst not refuse it, as holding himself obliged by the covenant of God and the public trust of his country reposed in him, although he was not ignorant of the danger he run as the condition of things then was.

In January 1648, the court sat, the king was brought to his trial, and a charge drawn up against him for levying war against the parliament and people of England, for betraying their public trust reposed in him, and for being an implacable enemy to the commonwealth.   But the king refused to plead, disowning the authority of the court, and after three several days persisting in contempt thereof, he was sentenced to suffer death.   One thing was remarked in him by many of the court, that when the blood spilt in many of the battles where he was in his own person, and had caused it to be shed by his own command, was laid to his charge, he heard it with disdainful smiles, and looks and gestures which rather expressed sorrow that all the opposite party to him was not cut off, than that any were : and he stuck not to declare in words, that no man's blood spilt in this quarrel troubled him but only one, meaning the Earl of Strafford. The gentlemen that were appointed his judges, and divers others, saw in him a disposition so bent on the ruin of all that opposed him, and of all the righteous and just things they had contended for, that it was upon the consciences of many of them, that if they did not execute justice upon him, God would require at their hands all the blood and desolation which should ensue by their suffering him to escape, when God had brought him into their hands. Although the malice of the malignant party and their apostate brethren seemed to threaten them, yet they thought they ought to cast themselves upon God, while they acted with a good conscience for him and their country. Some of them after, to excuse, belied themselves, and said they were under the awe of the army, and overpersuaded by Cromwell, and the like; but it is certain that all men herein were left to their free liberty of acting, neither persuaded nor compelled; and as there were some nominated in the commission who never sat, and others who sat at first, but durst not hold on, so all the rest might have declined it if they would, when it is apparent they should have suffered nothing by so doing. For those who then declined were afterwards, when they offered themselves, received in again, and had places of more trust and benefit than those who run the utmost hazard; which they deserved not, for I know upon certain knowledge that many, yea the most of them, retreated, not for conscience, but for fear and worldly prudence, foreseeing that the insolency of the army might grow to that height as to ruin the cause, and reduce the kingdom into the hands of the enemy; and then those who had been most courageous in their country's cause should be given up as victims. These poor men did privately animate those who appeared most publicly, and I knew several of them in whom I lived to see that saying of Christ fulfilled, " He that will save his life shall lose it, and he that for my sake will lose his life shall save it ; " when afterwards it fell out that all their prudent declensions saved not the lives of some nor the estates of others.   As for Mr. Hutchinson, although he was very much confirmed in his judgment concerning the cause, yet herein being called to an extraordinary action, whereof many were of several minds, he addressed himself to God by prayer; desiring the Lord that, if through any human frailty he were led into any error or false opinion in these great transactions, he would open his eyes, and not suffer him to proceed, but that he would confirm his spirit in the truth, and lead him by a right-enlightened conscience ; and finding no check, but a confirmation in his conscience that it was his duty to act as he did, he, upon serious debate, both privately and in his addresses to God, and in conferences with conscientious, upright, unbiassed persons, proceeded to sign the sentence against the king.   Although he did not then believe but that it might one day come to be again disputed among men, yet both he and others thought they could not refuse it without giving up the people of

God, whom they had led forth and engaged themselves unto by the oath of God, into the hands of
God's and their enemies ; and therefore he cast
himself upon God's protection, acting according to
the dictates of a conscience which he had sought
the Lord to guide, and accordingly the Lord did
signalise his favour afterwards to him.

After the death of the king it was debated and
resolved to change the form of government from
monarchical into a commonwealth, and the house
of lords was voted dangerous and useless thereunto, and dissolved. A council of state was to
be annually chosen for the management of affairs,
accountable to the parliament, out of which, consisting of forty councillors and a president, twenty
were every year to go off by lot, and twenty new
ones to be supplied. It is true, at that time every
man almost was fancying a form of government,
and angry, when this came forth, that his invention
took not place; and among these John Lilburne, a
turbulent-spirited man, that never was quiet in
anything, published libels ; and the levellers made
a disturbance with a kind of insurrection, which
Cromwell soon appeased, they indeed being betrayed by their own leaders.

But how the public business went on, how
Cromwell finished the conquest of Ireland, how the
angry presbyterians spit fire out of their pulpits,
and endeavoured to blow up the people against the

parliament, how they entered into a treasonable conspiracy with Scotland, who had now received and crowned the son of the late king, who led them in hither in a great army, which the Lord of hosts discomfited; how our public ministers were assassinated and murdered in Spain and Holland;[1] and how the Dutch, in this unsettlement of affairs, hoped to gain by making war, wherein they were beaten and brought to sue for peace,—I shall leave to the stories that were then written; and only in general say that the hand of God was mightily seen in prospering and preserving the parliament till Cromwell's ambition unhappily interrupted them. Mr. Hutchinson was chosen into the first council of state, much against his own will; for, understanding that his cousin Ireton was one of the commissioners to nominate that council,[2] he sent his wife to him, before he went to the house, that morning they were to be named, to desire him, upon all the scores of kindred and kindness that had been be-

---

[1] Dorislaus in Holland, and Ascham in Spain.

[2] Immediately after the death of the king, and the abolition of the House of Lords, the House of Commons deputed five members to nominate forty persons to form a Council of State. The five electors were Lisle, Holland, Robinson, Scott, and Ludlow. Out of the forty thus nominated the House selected thirty-six, to whom it added the five electors. This story is therefore not altogether accurate, though no doubt Ireton had considerable influence in the formation of the Council of State.

tween them, that he might be left out, in regard
that he had already wasted his time and his estate
in the parliament service ; and having had neither
recompence for his losses, nor any office of benefit,
it would finish his ruin to be tied by this employment to a close and chargeable attendance, besides
the inconvenience of his health, not yet thoroughly
confirmed, his constitution being more suitable to
an active than to a sedentary life. These and
other things he privately urged upon him ; but
he, who was a man regardless of his own or any
man's private interest wherever he thought the
public service might be advantaged, instead of
keeping him out got him in, when the colonel
had prevailed with others to have indulged him
that ease he desired. Mr. Hutchinson, after he
had endeavoured to decline this employment and
could not, thought that herein, as in other occasions,
it being put upon him without his own desire, God
had called him to his service in councils as formerly
in arms, and applied himself to this also, wherein
he did his duty faithfully, and employed his power
to relieve the oppressed and dejected, freely becoming the advocate of those who had been his
late enemies, in all things that were just and
charitable. Though he had now an opportunity to
have enriched himself, as it is to be feared some in
all times have done, by accepting rewards for even
just assistances, and he wanted not many who

offered them and solicited him therein, yet such
was his generous nature that he abhorred the mention of anything like reward, though never so justly
merited; and although he did a thousand high
obliging kindnesses for many, both friends and
enemies, he never had anything in money or
presents of any man.[1]   The truth is, on the contrary, he met with many that had not the good
manners to make so much as a civil verbal acknowledgment.   Among the rest one Sir John Owen
may stand for a pillar of ingratitude.   This man
was wholly unknown to him, and with Duke
Hamilton, the Earl of Holland, the Lord Capell,
and the Lord Goring, condemned to death by
a second high court of justice.   Of this, though
the colonel was nominated a commissioner, he
would not sit, his unbloody nature desiring to
spare the rest of the delinquents, after the highest
had suffered, and not delighting in the death of
men, when they could live without cruelty to better
men.   The parliament also was willing to show mercy
to some of these, and to execute others for example;
whereupon the whole house was diversely engaged,
some for one and some for another of these lords,
and striving to cast away those they were not con-

---

[1] The lists of the first two councils, which embraced
almost the whole duration of the republic, are preserved by
Whitelocke, and Colonel Hutchinson is in each of them;
he went out at the formation of the third.—J. H.

cerned in, that they might save their friends.
While there was such mighty labour and endeavour
for these lords, Colonel Hutchinson observed that
no man spoke for this poor knight; and, sitting
next to Colonel Ireton, he expressed himself to
him, and told him that it pitied him much to see
that, while all were labouring to save the lords, a
gentleman, that stood in the same condemnation,
should not find one friend to ask his life; "and
so," said he, "am I moved with compassion that,
if you will second me, I am resolved to speak for
him, who, I perceive, is a stranger and friendless."
Ireton promised to second him, and accordingly,
inquiring further of the man's condition, whether
he had not a petition in any member's hand, he
found that his keepers had brought one to the clerk
of the house; but the man had not found any one
that would interest themselves for him, thinking the
lords' lives of so much more concernment than this
gentleman's.   This the more stirred up the colonel's
generous pity, and he took the petition, delivered
it, spoke for him so nobly, and was so effectually
seconded by Ireton, that they carried his pardon
clear.   Yet although one who knew the whole circumstance of the business, how Mr. Hutchinson,
moved by mere compassion and generosity, had
procured his life, told him, who admired his own
escape, how it came about, yet he never was the
man that so much as once came to give him thanks;

nor was his fellow-prisoner Goring, for whom the colonel had also effectually solicited, more grateful.[1]

Some of the army, being very desirous to get amongst them a person of whose fidelity and integrity to the cause they had so good experi-

---

[1] There is no proof that Colonel Hutchinson took any important share in saving Sir John Owen's life. On the contrary, the evidence is all against the story. The Journals of the House name Ireton and Martyn as tellers for the "yeas." Clarendon and Ludlow both attribute his preservation to Ireton. "Ireton told them there had been great endeavours and solicitations used to save all those lords, but that there was a commoner, another condemned person, for whom no one man had spoke a word, nor had he himself so much as petitioned them; and therefore he desired that Sir John Owen might be preserved by the mere motive and goodness of the House itself (Clarendon, bk. xi. 260.) Ludlow states that Ireton, "observing no motion made for Sir John Owen, moved the House to consider that he was a commoner; and therefore more properly to have been tried in another way by a jury; whereupon the House reprieved him also (Ludlow, Memoirs, p. 111, folio). A second version is supplied by a contemporary newspaper, the *Moderate*, No. 35. "Sir John Owen carried it in the affirmative, by reason of a letter from Conway, intimating that one Captain Bartlet (a Washford pirate) came in at night on the coast of Keen, and at break of day landed some men under Mr. Griffith Jones (a well-affected gentleman and justice of the peace), his house, which they plundered sufficiently, and took the said Mr. Jones prisoner, giving out that as the High Court of Justice should do with Sir John Owen, the like would he do with the said Jones."

ence, had moved it to the general, my Lord Fairfax; who commanded to have it inquired in what
way he would choose to be employed; and when
he told them that, in regard of his family, which
he would not willingly be much absent from, he
should rather accept the government of some town
than a field employment, four governments were
brought to him, to select which he would have;
whereof Plymouth and Portsmouth, and one more
in the west, being at a vast distance from his
own country, Hull, in the north, though a less
beneficial charge than the other, he made choice
of, thinking they had not offered him anything
but what was fairly fallen into their dispose.
Soon after this, the lieutenant-general, Cromwell,
desired him to meet him one afternoon at a
committee, where, when he came, a malicious
accusation against the governor of Hull was
violently prosecuted by a fierce faction in that
town. To this the governor had sent up a very
fair and honest defence, yet most of the committee,
more favouring the adverse faction, were labour-

This story is confirmed by a letter from Nicholas to
Ormond, April 8, 1649, Carte's Original Letters, i. 247.
☞ Finally Sir John Owen himself, at the Restoration,
signed a certificate in favour of James Chaloner, asserting
that he was "the only instrument under God for the preservation of his life."—Seventh Report of Commission on
Historical MSS., 147.

ing to cast out the governor. Col. Hutchinson,
though he knew him not, was very earnest in his
defence, whereupon Cromwell drew him aside, and
asked him what he meant to contend to keep in
that governor? (it was Overton.) The colonel
told him, because he saw nothing proved against
him worthy of being ejected. "But," said Cromwell, "we like him not." Then said the colonel,
"Do it upon that account, and blemish not a man
that is innocent, upon false accusations, because
you like him not." "But," said Cromwell, "we
would have him out, because the government is
designed for you, and except you put him out you
cannot have the place." At this the colonel was
very angry, and with great indignation told him, if
there was no way to bring him into their army but
by casting out others unjustly, he would rather fall
naked before his enemies, than so seek to put himself into a posture of defence. Then returning to
the table, he so eagerly undertook the injured
governor's protection, that he foiled his enemies,
and the governor was confirmed in his place.
This so displeased Cromwell that, as before, so
much more now he saw that even his own interest would not bias him into any unjust faction,
he secretly laboured to frustrate the attempts of
all others who, for the same reason that Cromwell
laboured to keep him out, laboured as much to
bring him in.

But now had the poison of ambition so ulcerated Cromwell's heart, that the effects of it became more apparent than before; and while as yet Fairfax stood an empty name, he was moulding the army to his mind, weeding out the godly and upright-hearted men, both officers and soldiers, and filling up their rooms with rascally turn-coat cavaliers, and pitiful sottish beasts of his own alliance, and other such as would swallow all things, and make no question for conscience' sake. Yet this he did not directly nor in tumult, but by such degrees that it was unperceived by all that were not of very penetrating eyes; and those that made the loudest outcries against him lifted up their voices with such apparent envy and malice that, in that mist, they rather hid than discovered his ambitious minings. Among these, Colonel Rich and Commissary Staines and Watson had made a design even against his life, and the business was brought to the examination of the council of state. Before the hearing of it, Colonel Rich came to Colonel Hutchinson and implored his assistance with tears, affirming all the crimes of Cromwell, but not daring to justify his accusations, although the colonel advised him if they were true to stand boldly to it, if false to acknowledge his own iniquity. The latter course he took, and the counsel had resolved upon the just punishment of the men, when Cromwell, having only thus in a private council vindicated himself from their malice, and laid open what pitiful sneaking poor knaves they were, how ungrateful to him, and how treacherous and cowardly to themselves, he became their advocate, and made it his suit that they might be no farther published or punished. This being permitted him, and they thus rendered contemptible to others, they became beasts and slaves to him, who knew how to serve himself of them without trusting them. This generosity, for indeed he carried himself with the greatest bravery that is imaginable herein, much advanced his glory, and cleared him in the eyes of superficial beholders; but others saw he crept on, and could not stop him, while fortune itself seemed to prepare his way in sundry occasions. All this while he carried to Mr. Hutchinson the most open face, and made the most obliging professions of friendship imaginable; but the colonel saw through him, and forbore not often to tell him what was suspected of his ambition, what dissimulations of his were remarked, and how dishonourable to the name of God and the profession of religion, and destructive to the most glorious cause, and dangerous to overthrow all our triumphs, these things which were suspected of him, would be, if true. He would seem to receive these cautions and admonitions as the greatest demonstrations of integrity and friendship that could be made, and embrace the colonel in his arms, and

make serious lying professions to him, and often
inquire men's opinions concerning him, which the
colonel never forbore to tell him plainly, although
he knew he resented it not as he made show, yet
it pleased him so to discharge his own thoughts.

The islanders of Jersey wanting a governor, and
being acquainted, through the familiarity many of
their countrymen had with him, with the abilities
and honour of Colonel Hutchinson, they addressed
themselves to my Lord General Fairfax, and
petitioned to have him for their governor, which
my lord assented to : and accordingly commanded
a commission to be drawn up, which was done ;
but the colonel made not haste to take it out.   But
my lord, having ordered the commission, regarded
him as governor, and when the model of the castle
was brought to my lord to procure orders and
money for the repair of the fortifications, he sent
it to the colonel, and all other business concerning
the island.

In the meantime, the Scots having declared open
war against the parliament of England, it was concluded to send an army into Scotland, to prevent
their intended advance hither.   But when they
were just marching out, my Lord Fairfax, persuaded
by his wife and her chaplains, threw up his commission at such a time, when it could not have
been done more spitefully and ruinously to the
whole parliament interest.   Colonel Hutchinson

and other parliament men, hearing of his intentions
the night before, and knowing that he would thus
level the way to Cromwell's ambitious designs,
went to him and laboured to dissuade him; which
they would have effected, but that the presbyterian
ministers wrought with him to do it. He expressed
that he believed God laid him aside, as not being
worthy of more, nor of that glory which was
already given him.

To speak the truth of Cromwell, whereas many
said he undermined Fairfax, it was false; for in
Colonel Hutchinson's presence, he most effectually
importuned him to keep his commission, lest it
should discourage the army and the people in that
juncture of time, but could by no means prevail,
although he laboured it almost all the night with
most earnest endeavours.[1] But this great man
was then as immovable by his friends as pertina-
cious in obeying his wife; whereby he then died
to all his former glory, and became the monument
of his own name, which every day wore out.
When his commission was given up, Cromwell was
made general, and new commissions taken out
by all the officers from him. He finding that
Colonel Hutchinson's commission for the island was
not taken out, and that he did not address himself

---

[1] See Markham's Life of Lord Fairfax, 359–361.
Fairfax resigned his commission on June 25, 1650.

to him, made haste to prevent the islanders, and
gave a commission for the government to one of
his own creatures.   At this time the Lady Dormer
being dead, had left to her grandchild, a papist,
the Lady Anne Somerset, daughter to the Marquess
of Worcester, a manor in Leicestershire, which the
lady, being more desirous of a portion in money,
had a great mind to sell, and came and offered it
to Colonel Hutchinson, with whom she had some
alliance; but he told her he was not in a purchasing condition, whereupon she earnestly begged him,
that if he would not buy it himself, he would procure
of the parliament that she might have leave to sell
it.   This he moved and was repulsed, whereupon
both the lady, and one that was her priest, who negotiated for her, and other friends, most earnestly
solicited Colonel Hutchinson to buy it; who urging
that he had not money for such a purchase, they
offered him time of payment, till he could sell his
own land, and assured him it should be such a
penny-worth, that he should not repent the selling
his own land to buy it.   He urged to them the
trouble and difficulty it would be to obtain it,
and that it might so fall that he must lay a weight
upon it, more than the thing would be worth to
him, he never having yet made any request to the
house, and having reason to expect recompenses
for the loss of his estate, as well as others.   But
my lady still importuned him, promising a penny-

worth in it, that should countervail the difficulty
and the trouble; whereupon, at the last, he contracted with her, upon both her and her brother's
desire, the Lord Herbert, who was her next heir,
and was then at full age, and he gave˝ a release of
all claim to it, under his hand and seal; and my
lady, being between nineteen and twenty years old,
then passed a fine, and covenanted at her coming
to full age to pass another, and absolutely bargained
and sold the land to Colonel Hutchinson, who
secured the price of it to the Marquess of Dorchester, whom the lady and her friends had a
great hope and desire to compass for a husband, and
had thoughts, that when the portion was secured in
his hands, it would be easily effected.   This they
afterwards entrusted to Colonel Hutchinson, and
desired his assistance to propound the business to
my lord, as from himself, out of mutual well-wishes
to both parties; but my lord would not hearken to
it, though the colonel, willing to do her a kindness,
endeavoured to persuade him, as much as was fitting.   In the meantime the colonel could not, by all
the friends and interest he had in the house, procure
a composition and leave for my lady to sell her
land, because they said it would be a precedent to
other papists, and some moved, that what service
he had done, and what he had lost, might be some
other way considered, rather than this any way
suffered.   But he vigorously pursuing it, and laying

all the weight of all his merits and sufferings upon
it, all that he could obtain at last was, to be himself admitted, in his own name, for taking off the
sequestration, after he had bought it, which he did ;
and they took two thousand pounds of him for his
composition.[1]   By the interest of Sir Henry Vane
and several others of his friends, powerful in the
house, this too was with much difficulty wrought
out, though violently opposed by several others.
Of these Major-general Harrison was one, who,
when he saw that he could not prevail, but that, in
favour particularly to Colonel Hutchinson, it was
carried out by his friends ; after the rising of the
house, meeting the colonel, he embraced him, and
desired him not to think he did it in any personal opposition to him, but in his judgment who
thought it fit the spoil should be taken out of the
enemy's hands, and no composition admitted from
idolaters.   Whatever might be for a particular

---

[1] This was the manor of Loseby.   The sale to Colonel
Hutchinson took place on September 10th, 1650.   Colonel
Hutchinson's petition concerning it is dated November 6th,
1650, and the committee appointed to consider it reported
on December 10th.   On January 1st, 1651, the parliament
ordered that Colonel Hutchinson should be given leave to
compound for the interest of the State, in the manor and
tithes of Loseby, for which he hath contracted with the
Lady Anne Somerset, and the sequestration was accordingly removed on payment of £2000.—Commons'
Journals.

advantage to him, he envied not, but rejoiced in, only he so dearly loved him, that he desired he would not set his heart upon the augmenting of outward estate, but upon the things of the approaching kingdom of God, concerning which he made a most pious and seeming friendly harangue, of at least an hour long, with all the demonstrations of zeal to God and love to the colonel that can be imagined. But the colonel, having reason to fear that he knew not his own spirit herein, made him only a short reply, that he thanked him for his counsel, and should endeavour to follow it, as became the duty of a Christian, and should be glad to be as effectually instructed by his example as by his admonition. For at that time the major-general, who was but a mean man's son, and of a mean education, and no estate before the war, had gathered an estate of two thousand a year, besides engrossing great offices, and encroaching upon his under-officers ; and maintained his coach and family, at a height as if they had been born to a principality.

About the same time a great ambassador [1] was to have public audience in the house ; he came from the King of Spain, and was the first who had addressed to them owning them as a republic. The day before his audience, Colonel Hutchinson was set in the

---

[1] The ambassador was Alonzo de Cardenas, whose public audience took place on December 26, 1650.

house, near some young men handsomely clad,
among whom was Mr. Charles Rich, since Earl of
Warwick ; and the colonel himself had on that day
a habit which was pretty rich but grave, and no
other than he usually wore.   Harrison addressing
particularly to him, admonished them all, that now
the nations sent to them, they should labour to
shine before them in wisdom, piety, righteousness,
and justice, and not in gold and silver and worldly
bravery, which did not become saints ; and that the
next day when the ambassadors came, they should
not set themselves out in gorgeous habits, which.
were unsuitable to holy professions.   The colonel,
although he was not convinced of any misbecoming
bravery in the suit he wore that day, which was
but of sad-coloured cloth trimmed with gold, and
silver points and buttons ; ·yet because he would
not appear offensive in the eyes of religious persons,
the next day he went in a plain black suit, and so
did all the other gentlemen ; but Harrison came
that day in a scarlet coat and cloak, both laden with
gold and silver lace, and the coat so covered with
clinquant, that scarcely could one discern the ground,
and in this glittering habit set himself just under
the speaker's chair ; which made the other gentlemen think that his godly speeches, the day before,
were but made that he alone might appear in the
eyes of strangers.   But this was part of his weakness ; the Lord at last lifted him above these poor

earthly elevations, which then and some time after prevailed too much with him.[1]

After the colonel had bought my lady's land, some that were extremely vexed at her having that sum of money, dealt with the colonel to permit them to sequester it in his hands, and offered him he should have it all himself; which, he told them, he would be torn to pieces before he would do, and that it was a treachery and villany that he abhorred. Though, notwithstanding this, he was much pressed yet he would not yield, and to prevent force, which they threatened, after moving in the house, how dangerous it was to suffer such a sum of money to be in the hands of the daughter of an excepted person, especially at such a time (for now the king was crowned in Scotland, and the Scots ready to

[1] Harrison was always fond of being well dressed. Sir Thomas Herbert describes him meeting the king's escort on their way to London in 1648. Harrison was "gallantly mounted and armed, a velvet montero on his head, a new buff coat upon his back, and a crimson silk scarf about his waist, richly fringed" (Sir T. Herbert's Memoirs, p. 97). At his trial Harrison's courage was conspicuous. On the scaffold he justified the king's execution. "Take notice," he told the crowd, "that for being instrumental in that cause and interest of the Son of God which hath been pleaded amongst us, and which God hath witnessed to by appeals and wonderful victories, I am brought to this place to suffer death this day; and if I had ten thousand lives, I could freely and cheerfully lay down them all to witness to this matter."

invade, and the presbyters to join with them), the colonel put the money out of his own hands, to preserve it for my lady. All that time both she and her brother, and other friends, made all the acknowledgments of obligation that was possible. Not to confound stories, I finish the memorial of this here.

After the parliament was broken up by Cromwell, and after that my lady, seeing her project of marrying with my lord Dorchester would not take, had embraced an offer of Mr. Henry Howard, second son to the Earl of Arundel; and when, in the protector's time, the papists wanted not patrons, she began to repent the selling of her land, which before she thought such a blessing, and told her husband false stories, as he alleged, though his future carriage made it justly suspicious he was as unworthy as she.[1]

The colonel, presently after he had that land, had very much improved it, to a fourth part more than it was at when he bought it, and they, envying his good bargain, desired to have it again out of his hands, nor dealt fairly and directly in the thing, but employed a cunning person, Major Wildman,

---

[1] In the third vol. of Clarendon's State Papers, in a letter of his, dated August 1655, he says, "Cromwell hypocritically pretends kindness to the catholics, but the levellers have real candour towards them, and are implacable enemies to Cromwell."—J. H.

who was then a great manager of papists' interests,
to get the land again, which he was to have four
hundred pounds for, if he could do it.   Whereupon
he presently got money and came to the gentleman
who had a mortgage upon it for three thousand
pounds taken up to pay my lady, and tendered it.
But Mr. Ash, a great friend of the colonel's, was
so faithful that he would not accept it, and then
Wildman began a chancery suit, thinking that the
colonel, being out of favour with the present powers,
would be necessitated to take any composition.
When he had put the colonel to a great deal of
vain charge, and found he could do no good, at
last they desired to make up the business, and the
lady and Mr. Howard passed a new fine to confirm
the title, and the colonel was delivered from further
trouble with them, till after the change and the
return of the king.   Then, when the parliament
men began to come into question for their lives, my
Lord of Portland and Mr. Howard came to Mrs.
Hutchinson's lodgings three or four times, while
she was out soliciting for her husband, and my
lord left her a message, that he must needs speak
with her, upon a business of much concernment;
whereupon she sought out my lord, knowing that
he had professed much kindness and obligation to
her husband, and thinking he might have some
design now to acknowledge it by some real assistance.   But when she came to him, he told her, her

husband was in danger of his life, and that if he would resign back Loseby to Mr. Howard, he would help him to a good sum of money to fly, and Mr. Howard would stand to the hazard of buying it ; but she, being vexed that my lord should interrupt her with this frivolous proposition, told my lord that she would hazard it with the rest of her estate, rather than make up such desperate bargains. When Mr. Howard saw this would not do, he prepared a petition to get it excepted out of the act of oblivion, pretending that his wife being under age, the colonel had by power and fraud wrested her out of her estate. But when he showed this petition to his friends, they being informed of the falseness of the allegations, would none of them undertake either to deliver or back it. Only one Sir Richard Onslow was a violent man, railing against the colonel concerning this, but he not long after died by a blast of lightning. Others of his friends, when they understood that he himself had joined in the confirmation of the fine, after the colonel was retired, in the protector's reign, bade him for shame to make no more mention of his lady's being fooled or frightened to an act which he had voluntarily done. Many told the colonel how unsafe it was to displease a person who had so many powerful allies that might mischief him, but the colonel would neither be frighted nor flattered to give away his estate, which when Mr. Howard found, he let fall his purpose, and made no more vain endeavours.[1]

And now to return to his story where I left it. I shall not mention every particular action of his in the employment of a senator and councillor of the realms but only some which were more remarkable, to show the honour and excellency of his nature, among which this was one.   When his old opposites and enemies of the Nottingham committee had entered into the presbyterian conspiracy so deep, that their lives were forfeit to the law, had they been brought to public trial, and this was discovered to him, and also that Colonel Pierrepont was the chief of them, he took care to have the business so managed, that Colonel Pierrepont was passed by in the information, and others so favourably accused, that they were only restrained from the mischief they intended, and kept prisoners till the danger was over, and afterwards, through his mediation released, without any further punishment

---

[1] How, when, or by whom this estate at Loseby was sold again, the editor has not been able to discover, it never having come into the hands of his branch of the family, which purchased Owthorpe. One of the estates sold by Colonel Hutchinson in his lifetime, was that of Ratcliffe on Soar, which is spoken of in a note as given to Sir Thomas Hutchinson by his uncle Sacheverell; the purchaser was Alderman Ireton, and it was, in all probability, sold to enable him jointly with the money borrowed of Mr. Ash to purchase this estate.—J. H.

on their persons and estates, though Chadwick's eldest son was one of these. For Colonel Pierrepont, he only privately admonished him, and endeavoured to reclaim him, which the man, being good-natured, was infinitely overcome with ; insomuch, that ever after, to his dying day, all his envy ceased, and he professed all imaginable friendship and kindness to the colonel.[1] Indeed, his excellent gentleness was such, that he not only protected and saved these enemies, wherein there was some glory of passing by revenge, but was compassionately affected with the miseries of any poor women or children, who had been unfortunately, though deservedly, ruined in the civil war ; and without any interest of his own in the persons, whenever any ruined family came to seek relief,

---

[1] Francis Pierrepont died at Nottingham on January 30th, 1658. There is an interesting tract entitled " Elegies on the much lamented death of the honourable and worthy patriot, Francis Pierrepont, Esq." It is dated 1659, and contains verses by many persons mentioned in these Memoirs. Mr. Pigott contributes "An Elegy expostulating Death's arrest upon my honourable, dear, and noble friend," &c. He reflects that

> " The great, the good, the just, the wise, the high,
> Princes and Pierreponts too, they all must die."

Laurence Palmer contributes both Latin and English compositions, and Colonel White complains that the plumes of his muse have been so steept in tears, that he unfortunately cannot soar as high as others do.

where he was in power, he was as zealous in assisting all such, as far as it might be done with the safety of the commonwealth, as if they had been his brothers. As it was a misery to be bewailed in those days, that many of the parliament party exercised cruelty, injustice, and oppression to their conquered enemies, wherever he discovered it he violently opposed it, and defended even those enemies that were by might oppressed and defrauded of the mercies of the parliament. Upon this account he had contests with some good men, who were weak in these things, some through too factious a zeal, and others blinded with their own or their friends' interests. Among these Colonel Hacker's father, having married my Lady Biron's mother, was made a trustee for the estate of her son, which she had by Strelley her first husband.[1] He had about £1800 of the estate of young Strelley in his hands, which, he dying, his eldest son and heir, Colonel Francis Hacker, was liable and justly ought to pay. Young Strelley died in France, and left his estate to his half-brother, the son of Sir Richard Biron, who, all the time of the first war, was at school in Colonel Hutchinson's garrison at Nottingham, and after was sent

---

[1] Richard, second Lord Biron, married Elizabeth, daughter of George Russel of Ratcliff-on-Trent, Notts, and widow of Nicholas Strelley of Strelley in the same county (Collins' Peerage).

into France.   Being there, an infant, when this
estate fell to him, he returned and chose Colonel
Hutchinson for his guardian, who overcame Colonel
Hacker in the right of his pupil, and recovered
that money out of his hands, which he would not
have paid, if the infant had not found a friend that
was heartily zealous to obtain his just right.   Sir
Arthur Haslerig was a great patron of Colonel
Hacker's, and laboured to bear him out against
justice and the infant's right in this thing; and
when the colonel had overcome him, they were
both displeased ; for Hacker, on the other side,
was such a creature of Sir Arthur's, that without
questioning justice or honesty, he was more diligent
in obeying Sir Arthur's than God's commands.
Sir Allen Apsley had articles at the rendition of
Barnstaple, whereof he was governor, and contrary
to these he was put to vast expense and horrible
vexation by several persons, but especially by one
wicked woman, who had the worst and the
smoothest tongue that ever her sex made use of
to mischief.   She was handsome in her youth, and
had very pretty girls for her daughters, whom,
when they grew up, she prostituted to her revenge
and malice against Sir Allen Apsley, which was
so venomous and devilish, that she stuck not at
inventing false accusations, and hiring witnesses to
swear to them, and a thousand other as enormous
practices.   In those days there was a committee

set up, for relief of such as had any violation of
their articles, and of this Bradshaw was president;
into whose easy faith this woman, pretending herself religious, and of the parliament's party, had so
insinuated herself, that Sir Allen's way of relief
was obstructed.   Colonel Hutchinson, labouring
mightily in his protection, and often foiling this
vile woman, and bringing to light her devilish
practices, turned the woman's spite into as violent
a tumult against himself; and Bradshaw was so
hot in abetting her, that he grew cool in his kindness to the colonel, yet broke it not quite: but the
colonel was very much grieved that a friend should
engage in so unjust an opposition.   At last it was
manifest how much they were mistaken that would
have assisted this woman upon a score of being
on the parliament's side, for she was all this while
a spy for the king, and after his return, Sir Allen
Apsley met her in the king's chamber waiting for
recompense for that service.   The thing she sued
Sir Allen Apsley for, was for a house of hers in the
garrison of Barnstaple, which was pulled down to
fortify the town for the king, before he was governor
of the place.   Yet would she have had his articles
violated to make her a recompense out of his estate,
treble and more than the value of the house; pretending she was of the parliament's party, and that
Sir Allen, in malice thereunto, had without necessity
pulled down her house.   All which were horrible

lies, but so maliciously and so wickedly affirmed and sworn by her mercenary witnesses, that they at first found faith, and it was hard for truth afterwards to overcome that prepossession.

The colonel, prosecuting the defence of truth and justice in these and many more things, and abhorring all councils for securing the young commonwealth by cruelty and oppression of the vanquished, who had not laid down their hate, in delivering up their arms, and were, therefore, by some cowards, judged unworthy of the mercy extended to them, —the colonel, I say, disdaining such thoughts, displeased many of his own party, who in the main, we hope, might have been honest, although through divers temptations guilty of horrible slips, which did more offend the colonel's pure zeal, who detested these sins more in brethren than in enemies.

Now was Cromwell sole general, and marched into Scotland, and the Scots were ready to invade, and the presbyters to assist them in it. The army being small, there was a necessity of recruits, and the council of state, soliciting all the parliament-men that had interest to improve it in this exigence of time, gave Colonel Hutchinson a commission for a regiment of horse. He immediately got up three troops, well armed and mounted, of his own old soldiers, that thirsted to be again employed under him, and was preparing the rest of the regiment to carry after them himself, when he was informed, that as soon as his troops came into Scotland, Cromwell very readily received them, but would not let them march together, but dispersed them, to fill up the regiments of those who were more his creatures. The colonel hearing this, would not carry him any more, but rather employed himself in securing, as much as was necessary, his own country, for which he was sent down by the council of state, who at that time were very much surprised at hearing that the king of Scots was passed by Cromwell, and entered with a great army into England. Bradshaw himself, as stout-hearted as he was, privately could not conceal his fear; some raged and uttered sad discontents against Cromwell, and suspicions of his fidelity, they all considering that Cromwell was behind, of whom I think they scarce had any account, or of his intention, or how this error came about, to suffer the enemy to enter here, where there was no army to encounter him. Both the city and country (by the angry presbyters, wavering in their constancy to them and the liberties they had purchased) were all amazed, and doubtful of their own and the commonwealth's safety. Some could not hide very pale and unmanly fears, and were in such distraction of spirit, as much disturbed their councils.[1]   Colonel Hutchinson, who ever had

---

[1] The Scots entered England August 6th, 1651, the news reached the Council of State on the 9th, and a meeting of the council to decide on the measures of defence

most vigour and cheerfulness when there was most danger, encouraged them, as they were one day in a private council raging and crying out on Cromwell's miscarriages, to apply themselves to counsels of safety, and not to lose time in accusing others, while they might yet provide to save the endangered realm ; or at least to fall nobly in defence of it, and not to yield to fear and despair.   These and such like things being urged, they at length recollected themselves, and every man that had courage and interest in their countries, went down to look to them. Colonel Hutchinson came down into Nottingham-shire, and secured those who were suspicious to make any commotion, and put the country into such a posture of defence as the time would permit.   But it was not long before the king chose another way, and went to Worcester.   Cromwell following swiftly after with his army, and more forces meeting him from several other parts, they fought with the king

to be adopted, took place on the 10th.   Mr. Bisset (Commonwealth of England, ii. 155–8) conclusively proves that Mrs. Hutchinson exaggerates both in her description of the alarm of the republican leaders, and in her account of the share taken by Colonel Hutchinson in restoring them to confidence.   Orders were sent out on the afternoon of the 10th to the commanders of the militia in all the counties, to collect their forces to form an army under the command of Fleetwood or Harrison.   Colonel Hutchinson was the commander of the militia of Nottinghamshire (Calendar of Domestic State Papers, 1650, p. 506).

and his Scots, totally routed and subdued him, and
he, with difficulty, after concealment in an oak, and
many other shifts, stole away into France.

When the colonel heard how Cromwell used his
troops, he was confirmed that he and his associates
in the army were carrying on designs of private
ambition, and resolved that none should share with
them in the commands of the army or forts of the
nation, but such as would be beasts, and ridden
upon by the proud chiefs. Disdaining, therefore, that
what he had preserved, for the liberty of his country,
should be a curb upon them, and foreseeing that
some of Cromwell's creatures would at length be put
in, to exercise him with continual affronts, and to
hinder any man from standing up for the deliverance
of the country, if the insolence of the army (which
he too sadly foresaw) should put them upon it; for
this reason, in Cromwell's absence, he procured an
order for the remove of the garrison at Nottingham,
which was commanded by his kinsman Major Poulton,
into the marching army, and the demolishing of the
place; which accordingly was speedily executed.[1]

When Major Poulton, who had all along been
very faithful and active in the cause, brought his
men to the army, he was entertained with such
affronts and neglects by the general, that he volun-

---

[1] The Council of State ordered Nottingham Castle to
be demolished on May 9th, 1851, and the ordnance to be
sent to Hull and London.

tarily quitted his command, and retired to the ruined place, where the castle was which he had bought with his arrears.   When Cromwell came back through the country and saw the castle pulled down, he was heartily vexed at it, and told Colonel Hutchinson, that if he had been there when it was voted, he should not have suffered it.   The colonel replied, that he had procured it to be done, and believed it to be his duty to ease the people of charge, when there was no more need of it.[1]

When Cromwell came to London, there wanted not some little creatures of his, in the house, who had taken notice of all that had been said of him when he let the king slip by; how some stuck not in their fear and rage to call him traitor, and to threaten his head.   These reports added spurs to his ambition, but that his son-in-law, Ireton, Deputy of Ireland, would not be wrought to serve him, but hearing of his machinations, determined to come over to England to endeavour to divert him from such destructive courses.[2]   But God cut him short

---

[1] This conversation must have occurred in August 1651, during Cromwell's march to Worcester.   In " Mercurius Politicus " it is stated that two messengers arrived at London about five o'clock at night on August 23d.   " He that came from my Lord General saith he left his excellency yesterday morning at Mr. Pierrepont's house near Mansfield in Nottinghamshire, that his lordship would be at Nottingham last night with his foot and train."

[2] If this intention of Ireton is mentioned by any other

by death, and whether his body or an empty coffin was brought into England, something in his name came to London, and was to be, by Cromwell's procurement, magnificently buried among the kings at Westminster.   Colonel Hutchinson was, after his brother, one of the nearest kinsmen he had, but Cromwell, who of late studied him neglects, passed him by, and neither sent him mourning, nor particular invitation to the funeral, only the Speaker gave public notice in the house, that all the members were desired to attend him ; and such was the flattery of many pitiful lords and other gentlemen, parasites,

---

person, it has escaped the search of the editor ; it may have been known *with certainty* by Mr. Hutchinson alone, but something of the kind seems to have been in the *contempla-tion* of Whitelocke when he regrets his death, on account of the influence he had over the mind of Cromwell, which has been remarked in a former note ; as likewise the pro-bability that the prolongation of his life might have made a great difference in the conduct of Cromwell.   What is said of his funeral well agrees with what is said by Ludlow, who adds, that " Ireton would have despised these pomps, having erected for himself a more glorious monument in the hearts of good men, by his affection to his country, his abilities of mind, his impartial justice, his diligence in the public service, and his other virtues, which were a far greater honour to his memory than a dormitory among the ashes of kings ; who, for the most part, as they had governed others by their passions, so were they as much governed by them." For the rest, Colonel Hutchinson's reproof of Cromwell was a pithy one.—J. H.

that they put themselves into deep mourning; but Colonel Hutchinson that day put on a scarlet cloak, very richly laced, such as he usually wore, and coming into the room where the members were, seeing some of the lords in mourning, he went to them to inquire the cause, who told him they had put it on to honour the general; and asked again, why he, that was a kinsman, was in such a different colour? He told them, that because the general had neglected sending to him, when he had sent to many that had no alliance, only to make up the train, he was resolved he would not flatter so much as to buy for himself, although he was a true mourner in his heart for his cousin, whom he had ever loved, and would therefore go and take his place among his mourners. This he did, and went into the room where the close mourners were; who seeing him come in, as different from mourning as he could make himself, the alderman [1] came to him, making a great apology that they mistook and thought he was out of town, and had much injured themselves thereby, to whom it would have been one of their greatest honours to have had his assistance in the befitting habit, as now it was their shame to have neglected him. But Cromwell, who had ordered all things, was piqued horribly at it, though he dissembled his resentment at that time,

---

[1] Alderman John Ireton, brother of the general.

and joined in excusing the neglect; but he very well understood that the colonel neither out of ignorance nor niggardise came in that habit, but publicly to reproach their neglects.

After the death of Ireton, Lambert was voted Deputy of Ireland,[1] and commander-in-chief there, who being at that time in the north, was exceedingly elevated with the honour, and courted all Fairfax his old commanders, and other gentlemen; who, upon his promises of preferment, quitted their places, and many of them came to London and made him up there a very proud train, which still exalted him, so that too soon he put on the prince, immediately laying out five thousand pounds for his own particular equipage, and looking upon all the parliament-men, who had conferred this honour on him, as underlings, and scarcely worth the great man's nod. This untimely declaration of his pride gave great offence to the parliament, who having only given him a commission for six months for his deputyship, made a vote that, after the expiration of that time, the presidency of the civil and military power of that nation should no more be in his nor in any one man's hands again. This

---

[1] Ireton died on November 22, 1651, his funeral took place on February 6, 1652, and Lambert was appointed Lord Deputy on January 30, 1652. The vote of parliament referred to took place on May 19, and Fleetwood was appointed on July 9.

vote was upon Cromwell's procurement, who hereby designed to make way for his new son-in-law, Colonel Fleetwood, who had married the widow of the late Deputy Ireton. There went a story that as my Lady Ireton was walking in St. James's park, the Lady Lambert, as proud as her husband, came by where she was, and as the present princess always hath precedency of the relict of the dead prince, so she put my Lady Ireton below; who, notwithstanding her piety and humility, was a little grieved at the affront. Colonel Fleetwood being then present, in mourning for his wife, who died at the same time her lord did, took occasion to introduce himself, and was immediately accepted by the lady and her father, who designed thus to restore his daughter to the honour she was fallen from. His plot took as himself could wish; for Lambert, who saw himself thus cut off from half his exaltation, sent the house an insolent message, "that if they found him so unworthy of the honour they had given him as so soon to repent it, he would not retard their remedy for six months, but was ready to surrender their commission before he entered into his office." They took him at his word, and made Fleetwood Deputy, and Ludlow commander of the horse; whereupon Lambert, with a heart full of spite, malice, and revenge, retreated to his palace at Wimbledon, and sat there watching an opportunity to destroy the parliament.

Cromwell, although he chiefly wrought this business in the house, yet flattered with Lambert, and, having another reach of ambition in his breast, helped to inflame Lambert against those of the parliament who were not his creatures, and to cast the odium of his disgrace upon them, and profess his own clearness in it, and pity of him, that should be drawn into such an inconvenience as the charge of putting himself into equipage, and the loss of all that provision ; which Cromwell, pretending generosity, took all upon his own account, and delivered him of the debt. Lambert dissembled again on his part, and insinuated himself into Cromwell, fomenting his ambition to take the administration of all the conquered nations into his own hands ; but finding themselves not strong enough alone, they took to them Major-general Harrison, who had a great interest both in the army and the churches ; and these, pretending a pious trouble that there were such delays in the administration of justice, and such perverting of right, endeavoured to bring all good men into dislike of the parliament, pretending that they would perpetuate themselves in their honours and offices, and had no care to bring in those glorious things for which they had so many years contended in blood and toil. The parliament, on the other side, had now, by the blessing of God, restored the commonwealth to such a happy, rich, and plentiful condition, as it was not so flourishing

before the war, and although the taxes that were
paid were great, yet the people were rich and able
to pay them: they (*the parliament*) were in a way
of paying all the soldiers' arrears, had some hundred
thousand pounds in their purses, and were free
from enemies in arms within and without, except
the Dutch, whom they had beaten and brought to
seek peace upon honourable terms to the English:
and now they thought it was time to sweeten the
people, and deliver them from their burthens. This
could not be but by disbanding the unnecessary
officers and soldiers, and when things were thus
settled, they had prepared a bill to put a period to
their own sitting, and provide for new successors.
But when the great officers understood that they
were to resign their honours, and no more triumph
in the burthens of the people, they easily induced
the inferior officers and soldiers to set up for themselves with them; and while these things were
passing, Cromwell with an armed force, assisted by
Lambert and Harrison, came into the house and
dissolved the parliament, pulling out the members,
foaming and raging, and calling them undeserved
and base names; and when the Speaker refused to
come out of his chair, Harrison plucked him out.
These gentlemen having done this, took to themselves the administration of all things, and a few
slaves of the house consulted with them and would
have truckled under them, but not many. Mean-

while they and their soldiers could no way palliate their rebellion, but by making false criminations of the parliament-men, as that they meant to perpetuate themselves in honour and office, that they had gotten vast estates, and perverted justice for gain, and were imposing upon men for conscience, and a thousand such like things, which time manifested to be false, and truth retorted all upon themselves that they had injuriously cast at the others.

At the time that the parliament was broken up Colonel Hutchinson was in the country, where, since his going in his course out of the Council of State,[1] he had for about a year's time applied himself, when the parliament could dispense with his absence, to the administration of justice in the country, and to the putting in execution those wholesome laws and statutes of the land provided for the orderly regulation of the people. And it

---

[1] Colonel Hutchinson was a member of the Council of State during the first two years of its existence, until February 1651. He took little part in its deliberations, and served on committees of only trifling or temporary importance. During the first year he was twenty-ninth on the list of members drawn up according to the number of their attendances, and during the second, twenty-second. We find him in the first year serving on committees to consider the ordinances already made, the business of Jersey, and the petition of the sword blade makers. In the disposal of the king's goods and works of art he took a prominent part (Calendar of Domestic State Papers, 1650-1651).

was wonderful how, in a short space, he reformed
several abuses and customary neglects in that part
of the country where he lived, which being a rich
fruitful vale, drew abundance of vagrant people to
come and exercise the idle trade of wandering and
begging; but he took such courses that there was
very suddenly not a beggar left in the country, and
all the poor in every town so maintained and provided for, as they were never so liberally maintained and relieved before nor since.[1] He procured
unnecessary alehouses to be put down in all the
towns, and if any one that he heard of suffered any
disorder or debauchery in his house, he would not
suffer him to brew any more. He was a little
severe against drunkenness, for which the drunkards
would sometimes rail at him; but so were all the
children of darkness convinced by his light, that

---

[1] In spite of the success attributed to Colonel Hutchinson's exertions, Major-General Whalley complains, three
years later, of the amount of vagrancy in Nottinghamshire,
and afterwards claims for himself and his fellow-commissioners the credit of suppressing it. "This I may truly
say," he writes on April 21, 1656, "you may ride over all
Nottinghamshire, and never see a beggar or a wandering
rogue" (Thurloe State Papers, iv. 719).

The Justices of the Peace were generally, according to
Cromwell, negligent in the suppression of "the common
country disorders." "Really a Justice of the Peace, he shall
by the most be wondered at as an owl, if he go but one
step out of the ordinary course of his fellow-Justices in the
reformation of these things" (Speech, April 21, 1657).

they were in awe more of his virtue than his authority. In this time he had made himself a convenient house,[1] whereof he was the best ornament,
and an example of virtue so prevailing, as metamorphosed many evil people, while they were under

---

[1] About thirty years ago it was the fate of the editor to
visit this mansion of his ancestors, in order to bring away
a few pictures and some books, all that remained to him
of those possessions, where they had lived with so much
merited love and honour. Although he had not then read
these memoirs, yet having heard Colonel Hutchinson
spoken of as an extraordinary person, and that he had
built, planted, and formed, all that was to be seen there ;
the country adjoining being a dreary waste, many thousand
acres together being entirely overrun with gorse or furze ;
he viewed the whole with the utmost attention. He found
there a house, of which he has the drawing, large, handsome, lofty, and convenient, and though but little ornamented, possessing all the grace that size and symmetry
could give it. The entrance was by a flight of handsome
steps into a large hall, occupying entirely the centre of the
house, lighted at the entrance by two large windows, but
at the further end by one much larger, in the expanse of
which was carried up a staircase that seemed to be perfectly in the air. On one side of the hall was a long table,
on the other a large fireplace ; both suited to ancient
hospitality. On the right-hand side of this hall were three
handsome rooms for the entertainment of guests. The
sides of the staircase and gallery were hung with pictures,
and both served as an orchestra either to the hall or to a
large room over part of it, which was a ball-room. To the
left of the hall were the rooms commonly occupied by the
family. All parts were built so substantially, and so well
secured, that neither fire nor thieves could penetrate from

his roof, into another appearance of sobriety and holiness.

He was going up to attend the business of his country above, when news met him upon the road, near London, that Cromwell had broken the parlia-

---

room to room, nor from one flight of stairs to another, if ever so little resisted.

The house stood on a little eminence in the Vale of Belvoir, at a small distance from the foot of those hills along which the Roman fosse-way from Leicester runs. The western side of the house was covered by the offices, a small village, and a church, interspersed with many trees. The south, which was the front of entrance, looked over a large extent of grass grounds which were the demesne, and were bounded by hills covered with wood which Colonel Hutchinson had planted. On the eastern side, the entertaining rooms opened on to a terrace, which encircled a very large bowling-green or level lawn; next to this had been a flower-garden, and next to that a shrubbery, now become a wood, through which vistas were cut to let in a view of Langar, the seat of Lord Howe, at two miles', and of Belvoir Castle, at seven miles' distance, which, as the afternoon sun sat full upon it, made a glorious object: at the further end of this small wood was a spot (of about ten acres) which appeared to have been a morass, and through which ran a rivulet : this spot Colonel Hutchinson had dug into a great number of canals, and planted the ground between them leaving room for walks, so that the whole formed at once a wilderness or bower, reservoirs for fish, and a decoy for wild fowl. To the north, at some hundred yards' distance, was a lake of water, which, filling the space between two quarters of woodland, appeared, as viewed from the large window of the hall, like a moderate river, and beyond this the eye rested on the wolds or high wilds

ment.   Notwithstanding, he went on and found divers of the members there, resolved to submit to this providence of God, and to wait till he should clear their integrity, and to disprove those people who had taxed them of ambition, by sitting still,

---

which accompany the fosse-way towards Newark.   The whole had been deserted near forty years, but resisted the ravages of time so well as to discover the masterly hand by which it had been planned and executed.   But the most extraordinary and gratifying circumstance was the venera- tion for the family which still subsisted, and which, at the period when the last possessor had by his will ordered this and all his estates in Nottinghamshire to be sold, and the produce given to *strangers*, induced the tenants to offer a large advance of their rents, and a good share of the money necessary for purchasing the estates, in order to enable the remains of the family to come and reside again among them.   It was too late !   the steward had contracted with the executors, and resold the most desirable part, whereof the timber of Colonel Hutchinson's planting was valued at many thousand pounds !   The editor could only retire repeating Virgil's first Eclogue :

> *Nos patriæ fines, nos dulcia linquimus arva.*
>
> *   *   *   *
>
> *Impius hæc tam culta novalia miles habebit ?*
> *Barbarus has segetes ?   En, quo discordia cives*
> *Perduxit miseros ! en, queis consevimus agros.*

Round the wide world in banishment we roam,
Forced from our pleasing fields and native home :
Did we for these barbarians plant and sow,
On these, on these our happy fields bestow ?
Good heavens ! what dire effects from civil discord flow !

DRYDEN.

J. H.

when they had friends enough in the army, city, and country, to have disputed the matter, and probably vanquished these usurpers. They thought that if they should vex the land by war among themselves, the late subdued enemies, royalists and presbyterians, would have an opportunity to prevail on their dissensions, to the ruin of both : if these should govern well, and righteously, and moderately, they should enjoy the benefit of their good government, and not envy them the honourable toil; if they did otherwise, they should be ready to assist and vindicate their oppressed country, when the ungrateful people were made sensible of their true champions and protectors. Colonel Hutchinson, in his own particular, was very glad of this release from that employment, which he managed with fidelity and uprightness, but not only without delight, but with a great deal of trouble and expense, in the contest for truth and righteousness upon all occasions.

The only recreation he had during his residence at London was in seeking out all the rare artists he could hear of, and in considering their works in paintings, sculptures, gravings, and all other such curiosities, insomuch that he became a great virtuoso and patron of ingenuity. Being loth that the land should be disfurnished of all the rarities that were in it, whereof many were set to sale from the king's and divers noblemen's collections, he laid out about two thousand pounds in the choicest pieces of painting, most of which were bought out of the king's goods, which were given to his servants to pay their wages : to them the colonel gave ready money, and bought so good penny-worths, that they were valued at much more than they cost.[1] These he brought down into the country, intending a very neat cabinet for them; and these, with the surveying of his buildings, and improving by inclosure the place he lived in, employed him at home, and, for a little time, hawks abroad; but when a very sober fellow, that never was guilty of the usual vices of that generation of men, rage and swearing, died, he gave over his hawks, and pleased himself with music, and again fell to the practice of his viol, on which he played

---

[1] As a member of the Council of State, Colonel Hutchinson's lodgings at Whitehall were furnished from the ten thousand pounds' worth of the king's goods, which were reserved for the use of the council. He was appointed one of the committee of five to decide which of the king's goods should be so reserved, and also one of the committee to consider how the remainder might be disposed of to the best advantage. In the papers relating to the late king's goods, printed in the Seventh Report of the Historical Manuscripts Commission, is contained the information of Mr. Geldrop, who gives a list of various persons in possession of the king's goods. "Cornell Hutshanton" has "one Madone of Titian, and divers other pictures, and one naket boy of marbell very raerre" (Seventh Report, p. 89).

excellently well, and entertaining tutors for the
diversion and education of his children in all sorts
of music, he pleased himself in these innocent recreations during Oliver's mutable reign.[1] As he had
great delight, so he had great judgment, in music,
and advanced his children's practice more than
their tutors : he also was a great supervisor of
their learning, and indeed himself a tutor to them
all, besides all those tutors which he liberally entertained in his house for them. He spared not
any cost for the education of both his sons and
daughters in languages, sciences, music, dancing,
and all other qualities befitting their father's house.
He was himself their instructor in humility, sobriety,
and in all godliness and virtue, which he rather
strove to make them exercise with love and delight
than by constraint. As other things were his
delight, this only he made his business, to attend
to the education of his children, and the government of his own house and town. This he performed so well that never was any man more feared
and loved than he by all his domestics, tenants,

---

[1] Lady Catherine Hutchinson was also fond, too fond, of
music. In the presentment of the constables in October
1656, appears the following entry—"We present that the
Lady Hutchinson had music in her house on the sabbath-
day, the 12th of October" (Bailey, Annals of Nottinghamshire, p. 848).

and hired workmen. He was loved with such a fear and reverence as restrained all rude familiarity and insolent presumptions in those who were under him, and he was feared with so much love that they all delighted to do his pleasure.

As he maintained his authority in all relations, so he endeavoured to make their subjection pleasant to them, and rather to convince them by reason than compel them to obedience, and would decline even to the lowest of his family to make them enjoy their lives in sober cheerfulness, and not find their duties burthensome.

As for the public business of the country, he could not act in any office under the protector's power, and therefore confined himself to his own, which the whole country about him were grieved at, and would rather come to him for counsel as a private neighbour than to any of the men in power for greater help.

He now being reduced into an absolute private condition, was very much courted and visited by all of all parties, and while the grand quarrel slept, and both the victors and vanquished were equal slaves under the new usurpers, there was a very kind correspondence between him and all his countrymen. As he was very hospitable, and his conversation no less desirable and pleasant, than instructive and advantageous, his house was much resorted to, and as kindly open to those who had in public contests been his enemies, as to his continued friends; for there never lived a man that had less malice and revenge, nor more reconcilableness and kindness and generosity in his nature, than he.

In the interim Cromwell and his army grew wanton with their power, and invented a thousand tricks of government, which, when nobody opposed, they themselves fell to dislike and vary every day. First he calls a parliament out of his own pocket, himself naming a sort of godly men for every county, who meeting and not agreeing, a part of them, in the name of the people, gave up the sovereignty to him. Shortly after he makes up several sorts of mock parliaments, but not finding one of them absolutely for his turn, turned them off again.[1] He soon quitted himself of his triumvirs, and first thrust out Harrison, then took away

---

[1] Colonel Hutchinson served in none of these assemblies. There was, however, some thought of electing him in 1656. "For the town of Nottingham," writes Major-General Whalley to the Protector, "I have a great influence upon it; they will not choose any without my advice. The honest part of the county have of late, which I much wonder at, nominated Colonel Hutchinson to me, as not knowing better to pitch to make up the fourth man, he having satisfied some of them concerning his judgment of the present government; but I hope what I have hinted to them will cause them to think upon some other" (Thurloe State Papers, iv. 299).

Lambert's commission, and would have been king but for fear of quitting his generalship. He weeded, in a few months' time, above a hundred and fifty godly officers out of the army, with whom many of the religious soldiers went off, and in their room abundance of the king's dissolute soldiers were entertained ; and the army was almost changed from that godly religious army, whose valour God had crowned with triumph, into the dissolute army they had beaten, bearing yet a better name. His wife and children were setting up for principality, which suited no better with any of them than scarlet on the ape ; only, to speak the truth of himself, he had much natural greatness, and well became the place he had usurped. His daughter Fleetwood was humbled, and not exalted with these things, but the rest were insolent fools.[1]   Claypole, who married

---

[1] Many stories are told of the arrogance of the women of Cromwell's family. Captain Titus writes thus to Hyde in February 1656 :—"There was lately a wedding of a kins-woman of Laurence's, whither all the grandees and their wives were invited, but most of the major-generals and their wives came not. The feast wanting much of its grace by the absence of those ladies, it was asked by one there where they were ? Mrs. Claypole answered, 'I'll warrant you washing their dishes at home as they use to do.' This hath been extremely ill taken, and now the women do all they can with their husbands, to hinder Mrs. Claypole from being a Princess, and her Highness " (Clarendon State Papers, iii. 327).

his daughter, and his son Henry, were two debauched, ungodly cavaliers.   Richard was a peasant
in his nature, yet gentle and virtuous, but became
not greatness.   His court was full of sin and vanity,
and the more abominable, because they had not yet
quite cast away the name of God, but profaned it
by taking it in vain upon them.   True religion was
now almost lost, even among the religious party,
and hypocrisy became an epidemical disease, to the
sad grief of Colonel Hutchinson, and all true-
hearted Christians and Englishmen.   Almost all
the ministers everywhere fell in and worshipped
this beast, and courted and made addresses to him.
So did the city of London, and many of the degenerate lords of the land, with the poor-spirited gentry.
The cavaliers, in policy, who saw that while
Cromwell reduced all the exercise of tyrannical
power under another name, there was a door
opened for the restoring of their party, fell much
in with Cromwell, and heightened all his disorders.
He at last exercised such an arbitrary power, that
the whole land grew weary of him, while he set up
a company of silly, mean fellows, called major-
generals, as governors in every country.   These
ruled according to their wills, by no law but what
seemed good in their own eyes, imprisoning men,
obstructing the course of justice between man and
man, perverting right through partiality, acquitting
some that were guilty, and punishing some that

were innocent as guilty.[1]   Then he exercised
another project to raise money, by decimation of
the estates of all the king's party, of which action
it is said Lambert was the instigator.   At last he
took upon himself to make lords and knights, and
wanted not many fools, both of the army and gentry,
to accept of and strut in his mock titles.   Then
the Earl of Warwick's grandchild and the Lord
Falconbridge married his two daughters ; such
pitiful slaves were the nobles of those days.   At
last Lambert, perceiving himself to have been all

---

[1] The major-generals were appointed in the autumn of
1655.   Nottinghamshire, with the counties of Lincoln,
Derby, Warwick, and Leicester, was assigned to Whalley.
In each county the major-general was assisted by a council
of local commissioners.   The Nottinghamshire commissioners thanked the Protector for sending them as governor,
"a person so acceptable, who is our native countryman, of
an ancient and honourable family, and of singular justice,
ability, and piety."   The chief business of the major-generals
was to exact the tenth of their incomes from the royalist
gentry.   In Nottinghamshire this tax produced £1500 a
year.   They were also charged with the reformation of
meanness, and the ordinary duties of active magistrates.
"We have had many ploughs agoing," writes Whalley,
"that of ejecting scandalous ministers, depressing of rogues,
taking bonds, providing for the poor, depressing alehouses,
which were grown to incredible numbers, but could not
thoroughly end all, by reason this tax upon delinquents
hath taken up so much of our time" (Thurloe State Papers,
iv. 412).

this while deluded with hopes and promises of succession, and seeing that Cromwell now intended to confirm the government in his own family, fell off from him; but behaved himself very pitifully and meanly, was turned out of all his places, and returned again to plot new vengeance at his house at Wimbledon, where he fell to dress his flowers in his garden, and work at the needle with his wife and his maids, while he was watching an opportunity to serve again his ambition, which had this difference from the protector's; the one was gallant and great, the other had nothing but an unworthy pride, most insolent in prosperity, and as abject and base in adversity.[1]

The cavaliers, seeing their victors thus beyond their hopes falling into their hands, had not patience to stay till things ripened of themselves, but were every day forming designs, and plotting for the murder of Cromwell, and other insurrections,[2]

---

[1] A Life of Lambert has been very obligingly put into the hands of the editor, together with some other scarce tracts relating to those times, by Mr. White, jun., of Lincoln's Inn, who had collected them in the north of England, where Lambert resided. He seems to have enjoyed a better reputation among his countrymen: his horticulture is therein much spoken of, and he is said to have *painted* flowers, not to have *embroidered* them.—J. H.

[2] One of these abortive attempts at insurrection took place in Nottinghamshire in March 1655, in connection with Penruddock's rising. A midnight meeting of a few gentle-

which being contrived in drink, and managed by false and cowardly fellows, were still revealed to Cromwell, who had most excellent intelligence of all things that passed, even in the king's closet; and by these unsuccessful plots they were only the obstructors of what they sought to advance, while, to speak truth, Cromwell's personal courage and magnanimity upheld him against all enemies and malcontents. His own army disliked him, and once when sevenscore officers had combined to cross him in something he was pursuing, and engaged one to another, Lambert being the chief, with solemn promises and invocations to God, the protector hearing of it, overawed them all, and told them, "it was not they who upheld him, but he them," and rated them, and made them understand what pitiful fellows they were; whereupon, they all, like rated dogs, clapped their tails between their legs, and begged his pardon, and left Lambert to fall alone, none daring to own him publicly, though many in their hearts wished him the sovereignty. Some of the Lambertonians had at that time a plot to come with a petition to Cromwell, and, while he was reading it, certain of them had undertaken to cast him out of a window at

---

men was held at Rufford Abbey, and a cartload of arms brought thither, but they all dispersed on a sudden alarm, before they could collect any following.—Thurloe State Papers, iii. 229, 240, 264 ; iv. 599.

Whitehall that looked upon the Thames, where others would be ready to catch him up in a blanket, if he escaped breaking his neck, and carry him away in a boat prepared for the purpose, to kill or keep him alive, as they saw occasion, and then to set up Lambert. This was so carried on that it was near the execution before the protector knew anything of it. Colonel Hutchinson being at that time at London, by chance came to know all the plot.[1] Certain of the conspirators coming into a place where he was, and not being so cautious of their whispers to each other before him, but that he apprehended something; which making use of to others of the confederates, he at last found out the whole matter, without having it committed to him as a matter of trust, but carelessly thrown down in pieces before him, which he gathered together, and became perfectly acquainted with the whole design; and weighing it, and judging that Lambert would be the worse tyrant of the two, he determined to prevent it, without being the author of any man's punishment. Hereupon, having occasion to see Fleetwood (for he had never seen the protector since his usurpation, but publicly declared his testimony against it to all the tyrants' minions), he bade Fleetwood wish him to have a care of petitioners, by whom he apprehended danger to his

---

[1] I have not been able to find any trace of this plot.

life.   Fleetwood desired more particular information, but the colonel was resolved he would give
him no more than to prevent that enterprise which
he disliked.   For indeed those who were deeply
engaged rather waited to see the cavaliers in arms
against him, and then thought it the best time to
arm for their own defence, and either make a new
conquest, or fall with swords in their hands.
Therefore, they all connived at the cavaliers'
attempts, and although they joined not with them,
would not have been sorry to have seen them up
upon equal terms with the protector, that then a
third party, which was ready both with arms and
men, when there was opportunity, might have
fallen in and capitulated, with swords in their
hands, for the settlement of the rights and liberties
of the good people : but God had otherwise determined of things ; and now men began so to flatter
with this tyrant, so to apostatise from all faith,
honesty, religion, and English liberty, and there
was such a devilish practice of trepanning grown
in fashion, that it was not safe to speak to any man
in those treacherous days.

After Colonel Hutchinson had given Fleetwood
that caution, he was going into the country, when
the protector sent to search him out with all the
earnestness and haste that could possibly be, and
the colonel went to him; who met him in one of
the galleries, and received him with open arms and

the kindest embraces that could be given, and complained that the colonel should be so unkind as
never to give him a visit, professing how welcome
he should have been, the most welcome person in
the land, and with these smooth insinuations led
him along to a private place, giving him thanks for
the advertisement he had received from Fleetwood,
and using all his art to get out of the colonel the
knowledge of the persons engaged in the conspiracy
against him.   But none of his cunning, nor promises, nor flatteries, could prevail with the colonel
to inform him more than he thought necessary ·to
prevent the execution of the design, which when
the protector perceived, he gave him most infinite
thanks for what he had told him, and acknowledged
it opened to him some mysteries that had perplexed
him, and agreed so with other intelligence he had,
that he must owe his preservation to him: "But,"
says he, "dear colonel, why will not you come in
and act among us ? "   The colonel told him plainly,
because he liked not any of his ways since he broke
the parliament, being those which would lead to
certain and unavoidable destruction, not only of
themselves, but of the whole parliament party and
cause ; and thereupon took occasion, with his usual
freedom, to tell him into what a sad hazard all
things were placed, and how apparent a way was
made for the restitution of all former tyranny and
bondage.   Cromwell seemed to receive this honest

plainness with the greatest affection that could
be, and acknowledged his precipitateness in some
things, and with tears complained how Lambert
had put him upon all those violent actions, for
which he now accused him and sought his ruin.
He expressed an earnest desire to restore the
people's liberties, and to take and pursue more safe
and sober councils, and wound up all with a very
fair courtship of the colonel to engage with him,
offering him anything he would account worthy of
him. ' The colonel told him, he could not be forward to make his own advantage, by serving to the
enslaving of his country.   The other told him, he
intended nothing more than the restoring and confirming the liberties of the good people, in order
to which he would employ such men of honour
and interest as the people would rejoice, and he
should not refuse to be one of them.   And after
with all his arts he had endeavoured to excuse his
public actions, and to draw in the colonel, who
again had taken the opportunity to tell him freely
his own and all good men's discontents and dis-
satisfactions, he dismissed the colonel with such
expressions as were publicly taken notice of by all
his little courtiers then about him, when he went to
the end of the gallery with the colonel, and there,
embracing him, said aloud to him, " Well, colonel,
satisfied or dissatisfied, you shall be one of us, for
we can no longer exempt a person so able and

faithful from the public service, and you shall be satisfied in all honest things." The colonel left him with that respect that became the place he was in ; when immediately the same courtiers, who had some of them passed by him without knowing him when he came in, although they had been once of his familiar acquaintance, and the rest, who had looked upon him with such disdainful neglect as those little people use to those who are not of their faction, now flocked about him, striving who should express most respect, and, by an extraordinary officiousness, redeem their late slightings. Some of them desired he would command their service in any business he had with their lord, and a thousand such frivolous compliments, which the colonel smiled at, and quitting himself of them as soon as he could, made haste to return to the country. There he had not long been before he was informed, that notwithstanding all these fair shows, the protector, finding him too constant to be wrought upon to serve his tyranny, had resolved to secure his person, lest he should head the people, who now grew very weary of his bondage.[1] But though it was certainly confirmed to the colonel how much he was afraid of his honesty and freedom, and that he was resolved not to let him longer be at liberty, yet

---

[1] See the certificate and petition in the Appendix.

before his guards apprehended the colonel, death imprisoned himself, and confined all his vast ambition and all his cruel designs into the narrow compass of a grave. His army and court substituted his eldest son, Richard, in his room, who was a meek, temperate, and quiet man, but had not a spirit fit to succeed his father, or to manage such a perplexed government.

The people, being vexed with the pocket-parliaments and the major-generals of the counties, like bashaws, were now all muttering to have a free parliament, after the old manner of elections, without engaging those that were chosen to any terms. Those at Richard's court, that knew his father's counsels to prevent Colonel Hutchinson from being chosen in his own country, counselled Richard to prick him for sheriff of the county of Nottingham, which as soon as he understood, he writ him a letter, declaring his resentment in such a civil manner as became the person. Richard returned a very obliging answer, denying any intention in himself to show the least disfavour to him for former dissents, but rather a desire to engage his kindness. And soon after, when the colonel went himself to London and went to the young protector, he told him, that since God had called him to the government, it was his desire to make men of uprightness and interest his associates, to rule by their counsels and assistance, and not to enslave the nation to an army;

and that if by them he had been put upon anything
prejudicial or disobliging to the colonel in pricking
him for sheriff, he should endeavour to take it off,
or to serve him any other way, as soon as he had
disentangled himself from the officers of the army,
who at present constrained him in many things ;
and therefore if the colonel would please, without
unkindness, to exercise this office, he should receive
it as an obligation, and seek one more acceptable to
him after.   The colonel, seeing him herein good-
natured enough, was persuaded by a very wise
friend of his to take it upon him, and returned well
enough satisfied with the courteous usage of the
protector.[1] This gentleman who had thus counselled
the colonel, was as considerable and as wise a
person as any was in England, who did not openly
appear among Richard's adherents or counsellors,
but privately advised him, and had a very honourable design of bringing the nation into freedom
under this young man ; who was so flexible to good
counsels, that there was nothing desirable in a

---

[1] The very wise friend referred to was probably William
Pierrepont. Colonel Hutchinson remained sheriff of Nottingham until February 1660. On the 4th of that month
John Rayner was appointed sheriff, and on the 24th it was
ordered that Colonel Hutchinson should be discharged from
being sheriff of Nottinghamshire, and John Rayner stand
according to order.

prince which might not have been hoped in him, but a great spirit and a just title: the first of which sometimes doth more hurt than good in a sovereign ; the latter would have been supplied by the people's deserved approbation. This person was very free to impart to the colonel all the design of settling the state under this single person, and the hopes of felicity in such an establishment. The colonel, debating this with him, told him, that if ever it were once fixed in a single person, and the army taken off, which could not consist with the liberty of the people, it could not be prevented from returning to the late ejected family; and that on whatever terms they returned, it was folly to expect the people's cause, which, with such blood and expense, had been asserted, should not utterly be overthrown. To this the gentleman gave many strong reasons, why that family could not be restored, without the ruin of the people's liberty and of all their champions; and thought that these carried so much force with them, that it would never be attempted, even by any royalist that retained any love to his country, and that the establishing this single person would satisfy that faction, and compose all the differences, bringing in all of all parties that were men of interest and love to their country. Although the business was very speciously laid, and the man such a one whose authority was sufficient to sway in any state, the colonel was not

much opiniated of the things he propounded, but
willing to wait the event; being in himself more
persuaded that the people's freedom would be best
maintained in a free republic, delivered from the
shackles of their encroaching slaves the army.   This
was now not muttered, but openly asserted by all
but the army: although of those who contended
for it, there were two sorts; some that really
thought it the most conducible to the people's
good and freedom; others, that by this pretence,
hoped to pull down the army and the protectorian
faction, and then restore the old family.   It is believed that Richard himself was compounded with,
to have resigned the place that was too great for
him; certain it is that his poor spirit was likely
enough to do any such thing.   The army, perceiving they had set up a wretch who durst not
reign, and that there was a convention met, by their
own assent, who were ready, with a seeming face
of authority of parliament, to restore the Stewarts,
they were greatly distressed; finding also that the
whole nation was bent against them, and would not
bear their yoke; having therefore no refuge to save
themselves from being torn in pieces by the people,
or to deliver themselves from their own puppets
who had sold and betrayed them, they found out
some of the members of that glorious parliament
which they had violently driven from their seats
with a thousand slanderous criminations and un-

true.[1] To these they counterfeited repentance,
and that God had opened their eyes to see into
what a manifest hazard of ruin they had put the
interest and people of God in these nations, so that
it was almost irrecoverable; but if any hope were
left, it was that God would sign it, with his wonted
favour, in those hands out of which they had injuriously taken it.   Hereupon they opened the
house doors for them; and the Speaker, with some
few members, as many as made a house, were too
hasty to return into their seats, upon capitulation
with those traitors who had brought the commonwealth into such a sad confusion.   But after they
were met, they immediately sent summons to all the
members throughout all England, among whom the

---

[1] The last sitting of Richard's Parliament took place on
April 22d.   On May 7th, 1659, some forty-two members of
the Rump assembled in the House of Commons. Summonses
were sent to members resident in the country, and the
numbers of the House increased till it could be reckoned
to consist of about 120 members.   The highest number
ever present at a division was 76.   (Masson, Life of Milton,
v. 453.) Colonel Hutchinson's reply to the summons sent
him to attend, is given in the Appendix.   The certificate
presented in favour of the colonel after the Restoration says,
"when the army invited the remainder of the House of
Commons to return to Westminster, whither he was summoned, he declared to some of us before he went up that
he only went among them to endeavour to settle the kingdom by the king's return, and to improve all opportunities
to bend things that way.   See Appendix.

colonel was called up, and much perplexed, for now he thought his conscience, life, and fortunes were again engaged with men of mixed and different interests and principles ; yet in regard of the trust formerly reposed in him, he returned into his place, infinitely dissatisfied that any condescension had been made to the army's proposals, whose necessity rather than honesty had moved them to counterfeit repentance and ingenuity. This they did by a public declaration, how they had been seduced and done wickedly in interrupting the parliament, and that God had never since that time owned them and their counsels as before, and that they desired to humble themselves before God and man for the same, and to return to their duty in defending the parliament in the discharge of their remaining trust. According to this declaration, the army kept a day of solemn humiliation before the Lord ; yet all this, as the event after manifested, in hypocrisy.

Now the parliament were sat, and no sooner assembled but invaded by several enemies. The presbyterians had long since espoused the royal interest, and forsaken God and the people's cause, when they could not obtain the reins of government in their own hands, and exercise dominion over all their brethren. It was treason, by the law of those men in power, to talk of restoring the king ; therefore the presbyterians must face the design, and

accordingly all the members ejected in 1648, now
came to claim their seats in the house, whom
Colonel Pride, that then guarded the parliament,
turned back, and thereupon there was some heat
in the lobby between them and the other members.
Particularly Sir George Booth uttered some threats,
and immediately they went into their several counties, and had laid a design all over England, wherein
all the royalists were engaged, and many of the
old parliament officers ; and this was so dexterously,
secretly, and unanimously carried on, that before
the parliament had the least intimation of it, the
flame was everywhere kindled, and small parties
attempting insurrections in all places ; but their
main strength was with Sir George Booth in
Cheshire, who there appeared the chief head of
the rebellion. The city, at that time, was very
wavering and false to the parliament, yet the usual
presence of God, that was with them in former
times, never appeared so eminent as now, miraculously bringing to light all the plots against them,
and scattering their enemies before the wind, making
them fly when there was none to pursue them ;
although even in the parliament-house there wanted
not many close traitors and abettors of this conspiracy. It was presently voted to send an army
down into Cheshire ; but then it fell into debate
who should lead. Fleetwood, upon the deposing
his brother Richard (wherein he was most un-

worthily assistant), was made general, but not thought a person of courage enough for this enter- prize; whereupon many of Lambert's friends pro- pounded him to the house, and undertook for his integrity and hearty repentance for having been formerly assistant to the protector. Colonel Hut- chinson was utterly against receiving him again into employment;[1] but it was the general vote of

---

[1] Little can be learned respecting Colonel Hutchinson's parliamentary action during the next three months. The certificate before quoted represents him as, "openly oppos- ing the engagement to be true and constant to the Common- wealth, and endeavouring to bring the army under a civil authority, and for that end highly standing against Lambert's being put into employment against Sir George Booth." He does not seem to have been present in the House of Com- mons till the middle of June. On the 22d of June he was appointed one of a committee for inquiring into the vacant offices at the disposal of the Commonwealth, and during the months of July and August served on many other committees. He was a member of the committee appointed on July the 4th to consider "what is due for mourning for the late Lord Cromwell, and how the same may be paid for without prejudice or charge to the Commonwealth." During the whole month of September Colonel Hutchinson seems to have been absent from his place, and on the 30th September, when a call of the House took place, was fined twenty pounds for that reason. The Clarendon State Papers supply one small fact. On the 19th of July Mr. Broderick writes to Hyde—"Vane declines in reputation to that degree, as having set his heart and interest upon the promotion of

the house, and accordingly he was brought in to receive his commission from the Speaker; who, intending to accept an humble submission he then falsely made, with high professions of fidelity, and to return him an encouragement in declaring the confidence the house had in him,—through mistake made such a speech to him, as after proved a true prophecy of his perfidiousness. Many of the house took notice of it then only to laugh, but afterward thought some hidden impulse, the man was not sensible of, led his tongue into those mistakes. However, Lambert went forth, and through the cowardice of the enemy obtained a very cheap victory, and returned. In Nottinghamshire Colonel White rose, only to show his apostacy, and run away. The Lord Biron also lost himself and his companions in the forest, being chased by a piece of the county troop. And Mr. Robert Pierrepont, the son of the late colonel, went out to make up the rout, and run away, and cast away some good

---

one Captain Bishop, seconded by Salway, and all whom his power or persuasion could in any measure prevail on in the House, had but nineteen votes in his behalf, forty-nine against him; this drove him to an unusual passion, and taught hair-brained Haslerig more temper the day following, yielding to Hutchinson's single proposition against a dear creature of his own, and colonel of the present army (Hacker), whom he endeavoured to put into the militia of Nottinghamshire" (iii. 53).

arms into the bushes to make his flight more easy.[1]

During the late protectors' times Colonel Hutchinson, who thought them greater usurpers on the people's liberties than the former kings, believed himself wholly disengaged from all ties, but those which God and nature, or rather God by nature obliges every man of honour and honesty in to his country, which is to defend or relieve it from invading tyrants, as far as he may by a lawful call and means, and to suffer patiently that yoke which God submits him to, till the Lord shall take it off; and upon these principles, he seeing that authority, to which he was in duty bound, so seemingly taken quite away, thought he was free to fall in or oppose all things, as prudence should guide him, upon general rules of conscience. These would not permit him in any way to assist any tyrant or invader of the people's rights, nor to rise up against them without a manifest call from God ; therefore he stayed at home, and busied himself in his own domestic employments, having a very liberal heart, and a house open to all worthy persons of all parties. Among these the Lord Biron, who thought that no gentleman ought to be unprovided of arms, in such an uncertain time, had provided himself a trunk of

---

[1] This incident is related in a letter from the Mayor of Nottingham to the Speaker, which is given in the Appendix.

pistols, which were brought down from London; but some suspicion of it being entered in the protector's officers, he durst not fetch the trunk from the carrier's himself, but entreated the colonel to send for them to his house, and secure them there. This the colonel did; but afterward, when my Lord Biron had entered into a conspiracy with the enemies of the parliament, he knew that Colonel Hutchinson was not to be attempted against them, and was in great care how to get his arms out of the colonel's house.[1] The colonel, being of a very compassionate and charitable nature, had entertained into his service some poor people who on the enemy's side had been ruined, and were reduced from good estates to seek that refuge; and who counterfeited, so long as their party was down, such sobriety, love, and gratitude, and sense of their sins and miscarriages on the other side, that he hoped they had been converts, but could not believe they would have proved such detestable, unthankful traitors, as afterwards they did. Among these, Lord Biron corrupted a gentleman who waited then on the colonel, as the man after alleged; my lord

---

[1] The certificate presented in favour of Colonel Hutchinson says, "he received into his house, and secured there, arms prepared for the king's service, well knowing to what intent they were provided, and resolving to join with us when there had been occasion to use them." This is signed by Richard Lord Biron, and Robert Biron.

said he offered himself.   However it were, the plot
was laid that fifty men, near the colonel's house,
should be raised for him, and he with them should
first come to the colonel's house, and take away my
lord's arms, with all the rest of the colonel's that
they could find.   To raise him these men, certain
neighbours, who used to come to the house, were
very busy, and especially two parsons, he of
Plumtre and he of Bingham ; this had an active,
proud, pragmatical curate, who used to come to this
traitor in the colonel's house and help to manage
the treason, and the chaplain, the waiting-woman,
and two servants more, were drawn into the confederacy.   The colonel was then at the parliament-
house, and only his wife and children at home,
when, the night before the insurrection, Ivie (that
was the gentleman's name) came to a singing-boy
who kept the colonel's clothes, and commanded him
to deliver him the colonel's own arms and buff
coat.

The boy was fearful, and did not readily obey
him, whereupon he threatened immediately to pistol
him, if he made the least resistance or discovery
of the business ; so the boy fetched him the arms,
and he put them on, and took one of the best
horses and went out at midnight, telling the boy
he was a fool to fear, for the next night, before
that time, there would come fifty men to fetch away
all the arms in the house.

As soon as the boy saw him quite gone, his mistress being then in bed, he went to the chaplain and acquainted him; but the chaplain cursed him for breaking his sleep: then he went to the waiting gentlewoman, but she said she thought it would be unfit to disturb her mistress; so the boy rested till next day, when Ivie, having failed of his men, was come back again. Then the boy, finding an opportunity after dinner, told his mistress, that though he had been bred a cavalier he abhorred to betray or be unfaithful to those he served; and that he had reason to suspect there was some vile conspiracy in hand, wherein Ivie was engaged against them, and told his grounds. When Mrs. Hutchinson had heard that, she bade him keep it private, and called immediately a servant that had been a cornet of the parliament's party, and bade him go to the county troop's captain, and desire him to send her a guard for her husband's house, for she had intelligence that the cavaliers intended some attempt against it. Mrs. Hutchinson, ashamed to complain of her own family, thought of this way of security, till she could discharge herself of the traitor, not knowing at that time how many more were about her. Then calling her gentlewoman, whom she thought she might trust, upon her solemn protestations of fidelity, she took her to assist her in hiding her plate and jewels, and what she had of value, and scrupled not to let her see the *secret places in her house*, while the false and base dissembler went smiling up and down at her mistress's simplicity. Meantime, the man that was sent for soldiers came back, bringing news that the cavaliers had risen and were beaten, and the county troop was in pursuit of them. Then also the coachman, who finding himself not well, had borrowed a horse to go to Nottingham to be let blood, came home, bringing with him a cravat and other spoils of the enemy, which he had gotten. For when he came to the town, hearing the cavaliers were up, he got a case of pistols, and thought more of shedding than losing blood, and meeting the cavaliers in the rout, it is said, he killed one of them ; although this rogue had engaged to Ivie to have gone on the other side with him. Mrs. Hutchinson not being willing, for all this, to take such notice of Ivie's treason as to cast him into prison, took him immediately to London with her, and said nothing till he came there. Then she told him how base and treacherous he had been ; but to save her own shame for having entertained so false a person, and for her mother's sake whom he had formerly served, she was willing to dismiss him privately, without acquainting the colonel, who could not know but he must punish him. So she gave him something and turned him away, and told her husband she came only to acquaint him with the insurrection, and her own fears of staying in the country without him. He, being very indulgent, went immediately back with her, having informed the parliament, and received their order for going down to look after the securing of the country. His wife, as soon as she came down, having learned that the chaplain had been Ivie's confederate, told him privately of it, and desired him to find a pretence to take his leave of the colonel, that she might not be necessitated to complain, and procure him the punishment his treason deserved. He went away thus, but so far from being wrought upon, that he hated her to the death for her kindness.

The colonel having set things in order in the country, had an intent to have carried his family that winter with him to London; when just that week he was going, news was brought that Lambert had once more turned out the parliament, and the colonel rejoiced in his good fortune that he was not present.[1]

Lambert was exceedingly puffed up with his cheap victory, and cajoled his soldiers; and, before he returned to London, set on foot among them their old insolent way of prescribing to the parliament by way of petition.

The parliament, after the submission of the army, had voted that there should no more be a general

---

[1] Lambert turned out the Parliament on October the 13th, 1659.

over them, but to keep that power in their own hands,
that all the officers should take their commissions
immediately from the Speaker.   The conspiracy of
the army, to get a leader in their rebellion, was laid,
that they should petition for generals and such like
things as might facilitate their intents.   Among
others that were taken in arms against the parliament, Lord Castleton was one of the chief heads of
the insurrection.   Him Lambert brought along with
him in his coach, not now as a prisoner, but un-
guarded, as one that was to be honoured.   The
parliament hearing of this, sent and fetched him out
of his company and committed him to prison, and
then the army's saucy petition was delivered, and,
upon the insolent carriage of nine colonels, they
were by vote disbanded.   Lambert being one of
them, came in a hostile manner and plucked the
members out of the house; Fleetwood, whom they
trusted to guard them, having confederated with
Lambert and betrayed them.   After that, setting
up their army court at Wallingford-house, they
began their arbitrary reign, to the joy of all the
vanquished enemies of the parliament, and to the
amazement and terror of all men that had any honest
interest : and now were they all devising governments, and some honourable members, I know not
through what fatality of the times, fell in with them.[1]

---

[1] Vane, Ludlow, and Whitelocke.

When Colonel Hutchinson came into the country some time before Lambert's revolt, Mr. Robert Pierrepont, the son of the late Colonel Francis Pierrepont, sent friends to entreat the colonel to receive him into his protection.   Upon the entreaty of his uncle he took him into his own house, and entertained him civilly there, whilst he writ to the Speaker, urging his youth, his surrender of himself, and all he could in favour of him, desiring to know how they would please to dispose of him.   Before the letters were answered Lambert had broken the parliament, and the colonel told him he was free again to do what he pleased ; but the young gentleman begged of the colonel that he might continue under his sanctuary till these things came to some issue.   This the colonel very freely admitted, and entertained him till the second return of the parliament, not without much trouble to his house, of him and his servants, so contrary to the sobriety and holiness the colonel delighted in, yet for his father's and his uncle's sakes he endured it about six months.

Some of Lambert's officers, while he marched near Nottinghamshire, having formerly served under the colonel's command, came to his house at Owthorpe and told him of the petition that was set on foot in Lambert's brigade, and consulted whether they should sign it or no.   The colonel advised them by no means to do it, yet notwithstanding, they did, which made the colonel exceeding angry

with them, thinking they rather came to see how
he stood affected, than really to ask his counsel.
When Lambert had broken the house, the colonel
made a short journey to London to inform himself
how things were, and found some of the members
exceedingly sensible of the sad estate the kingdom
was reduced unto by the rash ambition of these
men, and resolving that there was no way but for
every man that abhorred it to improve their interest
in their countries, and to suppress these usurpers
and rebels.   Hereupon the colonel took measures
to have some arms bought and sent him, and had
prepared a thousand honest men, whenever he
should call for their assistance; intending to
improve his posse comitatus when occasion should
be offered.   To provoke him more particularly to
this, several accidents fell out.   Among the rest,
six of Lambert's troopers came to gather money,
laid upon the country by an assessment of parliament, whom the colonel telling that in regard it was
levied by that authority, he had paid it, but otherwise would not; two of them only who were in the
room with the colonel, the rest being on horseback
in the court, gave him such insolent terms, with
such unsufferable reproaches of the parliament, that
the colonel drew a sword which was in the room to
have chastised them.   While a minister that was
by held the colonel's arm, his wife, not willing to
have them killed in her presence, opened the door

and let them out, who presently ran and fetched in
their companions in the yard with cocked pistols.
Upon the bustle, while the colonel having disengaged
himself from those that held him, was run after
them with the sword drawn, his brother came out
of another room, upon whom, the soldiers pressing
against a door that went into the great hall, the
door flew open, and about fifty or sixty men
appeared in the hall,[1] who were there upon another
business.   For Owthorpe, Kinolton, and Hickling,
had a contest about a cripple that was sent from
one to the other, but at last, out of some respect
they had for the colonel, the chief men of the
several towns were come to him, to make some
accommodation, till the law should be again in
force.   When the colonel heard the soldiers were
come, he left them shut up in his great hall, who
by accident thus appearing, put the soldiers into a
dreadful fright.   When the colonel saw how pale
they looked, he encouraged them to take heart, and
calmly admonished them for their insolence, and
they being changed and very humble through their
fear, he called for wine for them, and sent them
away.   To the most insolent of them he said,
"These carriages would bring back the Stewarts."

---

[1] The description of the house, contained in a former
note (p. 194), will give a just idea of the position of all the
parties, and of the striking scene here described.—J. H.

The man, laying his hand upon his sword, said, "Never while he wore that." Among other things they said to the colonel, when he demanded by what authority they came, they showed their swords, and said, "That was their authority." After they were dismissed, the colonel, not willing to appear because he was sheriff of the county, and had many of their papers sent him to publish, concealed himself in his house, and caused his wife to write a letter to Fleetwood, to complain of the affronts had been offered him, and to tell him that he was thereupon retired, till he could dwell safely at home.[1] To this Fleetwood returned a civil answer, and withal sent a protection, to forbid all soldiers from coming to his house, and a command to Swallow, who was the colonel of these men, to examine and punish them. Mrs. Hutchinson had sent before to Swallow, who

---

[1] Probably this circumstance of Colonel Hutchinson concealing himself in his own home came at that time to be known at Nottingham, and gave rise to a tradition which is to be found in Throsby's edition of Thoroton, that he concealed himself in this manner after the Restoration, but was taken in his return from church ; both of which were untrue, as probably were some other tales, resembling the legends of romance, which the Editor heard of him at Owthorpe. But that there was an apartment so adapted for concealment, security, and convenience, as that he might have made a long residence in it without being discovered, the Editor had ocular demonstration.—J. H.

then quartered at Leicester, the next day after it was done, to inform him, who sent a letter utterly disowning their actions, and promising to punish them.   This Mrs. Hutchinson sent to show the soldiers who then lay abusing the country at Colson ; but when they saw their officer's letter they laughed at him, and tore it in pieces.   Some days after he, in a civil manner, sent a captain with them and other soldiers to Owthorpe, to inquire into their misdemeanours before their faces ; which being confirmed to him, and he beginning to rebuke them, they set him at light, even before Mrs. Hutchinson's face, and made the poor man retire sneaped [1] to his colonel ; while these six rogues, in one week's space, besides the assessments assigned them to gather up, within the compass of five miles, took away violently from the country, for their own expense, above five-and-twenty pounds.   Notwithstanding all this pretended civility, Fleetwood and his counsellors were afraid of the colonel, and the protection was but sent to draw him thither, that they might by that means get him into their custody.   But he, having intimation of it, withdrew, while men and arms were preparing, that he might appear publicly in the defence of the country, when he was strong enough to drive out the soldiers that were left in these parts.   Three hundred of them were one night drawn out of Nottingham to

---

[1] *Sneaped, i.e.* snubbed.

come to Owthorpe for him, but some of the party gave him notice, who was then at home, and immediately went out of the house. Neither wanted they their spies, who gave them notice that he was gone again, so that they turned off upon the wolds and went to Hickling; and the next day Major Grove, their commander, sent to Mrs. Hutchinson to desire permission for himself only to come down, which she gave, and so with only five or six of his party he came. With him Mrs. Hutchinson so easily dealt, that, after she had represented the state of things to him, he began to apologise that he had only taken this command upon him to preserve the country, and should be ready to submit to any lawful authority; and he and his men were not come for any other intent but to prevent disturbance of the peace and gatherings together of men, who, they were informed, intended to rise in these parts. Mrs. Hutchinson smiling, told him it was necessary for him to keep a good guard, for all the whole country would shortly be weary of their yoke, and, no question, find some authority to shelter them. At last he came to that as to desire her to let the colonel know he intended him no mischief, but he and all his men should be at her command to defend her from the insolencies of any others. She heard him without faith, for she knew the good will they pretended to her husband proceeded only from their fear. It is true that at that time the colonel had

met with Colonel Hacker, and several other gentlemen of Northampton and Warwickshire, and at the
same time Major Beque was to have reduced
Coventry, and another colonel Warwick Castle.[1]
Two regiments of horse should have marched to a
place within seven miles of Colonel Hutchinson's
house, where his men should have rendezvoused,
and the town of Nottingham at the same time
have seized all the soldiers there, and they of
Leicester the like.   These people had, through the
spies that were about the colonel, gotten some little
inkling of his rendezvous, but not right, neither

---

[1] Major Beque, or Beake, was a member for Coventry in
the parliament of 1654 and 1656, and for Peterborough in
that called by Richard Cromwell.   Colonel Hutchinson,
according to the before-mentioned certificate, acted vigorously against Lambert, and the pretended Council of Safety,
"against whom he had prepared considerable levies to assist
the Lord-General, if he had had occasion."   As for Hacker,
Mr. Ashton writes to Hyde on the 15th of July 1659:—
I have had occasion to be frequently of late with my old
acquaintance, Colonel Hacker, who hath the best regiment
of horse in the army, and by his discourse perceive they
find 'themselves in great confusion, and out of all hopes
of settlement, but it is not fit for me to enter into any
discourse with so great a rebel without leave; but if his
majesty give me leave to assure him pardon, and such
other conditions as may be fit to grant him, I will give you
further account of it" (Clarendon State Papers, iii. 526).
The king does not appear to have sanctioned any overtures
to Hacker.

could they have prevented it, had there been need. But just before it should have been put into execution the parliament were restored to their seats, Lambert was deserted by his men and fled, and Monk was marching on southwards, pretending to restore and confirm the parliament; insomuch that Colonel Hutchinson, instead of raising his country, was called up to his seat in parliament. Here there were so many favourers of Lambert, Fleetwood, and their partakers, that the colonel, who used to be very silent, could not now forbear high opposition to them; in whose favour things were carried with such a stream, that the colonel then began to lose all hopes of settling this poor land on any righteous foundation.

It was the 26th of December, 1659, that the parliament met again. The manner of it, and the contest and treaty in the north between Monk and Lambert, are too well known to be repeated; the dissimulations and false protestations that Monk made are too public; yet did the colonel and others suspect him, but knew not how to hinder him; for this insolent usurpation of Lambert's had so turned the hearts of all men, that the whole nation began to set their eyes upon the king beyond the sea, and think a bad settlement under him better than none at all, but still to be under the arbitrary power of such proud rebels as Lambert. The whole house was divided into miserable factions, among whom some would then violently have set up an oath of renunciation of the king and his family.[1] The colonel, thinking it a ridiculous thing to *swear out* a man, when they had no power to defend themselves against him, vehemently opposed that oath, and carried it against Sir Arthur Haslerig and others, who as violently pressed it; urging very truly that those

---

[1] On the question of imposing an oath of renunciation, Colonel Hutchinson was teller for the noes (January 3d, 1660), and performed the same function on January 2d, in the division on the question whether Lambert should be included in the vote of indemnity for officers who had returned to obedience. According to Ludlow, Hutchinson pressed the House "with an unbecoming importunity to proceed against Sir Henry Vane for not removing into the country, according to their order, when it was well known he was so much indisposed, that he could not do it without the apparent hazard of his life" (p. 313). The certificate in Colonel Hutchinson's favour claims also that he moved that the army might be put under the sole command of Monk, opposed the punishment of Sir George Booth and his friends, opposed the commitment of the gentlemen who presented petitions for a free Parliament, and opposed also the destroying and pulling down of the city gates. We find Hutchinson favouring the admission of the secluded members and taking part in the conference between the secluded members and sitting members of the Parliament on February 17 (Kennet. Register, p. 61). He also took part in a conference with the officers of the army (March 8th, 1660), in order to reconcile them with the policy pursued by Monk and his party in the Parliament (Clarendon State Papers, iii. 697).

oaths that had been formerly imposed had but multiplied the sins of the nation by perjuries; instancing how Sir Arthur and others, in Oliver's time, coming into the house, swore on their entrance they would attempt nothing in the change of that government, which, as soon as ever they were entered, they laboured to throw down. Many other arguments he used, whereupon many honest men, who thought till then he had followed a faction in all things, and not his own judgment, begun to meet often with him, and to consult what to do in these difficulties, out of which their prudence and honesty had found a way to extricate themselves, but that the period of our prosperity was come; hastened on partly by the mad rash violence of some that, without strength, opposed the tide of the discontented tumultuous people, partly by the detestable treachery of those who had sold themselves to do mischief, but chiefly by the general stream of the people, who were as eager for their own destruction as the Israelites of old for their quails.

One observation of the colonel I cannot omit, that the secluded members whom Monk brought in were, many of them, so brought over to a commonwealth that, if Sir Arthur Haslerig and his party had not forsaken their places because they would not sit with them, they had made the stronger party in the house, which by reason

of their going off were after in all things out-
voted.[1]

Sir Anthony Ashley Cooper at that time insinuated himself into a particular friendship with the
colonel, and made him all the honourable pretences
that can be imagined; called him his *dear friend*,
and caressed him with such embraces as none but
a traitor as vile as himself could have suspected;
yet was he the most intimate of Monk's confidants.
Whereupon some few days before the rising of that
house, when it began to be too apparent which way
Monk inclined, the colonel, upon the confidence of
his friendship, entreated him to tell him what were
Monk's intentions, that he and others might consider their safety, who were likely to be given up
as a public sacrifice. Cooper denied to the death
any intention besides a commonwealth; "but,"

---

[1] More than a third of the members staying in the House
had been members of the Rump, and thirty-three members
had refused to sit after the admission of the excluded members. Haslerig left the House for a time, but afterwards
returned to it. Ludlow refused to follow his example, being
resolved "to give no countenance to the secluded members
by sitting with them who had no right to any place in Parliament, having been expelled the House by more than a
quorum of lawful members." As the average attendance
during this portion of the session ranged from 100 to 120,
the two parts of the republican party combined would still
have formed a powerful party. But the secluded members
would nevertheless have outnumbered them considerably.
Vide Masson, Life of Milton, v. 544.

said he, with the greatest semblance of reality that can be put on, "if the violence of the people should bring the king upon us, let me be damned, body and soul, if ever I see a hair of any man's head touched, or a penny of any man's estate, upon this quarrel." This he backed with so many and so deep protestations of that kind, as made the colonel, after his treachery was apparent, detest him of all mankind, and think himself obliged, if ever he had opportunity, to procure exemplary justice on him, who was so vile a wretch as to sit himself and sentence some of those that died. And although this man joined with those who laboured the colonel's particular deliverance, yet the colonel, to his dying day, abhorred the mention of his name, and held him for a more execrable traitor than Monk himself. At this time the colonel, as before, was by many of his friends attempted every way to fall in with the king's interest, and often offered both pardon and preferment, if he could be wrought off from his party, whose danger was now laid before him : but they could no way move him. A gentleman that had been employed to tamper with him told me, that he found him so unmovable, that one time he and a certain lord being in the colonel's company, and having begun their vain insinuations, he, to decline them, seeing Cooper, went away with him ; upon which this lord, that had some tenderness for the colonel, "Well," said he, to this gentleman, "the colonel is a ruined man; he believes that traitor, which will ruin him." When they could not work into him one way, some, that were most kindly concerned in him, persuaded him to absent himself and not act for the parliament, and undertook with their lives to secure him, but he would not. He foresaw the mischief, and resolved to stay in his duty, waiting upon God, who accordingly was good to him. Some, when they saw Monk had betrayed them, would have fallen in with Lambert, but the colonel thought any destruction was to be chosen before the sin of joining with such a wretch.

Now was that glorious parliament come to a period, not more fatal to itself than to the three nations, whose sun of liberty then set, and all their glory gave place to the foulest mists that ever overspread a miserable people. A new parliament was to be chosen, and the county of Nottingham yet had such respect for Colonel Hutchinson, that they fixed their eyes on him to be their knight, but Mr. William Pierrepont having a great desire to bring in his son-in-law, the Lord Haughton, to be his fellow-knight, the colonel would not come into the town till the election was passed; which if he had, he had been chosen without desiring it; for many people came, and when they saw he would not stand, returned and voted for none, among whom were fifty freeholders of the town of Newark.

Some time before the writs for the new elections

came, the town of Nottingham, as almost all the
rest of the island, began to grow mad, and to declare themselves so, in their desires of the king.
The boys, set on by their fathers and. masters,
got drums and colours, and marched up and down
the town, and trained themselves in a military
posture, and offered many affronts to the soldiers
of the army that were quartered there, which were
two troops of Colonel Hacker's regiment. Insomuch that one night there were about forty of the
soldiers hurt and wounded with stones, upon the
occasion of taking away the drums, when the
youths were gathering together to make bonfires to
burn the Rump, as the custom of those mad days
was. The soldiers, provoked to rage, shot again,
and killed in the scuffle two presbyterians, whereof
one was an elder, and an old professor ; and one
that had been a great zealot for the cause, and
master of the magazine of Nottingham Castle.[1]
He was only standing at his own door, and
whether by chance or on purpose shot, or by

---

[1] The register of burials at St. Mary's Church, quoted
by Bailey, Annals of Nottinghamshire, p. 864, contains the
following entry :—"Mr. Richard Hawkins, an elder, who
was slain by the soldiers in the late tumults, whilst standing
at his own door." "Mercurius Publicus" for February 23,
March 1, 1660, notes that "his excellency sent Judge-Advo-
cate Margets to examine upon oath the differences at
Nottingham that lately happened betwixt the town and
soldiery."

whom, it is not certain; but true it is, that at that
time the presbyterians were more inveterately
bitter against the fanatics than even the cavaliers
themselves, and they set on these boys. But
upon the killing of this man they were hugely
enraged, and prayed very seditiously in their
pulpits, and began openly to desire the king; not
for good will to him neither, but for destruction to
all the fanatics. One of the ministers, who were
great leaders of the people, had been firmly
engaged in Booth's rebellion, and very many of the
godly led in, who, by the timely suppression of
those who began the insurrection in Nottingham,
were prevented from declaring themselves openly.
Colonel Hutchinson was as merciful as he could
safely be, in not setting on too strict inquisition;
but privately admonishing such as were not passed
hopes of becoming good commonwealth's men, if it
were possible that the labouring state might out-
live the present storm. Upon this bustle in the
town of Nottingham the soldiers were horribly
incensed, and the townsmen ready to take part
with the boys; whereupon the soldiers drew into
the meadows near the town, and sent for the
regiment, resolving to execute their vengeance on
the town, and the townsmen again were mustering
to encounter them. Mrs. Hutchinson by chance
coming into the town, and being acquainted with
the captains, persuaded them to do nothing in a

tumultuary way, however provoked, but to complain to the general, and let him decide the business.

The men, at her entreaty, were content so to do, the townsmen also consenting to restrain their children and servants, and keep the public peace; while it was agreed that both of them should send up together a true information to the general concerning the late quarrel. But one of the officers, more enraged than the rest, went immediately away to Monk, and complained to him of the malice of the presbyterian and cavalier against the soldiers. He, without asking more on the other side, signed a warrant to Colonel Hacker, to let loose the fury of his regiment upon the town, and plunder all they judged guilty; with which the officer immediately went away. Colonel Hutchinson being at that time at the general's lodging, my Lord Howard told him what order against the town of Nottingham had just been sent down. The colonel, who had been by his wife informed of the disorders there, went to the general, and prevailed with him for a countermand of all hostility against the town, till he should hear and determine the business; which countermand the colonel sent immediately by one of the townsmen, who, though he rid post, came not till Colonel Hacker, with all his regiment, were come into the town before him, and the soldiers were in some of the houses beginning to rifle them. Wherefore the counter-

mand coming so seasonably from Colonel Hutchinson, they could not but look upon him as their
deliverer; and this being done a very few days
before the election for the next parliament, when
the colonel came to town and had waived the
county, they generally pitched upon him for the
town. But then Dr. Plumptre laboured all he
could to get the burgess-ship for himself, and to
put by the colonel, with the basest scandals he and
two or three of his associates could raise. Mr.
Arthur Stanhope, in whose house the soldiers were
entered to plunder, being pitched upon for the
other burgess, and having a great party in the
town, was dealt with to desert the colonel, and
offered all Plumptre's party; but he, on the other
side, laboured more for the colonel than for himself, and at length, when the election day came,
Mr. Stanhope and the colonel were clearly chosen.

The colonel and Mr. Stanhope went up to the
parliament, which began on the 25th day of April,
1660; to whom the king sending a declaration from
Breda, which promised, or at least intimated, liberty
of conscience, remission of all offences, enjoyment
of liberties and estates; they voted to send commissioners to invite him. And almost all the gentry
of all parties went, some to fetch him over, some to
meet him at the sea side, some to fetch him into
London, into which he entered on the 29th day of
May, with an universal joy and triumph, even to

CHARLES II.

his own amazement; who, when he saw all the nobility and gentry of the land flowing in to him, asked where were his enemies? For he saw nothing but prostrates, expressing all the love that could make a prince happy. Indeed it was a wonder in that day to see the mutability of some, and the hypocrisy of others, and the servile flattery of all. Monk, like his better genius, conducted him, and was adored like one that had brought all the glory and felicity of mankind home with this prince.

The officers of the army had made themselves as fine as the courtiers, and everyone hoped in ·this change to change their condition, and disowned all things they before had advised. Every ballad-singer sung up and down the streets ribald rhymes, made in reproach of the late commonwealth, and of all those worthies that therein endeavoured the people's freedom and happiness.

The presbyterians were now the white boys,[1] and according to their nature fell a thirsting, then hunting after blood, urging that God's blessing could not be

---

[1] *i.e.,* favourites. Lord Willoughby writes to the Earl of Denbigh on June 30, 1644, and compares the earl's favour with the Parliament, with the unpopularity of other noble commanders. "You," he concludes, "are the only white boy I know." The expression is frequently used by the dramatists. In "The Knight of the Burning Pestle," Mrs. Merrythought calls her son Michael "my white boy" (Act II. 2).

upon the land, till justice had cleansed it from the late king's blood. First that fact was disowned, then all the acts made after it rendered void, then an inquisition made after those that were guilty thereof, but only seven nominated of them that sat in judgment on that prince, for exemplary justice, and a proclamation sent for the rest to come in, upon penalty of losing their estates.

While these things were debating in the house, at the first, divers persons concerned in that business sat there, and when the business came into question, every one of them spoke to it according to their present sense.[1] But Mr. Lenthall, son to the late Speaker of that parliament, when the presbyterians first called that business into question, though not at all concerned in it himself, stood up and made so handsome and honourable a speech in

---

[1] On the 12th of May 1660, passages from the Journals of the Commons concerning the king's trial, and a journal of proceedings at the trial itself were read in the House. "Divers members present who had been amongst the king's judges," did severally express how far they were concerned in the said proceedings and their sense thereon. "It was on this occasion that Lenthall made the speech referred to above, and the speech attributed to Colonel Hutchinson must have also been made at that time. The debate thus begun was continued on the 14th, and closed with a resolution, "that all those persons who sat in judgment upon the late king's majesty when the sentence was pronounced for his condemnation, be forthwith secured."

defence of them all, as deserves eternal honour. But the presbyterians called him to the bar for it, where, though he mitigated some expressions, which might be ill taken of the house, yet he spoke so generously, as it is never to be forgotten of him. Herein he behaved himself with so much courage and honour as was not matched at that time in England, for which he was looked on with an evil eye, and, upon a pretence of treason, put in prison; from whence his father's money, and the lieutenant of the Tower's jealousy, delivered him. When it came to Ingoldsby's turn, he, with many tears, professed his repentance for that murther, and told a false tale, how Cromwell held his hand, and forced him to subscribe the sentence, and made a most whining recantation, after which he retired; and another had almost ended, when Colonel Hutchinson, who was not there at the beginning, came in, and was told what they were about, and that it would be expected he should say something. He was surprised with a thing he expected not, yet neither then, nor in any the like occasion, did he ever fail himself, but told them, "That for his actings in those days, if he had erred, it was the inexperience of his age, and the defect of his judgment, and not the malice of his heart, which had ever prompted him to pursue the general advantage of his country more than his own; and if the sacrifice of him might conduce to the public peace and

settlement, he should freely submit his life and
fortunes to their dispose; that the vain expense of
his age, and the great debts his public employments
had run him into, as they were testimonies that
neither avarice nor any other interest had carried
him on, so they yielded him just cause to repent
that he ever forsook his own blessed quiet, to
embark in such a troubled sea, where he had made
shipwreck of all things but a good conscience; and
as to that particular action of the king, he desired
them to believe he had that sense of it that befitted an Englishman, a Christian, and a gentleman."
What he expressed was to this effect, but so very
handsomely delivered, that it generally took the
whole house; only one gentleman stood up and
said, he had expressed himself as one that was
much more sorry for the events and consequences
than the actions; but another replied, that when a
man's words might admit of two interpretations, it
befitted gentlemen always to receive that which
might be most favourable. As soon as the colonel
had spoken, he retired into a room where Ingoldsby
was with his eyes yet red, who had called up a little
spite to succeed his whinings, and embracing Col.
Hutchinson, "O colonel," said he, "did I ever
imagine we could be brought to this? Could I
have suspected it, when I brought them Lambert in
the other day, this sword should have redeemed us
from being dealt with as criminals, by that people

for whom we had so gloriously exposed ourselves?"
The colonel told him he had foreseen, ever since
those usurpers thrust out the lawful authority of
the land to enthrone themselves, it could end in
nothing else; but the integrity of his heart, in all
he had done, made him as cheerfully ready to suffer
as to triumph in a good cause.   The result of the
house that day was to suspend Colonel Hutchinson
and the rest from sitting in the house.   Monk, after
all his great professions, now sat still, and had not
one word to interpose for any person, but was as
forward to set vengeance on foot as any man.

Mrs. Hutchinson, whom to keep quiet, her husband had hitherto persuaded that no man would
lose or suffer by this change, at this beginning was
awakened, and saw that he was ambitious of being
a public sacrifice, and therefore, herein only in her
whole life, resolved to disobey him, and to improve
all the affection he had to her for his safety, and
prevailed with him to retire; for she said, she
would not live to see him a prisoner.   With her
unquietness, she drove him out of her own lodgings
into the custody of a friend, in order to his further
retreat, if occasion should be, and then made it her
business to solicit all her friends for his safety.
Meanwhile, it was first resolved in the house, that
mercy should be shown to some, and exemplary
justice to others; then the number was defined, and
voted it should not exceed seven; then upon the

king's own solicitation, that his subjects should be
put out of their fears, those seven named; and
after that a proclamation sent for the rest to come
in.   Colonel Hutchinson not being of the number
of those seven, was advised by all his friends to
surrender himself, in order to securing his estate,
and he was very earnest to do it, when Mrs.
Hutchinson would by no means hear of it: but
being exceedingly urged by his friends, that she
would hereby obstinately lose all their estate, she
would not yet consent that the colonel should give
himself into custody, and she had wrought him to
a strong engagement, that he would not dispose of
himself without her.   At length, being accused of
obstinacy, in not giving him up, she devised a way
to try the house, and writ a letter in his name to
the Speaker, to urge what might be in his favour,
and to let him know, that by reason of some in-
conveniency it might be to him, he desired not to
come under custody, and yet should be ready to
appear at their call; and if they intended any
mercy to him, he begged they would begin it in
permitting him his liberty upon his parole, till they
should finally determine of him.   This letter she
conceived would try the temper of the house; if
they granted this, she had her end, for he was still
free; if they denied it, she might be satisfied in
keeping him from surrendering himself.

Having contrived and written this letter, before

she carried it to the colonel, a friend came to her out of the house, near which her lodgings then were, and told her that if they had but any ground to begin, the house was that day in a most excellent temper towards her husband; whereupon she writ her husband's name to the letter, and ventured to send it in, being used sometimes to write the letters he dictated, and her character not much differing from his. These gentlemen who were moved to try this opportunity, were not of the friends she relied on; but God, to show that it was he, not they, sent two common friends, who had so good success that the letter was very well received; and upon that occasion all of all parties spoke so kindly and effectually for him, that he had not only what he desired, but was voted to be free without any engagement; and his punishment was only that he should be discharged from the present parliament, and from all office, military or civil, in the state for ever; and upon his petition of thanks, for this, his estate also was voted to be free from all mulcts and confiscations.[1] Many providential circumstances concurred in this thing. That which put

---

[1] The Commons Journals state, June 5, 1660, "Mr. Speaker communicates a letter, dated the 5th of June 1660, directed to himself and signed by Colonel John Hutchinson, who was one of those who sat in judgment upon the late king's majesty when sentence of death was pronounced against him, which was read. Resolved that Colonel John

the house into so good a humour towards the
colonel that day, was, that having taken the business of the king's trial into consideration, certain
committees were found to be appointed to order the
preparation of the court, the chairs and cushions,
and other formalities, wherein Colonel Hutchinson
had nothing to do;[1] but when they had passed
their votes for his absolute discharge and came to
the sitting of the court, he was found not to have
been one day away. A rogue that had been one
of their clerks had brought in all these infor-

Hutchinson be at liberty, on his own parole to be given to
Mr. Speaker."

On June 9th, the House went on to vote that Colonel
John Hutchinson,

"(1.) Be discharged from being a member of this House;

"(2.) Be incapable of bearing any office or place of public
trust in this kingdom;

"(3.) In respect of his signal repentance, shall not be
within that clause of exception in the Act of general pardon
and oblivion, as to any fine, or forfeiture of any part of his
estate not purchased of or belonging to the public."

A petition expressing this repentance had just been read.

[1] In Nalson's Trial of Charles I., it appears that on
Friday, January 12, when a committee was appointed for
ordering the trial, and many minute particulars agreed to
for the management of it, Colonel Hutchinson was absent,
but attended most other days. On January 25, however,
when the sentence was suggested, he was absent, but was
present at the signing, and himself signed the warrant for
execution.—J. H.

mations; and above all, poor Mrs. Hacker, thinking
to save her husband, had brought up the warrant
for execution, with all their hands and seals.[1]

Sir Allen Apsley too, who, with all the kindest
zeal of friendship that can be imagined, endeavoured to bring off the colonel, used some artifice
in engaging friends for him. There was a young
gentleman, a kinsman of his, who thirstily aspired
after preferment, and Sir Allen had given him
hopes, upon his effectual endeavours for the colonel,
to introduce him; who being a person that had
understanding enough, made no conscience of truth,
when an officious lie might serve his turn.[2] This
man, although he owed his life to the colonel, and
had a thousand obligations to Mrs. Hutchinson's
parents, yet not for their sakes, nor for virtue, nor

---

[1] To those who have not read or not remembered the
trials of the regicides, it may be useful to remark, that
Colonel Hacker was tried for superintending the execution
of the king in his military capacity, for which it seems this
warrant was expected to prove a sufficient justification:
and perhaps it ought to have been so considered: but it is
extraordinary that his wife, before she gave up an instrument which seemed so precious to those who were seeking revenge, had not stipulated for her husband's pardon.
—J. H.

[2] This gentleman, mentioned on p. 259 as Sir Allen
Apsley's candidate for preferment, was probably one of
those who signed the certificate in favour of Colonel Hutchinson.

for gratitude, but for his own hopes, which he had
of Sir Allen Apsley, told some of the leading men
among the court party, that it was the king's desire
to have favour shown to the colonel; whereupon
Mr. Palmer, since Castlemaine,[1] was the first man
that spoke for the colonel, whom Finch most
eloquently seconded. Then Sir George Booth and
his party all appeared for the colonel, in gratitude
for his civility to them. For when the parliament had passed by the rebellion of Lambert and
Fleetwood, and those who joined with them, and
would not make their offences capital, he had told
the house, they could not without great partiality
punish these, and had moved much in their favour.
Mr. Pierrepont, and all the old sage parliament men,
out of very hearty kindness, spoke and laboured very
effectually to bring him clear off; and there was
not at that day any man that received a more
general testimony of love and good esteem from all
parties than he did, not one of the most violent
hunters of blood opposing favour, and divers most
worthy persons giving a true and honourable testimony of him. Although they knew his principles to
be contrary to theirs, yet they so justified his clear
and upright carriage, according to his own persuasion, as was a record much advancing his honour,
and such as no man else in that day received.[1]

---

[1] Mr. Lassels (probably Lascelles) enjoyed exactly a

Yet though he very well deserved it, I cannot so much attribute that universal concurrence that was in the whole house to express esteem of him and desire to save him, to their justice and gratitude, as to an overruling power of Him that orders all men's hearts, who was then pleased to reserve His servant, even by the good and true testimony of some that after hated him and sought his ruin, for the perseverance in that goodness, which then forced them to be his advocates ; for even the worst and basest men have a secret conviction of worth and virtue, which they never dare to persecute in its own name.   The colonel being thus discharged, the house retired to a lodging further from Westminster, and lay very private in the town, not coming into any company of one sort or other, waiting till the act of oblivion were perfected, to go down again into the country; but when the act came to be passed in the house, then the Lord Lexington set divers friends on work in the commons' house to get a proviso inserted, that the Newarkers' money, which he paid into the committee of Haberdashers' Hall, and was by that committee paid to the colonel for his pay, might, with all the use of it, be paid out of the colonel's

---

similar exemption ; the peculiar reasons for it are not accurately known, but it is natural to suppose they were similar.—J. H.

estate. He forged many false pretences to obtain
this ; but it was rejected in the commons' house,
and the bill going up to the lords, was passed without any provisoes.   Only the gentlemen that were
the late king's judges, and who were decoyed to
surrender themselves to custody by the house's
proclamation, after they had voted only seven to
suffer, were now given up to a trial, both for their
lives and estates, and put into close prison ; where
they were miserably kept, brought shortly after
to trial, condemned, all their estates confiscated
and taken away, themselves kept in miserable
bondage under that inhuman, bloody jailor, the
lieutenant of the Tower, who stifled some of them
to death for want of air ; and when they had not
one penny, but what was given them to feed themselves and their families, exacted abominable rates
for bare, unfurnished prisons ; of some forty pounds
for one miserable chamber ; of others double,
besides undue and unjust fees, which their poor
wives were forced to beg and engage their join-
tures and make miserable shifts for; and yet this
rogue had all this while three pounds a week paid
out of the exchequer for every one of them.   At
last, when this would not kill them fast enough, and
when some alms were thus privately stolen in to
them, they were sent away to remote and dismal
islands, where relief could not reach them, nor
any of their relations take care of them : in this

a thousand times more miserable than those that
died, who were thereby prevented from the eternal
infamy and remorse, which hope of life and estate
made these poor men bring upon themselves, by
base and false recantations of their own judgments,
against their consciences; which they wounded for
no advantage, but lived ever after in misery themselves, augmented by seeing the misery of their
wretched families, and in the daily apprehension
of death, which, without any more formality, they
are to expect whenever the tyrant gives the word.
And these are the "*tender* MERCIES *of the wicked !*"
Among which I cannot forget one passage that
I saw. Monk and his wife, before they were removed to the Tower, while they were yet prisoners
at Lambeth House, came one evening to the
garden and caused them to be brought down
only to stare at them,—which was such a bar-
barism, for that man, who had betrayed so many
poor men to death and misery that never hurt him,
but who had honoured him, and had trusted their
lives and interest with him, to glut his bloody eyes
with beholding them in their bondage, as no story
can parallel the inhumanity of.

Colonel Scroope, who had been cleared by vote as
the colonel was, was afterwards rased out for nothing, and had the honour to die a noble martyr.[1]

---

[1] Colonel Scroope had used in conversation words justi-

Although the colonel was cleared both for life and estate in the house of commons, yet he not answering the court expectations in public recantations and dissembled repentance, and applause of their cruelty to his fellows, the chancellor was cruelly exasperated against him, and there were very high endeavours to have rased him out of the act of oblivion. But then Sir Allen Apsley solicited all his friends, as it had been for his own life, and divers honorable persons drew up a certificate, with all the advantage they could, to procure him favour;[1] who in all things that were not against the interest of the state had ever pitied and protected them in their distresses. The Countess of Rochester writ a very effectual letter to the Earl of

---

fying the king's death ; these words were reported against him by Sir Richard Browne, and to them he owed his death.

[1] See this certificate in the Appendix, signed by Lord Biron, the Countess of Rochester and others, including Anthony Ashley Cooper. The service mentioned, according to the certificate, was that Colonel Hutchinson "gave the Earl of Rochester notice and opportunity to escape when Cromwell's ministers had discovered him the last time he was employed in his majesty's service here in England."

This must refer to Rochester's visit to the north of England in the spring of 1655, but I can find no confirmation of the story in Clarendon's narrative, or in the accounts among the Clarendon State Papers. Wilmot was nearly arrested at Aylesbury, but escaped by bribing the innkeeper.

Manchester, making her request that the favour to him might be confirmed as an obligation to her, to quit some that she, and, as she supposed, her lord had received from him.   This letter was read in the house, and Sir Allen Apsley's candidate for preferment again made no conscience of deceiving several lords, that the preserving of the colonel would be acceptable to the king and the chancellor, who he now knew hated his life.   Many lords also of the colonel's relations and acquaintance, out of kindness and gratitude (for there was not one of them whom he had not in his day more or less obliged), used very hearty endeavours for him. Yet Sir Allen Apsley's interest and most fervent endeavours for him, was that which only turned the scales, and the colonel was not excepted in the act of oblivion to anything but offices.

The provisoes to the act of oblivion were all cut off, and it was determined that those things should pass in particular acts;[1] when the Lord Lexington

---

[1] On July 7th a proviso had been offered to the Bill of Indemnity, concerning money received by Colonel Hutchinson from Sir John Digby, lent unto Sir John Digby and others by John Chambers, William Barret, and Hercules Clay, deceased.   It was read twice and committed on the 7th, and finally agreed to on the 11th.   But by the resolution spoken of in the text this proviso was annulled, and Chambers and the rest were obliged to bring in a separate bill for the purpose, which failed to pass.   On June 8, 1661,

got one for that Newark money to be repaid
out of the colonel's estate, with all the interest for
fourteen years.   This act was committed, and
the colonel had counsel to plead against it, and
the Marquess Dorchester[1] having the chair,
was wonderful civil to the colonel.   The adverse
counsel, having been men that practised under the
parliament, thought they could no way ingratiate
themselves so well as by making invectives against
those they formerly clawed with, and when, quite
beside their matter, they fell into railings against
the injustice of the former times and scandals of
the colonel, the marquis checked them severely,
and bade them mind their cause : but Mr. Finch,
one of the colonel's counsel, after a lawyer had

---

a bill was brought into the House of Commons to enable
Clay and others to raise the sum of £2690 and damages out
of Colonel Hutchinson's lands, but it was rejected on the
third reading, February 22, 1662.

[1] The same whom, when Viscount Newark, Colonel Hutchinson rescued from the violence of the countrymen at
Nottingham ; to whom afterwards the colonel made, at the
request of her friends, the offer of the hand and fortune of
Lady Anne Somerset, and who so handsomely now evinces
his candour and gratitude.   His character is well contrasted
with that of Lord Lexington, who in the first place obtained
a peerage for the sacrifice of this very money ; next refused
payment of it to the Newarkers, of whom he had borrowed
it : then, upon being compelled to pay it, procured easy
terms by the colonel's interference ; and now attempts to
plunder his benefactor of the whole !—J. H.

made a long railing speech, which held them a
tedious while, he replying, "My lord," said he,
" this gentleman hath taken up a great deal of time
to tell your lordship how unjust that parliament
was, how their committees perverted judgment and
right, which he sets forth with all his power of language to make them odious, and in conclusion would
persuade your lordship therefore to do the same
things." After the hearing at the committee, a
report was made so favourable for the colonel that
the bill was cast aside, and the house being then
ready to adjourn, most of the colonel's friends went
out of town, which opportunity Lexington taking
notice of, the very last day in a huddle got the bill
past the lords' house.[1]

Then the colonel went down into the country,
and found it necessary to reduce and change his
family, which were many of them people he took
in for charity, when they could no where else be
received; and they had been more humble and
dutiful while they were under hatches, but now
might find better preferments, and were not to be
confided in; yet he dismissed not any of them
without bountiful rewards, and such kind dismis-
sions as none but that false generation would not

---

[1] The practice of parliament at that time must have
differed from what it is now, for such a bill to originate in
the House of Lords : we shall presently see it miscarry in
the Commons.—J. H.

have been obliged by. But some of them soon after betrayed him as much as was in their power, whose prudence had so lived with them, that they knew nothing that could hurt his person.

When the colonel saw how the other poor gentlemen were trepanned that were brought in by proclamation, and how the whole cause itself, from the beginning to the ending, was betrayed and condemned, notwithstanding that he himself, by a wonderfully overruling providence of God, in that day was preserved; yethe looked upon himself as judged in their judgment, and executed in their execution; and although he was most thankful to God, yet he was not very well satisfied in himself for accepting the deliverance. His wife, who thought she had never deserved so well of him, as in the endeavours and labours she exercised to bring him off, never displeased him more in her life, and had much ado to persuade him to be contented with his deliverance; which, as it was eminently wrought by God, he acknowledged it with thankfulness. But while he saw others suffer, he suffered with them in his mind, and, had not his wife persuaded him, had offered himself a voluntary sacrifice; but being by her convinced that God's eminent appearance seemed to have singled him out for preservation, he with thanks acquiesced in that thing; and further remembering that he was but young at that time when he entered

into this engagement, and that many who had
preached and led the people into it, and of that
parliament who had declared it to be treason not
to advance and promote that cause, were all now
apostatised, and as much preached against it, and
called it rebellion and murther, and sat on the
tribunal to judge it; he again reflected seriously
upon all that was past, and begged humbly of God
to enlighten him and show him his sin if ignorance
or misunderstanding had led him into error.   But
the more he examined the cause from the first, the
more he became confirmed in it, and from that time
set himself to a more diligent study of the scriptures, whereby he attained confirmation in many
principles he had before, and daily greater enlighten-
ings concerning the free grace and love of God in
Jesus Christ, and the spiritual worship under the
gospel, and the gospel liberty, which ought not to
be subjected to the wills and ordinances of men in
the service of God.   This made him rejoice in all
he had done in the Lord's cause, and he would
often say, the Lord had not thus eminently preserved him for nothing, but that he was yet kept
for some eminent service or suffering in this cause;
although having been freely pardoned by the present powers, he resolved not to do anything against
the king, but thought himself obliged to sit still
and wish his prosperity in all things that were not
destructive to the interest of Christ and his members

on earth; yet as he could not wish well to any ill
way, so he believed that God had set him aside,
and that therefore he ought to mourn in silence and
retiredness, while he lay under this obligation.

He had not been long at home before a pur-
suivant from the council was sent to fetch him from
his house at Owthorpe, who carried him to the
attorney-general.   He, with all preparatory insinuations, how much he would express his gratitude
to the king and his repentance for his error, if he
would now deal ingenuously, in bearing testimony
to what he should be examined, sifted him very
thoroughly; but the colonel, who was piqued at
heart that they should thus use him, to reserve him
with an imagination that he would serve their turns
in witnessing to the destruction of the rest, composed himself as well as he could, and resolved
upon another testimony than they expected, if they
had called him to any.   But the attorney-general
was so ill satisfied with his private examination
that he would not venture a public one.   He dealt
with him with all the art and flatteries that could
be, to make him but appear, in the least thing, to
have deserted his own and embraced the king's
party; and he brought the warrant of execution to
the colonel, and would fain have persuaded him to
own some of the hands, and to have imparted some
circumstances of the sealing, because himself was
present.   But the colonel answered him, that in a

business transacted so many years ago, wherein
life was concerned, he durst not bear a testimony,
having at that time been so little an observer, that
he could not remember the least tittle of that most
eminent circumstance, of Cromwell's forcing Colonel
Ingoldsby to set to his unwilling hand, which, if his
life had depended on that circumstance, he could not
have affirmed. "And then, Sir," said he, "if I have
lost so great a thing as that, it cannot be expected
less eminent passages remain with me." Then
being showed the gentlemen's hands, he told him he
was not well acquainted with them, as having never
had commerce with the most of them by letters;
and those he could own, he could only say they
resembled the writings which he was acquainted
with; among these he only picked out Cromwell's,
Ireton's, and my Lord Grey's. The attorney-general,
very ill-satisfied with his private examination, dismissed him; yet was he served with a writ to
appear in the court the next day. The colonel had
been told that, when they were in distress for
witnesses to make up their formality, Colonel Ingoldsby had put them upon sending for him, which
made him give that instance to the attorney. The
next day the court sat, and the colonel was fetched
in and made to pass before the prisoners' faces, but
examined to nothing; which he much waited for,
for the sight of the prisoners, with whom he
believed himself to stand at the bar, and the sight

of their judges, among whom was that *vile traitor*
who had sold the men that trusted him ; and he
that openly said he abhorred the word *accommodation*, when moderate men would have prevented the
war ; and the colonel's own *dear friend*, who had
wished damnation to his soul if he ever suffered
penny of any man's estate, or hair of any man's
head, to be touched ;—the sight of these [1] had so
provoked his spirit that, if he had been called to
speak, he was resolved to have borne testimony to
the cause and against the court ; but they asking
him nothing, he went to his lodging, and so out of
town, and would not come any more into their court,
but sent the attorney-general word he could witness nothing, and was sick with being kept in the
crowd and in the press, and therefore desired to
be excused from coming any more thither.   The
attorney made a very malicious report of him to the
chancellor and the king, insomuch as his ruin was
then determined, and only opportunity watched to
effect it. [2]

When Sir A. Apsley came to the chancellor he

---

[1] Monk, Ashley Cooper, and Hollis.

[2] The king intimated to the lords, when there were disputes on foot respecting the exceptions to the bill of
indemnity, that "*other ways* might be found to meet with
those of turbulent and factious spirits :" thereby showing
that he had, like the rest of his family, secret reserves for
rendering insignificant his public acts.—J. H.

was in a great rage and passion, and fell upon him
with much vehemence.   "O Nall," said he, " what
have you done ? [1] you have saved a man that would
be ready, if he had opportunity, to mischief us as
much as ever he did."   Sir Allen was forced to
stop his mouth, and tell him, that he believed his
brother a less dangerous person than those he had
brought into the king's council, meaning Maynard

---

[1] Sir Allen Apsley was both before and after the Restoration one of Clarendon's most trusted agents and friends.
Clarendon addresses him often, as also his namesake Sir
Allen Broderick, by the title of "Nall."   Broderick signed
the certificate in favour of Colonel Hutchinson, and his
name is frequently found associated with that of Apsley.
I am convinced that Apsley and Broderick are the two
persons referred to in a passage in "Clarendon's House-
warning," which Dr. Grosart is unable to explain.   It
describes the Chancellor planning his new house,

> "To proceed in the model he called in his Allans,
> The two Allons, when jovial, who ply him with gallons,
> The two Allons who served his blind justice for balance,
> The two Allons who served his injustice for talons."
> —Marvell's Poems, ed. Grosart.

Pepys tells a story of the two Allens "when jovial." On
the 19th of December 1666, Sir Richard Ford "did tell me,
and so did Sir W. Batten, how Sir Allen Broderick and Sir
Allen Apsley did come drunk the other day into the House,
and did both speak for half an hour together, and could not
be either laughed, or pulled, or bid to sit down and hold
their peace, to the great contempt of the king's servants and
cause."

and Glynne ; but the truth is, from that time, all kindness that any one expressed to the colonel was ill resented, and the Countess of Rochester was also severely rebuked for having appeared so kind to the colonel.

When the parliament sat again, the colonel sent up his·wife to solicit his business in the house, that the Lord Lexington's bill might not pass the lower house.   At her first coming to town a parliament-man, a creature of Worcester-house, being in his coach, she out of hers called to him, who was her kinsman, and desired his vigilancy to prevent her injury.   " I could wish," said he, " it had been finished last time, for your husband hath lately so ill behaved himself, that it will pass against him." She answered, " I pray let my friends do but their endeavours for me, and then let it be as God will." He, smiling at her, replied, " *It is not now as God will, but as we will.*"   However, she, notwithstanding many other discouragements, waited upon the business every day, when her adversaries as diligently solicited against her.   One day a friend came out of the house and told her that they were that day so engaged that she might go home and rest secure that nothing would be done ; and that day most of her friends were away, and her opposites took this opportunity to bring it into the house, which was now much alienated, especially all the court party, from the colonel ; but God, to show that not friends, nor diligence, preserved our estates, stirred up the hearts of strangers to do us justice, and the bill was thrown out when we had scarce one of those friends we relied on in the house.

Presently after Mrs. Hutchinson came to town, a kinsman of hers, fallen into the wicked counsels of the court, came to visit her one evening, and had been so freely drinking as to unlock his bosom, when he told her that the king had been lately among them where he was, and told them that they had saved a man, meaning Colonel Hutchinson, who would do the same thing for him he did for his father; for he was still unchanged in his principles, and readier to protect than accuse any of his associates, and would not discover any counsels or designs, or any party, though he were known to have hated them. Then this gentleman told her how contemptuous a carriage it was, that he would not own one but dead hands, and how they were resolved his pardon should never pass the seal, and what a desperate condition he was reduced to. Having thus affrighted her, then, to draw her in by examples, he told her how the late statesmen's wives came and offered them all the informations they had gathered from their husbands, and how she could not but know more than any of them; and if yet she would impart anything that might show her gratitude, she might redeem her family from ruin; and then he particularly told her how

her husband had been intimate with Vane, Pierrepont, and St. John, whose counsels they knew
how far they had gone in this matter, and that if
she would prevent others in the declaring them,
she might much advantage herself. But she told
him, she perceived any safety one could buy of
them was not worth the price of honour and conscience; that she knew nothing of state manage-
ments, or if she did, she would not establish herself upon any man's blood and ruin. Then he
employed all his wit to circumvent her in discourse,
and to have gotten something out of her concerning
some persons they aimed at, which, if he could, I
believe it would have been beneficial to him ; but
she discerned his drift, and scorned to become an
informer, and made him believe she was ignorant,
though she could have enlightened him in the very
thing he sought for ; which they are now never
likely to know much of, it being locked up in the
grave, and they that survive not knowing that their
secrets are removed into another cabinet.[1]   After

---

[1] The ingenious writer of the critique of this work in the
Annual Review, conjectures that the secret which this
friend of Mrs. Hutchinson endeavoured to extort from her
was, *the name of that considerable person who had formed
the design of settling the state under Richard Cromwell,* as
mentioned in p. 378 : this is highly probable, and still more
so that this person was Mr. William Pierrepont, and that
the royalists aimed peculiarly at his destruction, as will
appear from many passages that are to be found in the

all, natural affection working at that time with the gentleman, he in great kindness advised her that her husband should leave England. She told him he could not conveniently, and the act of oblivion being passed, she knew not why he should fear, who was resolved to do nothing that might forfeit the grace he had found. But he told her it was determined that, if there was the least pretence in the world, the colonel should be imprisoned, and never be loose again, which warning, though

---

third volume of Clarendon's State Papers. In one part the good will of Pierrepont to Richard Cromwell and Richard's respect for him is spoken of: in another Hyde instructs his spies to "gain Thurloe, whom he thinks considerable, and he would gain St. John and Pierrepont," adding significantly, "they have manifested that they have no inveterate objection to a *single person*, and the right heir is the best person." In another place it is said by one of the spies that "St. John, Pierrepont, and Thurloe, continue to cabal and press the general (Monk); *three such evil beasts do not exist.*" But when Pierrepont is reported to be ill, the most eager wishes are expressed for his death. No doubt but the *virtuous ministers* of Charles II. dreaded his abilities and integrity as they coveted his property : but supported by such connexions as he was, they could not venture to attack him without some clear and strong information against him. That these harpies were disappointed in their project of extinguishing this eminent patriot and his family, and pouncing on their possessions, may then most likely be attributed to the constancy and discretion of Mrs. Hutchinson.—J. H.

others of her friends said it was but an effect of his wine, the consequence proved it but too true.

She advertised the colonel and persuaded him, being also advised to the same by other friends, to go out of England, but he would not : he said this was the place where God had set him, and protected him hitherto, and it would be in him an ungrateful distrust of God to forsake it. At this time he would have sold part of his estate to pay his debts, but the purchasers scrupled, desiring to see his pardon, which he not having, was fain to break off the treaty ; and though all the friends he had laboured it, the chancellor utterly refused it.

There was a thousand pounds offered to one to procure it, but it was tried several times and would not pass, by reason of which he was prevented of the opportunity then to settle his estate ; yet a year after a little solicitor shuffled it in among many others, and managed it so dexterously that it passed all the seals. The colonel's estate being in mortgage with a peevish alderman, who designed to have bought it for little or nothing, he had a great trouble with him ; for having procured him his money, he would not assign the mortgage, and the others would not lend the money without assignment from him, so that it put the colonel to many inconveniences and great expense.

This parliament being risen, another was called by the king's writ, wherein the act of oblivion was again confirmed, not without some canvassing and opposition; and here again another act about that money of the Lord Lexington's was prepared and twice read in the house, through divers abominable untruths which they had forged and possessed the members withal. The colonel himself solicited his own defence, and had all the injustice and foul play imaginable at the committee appointed to examine it, and it was so desperate that all his friends persuaded him to compound it; but he would not, though his enemies offered it, but he said he would either be cleared by a just, or ruined by an unjust sentence, and, pursuing it with his usual alacrity and vigour in all things, he at last removed that prepossession that some of the gentlemen had against him; and clearing himself to some that were most violent, it pleased God to turn the hearts of the house at last to do him justice, and to throw out the bill for evermore, which was a great mercy to him and his family, for it was to have thrown him out of possession of all the estates he had, and to have put them into his enemies' hands till they had satisfied themselves. But the defending himself was very chargeable to him, and not only so, but this rumour of trouble upon his estate, and the brags of his enemies, and the cloud he lay under, hindered him both from letting and selling, and improving his estate, so that it very much augmented his debt.

Before this time, in December, 1660, Captain

Cooper sent one Broughton, a lieutenant, and Andrews, a cornet, with a company of soldiers, who plundered his house at Owthorpe, while he was absent, of all the weapons they found in it, to his very wearing-swords, and his own armour for himself, although at that time there was no prohibition of any person whatsoever to have or wear arms. The colonel was not then at home, and the arms were laid up in a closet within his chamber, which they searched, and all the house over, to see if they could have found plate or anything else; but when they could not, they carried these away, which one of his servants, whom he had dismissed with a good reward, betrayed to them. His eldest son went to the Marquis of Newcastle, lord-lieutenant of the county; and complained of the violence of the soldiers, and my lord gave him an order to have the swords and other things back, and some pistols which were the Lord Biron's, but Mr. Cooper contemned my lord's order, and would not obey it. The arms were worth near £100.

Also an order came down from the secretary, commanding certain pictures and other things the colonel had bought out of the late king's collection, which had cost him in ready money between £1000 and £1500, and were of more value; and these, notwithstanding the act of oblivion, were all taken from him.

After these troubles were over from without, the

colonel lived with all imaginable retiredness at home, and, because his active spirit could not be idle nor very sordidly employed, took up his time in opening springs, and planting trees, and dressing his plantations; and these were his recreations, wherein he relieved many poor labourers when they wanted work, which was a very comfortable charity to them and their families: with these he would entertain himself, giving them much encouragement in their honest labours, so that they delighted to be employed by him. His business was serious revolving the law of God, wherein he laboured to instruct his children and servants, and enjoyed himself with much patience and comfort, not envying the glories and honours of the court, nor the prosperity of the wicked; but only grieved that the straitness of his own revenues would not supply his large heart to the poor people in affliction. Some little troubles he had in his own house. His son, unknown to him, married a very worthy person,[1] with the manner of which he was so discontented that he once resolved to have banished them for ever, but his good nature was soon overcome, and he received them into his bosom, and for the short time he enjoyed her, had no less love for her than for any of his own

---

[1] The daughter of Sir Alexander Ratcliffe, of the Royalist party.—J. H.

children.   And indeed she was worthy of it, applying herself with such humble dutifulness and kindness to repair her fault, and to please him in all
things he delighted in, that he was ravished with
the joy of her, who loved the place not as his own
wife did, only because she was placed in it, but
with a natural affection, which encouraged him in
all the pains he took to adorn it, when he had one
to leave it to that would esteem it.   She was
besides naturalised into his house and interests, as
if she had had no other regard in the world; she
was pious and cheerful, liberal and thrifty, com-
plaisant and kind to all the family, and the freest
from humour of any woman; loving home, without
melancholy or sullenness, observant of her father
and mother, not with regret, but with delight, and
the most submissive, affectionate wife that ever
was.   But she, and all the joy of her sweet, saint-
like conversation, ended in a lamented grave, about
a year after her marriage, when she died in child-
birth, and left the sweetest babe behind her that
ever was beheld, whose face promised all its mother's
graces, but death within eight weeks after her
birth, ravished this sweet blossom, whose fall
opened the fresh wounds of sorrow for her mother,
thus doubly lost.   While the mother lived, which
was ten days after her delivery, the colonel
and his wife employed all imaginable pains and
cares for her recovery, whereof they had often

hopes, but in the end all in vain ; she died, and left the whole house in very sensible affliction, which continued upon the colonel and his wife till new strokes awakened them out of the silent sorrow of this funeral. Her husband having no joy in the world after she was gone, some months shut himself up with his grief in his chamber, out of which he was hardly persuaded to go, and when he did, every place about home so much renewed his remembrance of her that he could not think of but with deep affliction, that being invited by his friends abroad to divert his melancholy,[1] he grew a little out of love with home, which was a great damping to the pleasures his father took in the place : but he, how eager soever he were in the love of any worldly thing, had that moderation of spirit that he submitted his will always to God, and endeavoured to give Him thanks in all things.

This winter, about October and the following months, the papists began to be very high, and a sort of strangers were come into Nottingham, who were observed to distinguish themselves by scarlet ribbons in their hats ; and one night, in a drunken humour, a papist fired a hay barn in a wood-yard in Nottingham, which, if not discovered and prevented by many providences, might have endangered

---

[1] Mr. Thomas Hutchinson did not marry again, but died without issue.

much of the town: but it did £200 worth of mischief; but the matter was shuffled up and compounded, although the same night several other towns were attempted to be fired.   A great papist, at Eastwold, was known to assemble two hundred men in arms in the night, and some of the Lord Carrington's tenants, that went to Arundel House to speak with their landlord, observed very strange suspicious signs of some great business on foot among the papists, who, both in Nottinghamshire and Leicestershire, were so exalted, that the very country people everywhere apprehended some insurrection.   Among the rest, there was a light-headed, debauched young knight, that lived in the next town to Owthorpe, who vapoured beyond all bounds, and had twelve pair of holsters for pistols at one time of the colonel's saddler, and rid at that time with half a dozen men armed, up and down the country, and sent them, and went himself, to several men who had been soldiers in the army, to offer them brave terms to enlist under him, telling them, they, meaning the papists, should have a day for it. Besides, he, with the parson of the parish, and some other men, at an alehouse, began a health to the confusion of all the protestants in England; and one of the colonel's maids going to Colson, to have a sore eye cured by a woman in the town, heard there that he had vapoured that the papists should shortly have their day, and that he would

not leave one alive in the colonel's house.   He sent
to the preacher of Cotgrove, to forbid him to preach
on gunpowder-treason day, threatening to kill him
if he did, insomuch that the town were forced to
keep a guard all that day upon the steeple.

The men whom the papists had endeavoured to
enlist, acquainted the colonel with it, whereof some
being in Leicestershire, the colonel sent his son to
Sir George Villiers, one of the deputy-lieutenants
of that county, to acquaint him with it; but he
slighted the matter, although at that time it would
have been proved that Golding brought a whole
coach laden with pistols, as many as they could
stuff under the seats and in the boots, to the house
of one Smith, a papist, dwelling at Quineborough,
in Leicestershire.   The colonel also sent to the
deputy-lieutenants of our county to acquaint them
the public danger, and how himself was threatened ; and, by reason that his house had been
disarmed, desired that he might have leave to
procure some necessary arms to defend it; but
they sent him word that the insurrection of the
papists was but a fanatic jealousy, and if he were
afraid, they would send him a guard, but durst not
allow him to arm his house.   He, disdaining their
security that would not trust him with his own,
would have taken a house at Nottingham for his
wife to lie in, who being then big with child, was
near her account ; but although she were fearful,

yet when she found him resolved to stay in his
own house, she would not go; whereupon he made
strong shutts to all his low windows with iron
bars; and that very night that they were set up,
the house was attempted to be broken in the night,
and the glass of one of the great casements broken,
and the little iron bars of it crashed in sunder.
Mrs. Hutchinson being late up, heard the noise, and
thought somebody had been forcing the doors, but,
as we since heard, it was Golding who made the
attempt. The common people, everywhere falling
into suspicion of the papists, began to be highly
offended at their insolence, and to utter strange
words; whether it were this, or what else we know
not, but their design proceeded no further; yet
there is nothing more certain than that at that
time they had a design of rising generally all over
England in arms. But the colonel lived so retired
that he never understood how it was taken up,
and how it fell off, yet, although they would not
take the alarm from him, even the gentlemen of
the county afterwards believed they were hatching
some mischief, and feared it.

The colonel continued his usual retiredness all
that winter and the next summer, about the end of
which he dreamt one night that he saw certain
men in a boat upon the Thames, labouring against
wind and tide, to bring their boat, which stuck in
the sands, to shore; at which he, being in the

boat, was angry with them, and told them they toiled in vain, and would never effect their purpose; but said he, let it alone and let me try ; whereupon he laid him down in the boat, and applying his breast to the head of it, gently shoved it along, till he came to land on the Southwark side, and there, going out of the boat, walked in the most pleasant lovely fields, so green and flourishing, and so embellished with the cheerful sun that shone upon them, as he never saw anything so delightful, and there he met his father, who gave him certain leaves of laurel which had many words written in them which he could not read.   The colonel was never super- stitious of dreams, but this stuck a little in his mind, and we were therefore seeking applications of it, which proved nothing in the event, but that having afforded one, I know not whether the dream might not be inspired.   The boat representing the commonwealth which several unquiet people sought to enfranchise, by vain endeavours against wind and tide, paralleling the plots and designs some impatient people then carried on without strength, or counsel, or unity among themselves ; his lying down and shoving it with his breast, might signify the advancement of the cause by the patient suffer- ing of the martyrs, among which his own was to be eminent, and on the other side of the river to land him into walks of everlasting pleasure, he dying on that shore, and his father's giving him these laurel leaves with unintelligible characters, foretold him those triumphs which he could not read in his mortal estate. But to let dreams pass,—

I cannot here omit one story, though not altogether so much of the colonel's concern, yet happening this summer, not unworthy mention. Mr. Palmer,[1] a certain nonconformist preacher, was taken at his own house in Nottingham, by the mayor of the town, for preaching upon the Lord's day, and some others with him (whereof one was formerly a servant of the colonel's, and had married one of his maids), and put into the town's gaol, where they continued about two or three months. There being a grated window in the prison, which was almost even with the ground, and looked into the street, all people coming by might see these poor people, kept in a damp, ill-favoured room, where they patiently exhorted and cheered one another. One Lord's day, after sermon time, the prisoners were singing a psalm, and the people as they passed up and down, still when they came to the prison, stood still, till there were a great many

---

[1] Mr. Thomas Palmer. He was at one time minister of St. Lawrence Poultney Church in London, then of Ashton-upon-Trent in Derbyshire. He was ejected soon after the Restoration, to make room for the sequestered clergyman, Mr. Clark. About July 1663 he was imprisoned at Nottingham for preaching in conventicles (Calamy's " Nonconformist's Memorial," vol. i. p. 392, ed. 1802).   .

gathered about the window at which Mr. Palmer
was preaching ; whereupon the mayor, one Toplady,
who had formerly been a parliament officer, but was
now a renegado, came violently with his officers,
and beat the people, and thrust some into prison
that were but passing the streets, kicked and
pinched the men's wives in his rage, and was the
more exasperated, when some of them told him;
how ill his fury became him who had once been one
of them.   The next day, or few days after, having given order the prisoners should every Lord's
day after be locked in the coal-house, he went to
London and made information, I heard oath, to the
council, that a thousand of the country came in
armed to the town, and marched to the prison
window to hear the prisoner preach ; whereupon he
procured an order for a troop of horse to be sent
down to quarter at Nottingham to keep the fanatics
in awe.   But one who had relation to the town,
being then at court, and knowing this to be false,
certified to the contrary and prevented the troop.
After the mayor came down, he was one night taken
with a vomiting of blood, and being ill, called his
man and his maid, who also at the same time fell
a bleeding, and were all ready to be choked in
their own blood, which at last stopping, they came
to assist him ; but after that he never lift up his
head, but languished a few months and died.
   While these poor people were in prison, the

colonel sent them some money, and as soon as their
time was expired, Mr. Palmer came to Owthorpe to
give him thanks, and preached there one Lord's
day.   Whether this were taken notice of is not
evident, but within a short time after, upon the Lord's
day, the 11th of October, 1663, the colonel having
that day finished the expounding of the Epistle to
the Romans to his household, and the servants
being gone out of the parlour from him, one of them
came in and told him soldiers were come to the town.[1]
He was not at all surprised, but stayed in the room
till they came in, who were conducted by Atkinson,
one of those Newark men, who had so violently
before prosecuted him at the parliament, and he
told the colonel he must go along with them, after
they had searched the house ; for which the colonel
required their commission, which at the first they
said they need not show, but after they showed him
an order from Mr. Francis Leke, one of the deputy-
lieutenants, forthwith to repair to his house, to
search for and bring away what arms they could
find, and to seize his person.   All which they did,
and found no arms in the house but four birding-
guns, that hung open in the kitchen, which being

---

[1] The account of Colonel Hutchinson's arrest and imprisonment here given by Mrs. Hutchinson should be
compared with that written by the colonel himself, printed
in vol. iii. of the Harleian Miscellany, the title of which
is given at length in a later note.

the young gentleman's, at that time they left. It was after sunset when they came, and they were at least two hours searching every corner and all about the house, and the colonel was not at that time very well in health, and not having been for six months before on horseback, had neither horses nor saddles at that time in the house ; the coachman was also gone away, and the coach-horses turned out, and it was as bitter a stormy, pitchy, dark, black, rainy night as any that year ; all which considered, the colonel desired that they would but stay for the morning light, that he might accommodate himself; but they would not, but forced him to go then along with them, his eldest son lending him a horse, and also voluntarily accompanying him to Newark, where, about four of the clock in the morning, he was brought into the Talbot, and put into a most vile room, and two soldiers kept guard upon him in that room.

And now what they ailed we knew not, but they were all seized with a panic fear, and the whole country fiercely alarmed, and kept at Newark many days at intolerable charges, and I think they never yet knew what they were sent for in to do, but to guard Colonel Hutchinson ; who being at first put into a room that looked into the street, was afterwards removed into a back room, worse, if worse could be, and so bad that they would not let the Duke of Buckingham's footmen lodge in it ; and here he continued, no man coming at him nor letting him know why he was brought in. The next day Mrs. Hutchinson sent him some linen, and as soon as the man came, Tomson, the host of the inn, would not suffer him to see his master, but seized him and kept him prisoner two days. Mr. Thomas Hutchinson had a mare which the innkeeper had a desire to buy, and his father persuaded him to let him have her worth money, who thereupon agreed on the price, only Tomson desired him to let him try the mare six miles, which he condescended to, upon condition that if Tomson rid the mare above six miles he should pay the money for her, and furnish Mr. Hutchinson with a horse home, or to my Lord of Newcastle's, or any other occasion he had while he was at Newark. Upon this bargain Tomson had the mare, but instead of going but six miles, he led a greater party of horse than those who first seized the colonel, to Owthorpe, and coming in after sunset, to the affright of Mrs. Hutchinson and her children, again searched their house more narrowly if possible than at first, with much more insolent behaviour, although they found no more than at first; but they took away the birding-guns they had left before, and from Owthorpe went to Nottingham, where they took one Captain Wright [1] and Lieutenant Franck,

---

[1] Captain Wright had been a captain in Hutchinson's

who had been Lambert's adjutant-general, and
brought the poor men to Newark, where they are
yet prisoners, and to this day know not why.
Several others were taken prisoners, among the
rest one Whittington, a lieutenant, who, being
carried to prison, " Col. Hutchinson," said he, " hath
betrayed us all ; " such were the base jealousies of
our own party over him, who, because he was not
hanged at first, imagined and spoke among themselves all the scandals that could be devised of him,
as one that had deserted the cause, and lay private
here in the country to trepan all the party, and to
gather and transmit all intelligence to the court,
and a thousand such things, giving each other
warning to take heed of coming near him.   Those
who began to render him thus odious among his
own party were the Lambertonians, in malice because he had openly opposed their rebellious insolencies against the parliament.   Franck and Whittington, &c., were of these, but the colonel would

---

regiment. Mr. Bailey gives a long account of him in his
"Annals of Nottinghamshire," pp. 908-9.   Mr. Bailey states
that on the 7th of July 1671, Captain Wright was arraigned
before Judge Hale at the King's Bench, and, as no evidence
was adduced against him, discharged.   But Mr. Bailey
unfortunately gives no authority for this statement. Colonel
Hutchinson died September 11, 1664. Since Captain Wright
is described as being still a prisoner, this memoir must have
been written between 1664 and 1671, as Mr. Bailey does not
forget to point out.

not put himself in hazard to rectify their unjust thoughts, and had no resort of his own friends, the soberer and honester men of the party; only, as much as the straits that were upon him would allow, when any of them were in distress, would send them relief. Hereupon some, convinced of the injuries they did him, about this time sought to do him right, in some meeting where one of the Buckingham's trepans was, and said he was unchanged in his principles, which was all that ever I could hear was informed against him, but anything would serve for those who sought a pretence.

While the colonel was at Newark, Golding, the papist, was a very busy fellow in spying and watching his house at Owthorpe, and sending in frivolous stories, which amounted to nothing, but declaring his pitiful malice, as they that received it afterwards told the colonel.

When Tomson came back, Mr. Hutchinson, out of the window, spied his own gun, which some of the men brought in, and soon understood that this rogue had màde use of his own horse to plunder him. At night Tomson, the host, came up into the colonel's chamber, and behaved himself most insolently, whereupon the colonel snatched up a candlestick and laid him over the chaps with it; whereupon Mr. Leke, being in the house, and hearing the bustle, with others, came in with drawn swords, and the colonel took that opportunity to tell him that he stood upon his justification, and desired to know his crime and his accusers, and that till then he was content to be kept as safe as they would have him, but desired to be delivered out of the hands of that insolent fellow, and to have accommodation fit for a gentleman; which when they saw he would not be without, for he would eat no more meat in that house, they after two days removed him to the next inn, where he was civilly treated, with guards still remaining upon him.

It was not passion which made the colonel do this, for he was not at all angry, but despised all the malice of his enemies; but he having been now four days in Newark, Mr. Leke came every day to the house where he was kept by Leke's warrant, and never vouchsafed so much as to look on him, but put him into the hands of a drunken insolent host, who daily affronted him; which, if he would have suffered, he saw would be continued upon him, therefore knowing that Leke was then in the house, he took that occasion to make him come to him, and thereupon obtained a remove to an accommodation more befitting a gentleman.

While he was at the other inn, several gentlemen of the king's party came to him, some whom he had known, and some whom he had never seen, complimenting him, as if he had not been a prisoner; which he very much wondered at, and yet could never understand, for by his former usage he saw it was not their good nature: but whether this carriage of his had made them believe innocency was the ground of his confidence, or whether the appearance of his great spirit had made them willing to oblige him, or whether even his virtue had strucken them with a guilty dread of him, though a prisoner, certain it is, that some who had been his greatest enemies began to flatter him; whereupon, in a Bible he carried in his pocket, and marked upon all occasions, he marked that place, Prov. xvi. 7, " When a man's ways please the Lord, he maketh his enemies to be at peace with him."

The 19th of October, Mr. Leke, with a party of horse, carried the colonel to the Marquess of Newcastle's, who treated him very honourably; and then falling into discourse with him, " Colonel," saith he, " they say you desire to know your accusers, which is more than I know." And thereupon very freely showed him the Duke of Buckingham's letter, commanding him to imprison the colonel, and others, upon suspicion of a plot; which my lord was so fully satisfied the colonel was innocent of, that he dismissed him without a guard to his own house, only engaging him to stay there one week, till he gave account to the council, upon which he was confident of his liberty.[1]   The colonel, thus dis-

---

[1] Here shines out the genuine spirit of a noble Briton ! This was the same man, who, commanding a host, against which the forces Colonel Hutchinson had to defend Not-

missed, came home, and upon the 22d day of October a party of horse, sent only with a wretched corporal, came about eleven o'clock with a warrant from Mr. Leke, and fetched him back to Newark, to the inn where he was before, Mr. Twentyman's, who being still civil to him, whispered him as soon as he alighted, that it was determined he should be close prisoner; whereupon the colonel said he would no more pay any sentinels that they set upon him, yet they set two hired soldiers, having now dismissed the county, but the colonel forbade the inn to give them any drink, or anything else upon his account.

---

tingham Castle with were but as a dwarf before a giant, yet saw his fidelity to be proof both against danger and the temptation of great rewards, and had generosity enough to see and value virtue in an adversary; he well knew that such a person as the colonel was safer in the keeping of his own honour than of all the guards or prisons of his enemies. Who can fail to regret that such a man should have been so long the dupe of his loyalty to the Stuarts, and above all that he should have to receive mandates from the infamous sycophants of Charles the Second? If a man were inevitably to be persecuted, it made much for his honour, and somewhat for his satisfaction, to have two men of such opposite characters as Newcastle and Buckingham, the one for his protector, the other for his persecutor.

Of Buckingham we shall again have occasion to speak.

As we shall not again see anything more of this *truly noble* man, the Marquis of Newcastle, we take this opportunity to cite, from a tradition preserved by Deering in his "History of Nottingham," that at the time of the great

The next day, being the 23rd, Mr. Leke came to him and showed him a letter from my Lord New-castle, wherein my lord writ that he was sorry he could not pursue that kindness he intended the colonel, believing him innocent, for that he had received a command from Buckingham to keep him a close prisoner, without pen, ink, or paper; and to show the reality of this, with the order he sent a copy of the duke's letter, which was also shown the colonel; and in it was this expression, *"that though he could not make it out as yet, he hoped he should bring Mr. Hutchinson into the plot."* Mr. Leke

---

Revolution, another Cavendish, Earl, and afterwards Duke of Devonshire, together with Lord Delamere, son of that Sir George Booth whose life and fortunes Colonel Hutchinson preserved, together with Colonel Hutchinson's half-brother, and others of that country, set up their standard at Notting-ham; there waked again the soul of liberty and patriotism, which had slept ever since Colonel Hutchinson's days, and causing the trumpet to sound to arms, and telling the inhabitants a Stuart was at hand with all his army, saw the whole people fly to arms, some on horseback, some on foot, with all the various weapons they could find, march all as one man to meet him, and take their determined stand at that pass of the Trent where their old governor had repeatedly fought and conquered, and whose spirit they imagined to hover over and inspire them with its wonted energy. Having thus tried their temper, he committed to the guard of these true-born sons of freedom, that princess (Anne) who was to carry the British name to its highest pitch of glory.—J. H.

having communicated these orders to Mr. Hutchinson, told him he was to go to London, and should leave him in the charge of the mayor of Newark.

Because here is so much noise of a plot, it is necessary to tell what it hath since appeared. The Duke of Buckingham set a-work one Gore, sheriff of Yorkshire, and others, who sent out trepanners among the discontented people, to stir them up to insurrection to restore the old parliament, gospel ministry, and English liberty; which specious things found very many ready to entertain them, and abundance of simple people were caught in the net; whereof some lost their lives, and others fled.[1] But the colonel had no hand in it, holding himself obliged at that time to be quiet. It is true he still suspected insurrections of the papists, and had secured his house and his yards, better than it was the winter before, against any sudden night assaults.

After Mr. Leke was gone, the mayor, one Herring, of Newark, a rich but simple fellow, sent the jailer to Mr. Hutchinson, to tell him he must go to his house; which the colonel refusing to do voluntarily, without a mittimus from some magistrate, the mayor sent five constables and two soldiers, who by violence both forced the colonel out of his

---

[1] Rapin speaks slightly and cursorily of this, under the name of the Northern Plot; but plainly shows that some of the principal persons whom it was pretended had been concerned in it, neither were nor could be.—J. H.

quarters, and into the gaol without any legal commitment, although the colonel warned both the
jailer and the men of the danger of the law, by
this illegal imprisonment. The colonel would not
advance at all into the prison, into which the men
would fain have entreated him ; but when they saw
they could not persuade, they violently thrust him
in, where the jailer afterwards used him pretty
civilly : but the room being unfit for him, he got
cold and fell very sick, when, upon the 27th of
October, Mr. Leke, with the marquess's secretary,
came to him, and found him so, and acquainted him
that the marquess had received express orders from
the king to send him up in safe custody to London.
Mr. Leke finding him so ill, was so civil as to
permit him to go by his own house, which was as
near a road, that he might there take accommodations
for his journey, and be carried up at more ease in
his own coach ; Mr. Leke himself, being necessitated
to make more haste than he could have done if
he had stayed for the party that was to guard the
colonel, went away before, and left his orders for
sending him away with Mr. Atkinson, who first
seized him. The same 27th day, at night, his
house at Owthorpe was again searched, and he and
his wife being abroad, all their boxes and cabinets
were broken open, and all their papers rifled, but
yet for all this they could find nothing to colour
their injustice to him.

Having been falsely and illegally imprisoned, from six o'clock on Friday night, the 23rd of October, till ten o'clock in the morning, October 28th, he was then, in order to his going to London, brought by Beek, the jailer, to Twentyman's, the inn from whence he was haled, to stay there till a commanded party of the county horse came to guard him to London. But one division of the county who had warrants sent them, not coming in, Atkinson sent into that part where the colonel lived, and his own neighbours coming slowly and unwillingly to that service, he was forced to stay there all that day till night in the custody of the jailer.   At night, when he was in bed, the mayor being drunk, commanded him to be carried back to the jail ; but the jailer, weary of his drunken commands, sat up with two soldiers, and guarded him in the inn.

The next day, the party not being come in, a mean fellow, that was appointed to command the colonel's guard, one Corporal Wilson, came and told him that he must not go by his own house, nor have the privilege of his coach, but be carried up another way ; whereupon the colonel sent to Atkinson, to desire him he might not be denied that civility Mr. Leke had allowed him ; but he was so peevish and obstinate that the colonel was sending his son post to the Marquess of Newcastle's to complain of his malicious inhumanity, who would have forced him on horseback without any accommodation, when he was so taken ill that he could not have ridden one stage without manifest hazard of his life: and yet Mr. Cecil Cooper and Mr. Whalley, though justices and deputy-lieutenants, could not prevail with him, till he saw the colonel as resolute as himself: and then at last, by their mediation (wherein Mr. Cecil Cooper did something to redeem his former causeless hatred, which made him plunder the house, and detain the plunder when it was ordered back), the colonel, about sunset, was sent out of Newark, with those horse that were come in, to stay for the rest at his own house. Being driven in the night by an unskilful coachman, the coach was overturned and broken; but about twelve of the night they came safe home. Thus the colonel took his last leave of Newark, which being a place he had formerly subdued, and replete with so many malicious enemies to the whole party, and more particularly to him, upon no other account but that he had been the most formidable protector of the other party in this country, he expected far worse treatment from the generality of the town; who were so far from joining in joy of his captivity, that when he was forced through their streets, they gave him very civil respect, and when he came away, civil farewells, and all muttered exceedingly at their mayor, and said he would undo their town by such simple illegal proceedings. The colonel regarded all these civilities from the town, who were

generally much concerned in his injuries, and from
Cooper and others, not as of themselves, but as
from God, who at that time overawed the hearts of
his enemies, as once he did Laban's and Esau's ;
and was much confirmed in the favour of God
thereby, and nothing at all daunted at the malice of
his prosecutors, but went as cheerfully into captivity
as another would have come out of it.

They were forced to stay a day at Owthorpe,
for the mending of the coach and coming in of the
soldiers, where the colonel had the opportunity to
take leave of his poor labourers, who wept all
bitterly when he paid them off; but he comforted
them and smiled, and without any regret went
away from his bitterly weeping children, and
servants, and tenants, his wife and his eldest son
and daughter going with him, upon Saturday, the
31st of October.

Golding, the night before he went, had sent him
a pot of marmalade to eat in the coach, and a letter
to desire all grudges might be forgotten, and high
flattering stuff, by his man, who was to be one of
the guard, which, he said, he had chosen out the
best he had, and his best horse, and if he did not
pay him all respect, he would turn him away ; and
as the colonel came by his door, came out with
wine, and would fain have brought him into the
house to eat oysters, but the colonel only drank with
him, and bid him friendly farewell, and went on, not

guarded as a prisoner, but waited on by his neighbours. Mrs. Hutchinson was exceedingly sad, but he encouraged and kindly chid her out of it, and told her it would blemish his innocence for her to appear afflicted, and told her if she had but patience to wait the event, she would see it all for the best, and bade her be thankful for the mercy that she was permitted this comfort to accompany him in the journey ; and he with divers excellent exhortations cheered her, who was not wholly abandoned to sorrow, while he was with her, who, to divert her, made himself sport with his guards, and deceived the way, till upon the 3rd of November he was brought to the Crown, in Holborn. From thence, the next day, he was carried by Mr. Leke to the Tower, and committed there close prisoner, by warrant, signed by Secretary Bennett, the 20th of October, whereby he stood committed for treasonable practices, though he had never yet been examined by any magistrate, one or other. His wife, by his command, restrained herself as much as she could from showing her sadness, whom he bade to remember how often he had told her that God never preserved him so extraordinarily at first, but for some great work he had further for him to do or to suffer in this cause ; and bade her be thankful for the mercy by which they had so long in peace enjoyed one another since this eminent change, and bade her trust God with him ; whose faith and cheerfulness were so encouraging that it a little upheld her; but, alas! her divining heart was not to be comforted : she remembered what had been told her of the cruel resolutions taken against him, and saw now the execution of them.

On Friday, November the 6th, he was sent for by Secretary Bennett to his lodgings at Whitehall, which was the first time he was examined, and the questions he asked him were : 1st. "Where he had lived this four or five months?" To which he answered, "Constantly at home, at his own house in Nottinghamshire." 2nd. "What company used to resort to his house?" He told him, "None, not so much as his nearest relations, who scarce ever saw him." 3rd. "What company he frequented?" He told him, "None; and that he never stirred out of his own house to visit any." Bennett said, "That was very much." 4th. "Whether he knew Mr. Henry Nevill?" He answered, "Very well." 5th. "When he saw him?" He said, "To his best remembrance never since the king came in." 6th. "When he wrote to him?" He said, "Never in his life." 7th. "When Mr. Nevill wrote to him?" He said, "Never." 8th. "Whether any messages had past between them?" He said, "None at all." 9th. "Whether none had moved anything to him concerning a republic?" He said, "He knew

none so indiscreet." 10th. "What children he
had?" He said, "Four sons and four daughters."
11th. "How old his sons were?" He said, "Two
were at men's estate, and two little children."
12th. "Whether his sons had not done anything to
injure him?" He replied, "Never that he knew
of, and he was confident they had not." 13th.
"Where he went to church to hear divine service,
common prayer?" He said, "Nowhere, for he
never stirred out of his own house." 14th.
"Whether he heard it not read there?" He
answered, "To speak ingenuously, no." 15th.
"How he then did for his soul's comfort?" He
replied, "Sir, I hope you leave me that to account
between God and my own soul." Then Bennett
told him his answers to these had cut him off of
many questions he should have asked, and he
might return. So he was carried back to the
Tower with only two of the warders which brought
him thither.

Not long after one Waters was brought prisoner
out of Yorkshire, a fellow of a timorous spirit,
who, being taken, was in so great a fear, that
he accused many, guilty and not guilty, to save
himself; and caused his own wife to be put in
prison, and hanged the dearest friend he had in
the world, and brought his wife's brother into the
same danger; some say through fear, others that he
was a trepanner from the beginning, for he drew

in all the people whom he accused.[1] Whatever
he was, he was so utter a stranger to Colonel
Hutchinson, that he never saw his face; yet that
day he was examined at Whitehall, Colonel Hutchinson was in great haste fetched away from his
dinner at the Tower, and told he should be examined
in the king's own hearing; which he was very glad
of, and with great haste, and formality, and strictness he was carried by the deputy-lieutenant and a
strong guard by water from the Tower to Whitehall; and when he came to land at Whitehall
Stairs, one Andrews, an officer, with two files of
musketeers, was ready to receive him, and led him
to Bennett's lodgings, where he observed a great
deal of care to place the guard at the outward door
in the court, and to keep the chamber door continually shut, that none might peep in, but a few
gentlemen who were admitted to come now and
then and stare him in the face at the door, but
none were in the room for a long space but Andrews
and himself, till at the last his keeper thrust himself
in. The colonel, having stayed two hours, concluded
that he should now be confronted by some accuser,

---

[1] Richard Walters, an abstract of whose examination is
to be found in the Calendar of Domestic State Papers for
1663, p. 391. He stated that all he knew of the plot he had
learned from Colonel Hutchinson. The colonel was also
implicated by a witness called Carr, p. 392. In neither
case does the evidence appear trustworthy.

or at least have an examination more tending to
treasonable practices than his first seemed to do,
especially understanding that Mr. Waters had been
many hours before in the house, and was yet there.
But at last, *parturiunt montes!* and out comes
Secretary Bennett! who, taking him to a window
apart from Mr. Andrews and the keeper, most
formally begins thus : " Mr. Hutchinson, you have
now been some days in prison, have you recollected
yourself any more to say than when I last spoke to
you ? " Mr. Hutchinson answered, " He had nothing to recollect, nor more to say." " Are you sure
of that ? " said the secretary. " Very sure," said
Mr. Hutchinson. " Then," said Bennett, " you
must return to prison." And accordingly he was
carried by the same guard back again to the Tower,
where he was kept with a great deal of strictness,
and some weeks passed before his wife was admitted
to see him ; for whom, at the last, Sir Allen Apsley
procured an order that she might visit him, but
they limited it that it must not be but in the presence of his keeper. The lieutenant, in hope of a
fee, gave leave that her son and daughter might go
into the room with her, who else must have stood
without doors ; but he would not permit her to take
lodgings in the Tower, which, being in a sharp
winter season, put her to great toil and inconvenience, besides excessive charge of providing his
meat at the Tower, and her company in another

place : meanwhile he was kept close prisoner, and had no air allowed him, but a pair of leads over his chamber, which were so high and cold he had no benefit by them ; and every night he had three doors shut upon him, and a sentinel at the outmost. His chamber was a room where it is said the two young princes, King Edward the Fifth and his brother, were murthered in former days, and the room that led to it was a dark great room, that had no window in it, where the portcullis to one of the inward Tower gates was drawn up and let down, under which there sat every night a court of guard. There is a tradition, that in this room the Duke of Clarence was drowned in a butt of malmsey ; from which murther this room, and that joining it, where Mr. Hutchinson lay, was called the Bloody Tower. Between Mr. Hutchinson's chamber and the dark room there was a door, which Mr. Hutchinson desired the lieutenant might be left open in the night, because it left a little necessary house open to the chamber, which he and his man had occasion of in the night, having gotten fluxes with their bad accommodations and diet : but the lieutenant would not allow it him, although, when that was open, there were two doors more shut upon him, and he could not have any way attempted any escape, but he must, if it had been possible to work through the walls, have fallen upon a court of guard.

Notwithstanding all this strictness, which was

also exercised on most of the other prisoners, yet
their own sentinels hated the lieutenant, and his
Cerberus, Cresset, because they cheated them, and
had nothing of generosity or bounty to engage the
hearts of their soldiers, who, seeing so much of
their wickedness, abhorred them, and pitied the
poor gentlemen that were so barbarously used by
them; and whether out of humanity, or necessity,
or villainy, I know not, but they would offer the
prisoners many courtesies, and convey letters between them. Mr. Hutchinson was never so impru-
dent to trust any of them with his, having within
an hour of his imprisonment been instructed by
another prisoner a safer and more convenient way;
yet was it their interest to use courteously all those
that offered themselves to do them service. Among
the rest, as he was one day sitting by the fire, the
sentinel at the door peeped in his head and called
to him: " Sir," said he, " God bless you! I have
sometimes guarded you in another manner at the
parliament house, and am grieved to see the change
of your condition, and only take this employment
now, to be more able to serve you, still hoping to
see you restored to what I have seen you." The
colonel, not turning his head, told the man that
language suited not the coat he wore, bade him
mind his present duty, and told him he had no
employment of his service. " Well," said the soldier,
" I perceive, sir, you dare not trust me, but my

Lady Vane and my Lady Lambert know me, and
if you have any service to command me to them,
I will bring you a testimony from them." The
colonel took no more notice of him, but the fellow,
officious, or hoping to get money, went to my Lady
Lambert's house, and told her that he had formerly
been her husband's soldier, and that he wished his
restitution, and that he used sometimes to guard
the prisoners, and would carry her letters to any
of them, and that he had been sentinel lately at
Colonel Hutchinson's chamber, and would carry
anything she would send to him. She only bade
him remember her service to him, and tell him she
wished him liberty; and the fellow flattering her
with professing his love to her lord, she expressed
some pleasure with his speeches, and gave him some
money; which her daughter considering, as soon
as he was gone out told her that she had done
unwarily to open herself so much to one of the
soldiers in present employment, whom she did not
know but he might be set on purpose to trepan
her. My lady, to prevent any inconvenience of her
error, thought it the best way to go immediately
and complain that one of the soldiers had come to
her to trepan her, under colour of a message from
Colonel Hutchinson, which she had not entertained;
and desired they might not be allowed in any
such thing, protesting her own loyalty and readiness to discover any that were false to them. This

was extremely well represented of her at the court, and as ill of Colonel Hutchinson, that he had not done the like; and Colonel Legge, whose company it was that then had the guard of the Tower, was commanded to find out and punish this soldier, who, it proved after, was a good honest fellow, and was the only protestant in that company, the rest being most of them Irish and papists, and some rebels. This poor fellow, having been a parliament soldier, listed among them to get a living, but was very tender-hearted to the prisoners, and had a desire to do them kindness. Hereupon he came to the colonel's man, and desired his master would not own him, and that he would send to my Lady Lambert to do the same, which the colonel did; but when she was sent to by him, she sent a maid to see all the soldiers, who owned the man, and he was put in prison, and cashiered and undone, for nothing but offering his service to have done the prisoners slight services. And Colonel Hutchinson was ill thought of at the court, because when Colonel Legge brought his men under the window of his prison, and came up to Mr. Hutchinson and desired him to view them all, he would not accuse any of them; which if he had, he would not only have cut off his own, but all the other prisoners' ways of sending to their friends abroad; yet he never made use of this fellow, nor any of them, in any business of trust, although he thought it not good to discourage

any that appeared to wish them well, among so many
bloody murtherers as they were given up to.

The colonel endured his prison patiently till the
trial of those they called conspirators in Yorkshire
was over; but when he had lain from November
till Candlemas term in prison, he sent his wife to
Secretary Bennett to desire that such persons as had
business with him might have the liberty to come
to him.   She had before been with some of the
privy council who were her husband's friends and
allies, to complain of his unjust imprisonment, and
his harsh usage there, contrary to all law from the
beginning to the ending, even their own laws; and
they had told her that they were sensible of it, but
that they only stood for cyphers, while the chancellor
and Bennett managed all things without their privity,
in most oppressive and illegal ways.   She, as she
was advised, went therefore to Bennett and told him
that, by reason of some engagements for money her
husband had upon his estate, this very close imprisonment had been infinitely prejudicial to him,
both his tenants and his creditors taking advantage
of his incapacity (by reason of his close restraint)
to defend himself, or to speak with lawyers or
others about affairs that nearly concerned his
estate; besides the neglect of all his business, and
the intolerable charge and inconvenience of his disordered family, dispersed into three several places,
which would suddenly bring ruin upon his whole

family, besides the destruction of his health.
Bennett told her, her husband was a very unfortunate person in regard of his former crimes. She
told him she had rather hoped he had been happy
in being comprised in the act of oblivion, which
allowed him not to be remembered as a criminal;
and that she had chosen to make her addresses to
him in this occasion, because some of the council
had told her the king left all the management of
these things to him. He was very urgent with
her to know who it was that informed her that he
was the sole actor in these businesses; but she
desired to be excused from naming any author in
that thing, which she had not mentioned but that
she thought it his honour to own; but he told her
he would not move for any more liberty for her
husband than he had, unless he could be secured it
might be done with more safety to his majesty
than he could apprehend it. "But," said he,
"Mrs. Hutchinson, I have some papers of yours
which I would show, not to examine you, but to
see whether you will inform me anything of them."
She told him she had curiosity enough to see anything that passed under her name; whereupon he
called forth his man, who brought out a great
bundle of papers, called examinations, taken at
Grantham, of passages between Mrs. Hutchinson
and Mrs. Vane. First he showed her a character
which contained cyphers for the names of many

gentlemen and women who were not very distant neighbours, with others whom she knew not at all. She told him she understood nothing at all of that paper; then he turned down the rest, and showed her a letter, beginning, "My dear Amaranta;" which she told him she knew not at all. "But," said he, "you will yet own your own hand;" and showed her among these papers the copy of the letter that was sent to the house of parliament in her husband's name, written in her hand, which when she saw she was a little confounded, wondering how it should come into his hands;[1] but she told him that she could not absolutely say that was her writing, though it had some resemblance. So when she had again urged the business she came for, and could obtain nothing from him, she went away, and left in the room with the secretary, Sir

---

[1] This is explained by a letter amongst the Domestic State Papers. Sir Allen Apsley writes to Secretary Bennett, sending a letter of his sister's, Mrs. Hutchinson, in her own hand, to show whether the cypher mentioned or the other papers are her writing. "It is a copy of a letter written to the House of Commons by her husband: it may in some measure explain how he escaped then; if it were printed nothing could more lessen his credit amongst those who continue in rebellious principles, for no man can express more repentance, or a greater detestation of those ill men. Wishes Hutchinson to know that he keeps the paper as a testimony against him, should he make the least failing."—"Calendar of Domestic State Papers," January 14, 1664.

Robert Biron, a cousin-german of her husband's,
who had by chance come in thither upon some
business of his own, and had stood by while she
urged to the secretary the mischief and ruin her
husband's imprisonment brought upon his family
and estate. As soon as she was gone, the secretary told Sir Robert that he had heard Mrs.
Hutchinson relate the sad condition of her husband
and his house; "and," said he, "you may here
take notice how the justice of God pursues those
murtherers, that, though the king pardoned both
his life and estate, yet by the hand of the divine
justice they were now like to come to ruin for
that crime;" which words being told Mr. Hutchinson, he laughed much at the simple folly of
the man, who could call his own illegal persecu-
tions and oppressions of innocence the judgments
of God. The papers which he showed Mrs. Hutchinson she after learned to have been some letters
between Mrs. Vane, one of Sir Henry Vane's
daughters, and one Mrs. Hutchinson, a gentlewoman that used to come thither, filled with such
frivolous intelligence of private amours and intrigues
as young people used to communicate to their confidants, and such as any wise statesman would
have believed himself affronted to have had brought
to him, and not made such politic inquiries, and
imprisoned those with whom they were found,
about so unconcerning a matter.

Mr. Henry Nevill and Mr. Salloway had been put into the Tower about the same suspicion which they had of Mr. Hutchinson—a northern plot, for which there was a peculiar assizes, and some men were executed; and the judges, at their return, said that their confessions almost amounted to treason; but that *almost* served their turns. As soon as those assizes were past, Mr. Hutchinson sent to Mr. Nevill and Mr. Salloway, that he thought it now time for them to endeavour their liberty, and therefore desired to know what course they intended to proceed in, that they might all take one way. They both sent Mr. Hutchinson word that they looked upon him as the best befriended, and they were resolved to see first what success he had, and to make him their leading card. Hereupon he, fearful of doing anything which they could not, sat still deliberating, while they, without giving him the least notice, wrought their own liberties secretly, Mr. Nevill desiring to travel, and Mr. Salloway making such a false, flattering petition, that no honest man could make such another, and a less after his would have but more exasperated. It took so, that immediately he had his liberty, both of them taking some oaths to confirm their loyalty, which were given them by the clerk of the Tower.[1]

---

[1] Mr. Nevill, as just before mentioned, had acted with steadiness and integrity; Mr. Salloway had been more variable, and had been successively of the council of state,

They had a mind at court Mr. Hutchinson should have made such another petition, and therefore Salloway's was showed to a friend of his; the words of which were, "That since God by his miraculous providence had set his majesty over us, he had acquiesced thankfully under it, and never, not so much as in thought, made a wish against it;" and promises of the like nature: which perhaps were no truer than the professions, for they were utterly false; for at his first coming into the Tower no man had muttered more than he, who scarce refrained even blasphemies against God himself for bringing him into bondage. After his release he went to their common prayer, and pleased them so well that it was said they would give him an office. But when they found that, notwithstanding their hint, Mr. Hutchinson would not follow his example, their malice grew very bitter against him at the court, insomuch that a gentleman having treated with Mrs. Hutchinson for a niece of his, to whom he was guardian, that would have been a convenient fortune for her son, the Chancellor sent for the gentleman and peremptorily forbade him to proceed in the affair, and openly said, "*he must keep their family down.*"

Mr. Hutchinson was not at all dismayed, but

---

of the Rump parliament, of the committee of safety, and council of officers.—J. H.

wonderfully pleased with all these things, and told
his wife this captivity was the happiest release
in the world to him ; for before, although he had
made no express engagement, yet, in regard his
life and estate had been freely left him when they
took away others, he thought himself obliged to
sit still all the while this king reigned, whatever
opportunity he might have ; but now he thought
this usage had utterly disobliged him from all ties
either of honour or conscience, and that he was
free to act as prudence should hereafter lead him,
and that he thought not his liberty out of prison
worth the purchase by any future engagement,
which would again fetter him in obligations to
such persons as every day more and more manifested themselves enemies to all just and godly
interests.   He therefore charged his wife that she
should not make applications to any person whatsoever, and made it his earnest request to Sir Allen
Apsley to let him stand and fall to his own innocency, and to undertake nothing for him, which, if
he did, he told him he would disown.   Mrs. Hutchinson, remembering how much she had displeased
him in saving him before, submitted now to suffer
with him, according to his own will, who, as he
would do nothing that might entangle him for his
freedom, so he patiently suffered their unjust bondage, and had no guilt found in him ; yet was
cruelly and maliciously persecuted and hated ; and

criminals, with threats and promises, were tried all ways to see if they could have brought out any accusation against him, but all they could arrive to was only that he was an unchanged person, yet they kept him still as close prisoner as at the first. After Salloway was released, Sir Allen Apsley asking the Chancellor why his brother was not let out as Salloway; "What!" said the Chancellor, "make you no difference between your brother and Salloway?" Sir Allen replied, he thought his brother as innocent. "Surely," said the Chancellor, "there is a great difference; Salloway conforms to the government, and goes to church, but your brother is the most unchanged person of the party."

The colonel, at last, with some other prisoners were deliberating to sue out a habeas corpus, and in order thereunto sent to the lieutenant of the Tower to desire a copy of the warrant whereby he stood committed, which indeed was so imperfect that he could not legally be kept upon that, for there was neither his Christen name nor any place of residence mentioned in it, so that any other Hutchinson might have as well been kept upon it as he; but the lieutenant refused to give him a copy, and his jailer told the prisoner it was altered after they had kept him four or five months in prison : then the colonel writ to Bennett, but neither could he obtain any copy of his commitment from him.

After this a friend gave him notice that they had

a design to transport him to some island or planta-
tion ; whereupon he wrote a narrative of his imprisonment, and procured it to be secretly printed,[1]
to have left behind him, if he had been sent away,
to acquaint the parliament, which was then shortly
to assemble, and to leave with his friends ; but he
kept it in the meantime privately.

At length, through the lies that the lieutenant of
the Tower made of his prisoners, and the malice of
their wicked persecutors, who envied even the
bread which charity sent in to feed some of the
men whose estates were wholly taken away,
warrants were signed for carrying away most of
the prisoners, some to Tangier, and to other barbarous and distant places : among the rest Colonel

---

[1] This is the narrative reprinted in the Harleian Miscellany, vol. iii. ed. 1745.

"A narrative of the imprisonment and usage of Colonel
John Hutchinson of Owthorp in the county of Nottingham,
Esq., now close prisoner in the Tower of London. Written
by himself on the 6th of April 1664, having then received
intimation that he was to be sent away to another prison ;
and therefore he thought fit to print this, for the satisfying
his relations and friends of his innocence."

"Let the proud be ashamed, for they dealt perversely with
me without a cause ; but I will meditate in thy precepts."
Psal. cxix. 78. (1664, 12 pages quarto.)

The account given in the text is evidently based on this,
and both are confirmed by the official records of his imprisonment and examination in the State Paper Office.

Hutchinson was destined to the Isle of Man, which Sir Allen Apsley hearing of, told the king he had some private business of trusts with the colonel concerning his own estate, for which he obtained that he might be respited three months, and have liberty for lawyers to come to him.[1] But when the colonel heard of it, he was more displeased with this petty favour than with all their rigour, and had resolved to have done something to reverse it, but that his wife persuaded him to rest till she made a short voyage into the country to fetch him supplies, which he did.

As soon as she was gone, the lieutenant of the Tower sent his jailer, Mr. Edward Cresset, early in the morning, upon the 16th day of April, 1664, to fetch Mr. Hutchinson to his lodgings, whither being come, Cresset withdrew, and the lieutenant told Mr. Hutchinson that he had been civil to him in permitting his children to come to him with their mother, and yet he had not paid him his fees and dues, although that warrant which allowed the access of his wife did not mention his children, and therefore he now demanded his dues. Mr. Hutchin-

---

[1] Warrants had actually been prepared to the lieutenant of the Tower to deliver up Hutchinson to be conveyed to the custody of the Earl of Derby at the Isle of Man, and to the Governor of Chester to keep him till he could be transported to the island.—"Calendar of Domestic State Papers, 1664," p. 575–9.

son told him, "At his departure out of the Tower
he should not be behindhand with him for the
civility of suffering his children to come to him."
Robinson replied, "That signified nothing, he expected his dues, and would have them." Mr.
Hutchinson answered, "His was not every prisoner's
condition, for he had been now twenty-four weeks
kept close prisoner, and yet never knew accuser
nor accusation against him, and therefore he should
desire to consider before he parted from his money ;
but for any civilities he should repay them." Robinson said, "He meddled with no man's crimes, but
whether guilty or not guilty, he expected his dues,
which he could recover by law if they were refused."
Mr. Hutchinson asking, "What they were ?" He
said, "Fifty pounds." Further demanding, "By
what law they were due, so as he could recover
them ?" Robinson answered, "By custom." Mr.
Hutchinson told him, "He was confident that pretence would not recover them ; and if he thought
it would, he would go to a civil and fair trial with
him the next term; yet due or not due, what
civilities he either had or should afford him, he
would recompense at parting." Robinson answered,
"He stood upon his right, and he would make Mr.
Hutchinson, or somebody else, pay it." Mr.
Hutchinson told him, "He knew not whom he
meant by somebody else, but if his liberty were
taken from him without any reason that he knew,

he would not so part with his money, if he could
help it." He then, in anger, said, "He would lock
him up close, and let nobody come at him." Mr.
Hutchinson told him, "He could be locked no
closer than he had been all this time, and he hoped
he would not forbid those coming to him who had
warrant from the secretary; for the rest he might
use his pleasure." He, in fury, commanded to take
away Mr. Hutchinson and lock him up, that no
person might come at him; and gave order at the
Tower Gates to keep out his children and all his
relations that should come to inquire for him; and
he sent word to Serjeant Fountaine [1] who had an
order to come in, that he should not be admitted,
although his business was of great concernment to
others, and not to Colonel Hutchinson, who being
a trustee for some of his relations, was to have
made some settlements in their affairs; which could
not be done, but they, to their prejudice, were forced
to go without it. [2] Although his commands were

---

[1] John Fountaine, made a serjeant-at-law by Richard
Cromwell, and appointed June 3, 1659, one of the Com-
missioners of the Great Seal. He died in 1671.—Foss,
"Judges of England."

[2] The same respectable friend who, proceeding upon an
intimation contained in the Annual Review, communicated
to the editor the particulars of the deliverance of George
Fox, given in page 201, has upon a similar intimation
pointed out several passages in the life of William Penn,
demonstrating the officious readiness of this same Sir John

executed to the full, yet Mr. Hutchinson's eldest son found means to steal into the Tower, and to inform his father of a malicious lie which the lieutenant had made of him at court, that day that he fell out with him ; which was this.—Robinson told the king, that when Mr. Henningham and others were carried out of the Tower to be shipped away, Mr. Hutchinson, looking out of his window, bade them take courage, they should yet have a day for it.

Robinson to act as the minister of oppression and persecution. He first sends a serjeant from the Tower to watch Penn ; the serjeant finds him preaching to *friends,* seizes him, drags him away to the Tower, and sends to Whitehall for Robinson—Robinson comes, sits as magistrate, overrules the just and legal objections of Penn, and commits him to gaol. Penn, whilst in prison, writes a very sensible and moderate letter to Bennett, Earl of Arlington, complaining of coarse treatment in prison, although the secretary had pretended to give orders for his decent accommodation. At the trial of Penn, Sir John Robinson sits as assessor to the recorder, and at the same time obtrudes himself upon the court as an evidence, interferes to influence the jury against the prisoner, and abuses the foreman because he will not suffer himself to be browbeaten nor biassed. At last, when a verdict could not be obtained comformable to the views of the judges, they fine the jury for that which they have given, and Penn for contempt of the court. To enumerate, from the " Histories of the Sufferings of the Quakers," the instances of his oppression and cruelty, would fill a volume. Suffice it to hold him up here to infamy as lasting as the fame of those two virtuous men, in the hope of deterring other ministers of injustice from doing the like.—J. H.

This lie coming to Mr. Hutchinson's knowledge the 19th of April, moved him more than all his other base usage; whereupon he wrote a letter to Robinson, to tell him he should have had a care of provoking his prisoners to speak, who had so much exposed himself to every one of them; and to let him know what he himself had observed and could prove, he drew it up under certain heads, which he told him, if he continued his vile usage of him, he would publish. The articles were :—

1st. That Robinson had affirmed that the king gave no allowance to his prisoners, not so much as to those who had all their estates taken from them; and accordingly he gave them none, but converted what the king allowed to his own use and threatened some of the prisoners with death, if they offered to demand it; and suffered others, at twelve of the clock at night, to make such a miserable outcry for bread, that it was heard into some parts of the city, and one was absolutely starved to death for want of relief; although the king at that time told a prisoner, that he took more care for the prisoners than for his own table.

2nd. That he set down to the king seven pounds a week for one prisoner, for whom he never laid out about twenty-seven or thirty shillings a week at the most.

3rd. That he not only kept back the prisoners' allowances, but exacted of them excessive rents for bare prison lodgings, and empty warders' houses, unfurnished ; and if they have not punctually paid him, hath stifled them up by close imprisonment, without any order, although he knew they had not a penny to buy bread, but what came from the charity of good people.

4th. That he received salary of the king for forty warders, and had not near so many, but filled up the list with false names, and took the pay to himself.

5th. That when he had received money for those warders he kept, he had detained it many months, to his own use, while the poor men were thereby in miserable wants.

6th. That he sold the warders' places, and let them houses at a dear rate, and yet took the most considerable prisoners, which ought to have been committed to them, into his own house, and made them pay him excessive rates for bed-rooms, and set his man, Cresset, over them, making them pay him for attendance what the warders should have had.

7th. That he made many false musters in his own company belonging to the Tower, and though he had received the soldiers' money, was run in arrears to them five or six pounds a man ; at which they cruelly murmured, because by this means their maintenance was straitened, and their duty brought more frequent upon them.

8th. That notwithstanding all his defrauding, oppressive, and exacting ways of raising money, he had ungratefully complained of the king's scanty recompense of his service.

9th. That after the starving of the poor prisoners and their miserable outcry, when shame forced him to allow about a dozen poor tradesmen ten shilling a piece, though at that time he received forty from the king for each of them, he and his man, Cresset, denied the king's allowance, and said it was his own charity.

10th. That he was frequently drunk, out of the Tower till twelve, one, and two of the clock, and threatened one of the warders, who came one night to fetch him home, with Newgate, and spited him ever after.[1]

All these things being notoriously true, this letter put him into a great rage, and a no less dread that

---

[1] The Tower, like other English prisons, was a place of oppression and extortion. The volume published by Dr. Jessopp for the Camden Society, "The Economy of the Fleet," gives an account of the state of that prison at the beginning of the 17th century. Lilburn in his "Christian Man's Trial" describes its condition in 1637. In the pamphlet entitled "The Oppressed Man's Oppressions Declared" (1646) he sets forth, in the form of a letter to the lieutenant of the Tower, the "oppressing cruelty of all the gaolers of England, and particularly the lieutenants of the Tower." He, like Colonel Hutchinson, refuses to pay the fees and room rent demanded by the lieutenant. "Therefore I desire you, according to your duty which by law you are bound unto, to provide me a prison gratis ; for I profess unto you no

the colonel, as he had threatened him, would publish it ; [1] whereupon, as soon as these things were laid to his charge, within ten days he paid his soldiers fifteen months' pay out of twenty-two due to them when the letter was written, he having all that while kept back eighteen pence a week out of every soldier's pay ; and the soldiers, understanding that Colonel Hutchinson's observations of his fraud had procured them this satisfaction, used to give him thanks when they came to stand sentinels at his door.

Presently after he received the letter, he went to · Sir Allen Apsley and complained to him that the colonel had sent him a vile letter, but did not show it Sir Allen, as he sent word to the colonel he would ; whereupon Sir Allen Apsley sent Mr. George Hutchinson with a letter to Sir John Robinson, to tell him that if he would let him go to his brother, he doubted not but it would be a good means to persuade the colonel to pay him his fees, and to reconcile differences between them. Sir John, upon the 21st of April, went along with Mr. George Hut-

---

more rent I can nor will pay, though it cost me a dungeon, or as bad, for my pains."

See also "A Relation of the cruel and unparalleled oppressions on the gentlemen prisoners in the Tower" (1647). It is signed by some eighteen royalist prisoners.

[1] The letter, dated April 20, 1664, is amongst the Domestic State Papers, 561, 14.

chinson to his brother, and at his entrance, in a
passion began to quarrel at the colonel's sour looks ;
who told him, if he had known they would not
have pleased him, and had had notice of his coming,
he would have set them in a glass for him. Then
Robinson told him, in a rage, he had written him
a libel. Mr. Hutchinson answered it was no libel,
for he had set his name to it, and they were truths,
which if he put him to, he could prove by sufficient
testimonies. Whereupon he fell into horrible railing
and cruel language, but by Mr. George Hutchinson's interposition at length all was pacified, and he
was fairly going out of the room with Mr. George
Hutchinson, when his man Cresset, reminding him
that the colonel had a foul copy of his letter, and
had said he would send to Sir Allen, who had
desired to see it ; Robinson resolved to take that
draught away from him ; but the colonel, foreseeing
that, had sent copies of it long before out of the
Tower, which Robinson's dull head not dreaming
of, came back and insolently commanded the colonel
to give him the first draught of the letter. The
colonel desired to be excused, whereupon Robinson
said he would have his pockets searched, and
accordingly bade Cresset feel in them. He, a little
moved, took a bottle in his hand, and bade Cresset
forbear, if he loved his head, and told Sir John if
he had any warrant to search him from the king or
council, he would submit to it, but otherwise he

would not suffer it, especially for a paper which was only of private concernment between them ; for all this, when Sir John saw that Cresset durst not approach the colonel, he commanded one Wale, a warder, to search his pockets, who coming with entreaties to the colonel to permit it, he suffered him. And then the lieutenant caused a little dressing-box which the colonel had to be opened, and took away all the papers he found in it, among which there was one wherein the colonel had written a verse out of the 43d Psalm, it was the first.verse, to be joined with the narrative of his imprisonment, that he had provided to leave behind him for the satisfaction of his friends.[1] This paper Robinson carried to court, and said, that by the deceitful and unjust man the colonel intended the king, although the application was of his own making. In the meantime, while they were ransacking his box and pockets Robinson fell a-railing at the colonel, giving him the base terms of rebel

---

[1] The narrative printed in the Harleian MSS. ends thus :— "And whilst I am yet suffered to breathe, having no other refuge on earth, putting up my petitions to the great Judge of heaven and earth, as one not without hope in God, in the words of the prophet David, Psal. xliii.—"Judge me, O God, and plead my cause against an ungodly nation : O deliver me from the deceitful and unjust man."

Probably at this time the imperfect draft of this narrative, now amongst the Domestic State Papers, was seized.—Dom. S. P. 539, 103.

and murtherer, and such language as none could
have learned, but such as had been conversant among
the civil society of Picked-hatch, Turnbull-street,[1]
and Billings-gate, near which last place the hero
had his education.   When the colonel patiently told
him he transgressed the act of oblivion, he said he
knew that well enough, and bade him sue out
his remedy; then in fury and rage turned the
colonel's servant out of his chamber, who had been
locked up with him all the time of his imprisonment, and left him altogether unattended, which
having never been before in his whole life, put him
into a cold and a flux, with a feverish distemper:
but the greatness of his mind was not broken by
the feebleness of his constitution, nor by the barbarous inhumanity of his jailers, which he received
with disdain, and laughed at them, but lost not
anger on them.

After these things, Mrs. Hutchinson coming out
of the country was, by the lieutenant's order, denied
to see her husband, but at her lodgings she found
letters from him conveyed to her every day, in spite
of all his guards; and thereupon she writ to Robinson to desire to know whether the secretary had

---

[1] "Turnbull Street, now, and indeed originally, Turnmill
Street, near Clerkenwell, only corrupted into Turnbull.
Anciently the resort of bullies, rogues, and other dissolute
persons.   Pict-Hatch, a noted tavern or brothel in Turnbull Street" (Nares' Glossary).

countermanded his first order for her to see her husband, or whether he denied obedience to it ; whereupon Robinson sent to her to come to him the next day, but when she came he was gone forth, and she was not admitted within the gates, and thereupon she went back to her lodgings and writ him a smart letter, and sent him with it a copy of her husband's letter, which she told him she would publish, and not suffer him to be murthered to extort undue money from him. The next day, being the Lord's day, he sent one of the warders to entreat her to come to her husband, and the blood-hound Cresset met her at the gate, and led her to her husband, and left her all the day alone with him, which they had never before done all the time of his prison ; and in the evening Sir John Robinson sent for her, and partly expostulated with her and partly flattered, and told her her husband had been sent to the Isle of Man, but that he in kindness had procured a better place for him, and that he was not covetous, but since her husband would not pay him his fees, he might use his pleasure, and she and his children and relations might freely go to him. She received this as befitted her, being in his hands, and knowing that not good nature, but fear she would have printed him, moved him to this gentler course ; and this she understood, both by the inquiries his servants made of the colonel's warder concerning her

intentions, and by Robinson's continuing, notwithstanding all his dissimulation, to make a thousand
false insinuations of the colonel. everywhere, and
to do him all ill offices at court ; if there were not
a more abominable wickedness than all this practised, a lingering poison given him, which, though
we had not wickedness enough to suspect then,
the events that have since ensued make a little
doubtful. It is certain that Cresset did make that
attempt upon Sir Henry Vane and others, and two
or three days before the colonel was sent away,
he brought into his chamber, when he came to lock
him up at night, a bottle of excellent wine, under
pretence of kindness, which he, the colonel, and the
warder drunk together, and the warder and the
colonel both died within four months ; the colonel
presently after falling sick, but very unsuspicious,
and we must leave it to the great day, when all
crimes, how secret soever, will be made manifest,
whether they added poison to all the other iniquity,
whereby they certainly murthered this guiltless
servant of God.

A few days after, at nine of the clock at night,
after his wife was gone from him, Cresset brought
the colonel a warrant, to tell him that he must, the
next morning tide, go down to Sandown Castle, in
Kent ;[1] which he was not surprised at, it being the

---

[1] The warrant for the removal of Colonel Hutchinson

barbarous custom of that place to send away the prisoners, when they had no knowledge nor time to accommodate themselves for their journey.   But instead of putting him into a boat at the morning tide, about eight of the clock Sir Henry Wroth came with a party of horse to receive him of the lieutenant, and finding him sick, and not well able to endure riding in the heat of the day, he was so civil as to let him go by water in the evening tide to Gravesend, with a guard of soldiers in boats hired at his own charge, where the horse guard met him.   By these means he got opportunity to take leave of his children that were in town, and about four o'clock he was sent out of the Tower, with one Gregory, designed to be his fellow-prisoner; who going over the drawbridge, turned back to the lieutenant, and told him he would have accepted it as a greater mercy if the king had commanded him to be shot to death there, rather than to send him to a distant place to be starved, he having nothing but his trade to maintain him, and his friends, from whom he should now be so far removed that he could expect nothing.   The lieutenant in scorn told him, he went with a charitable man who would not suffer him to starve, whereby he exposed

and Captain John Gregory to Sandown Castle is dated May 3, 1664.—" Calendar of Domestic State Papers, 1664," p. 579.

the malice of their intentions to the colonel; who
thought it not enough to send him to a far prison
not much differing from exile, but to charge with
a companion, whom however his kindness might
have rendered him charitable to, yet they ought not
to have put upon him; neither would the colonel
take notice of their imposition, though he designed
kindness to the man, had he been worthy of it.

The colonel's wife and children got a boat and
followed him to Gravesend, whither also Gregory's
wife, and one that called him brother, went; and
that night all the company and all the guards supped
at the colonel's charge, and many of the guards lay
in the chamber with him, who, with the refresh-
ment of the evening air, and the content he took
to be out of Robinson's claws, found himself, or
through the liveliness of his spirit fancied himself,
something better than he was in the Tower. The
next morning, very early, his guards hurried him
away on horseback; but, to speak truth, they were
civil to him. His son went along with him to see
the place he was sent to, and Sir Allen Apsley had
procured an order for his servant to continue with
him in the prison; his wife went back to London,
to stay there to provide him such accommodation as
she could hear he had need of.

When he came to the castle, he found it a
lamentable old ruined place, almost a mile distant
from the town, the rooms all out of repair, not

weather-free, no kind of accommodation either for lodging or diet, or any conveniency of life. Before he came, there were not above half a dozen soldiers in it, and a poor lieutenant with his wife and children, and two or three cannoniers, and a few guns almost dismounted, upon rotten carriages ; but at the colonel's coming thither, a company of foot more were sent from Dover to help guard the place, pitiful weak fellows, half-starved and eaten up with vermin, whom the governor of Dover cheated of half their pay, and the other half they spent in drink. These had no beds, but a nasty court of guard, where a sutler lived, within a partition made of boards, with his wife and family, and this was all the accommodation the colonel had for his victuals, which were bought at a dear rate at the town, and most horribly dressed at the sutler's. For beds he was forced to send to an inn in the town, and at a most unconscionable rate hire three, for himself, and his man, and Captain Gregory ; and to get his chamber glazed, which was a thoroughfare room, that had five doors in it, and one of them opened upon a platform, that had nothing but the bleak air of the sea, which every tide washed the foot of the castle walls ; which air made the chamber so unwholesome and damp, that even in the summer time the colonel's hat-case and trunks, and everything of leather, would be every day all covered over with mould,—wipe them as

clean as you could one morning, by the next they
would mouldy again ; and though the walls were
four yards thick, yet it rained in through cracks
in them, and then one might sweep a peck of
saltpetre off of them every day, which stood in a
perpetual sweat upon them. Notwithstanding all
this, the colonel was very cheerful, and made the
best shifts he could with things as he found them ;
when the lieutenant's wife, seeing his stomach
could not well bear his food, offered to board him,
and so he and his man dieted with her for twenty
shillings a week, he finding wine besides, and linen,
&c. Whilst the sutler provided his meat, Gregory
ate with him ; but when he tabled with the captain,
Gregory's son coming to him, he had his meat
from the town, and soon after a woman came down
who left not the man destitute and comfortless.
The worst part of the colonel's sufferings in this
prison, was the company of this fellow, who being
a fellow-prisoner and poor, and the colonel having
no particular retreat, he could not wholly decline his
company ; and he being a carnal person, without
any fear of God, or any good but rather scandalous
conversation, he could take no pleasure in him ;
meanwhile, many of his friends gave caution to his
wife concerning him, as suspecting him to be a trepanner, which we had after some cause to fear.

The captain of the castle, one Freeman, had all
this while a chamber which was a little warmer,

and had a bed in it, but this he reserved, intending
to set a rate upon it, and this too was so dark one
could not have read by the fire or the bedside
without a candle at noonday.

When the colonel's wife understood her husband's
bad accommodation, she made all the means she
could through her friends to procure liberty that
she might be in the castle with him, but that was
absolutely denied; whereupon she and her son
and daughter went to Deal, and there took lodgings, from whence they walked every day on foot
to dinner and back again at night, with horrible
toil and inconvenience; and they procured the
captain's wife to diet them with the colonel, where
they had meat good enough, yet through the
poverty of the people, and their want of all neces-
saries, and the faculty to order things as they
should be, it was very inconvenient to them; yet
the colonel endured it so cheerfully that he was
never more pleasant and contented in his whole
life. When no other recreations were left him, he
diverted himself with sorting and shadowing cockle-
shells, which his wife and daughter gathered for
him, with as much delight as he used to take
in the richest agates and onyxes he could compass
with the most artificial engravings, which were
things, when he recreated himself from more
serious studies, he as much delighted in as any
piece of art. But his fancy showed itself so excel-

lent in sorting and dressing these shells, that none
of us could imitate it, and the cockles began to be
admired by several persons that saw them.   These
were but his trifling diversions, his business and
continual study was the Scripture, which the more
he conversed in, the more it delighted him ; insomuch that his wife having brought down some
books to entertain him in his solitude, he thanked
her, and told her that if he should continue as long
as he lived in prison, he would read nothing there
but his bible.   His wife bore all her own toils joy-
fully enough for the love of him, but could not but
be very sad at the sight of his undeserved sufferings ; and he would very sweetly and kindly chide
her for it, and tell her that if she were but cheerful,
he should think this suffering the happiest thing
that ever befell him ; he would also bid her consider
what reason she had to rejoice that the Lord supported him, and how much more intolerable it
would have been, if the Lord had suffered his spirit
to have sunk, or his patience to have been lost
under this.   One day when she was weeping, after
he had said many things to comfort her, he gave
her reasons why she should hope and be assured
that this cause would revive, because the interest
of God was so much involved in it that he was
entitled to it.[1]   She told him she did not doubt but

---

[1] The notion of the revival of The Cause, and of the

the cause would revive; but, said she, notwithstanding all your resolution, I know this will conquer the weakness of your constitution, and you
will die in prison. He replied, I think I shall not,
but if I do, my blood will be so innocent, I shall
advance the cause more by my death hasting the
vengeance of God upon my unjust enemies, than I
could do by all the actions of my life. Another

---

advancement of it by their sufferings, seems to have been
very prevalent with those who fell in these times; accordingly they supported their fate with the true spirit of
martyrs. The speech of Colonel Okey at the time of his
execution, preserved in the "Trials of the Regicides,"
maintains the style of prophetic eloquence with so much
dignity and firmness, as almost to captivate the imagination
of the coolest reasoner. These sentences following are
extracted from it :—

"And truly, as to the Cause, I am as confident, even as
I am of my resurrection, that that cause which we first took
up the sword for, which was for righteousness and justice,
and for the advancement of a godly magistracy and a good
ministry (however some men turned about for their own
ends), shall yet revive again. I am confident, I say, that
cause for which so much blood hath been shed, will have
another resurrection, and that you will have a blessed fruit
of those many thousands that have been killed in the late
war. I would say to all good men, rather to suffer than
take any indirect means to deliver themselves; and God,
when it shall make most for his own glory and the good of
his people, will deliver, and that in such a way that himself
shall have glory in, and the gospel have no reproach
by."—J. H.

time, when she was telling him she feared they had placed him on the sea-shore but in order to transport him to Tangier, he told her, if they had, God was the same God at Tangier as at Owthorpe; prithee, said he, trust God with me; if he carry me away, he will bring me back again.

Sometimes when he would not be persuaded to do things wherein he had a liberty, for fear of putting a snare and stumbling-block before others that had not so, and when she would expostulate with him, why he should make himself a martyr for people that had been so censorious of him, and so unthankful and insensible of all his merits, he would say, he did it not for them, but for the cause they owned. When many ill usages he had received from godly people have been urged to him, he would say, that if they were truly the people of God, all their failings were to be borne; that if God had a people in the land, as he was confident he had, it was among them, and not among the cavaliers, and therefore although he should ever be severe against their miscarriages in any person in whomsoever he found them, yet he would adhere to them that owned God, how unkindly soever they dealt with him. Sometimes he would say, that if ever he should live to see the parliament power up again, he would never meddle any more either in councils or in armies; and then sometimes again, when he saw or heard of any of the debaucheries of the times, he would say, he would act only as a justice of the peace in the country, and be severe against drunkards, and suffer none in his neighbourhood. Oftentimes he would say, if ever he were at liberty in the world, he would flee the conversation of the cavaliers, and would write upon his doors,

Procul hinc, procul este, profani!

and that, though he had in his former conversation with them never had any communication with their manners nor vices, yet henceforth he would never, in one kind or other, have any commerce at all with them ; and indeed it was a resolution he would oftener repeat than any other he had, telling us that he was convinced there was a serpentine seed in them. Yet he had many apprehensions of the rash, hot-heated spirits of many of our party, and fears that their pride and self-conceit of their own abilities would again bring us to confusion, if ever they should have the reins again in their hands ; and therefore he would bid us advise his son, if ever we lived to see a change, and would himself advise him, not to fall in with the first, how fair soever their pretences were ; but to wait to see how their practices suited them. For he would say, that a hot-spirited people would first get up and put all into confusion, and then a sober party must settle things ; and he would say, Let my son stay to fall in with these. He foresaw that the courses which the

king and his party took to establish themselves
would be their ruin, and would say, that whenever
the king had an army it would be his destruction.
Once when his wife was lamenting his condition,
having said many things to comfort her, he told her
he could not have been without this affliction, for
if he had flourished while all the people of God
were corrected, he should have feared he had not
been accounted among his children, as he had not
shared their lot. Then would he with thankfulness
repeat the kind and gentle dealings of the Lord at
all times toward him, and erect a firm and mighty
hope upon it, and wonderfully encourage her to
bear it patiently, not only by words, but by his
own admirable example.

After Mr. Hutchinson had been some time prisoner
at Sandown, the governor of the Castle came over,
and would fain have let him his chamber for 20s. a
week, which Mr. Hutchinson told him he would
give him, if his wife might come there to him; but
the governor refused that without an express order,
which was endeavoured but could not be obtained.
Then Freeman demanded a mark a week of the
colonel for fees, but the colonel told him, except he
could show how it was due by any known law, he
would not pay it. Some time after, the governor
of Dover came over, with the governor of Sandown
and one Mr. Masters, and Freeman consulting his
master of Dover how he should get money of the

colonel, the governor of Dover advised him to put him into a dungeon, but the fellow durst not attempt it. Yet some time after he came to the castle, and passing into his own chamber, through Mr. Hutchinson's, who was there,—as he went by with his lieutenant, Moyle, at his heels, he called out to Mr. Hutchinson's man, and bade him bid Hutchinson come to him, without any addition of so much as the title of a gentleman. Mrs. Hutchinson being then in the room with her husband, desired him she might go in with him and answer the captain's insolency, and that he would take no notice of it, which he told her he would not, neither should she, and so they both went into the captain's chamber, who had also called Gregory. When they were both there, the captain, turning to Moyle, said, " Captain Moyle, I ordain you to quarter Hutchinson and Gregory together in the next room ; and if Hutchinson will make a partition at his own charge, he may have that part of the chamber that has the chimney, and for this expect a mark a week of Hutchinson, and a noble of Gregory; and if they will have any enlargement besides, they must pay for it."[1] Mr. Hutchinson laughed at him, and bade

---

[1] In speaking of the persons who had the command of the castle, and the custody of the prisoners, there seems in some parts of the narrative to be a little perplexity ; but this passage shows clearly that Freeman was captain, but

his wife report his usage of him to the secretary at London, to whom she presently writ an account of it, and sent it to Sir Allen Apsley, desiring him either to procure a remove or an order for better accommodation, and showed this letter to Gregory before it went, representing equally his condition with her husband's : and · seeing she could not get admission into the castle, she took a house in the town, to which she intended to bring her children for the winter, had not God prevented.

Not long after, the colonel's brother, Mr. George Hutchinson, came down, and brought with him an order, signed by Secretary Bennett, to allow the colonel leave to walk by the sea-side with a keeper, which order Sir Allen Apsley and his lady[1] had at length procured with some difficulty and sent him ; wherein he was so well satisfied, that he thought not his prison now insupportable ; neither indeed was it so to him before, for his patience and faith wonderfully carried him on under all his sufferings. As it now drew nigh to the latter end of the year,

---

did not reside at it ; and that Moyle was his lieutenant, and did reside at it. The former was the person who, on this and some other occasions, attempted to extort money from Colonel Hutchinson and his family ; the latter was the person whose wife boarded and accommodated them. —J. H.

[1] This warrant is dated August 8, 1664.—"Calendar of Domestic State Papers for 1664," p. 662.

Mrs. Hutchinson, having prepared the house, was
necessitated to go to Owthorpe to fetch her children,
and other supplies to her husband ; whom, when
the time of her departure came, she left with a
very sad and ill-presaging heart, rather dreading
that while he lay so ready on the sea-coast, he
might some time or other be shipped away to some
barbarous place in her absence, than that which
after ensued.   The colonel comforted her all · he
could, and that morning she went away, " Now,"
said he, " I myself begin to be loth to part with thee."
But yet, according to his usual cheerfulness, he encouraged himself and her, and sent his son along
with her.   His daughter and his brother stayed
at Deal, who, coming to him every day, he walked
out with them by the sea-side, and would discourse
of the public concernments, and say that the ill-
management of the state would cause discontented
wild parties to mutiny and rise against the present
powers, but that they would only put things in
confusion ; it must be a sober party that must then
arise and settle them.   He would often say to his
son and his wife, as he did now to his brother,
" Let not my son, how fairly soever they pretend,
too rashly engage with the first, but stay to see
what they make good, and engage with those who
are for settlement, who will have need of men of
interest to assist them ; let him keep clear and
take heed of too rash attempts, and he will be

courted if he behave himself piously and prudently, and keep free of all faction, making the public interest only his." He would sometimes in discourse say, that when these people once had an army up, which they seemed to aim at, that army would be their destruction, for he was very confident God would bring them down; he would often say they could not stand, and that whoever had anything to do with them could not prosper. He once made this expression, " Although," said he, " I am free from any trucking with them, yet even that consenting submission that I had, hath brought this suffering upon me." And he would often say, he would never have so much as a civil correspondence with any of them again; yet when he mentioned Sir Allen Apsley, he would say, he would never serve any that would not for his sake serve the person that had preserved him. When his wife went away he was exceeding well and cheerful, and so confident of seeing Owthorpe, that he gave her directions in a paper for planting trees, and many other things belonging to the house and gardens. " You give me," said she, " these orders, as if you were to see that place again." " If I do not," said he, " I thank God I can cheerfully forego it, but I will not distrust that God will bring me back again, and therefore I will take care to keep it while I have it."

The third of September, being Saturday, he had

been walking by the sea-side, and coming home
found himself aguish, with a kind of shivering and
pain in his bones, and went to bed and sweat
exceedingly : the next day was a little better,
and went down, and on the Monday, expecting
another fit, which came upon him, lay in bed all
day, and rose again the next day, but went not
down ; and after that he slept no more till his last
sleep came upon him, but continued in a feverish
distemper, with violent sweatings, after which he
used to rise out of his bed to refresh him, and when
he was up used to read much in his Bible. He had
appointed his wife, when she went away, to send
him the Dutch Annotations on the Bible, and she
had sent it down with some other things ; which he
presently caused to be brought him, though he was
in his bed, and some places in the Epistle to the
Romans read, which having heard, "these annota-
tors," said he, "are short ; " and then looking over
some notes upon that Epistle, which his wife had
left in a book she had gathered from him ; "I have,"
said he, " discovered much more of the mystery of
truth in that Epistle, and when my wife returns I
will make her set it down ; for," said he, "I will no
more observe their cross humours, but when her
children are near, I will have her in my chamber
with me, and they shall not pluck her out of my
arms ; and then, in the winter nights, she shall
collect several observations I have made of this

Epistle since I came into prison." The continual
study of the Scriptures did infinitely ravish and
refine his soul, and take it off from all lower
exercise, and he continued it in his sickness even
to the last, desiring his brother, when he was in
bed and could not read himself, to read it to him.
He found himself every day grow weaker, yet was
not exceeding sick, only he could not sleep at all,
day nor night. There was a country physician at
Deal, who had formerly belonged to the army, and
had some gifts, and used to exercise them among
godly people in their meetings ; but having been
taken there once by the persecutors, and being
married to a wicked unquiet woman, she and the
love of the world had perverted him to forsake all
religious meetings ; yet the man continued civil and
fair-conditioned, and was much employed thereabouts. He being sent for to Mr. Hutchinson,
found that on Friday his mouth grew very sore,
whereupon he told Mr. George Hutchinson that he
distrusted his own skill in looking to it, and apprehended some danger, and advised him to send for
a very famous physician that was at Canterbury,
which they did, and he came on Saturday. As
he came along he inquired of the messenger that
fetched him what kind of person the colonel was,
and how he had lived, and been accustomed, and
which chamber of the castle he was now lodged in ?
Which when the man had told him, he said his

journey would be to no purpose, for that chamber had killed him. Accordingly, when he came, he told the colonel's brother, on Saturday night, that he apprehended danger, and appointed some remedies, and some applications to his temples, and a cordial to procure rest, but it had no effect. There was a nurse watched in his chamber, and she told them after his death, that she heard him pray in the night, with the deepest sighs that ever she heard. The next morning, before the doctor and his daughter, and brother and servants came to him, the gentlewoman of the castle came up and asked him how he did? He told her, incomparably well, and full of faith.

Some time after, when the doctor came, he told his brother that the fever had seized his head, and that he believed he would soon fall into ravings and die, and therefore wished him, if he had anything to say to him, to speak while he was in perfect sense. So Mr. George Hutchinson came to him, and told him he believed he could not live, and therefore desired him if he had anything to do, to despatch it, for he believed his end was approaching. The colonel, without the least dejection or amazement, replied, very composedly and cheerfully, " The will of the Lord be done : I am ready for it." And then he told them that he did now confirm the will he wrote in the Tower for his last will and testament, and all others to be void. The doctor, who

had, when religion was in fashion, been a pretender
to it, came to him and asked him if his peace was
made with God ; to which he replied, " I hope you
do not think me so ill a Christian, to have been
thus long in prison, and have that to do now ! "
The doctor asked him concerning the ground of his
hope ; to which he answered, " There's none but
Christ, none but Christ, in whom I have unspeak-
able joy, more than I can express ; yet I should
utter more, but that the soreness of my mouth
makes it difficult for me to speak."   Then they
asked him where he would be buried ?   He told
them, in his vault at Owthorpe ; his brother told
him it would be a long way to carry him : he answered, " Let my wife order the manner of it as
she will, only I would lie there."   He left a kind
message to his wife, " Let her," said he, " as she is
above other women, show herself, in this occasion,
a good Christian, and above the pitch of ordinary
women."[1]   He commanded his daughter who was
present to tell the rest, that he would have them
all guided by her counsels ; and left with his
brother the same message to his eldest son.   " I
would," said he, " have spoken to my wife and

---

[1] This is that command of her husband which Mrs.
Hutchinson speaks of at the beginning of her narrative,
where she says she has determined to employ her thoughts
upon the preservation of his memory, not the fruitless
bewailing of it.—J. H.

son, but it is not the will of God;" then, as he was going to utter something, "here's none but friends;" his brother minded him that the doctor was present; "Oh, I thank you," said he; and such was their amazement in their sorrow, that they did not think of speaking to the doctor to retire, but lost what he would have said, which I am confident was some advice to his son how to demean himself in public concernments. He lay all the day very sensible and very cheerful, to the admiration of both the doctors and of all that saw him; and as his daughter sat weeping by him, " Fie, Bab," said he, "do you mourn for me as for one without hope? There is hope." He desired his brother to remember him to Sir Allen Apsley, and tell him that he hoped God would reward his labour of love to him. While he was thus speaking to them, his spirits decayed exceedingly fast, and his pulse grew very low, and his head already was earth in the upper part; yet he raised himself in his bed, "And now," said he to the doctor, "I would fain know your reason why you fancy me dying; I feel nothing in myself, my head is well, my heart is well, and I have no pain nor sickness anywhere." The doctor, seeing this, was amazed; " Sir," said he, "I would be glad to be deceived; " and being at a stand, he told Mr. George Hutchinson he was surprised, and knew not what to think, to see him so cheerful and undisturbed, when his

pulse was gone ; which if it were not death, must
be some strange working of the spleen, and therefore advised him to send away for Dr. Ridgely,
which he would before have done, but that the
doctor told him he feared it would be vain, and
that he would be dead before the doctor could
come.   While they were preparing to write, the
colonel spoke only these two words : " 'Tis as I would
have it : 'tis where I would have it :" and spoke no
more, for convulsions wrought his mouth, yet did
his sense remain perfect to his last breath ; for
when some named Mrs. Hutchinson, and said,
" Alas, how will she be surprised !" he fetched a
sigh, and within a little while departed ; his countenance settling so amiably and cheerful in death,
that he looked after he was dead as he used to do
when best pleased in life.   It was observable that
at the same hour, and the same day of the month,
and the same day of the week, that the wicked
soldiers fetched him out of his own rest and
quiet condition at home, eleven months before, the
Lord of hosts sent his holy angels to fetch him out
of their cruel hands up to his everlasting and
blessed rest above ; this being the Lord's day,
about seven o'clock at night, the eleventh day of
September, 1664 ; that, the same day and hour,
the eleventh of October, 1663.

The two doctors, though mere strangers to him,
were so moved that they both wept as if it had

been their brother; and he of Canterbury said, he
had been with many eminent persons, but he never
in his whole life saw any one receive death with
more Christian courage, and constancy of mind,
and stedfastness of faith, than the colonel had
expressed from the first to the last; so that, considering the height of his fever, and his want of
rest, there was an evidence of a divine assistance
that overruled all the powers and operations of
nature. This doctor, who was called Dr. Jachin,
had most curiously and strictly observed all his
motions. I know not by what impulse, but he
after said, in regard of the colonel's former engagements, he knew he should be examined of all circumstances, and therefore was resolved diligently
to observe them; and as he guessed, it after fell
out, for the gentlemen of the country, being of the
royal party, were busy in their inquiries, which the
doctor answered with such truth and clearness as
made them ready to burst with envy at the peace
and joy the Lord was pleased to give his servant,
in taking him out of this wicked world. I am apt
to think that it was not alone tenderness of nature,
but conviction of their own disturbed peace, which
drew those tears from the doctors, when they saw
in him that blessed peace and joy which crowns the
Lord's constant martyrs : whatever it were, the men
were faithful in divulging the glory of the Lord's
wonderful presence with his servant.

As soon as the colonel was dead, his brother
sent away a messenger to carry the sad news to
his house, and caused his body to be embalmed in
order to his funeral, as he had thrice ordered.
When he was embowelled, all his inwards were
found exceeding sound, and no taint in any part,
only two or three purple spots on his lungs: his
gall, the doctor said, was the largest that ever he
saw in any man, and observed it to be a miracle
of grace that he had been so patient as he had
seen him.

Some two or three days before the colonel fell
sick, Freeman, the captain of the castle, had sent
down a very strict order that the colonel should
carry nothing out of the castle; in pursuance of
which the soldiers would not suffer them to take
out his beds, and furniture, and clothes, which Mr.
Hutchinson forbore till an order came for them.[1]

As soon as the news came to Owthorpe, the
colonel's two eldest sons and all his household
servants went up to London with his horses, and
made ready a hearse, tricked with scutcheons and
six horses in mourning, with a mourning coach and
six horses to wait on it, and came down to Deal
with an order from the secretary for the body; but

---

[1] On September 20, 1664, a warrant was signed by Secretary Bennett to the governor of Sandown Castle, to deliver
up to Mrs. Hutchinson her husband's body, and his trunks
and clothes.

when they came thither, Captain Freeman, in spite, would not deliver it, because Mrs. Hutchinson herself was not come to fetch it; so they were forced, at an intolerable expense, to keep all this equipage at Deal, while they sent to the secretary for another order, which they got directed to the lieutenant in the absence of the captain, and as soon as it came they delivered it to him, who immediately suffered them to take away the body, which they did at that very hour, though it was night, fearing a further dispute with Freeman. For he, after the body had been ten days embalmed, said he would have a jury empannelled, and a coroner to sit upon it, to see whether he died a natural death. Mr. Hutchinson asked him why he urged that, when it lay on their side to have sought satisfaction. He said he must do it to clear the king's garrison. Mr. Hutchinson told him he had slipped his time; it should have been done at the first, before the embalming. He said he would have it unlapped, and accordingly he sent for a coroner and a jury, who, when they came, would not unlap the body, but called those persons that were about him, and examined them as to the occasion of his death. They made affidavit, which remains yet upon record, that the doctor said *the place had killed him*, and, satisfied with this, they did not unlap the body. As it came into Deal, Freeman met it, and said, if he had been in the castle they should not have had it till they had

paid the money he demanded ; which, when he could
not justify any right to by any law, he began to
beg most basely and unworthily, but neither had
anything given him for that. However, though the
secretary had also ordered the colonel should have
his things out, yet he detained all he found in the
castle, his trunks, and beds, and furniture, which
could never be gotten out of his hands. Although
this spite of his put the colonel's family to an excessive charge in staying so long in that cut-throat town
of Deal, yet there was a providence of the Lord in
it ; for the colonel's daughter who was there, through
grief had contracted a violent sickness, which took
her with great severity, and wrought off of her
stomach in black vomits, that made her for the present desperately ill, and the doctor that was with her
said that if she had then been in her journey, as she
would have been had they not been delayed by
his cruel spite, she could not have lived.

The next day after they had gotten out the body,
they brought it with a handsome private equipage
to Canterbury, and so forward towards London,
meeting no affronts in their way but at one town,
where there was a fair, and the priest of the place
came out, with his clerk in his fool's coat, to offer
them burial, and to stop their hearse laid hold on
the horses, whom when the attendants put by, the
wicked rout at the fair took part with them, and set
upon the horsemen ; but they broke several of their

heads, and made their way clear, having beaten off all the town and the fair, and came on to London. They passed through Southwark, over the bridge, and through the whole heart of the city, to their lodging in Holborn, in the day time, and had not one reviling word or indignity offered them all the way, but several people were very much moved at that sad witness of the murderous cruelty of the men then in power.

From London he was brought down to Owthorpe, very seriously bewailed all the way he came along by all those who had been better acquainted with his worth than the strangers were among whom he died, and was brought home with honour to his grave through the dominions of his murtherers, who were ashamed of his glories, which all their tyrannies could not extinguish with his life.

Inscription on the Monument of Col. Hutchinson,

AT OWTHORPE, IN NOTTINGHAMSHIRE.

(Supposed to have been written by Mrs. Hutchinson.)

———

Quousque Domine!

In a vault under this wall lieth the body of

JOHN HUTCHINSON,

Of Owthorpe, in the county of Nottingham, Esq.,

Eldest son and heire of Sir Thomas Hutchinson, by his first wife, the
Lady Margaret, daughter of Sir John Biron, of Newstead,
in the said county.

This monument doth not commemorate
Vain airy glorious titles, birth, and state;
But sacred is to free, illustrious grace,
Conducting happily a mortal's race;
To end in triumph over death and hell,
When, like the prophet's cloak, the frail flesh fell,
Forsaken as a dull impediment,
Whilst love's swift fiery chariot climb'd th' ascent.
Nor are the reliques lost, but only torn,
To be new made, and in more lustre worn.

Full of this ioy he mounted, he lay downe,
Threw off his ashes, and took up his crowne.
  Those who lost all their splendour in his grave,
Ev'n there yet no inglorious period have.

He married Lucy, the daughter of Sir Allen Apsley, lieu-
tenant of the Tower of London, by his third wife, the
Lady Lucy, daughter of Sir John St. John of Lidiard
Tregooze, in the county of Wilts, who [1] dying at Owthorpe,
October 11, 1659, lieth buried in the same vault.

He left surviving by the said Lucy 4 sons ; Thomas, who
married Jane, the daughter of Sir Alexander Radcliffe,
buried in the same vault : and Edward, Lucius, and John :
and 4 daughters ; Barbara, Lucy, Margaret, and Adeliza ;
which last lies buried in the same vault.

He died at Sandown Castle, in Kent, after 11 months'
harsh and strict imprisonment,—without crime or accusation,—upon the 11th day of Sept. 1664, in the 49th
year of his age, full of joy in assured hope of a glorious
resurrection.

---

[1] Who refers to the Lady Lucy Apsley.

Verses written by Mrs. Hutchinson,

In the small Book containing her own Life, and most probably composed by her during her Husband's retirement from public business to his seat at Owthorpe.

———————

ALL sorts of men through various labours press
To the same end, contented quietness ;
Great princes vex their labouring thoughts to be
Possessed of an unbounded sovereignty ;
The hardy soldier doth all toils sustain
That he may conquer first, and after reign ;
Th' industrious merchant ploughs the angry seas
That he may bring home wealth, and live at ease.
These none of them attain : for sweet repose
But seldom to the splendid palace goes ;
A troop of restless passions wander there,
And private lives are only free from care.
Sleep to the cottage bringeth happy nights,
But to the court hung round with flaring lights,
Which th' office of the vanished day supply,
His image only comes to close the eye,
But gives the troubled mind no ease of care,
While country slumbers undisturbed are ;
Where, if the active fancy dreams present,
They bring no horrors to the innocent.

Ambition doth incessantly aspire,
And each advance leads on to new desire ;
Nor yet can riches av'rice satisfy,
For want and wealth together multiply :
Nor can voluptuous men more fulness find,
For enjoyed pleasures leave their stings behind.
He's only rich who knows no want ; he reigns
Whose will no severe tyranny constrains ;
And he alone possesseth true delight
Whose spotless soul no guilty fears affright.
This freedom in the country life is found,
Where innocence and safe delights abound.
Here man's a prince ; his subjects ne'er repine
When on his back their wealthy fleeces shine :
If for his appetite the fattest die,
Those who survive will raise no mutiny :
His table is with home-got dainties crowned,
With friends, not flatterers, encompassed round ;
No spies nor traitors on his trencher wait,
Nor is his mirth confined to rules of state ;
An armed guard he neither hath nor needs,
Nor fears a poisoned morsel when he feeds ;
Bright constellations hang above his head,
Beneath his feet are flow'ry carpets spread ;
The merry birds delight him with their songs,
And healthful air his happy life prolongs ;
At harvest merrily his flocks he shears,
And in cold weather their warm fleeces wears ;
Unto his ease he fashions all his clothes ;
His cup with uninfected liquor flows :
The vulgar breath doth not his thoughts elate,

Nor can he be o'erwhelmed by their hate.
Yet, if ambitiously he seeks for fame,
One village feast shall gain a greater name
Than his who wears the imperial diadem,
Whom the rude multitude do still condemn.
Sweet peace and joy his blest companions are ;
Fear, sorrow, envy, lust, revenge, and care,
And all that troop which breeds the world's offence,
With pomp and majesty, are banish'd thence.
What court then can such liberty afford ?
Or where is man so uncontroll'd a lord ?

APPENDIX.

APPENDIX.

I.

The Quarrel between Colonel Hutchinson and the Committee of Nottingham.

THE following documents illustrate and explain the progress of the quarrel related in the text of the Memoirs.

Letter of Lord Fairfax from York.   October 4, 1644.

For the right honourable the Lords and others of the committee of both kingdoms, &c.

" MY LORDS,—Upon very large testimony of Colonel John Hutchinson's good services, and fidelity unto the Parliament, I sent him a commission for the guarding of the castle at Nottingham, not knowing any at that time of more trust for such an employment : I hear now he is questioned, and that authority I gave him conceived by the committee of that county, either as too much trenching upon their authority, or as not well employed by that person.   I never heard anything but very well of the gentleman, both for his discreet carriage and fidelity to the cause.   I humbly desire your lordships will be pleased to consider him in that place, and not let him suffer without proof testifying his ill deservings.   I am not only a suitor in his behalf but in my own. I have not willingly done, or intend to do, anything which may be prejudicial to the public. Thus waiting your lordships' pleasure and commands, I remain, my lords, your lordships' most humble servant,

FER. FAIRFAX."

YORK, *October* 4, 1644.

The dispute between the governor and the committee came before the committee of both kingdoms in October 1644, and a sub-committee was at once appointed to consider the business and report to the committee. The sub-committee consisted of Lord Say, Sir Henry Vane the younger, Sir Gilbert Gerrard, Mr. Pierrepont, some of the Scotch commissioners, and two lawyers, viz., the Solicitor-General, and the Recorder. (Day Book of the Derby House Committee, October 11, 1644.)

The sub-committee made its first report on November 11, 1644. (*Vide* Memoirs, vol. ii. pp. 41–51.)

First Report.

"*November* 11, 1644.—The Report of the sub-committee concerning the business of Nottingham.

That having heard and considered the several matters in difference between Colonel John Hutchinson, governor, and some of the committee of Nottingham, they do conceive it most conducible to the public good, and the safety of that castle and garrison, that the things objected on either part, by soldiers or others, or that may anyways relate to the said differences, be laid aside, and no further made use of, and that both parties be required to order themselves accordingly.

Letters to be written to all parties concerned to the effect above mentioned by the committee of both kingdoms.

That for the avoiding of any disputes for the future about

the former or the like differences, and for the safe keeping
of the said town and garrison, and best employing those
forces for the public service, the committee of both kingdoms are to appoint and authorise Colonel John Hutchinson,
governor, Colonel Francis Thornhagh, Gilbert Millington,
Esq., Major Joseph Widmerpoole, Jervois Piggot, Esq.,
Captain Charles White and the Mayor of Nottingham for
the time being, or the major part of such of them as shall
be present in the castle and town, shall be a committee to
put in operation these following instructions :

That the governor shall not undertake any design or
service against the enemy, (except an opportunity be offered
him, or the commander-in-chief whom he sends out, when
he is upon any other service or employment, and that then
a council of war of those officers in the field advise him to
it), without the approbation or consent of the aforesaid
persons, or the major part of them as aforesaid.

That the governor shall not send forth any horse or foot
out of the garrison, to assist or join with any other county
or force upon any other design or service, without the
approbation or consent aforesaid.

That the forces so sent forth shall not be commanded
back without the approbation and consent as aforesaid, but
the orders for sending out and commanding in such forces,
after the approbation and consent as aforesaid, shall be
signed with the governor's hand only.

No works or fortifications shall be made in or about the
garrison without the consent or approbation as aforesaid.

The managing or carrying on of any design or service,
shall be left wholly to the governor, or commander-in-chief
whom he shall appoint, after it is agreed and consented to
as aforesaid. Except the persons above mentioned, or the
major part of them, shall march into the field with them,
and then he is to be regulated in the prosecution of any
service according to their votes and direction.

That in all other things appertaining to the charge and duty of the governor, the governor shall be left to act singly by himself, according to the authority of Parliament and his commission.

Letters to be written from the committee of both kingdoms to the several commanders within the garrison, declaring to them that they have given instructions for the carrying on the affairs of that garrison, which they doubt not will be carefully observed by the governor and those whom they shall concern, and therefore to require them to be obedient from time to time, to such orders as they shall receive from the houses in pursuance of the said instructions.

The same course above mentioned, for the settling the differences between the governor and some of the committee and officers of the garrison, is also to be held (*mutatis mutandis*), for the settling the differences between Colonel Thornhagh and some of the committee and the officers of the horse.

It is further thought fit that the public table, formerly kept in the castle for the committee and governor, be still continued for them in the same place, until some other course be settled, which is now in consideration.

That the committee of Nottingham be desired to take care of providing monies, that the garrison may not suffer prejudice for want of their pay."

The malcontents, however, were still dissatisfied, and sent up fresh complaints (January 1645), so that the governor was again summoned to London, and, after some deliberation, a second report was drawn up by the sub-committee, reiterating the instructions formerly given (January 27, 1645).—Memoirs, vol. ii. pp. 62–67.

Second Report.

"*January* 27, 1644.—Report of the sub-committee con‑cerning the business of Nottingham.

That the order and instructions hereafter mentioned were made by the committee of both kingdoms, the 11th day of November, for the composing the differences between the governor of Nottingham and some of the gentlemen of the committee there, which the committee of both kingdoms found to be at a very great height.

That the governor with divers of the gentlemen of the committee of Nottingham, in pursuance of the said order and instructions, did make their repair to Nottingham, and demeaned themselves as was directed by the said instructions.

That others of the gentlemen of the committee of Not‑tingham, instead of observing the said order and instruc‑tions, made their way to London with complaints against the governor and others, and with desires that an order and instructions might be framed according to propositions offered by them, or else the whole matter to be reported to the House.

It is the opinion of the sub-committee that the whole matter be reported to the House with the last petition of those gentlemen, and the opinion of the House desired for the settling those matters.

That the said orders formerly made be observed till the House do otherwise order."

It was further ordered by the committee of both kingdoms on February 14th, "that the business of Nottingham, with the opinion of this committee concerning it, may be reported to the House." This, however, as we are told in the Memoirs, vol. ii. p. 68, Mr. Millington contrived to delay for nearly three months. During this period of delay Colonel Hutchinson remained in London. At length the capture of the bridge and fort obliged the colonel to take the decisive step mentioned in the Memoirs, vol. ii. p. 72, and the House, after hearing his relation, passed an order which was practically a judgment in his favour. The Journals of the House, of Commons for April 22, 1645, contain the following entry :—

"Colonel Hutchinson, governor of Nottingham, was called in ; and acquainted the House, that the enemy from the garrison of Newark and the garrisons round abouts, drew out to the number of 1600 on sabbath-day last; and have possessed themselves of the fort at the bridge, and have put the town into great danger.

Ordered, that the governor of Nottingham be forthwith sent down with order, that the instructions made by the committee of both kingdoms, for the present, may be pursued, and that a letter be written to the committee resident there, to this effect, and to acquaint them, that, upon their last petition, the House had taken the whole matter into consideration. Mr. Knightley and Mr. Millington are appointed to prepare this letter for Mr. Speaker to sign. And Mr. Millington is to apply himself to further a reconcilement between the governor and the committee, and a settlement of matters for the present for the safety of the place. And to that end it is ordered, that the governor and those of the committee that are here, do come to the committee of both kingdoms this afternoon, to whom it is referred to make a reconcilement, and to persuade a compliance in the committee of Nottingham to the instructions formerly made by the committee of both kingdoms ; and it is left to the committee of both kingdoms, if they shall find that committee to comply, to send them down also."

II.

Colonel Hutchinson's Orders to the Garrison at Nottingham.

Amongst the Shelton MSS. in the Nottingham Free Library is the following series of orders for the proper management of the garrison, which was communicated to "Notes and Queries" for January 29, 1876, by Mr. J. P. Briscoe.

"Mr. Mayor and the governor do require all persons whatsoever within this garrison, (for the better ordering and governing of the same), to take notice of their orders here following, as they will answer the contrary :—

1. If anyone shall be found idly standing or walking in the street in sermon time, or playing at any games upon the sabbath or fast-day, he shall pay half-a-crown, or suffer imprisonment till he pay the same.

2. If anyone shall be found drinking in any tavern, inn or alehouse, on the sabbath or fast-day, he shall pay one shilling, or suffer imprisonment till he pay the same ; and the master of that house shall pay for every person so taken in at one shilling, and if he offend the second time, he shall be disenabled for selling wine, ale, or beer any more.

3. If any tavern, inn, or alehouse soever, shall sell any wine, ale, or beer, out of their houses upon the sabbath or fast-day, (except to any one who is sick), for the first offence he shall pay ten pence (?), for the second one shilling, and for the third be disenabled for selling any wine, ale, or beer any more.

4. If any tradesman shall carry home any work to any of their customers on the sabbath-day, they shall forfeit their work, and suffer a week's imprisonment.

5. If anyone shall keep open any shop, or buy or sell any

commodities whatsoever, on the sabbath or fast-day, the buyer shall pay one shilling, and the seller one shilling, and suffer imprisonment till he pay the same, (unless it be upon an extraordinary occasion for one that is sick).

6. If any one shall swear, he shall pay threepence for every oath, or suffer imprisonment till he pay the same.

7. If any one shall be drunk, he shall pay five shillings, or suffer imprisonment till he pay the same : and the master of the house where he was made drunk shall pay one shilling, and likewise suffer imprisonment till he pay the same.

8. If any one shall be found tippling, or drinking in any tavern, inn, or alehouse after the hour of nine of the clock at night, when the tattoo ("taptoo") beats, he shall pay half-a-crown ; and the house for the first time shall pay half-a-crown for every man so found, and the second time five shillings, and for the third time be disenabled for selling wine, ale, or beer any more.

9. If any soldier shall be found drinking in their quarters after nine of the clock at night, when the tattoo hath beaten, they shall pay two shillings, or suffer twenty-four hours' imprisonment with bread and water.

10. If any tavern, inn, or alehouse soever shall sell any wine, ale, or beer, (except upon an extraordinary occasion to one that is sick), after the tattoo hath beaten, until the reveille ("revelly") hath beaten the next morning, he shall pay one shilling or suffer imprisonment till he pay the same, and he who fetches the drink after the aforesaid hour, shall pay half-a-crown, or suffer imprisonment till he pay the same.

Whosoever shall give information of any person who shall commit any of these offences, he shall have half the penalties set upon them for his reward,

WILL. NIX, *Mayor.*
JOHN HUTCHINSON."

"On the back of the sheet on which the above is written," says Mr. Briscoe, "there is a note giving instructions for a corporal to 'see to the executing these orders to-day,' and dated Sabbath, December (erasure) 1644."—"Notes and Queries," 5th series, vol. v. p. 84.

III.

On the treatment of prisoners, &c.

"Wednesday, Shelford men came and thought to have driven the horses that were turned out to grass, but the alarum being timely given, Lieutenant Chadwick went out with a party and took twenty of them, and killed some four or five without any loss on our side.

Saturday, a boy was taken gazing in the town, and brought up upon suspicion of being a spy, and being burnt with match confessed that he came from Newark, and brought two letters to the town, and delivered them to a man in the town who formerly had been a corporal at Wiverton, and was sent hither to list himself as a soldier, that he might have the more opportunity to do mischief here; he said he knew the man (but knew not his name), and the place where he lived, and that at four o'clock of the afternoon he should have had an answer of the letters; he owned the man among forty others, but the fellow, who was one Griffith, a soldier in the major's company, utterly denied that he knew, or had ever seen the boy, or received any letters from him; which yet the boy with so many circumstances so constantly affirmed, that the man was first tortured with match between his fingers, and then with a rope round his head; then he confessed that he had had letters twice from the boy, and had delivered them one Brinsly, who was a butcher in this town, of a lewd life and conversation and most malignant to this cause, and had from the beginning been a trooper under Sir Richard Biron at Newark, but came in before the first of March, and took the Covenant, and so was received into the town, but the governor had ever held him in such distrust that when there was any danger he still clapped him in close prison. He was upon this tortured, but would confess nothing, and though many other circumstances were proved against him, yet would he not be persuaded to confess anything.

Tuesday there was a day of rejoicing for the success of the fight at York, and the boy, being that day carelessly looked to, being kept only in the court of guard in the castle, got away when the soldiers marched out of the castle to church."

The use of torture to extract information from spies or prisoners was unfortunately by no means uncommon. Vicars gives an account of its employment by Col. Hutchinson in another case, viz., when the cavaliers attempted to seize Nottingham Bridge. According to him, when some of them were seized, and their disguise discovered, "these cozening cormorants were further examined, but were very unwilling to confess the plot for all this, only they said they were sent as spies from Newark, but the prudent governor seriously examining the business, and being too old a bird to be caught or cozened with such chaff, took match and caused their fingers to be tied therewith, and told them what they must trust to, except they would speedily discover the plot." Hereupon the prisoners confessed (Vicars, "God's Ark," p. 164). In the fragment of Col. Hutchinson's letter concerning the plot, Vol. I., Appendix XIX., it is simply stated that he had received notice of the attempt beforehand, so the account given by Vicars is probably inaccurate, but it is to be observed that Vicars thoroughly approves the use of torture.

The Note-Book also supplies an instance of the punishment of a renegade :—

"When the Nottingham horse were in the vale of Belvoir, Captain Palmer's troop took one Captain Deane, who had formerly received a commission from the Earl of Essex to raise a troop of horse in Nottinghamshire, and endeavoured to do it, but before he had gotten any men went away with some six case of pistols to the enemy, and there continued about Belvoir and Wiverton till at length Captain Palmer's men met with him, and brought him prisoner to Nottingham. This and some other trials upon life being to be determined, the governor would not call a council of war upon them till he had a special commission from my lord-general, which he writ to him for, and my lord sent it to him, and after it was come a council was called, where he, being brought before them and examined, confessed his fault and desired mercy of the council, and was condemned to be shot to death four months after, this respite of time being all the favour they would afford him."

IV.

Two Letters from Colonel Hutchinson to Lord Fairfax in May 1645.

At the time when these letters were written the New Model under the command of Sir Thomas Fairfax had just commenced the investment of Oxford (May 22, 1645). The king had left Oxford on the 7th of May with the intention of relieving Chester. He found the siege raised, and was on the 23d and 24th of May in Staffordshire meditating an attack on Leicester. Cromwell, who in company with Browne had been detached to observe the king's movements, and had proceeded as far as Warwick, was then recalled to take part in the siege of Oxford.

(1.)

For the right honourable Lord Fairfax, commander-in-chief of the northern forces.

" MY LORD,—I have received this letter from Lieutenant-general Cromwell this day. I do not know of what concernment it may be, and therefore I despatch it with such haste to your lordship that I have not leisure at present to give you an account of some passages in this garrison as I ought to do. I hope I shall have leisure shortly, either to wait on your lordship myself, or at least fully to acquaint you how things are here with us. In the meantime I beseech you be pleased to pardon the haste of your most faithful and humble servant,

JOHN HUTCHINSON.

NOTTINGHAM, *May 23d,* 1645.

Colonel Rossiter is not joined with us, and hath this day sent us word, that he hath given your lordship a reason for it, which your lordship is well satisfied in.

Newark do not stir, but be ready prepared with their dragoons."

(2.)

" May it please your Lordship,—I have intelligence at this instant that the enemy at Newark are drawing out this night with all their horse and dragoons, whether to the north or to the king is uncertain, and another messenger tells me they are now drawn out and are marching this way. Derby and Lincoln horse are not yet united with those of this garrison, which are in such ill ease to march for want of pay, that they will rather mutiny than obey commands. Colonel Vermuden, I hear, is upon his march northward at Elvaston, in Derbyshire, within nine miles of

this garrison. I have given him notice hereof, and have no
more to your lordship but that I am, my lord, your lordship's humble servant, JOHN HUTCHINSON.

I have intelligence even now, by a drummer of mine from
Newark, that they are designed for Pontefract."

NOTTINGHAM, 24*th May* 1645, at
  one of the clock, afternoon

Colonel Hutchinson was mistaken as to the intentions of
the Newark troops, for Sir Richard Willis, with 1200 horse,
joined the king on May 28th, and took part in the capture
of Leicester on the 30th (Symonds's Diary, p. 179). The
horse of Derbyshire, Lincolnshire, and Nottinghamshire,
the Lincolnshire troops being commanded by Colonel
Rossiter, had been ordered to unite and join with the
advancing Scotch army. Colonel Vermuden, with 2500
horse and dragoons, part of the forces lately commanded by Cromwell, was detached for the same purpose,
by order of the committee of both kingdoms dated May 15.
By the same letter Cromwell was recalled to take part in
the siege of Oxford (Rushworth, vi. 33). These two letters
of Colonel Hutchinson's are from the Fairfax Correspondence,
" Memorials of the Civil War," vol. i. pp. 221, 222.

V.

*Two Letters relating to Skirmishes near Nottingham, in
the Autumn of 1645.*

To my honoured friend, Gilbert Millington, Esq.

" SIR,—I know you will be glad to hear in what conditions we are in this place. The king quarters at this presen

about Welbeck and Worksop Manor, where he hath not above fifteen hundred horse, and those so tired and ill armed, that he is able to do little service with them. During their time of quartering on the south side Trent near us (which hath been for the space of eight days or thereabouts), we from hence continually alarmed them, and found them of so daunted and dejected spirits, that twenty of our men charged fifty of them in a town where the queen's regiment is quartered, and killed and took thirty of them, and if they had had more strength, might have brought away many more ; they took and brought away with them thirty horse with some good luggage ; another time since that, forty of ours charged one hundred and twenty of them at Langar, routed them, killed near twenty, took fourteen, one whereof is a major who is sore wounded. I cannot certainly acquaint you what the king intends : the reports are some for the relief of Skipton, others Chester, and some others say that Colonel Rossiter and we so visited their quarters, that they make trial of other for more security. I have made some more discoveries of other countrymen, who were engaged in the betraying of the Trent Bridges ; and they likewise testify that Sir Gervase Clifton was engaged in the plot against the castle, Kirke, the chief actor, is condemned by a council of war to be hanged on Saturday next ; I know, sir, tedious letters are a trouble to you, than which I shall rather choose to break off abruptly, remaining, sir, your obliged friend and humble servant,

JOHN HUTCHINSON."

NOTTINGHAM, *October* 15, 1645.

For the Honourable Colonel Thornhagh, at the King's Head, in the Strand, these, with my humble service.

" SIR,—Since your departure hence, parties have been sent out every night, but the enemy have drawn into their garrisons continually, that nothing could be attempted; only on Friday morning last, Corporal Cross, who is one of my corporals, with twenty horse of Captain Pendock's and mine did fall into Bridgeford super Mount, whither the queen's regiment were newly come and all mounted, they charged through them, routed the whole regiment, killed eight besides what were wounded, and brought off sixteen prisoners, twenty-eight horse, without loss of one man. And on Saturday following, my lieutenant, with forty-two men going to secure the market, fell into Langar, where the Earl of Northampton's regiment were drawing out to a rendezvous, being about two hundred horse; thirty of our men charged about eighty of them, and routed them, and falling into the town with them, they killed between twenty and thirty, and a captain: they took a major, nine others, and twenty-seven horse, without loss of one man. I desire that God may have the praise of all, for He is worthy. On Sunday, Captain Pendock and my lieutenant, with a hundred and fifty horse, went to Ekering to gain intelligence, and the king quartered at Tuxford, Laxton, and Lymonton with his whole army, but they wanted men to fall upon any quarters. I am just now sending a small party to Ekering.

Since I began this letter, I hear that the king quarters this night about Welbeck and Worksop, and (as report gives it) he is for the north. Sir, be pleased to procure some arms, if it be possible, and some money, for the country is impoverished, and the soldiers in great want. Sir, I have no more but to assure you, that I am, sir, your most humble servant, CHARLES WHITE.

NOTTINGHAM, *October* 13th,
about 8 at night.

Sir, I beseech you present my service to Master Millington, and excuse my not writing to him."

These two letters are printed in a pamphlet entitled " Several Letters from Colonel-general Poyntz, Lieutenant-general Cromwell, Colonel Hutchinson, and Colonel White, of the late great victory near Sherborne in the north, with some other happy successes in the west." The original of Colonel Hutchinson's letter is amongst the papers of the House of Lords, and is printed in an abridged form, in the Sixth Report of the Historical MSS. Commission, Appendix, p. 80.

The king and his forces were about Nottingham from August 15th to 22d, 1645, and from October 4th to November 3d (*vide* Iter Carolinum, and the Diary of Richard Symonds, published by the Camden Society). The king formed the plan of marching north to join Montrose, but during his march received at Welbeck (October 13) the news that Montrose had retired further north, and that the Scotch army lay between Northallerton and Newcastle. On this the king retired again to Newark, and detached Lord Digby with fifteen hundred horse to join Montrose. Digby was defeated at Sherborne on the 15th of October, and the king, finding himself in danger of being blockaded in Newark by Colonel Poyntz and Colonel Rossiter, returned to Oxford, which he reached on the 5th of November (Clarendon, ix. 122, 132).

VI.

The Capture of Shelford and other Garrisons.

Letter from Col. Poyntz to Speaker of the House of Lords.

" MY LORD,—I am to render your honour this brief account of what it pleased God to do for us in the late storming of Shelford House. On Saturday, having sent a strong party of horse and dragoons to attend the King's motion in case he seeks to break away from Newark, I advanced towards Shelford, where Colonel Rossiter joining with me, I presently clapped down before it, and took divers of their men prisoners, who were got into the church. This day, being prepared for a storm, I summoned the House, whereunto the young governor returned me a very peremptory answer ; whereupon we fell on with much resolution on all sides, and were entertained for half an hour with like courage ; but at length they were forced to leave that hot service. They were in all near two hundred, most of the queen's regiment being there. About forty of them escaped with their lives and are brought prisoners into this town ; the rest put to the sword. The Governor, being dangerously shot and wounded, was stripped for dead ; but some officers took pity upon the young gentleman, and got him off; peradventure it may recover him. The London brigade behaved themselves very faithfully in this service ; the rest wanted no courage. To God be the praise. Our next design is against Werton House ; and I hope it will be the next news, that it is reduced. However, I shall use my faithful endeavours therein ; and in all other respects continue, my lord, your obedient and faithful servant till death, SYDENHAM POYNTZ."

BINGHAM, *November* 3, 1645.

—Journals of the House of Lords, Nov. 6th, 1645.

A Letter from Col. Sandys on the Storming of Shelford.

"SIR,—I suppose you have a particular relation of this day's service, but thus much from your friend : we assaulted Shelford House this day about four of the clock; it was defended gallantly, and disputed half an hour at sword's point after we got to the top of the works, but our men growing faint, I dismounted, and being assisted by some troopers that dismounted with me, stormed, and was one of the first that entered in. We killed about 140, and gave quarter to about 30. The governor, son to the Earl of Chesterfield, received many wounds, and I believe some mortal, but I coming in gave him a longer time to repent, for he is not likely to live. We are to-morrow for Worton. I trust God will go along with us. The king is yet in Newark and cannot probably escape, the two princes with their party about Belvoir, and keep guards against Newark, and do hostile acts on the king's party. Your servant,

RICHARD SANDYS."

November 3, 9 at night.

> —From a pamphlet entitled : " A full relation of the desperate charge of the malignants for the betraying of Monmouth, also how Lieut.-Col. Kyrle fell into the enemy's quarters near Hereford,— likewise a copy of Col. Sandys' letter of the manner of taking Shelford House." 4to, 1646.

The fall of the other little garrisons of the royalists in Nottinghamshire may be briefly summarised. According to Vicars, news arrived about the 6th of November that the garrison of Worton House and Wiverton House were both so afraid of "Shelford quarter," that they surrendered directly Poyntz came before them. Welbeck followed their example, it being agreed that Tickhill Castle and Welbeck should both be slighted. (Vicars, "Burning Bush," p. 316.) Wiverton was Lord Chaworth's house, the other probably Whatton, which belonged to the Earl of Chesterfield.

VII.

Plot to betray Nottingham Castle.

The *Moderate Intelligencer*, No. 17, gives an account of the plot, probably based on the letter of Poulton's which was read in the House on the 13th of June :—

"The first thing that offers itself unto view is the long intended and late acted design upon Nottingham Castle, in brief thus :—The royal party in that country taking advantage of some discontents lying upon the governor, Captain Poulton, occasioned by some, no friends, violent solicitations to the army to eject him, which in part was effected, though soon after recalled. In steps Gilbert Biron, (upon premedi-. tated advice of a royal committee met for this purpose), and aggravates the endeavours of that discourtesy to the highest of incivilities, and at a second meeting makes an overture of a considerable gratuity in hand ; with the annuity of £300 to be settled upon him and heirs for ever ; and to this, the honour of knighthood, and now was the time to make a revenge and to regain the favour of his Majesty. The governor's modesty, or rather integrity, admits at present but of a dubious response, and defers his further resolution herein to second thoughts. The gentleman desired no delay, for that it was in order to a further design of his Majesty, which was within six weeks to be put into execution. The governor imparting all this discourse to a member of the House then resident there, desires his advice to lay the bait, well knowing the greediness of the creature would soon gorge it ; upon debate their result was to carry the thing modestly, and to give him some encouragement of possibility of an assent, that thereby the secret of the grand design of his Majesty might be discovered with the chief actors thereof in that county. The governor now comes to an inclining condition, and the royal friend is free in opening the secrets of the design, which was that Kent, Surrey, Essex and that association, should, upon the House's denial of their petition, rise as one man, in order to which a subscription went through the kingdom of such as would appear herein ; the governor giving notice hereof to Derby House, and promising to betray the castle on such a night to the gentleman, who was to bring fifty men to enter, casts in the bait, which the cormorants coming to take are caught in a net, and lie at mercy to a party of horse and foot, which surprised them, and are now imprisoned in Nottingham gaol."

The member of the House of Commons referred to was most likely Colonel Hutchinson. This account, however, differs considerably from that in the Memoirs, which was written much later. The editor of the *Moderate Intelligencer* (if the same as the editor of *The Moderate, impartially communicating martial affairs to the kingdom of England*) was Gilbert Mabbot, whom "Mercurius Elencticus" (No. 44) terms "the cobbler's son of Nottingham." If this conjecture is correct it would account for the excellence of his intelligence from Nottingham.

Another attempt against Nottingham Castle is described under the title of " A dangerous fight near Newark between the Parliament's forces and the Scotch cavaliers, and how they would have surprised Newark and Nottingham Castle."

VIII.

The Fight in Willoughby Field, July 5th, 1648.

As this fight was of considerable importance, and has hardly received sufficient attention from later historians of the second civil war, I have thought right to give an extract from a pamphlet on it. It contains interesting details concerning many persons mentioned in these Memoirs.

> "An impartial and true relation of the great victory obtained, through the blessing of God, after a very sharp dispute, by the conjoined forces of Lincoln, Nottingham, Leicester, Derby, and Rutland, under the command of Colonel Edward Rossiter."

"On Friday the 30th of June, about 400 horse from Pomfret Castle, most of them gentlemen of several counties and reformado officers, and 200 foot, ferried over Trent, and made incursion into Lincolnshire, marching forthwith to the city of Lincoln ; where, after they had by warrant under the. hand of Sir Philip Monckton, their general, released all the prisoners in the Castle for debt, murther, felony, and other crimes, who took up arms presently with them, they went to the Bishop's Palace, wherein lay several arms and some monies of the country's : which place Captain Bee, a woollen draper of that city, with 30 men had taken possession of and defended for three hours, until the Cavaliers had fired one part of the house. In which Captain Bee resolved, and so told them, he would be consumed, unless he might surrender upon conditions propounded by him, amongst which the protection of his person and estate, the which they agreed to ; no sooner was the palace delivered, but all conditions broke, the captain seized and carried away prisoner until released in the field at the following fight, all his wares and goods put in carts, with which and the arms and money found in the palace, together with the plunder and persons of other honest men of the town, they marched on Saturday night to Gainsborough, twelve miles off. This alarum coming that Friday night to Belvoir Castle to Col. Rossiter, who was there upon some occasions of the country, he forthwith gave the alarum to Northampton, Leicester, Nottingham, Derby, and Rutland, and desired them to spare what horse they could, to join with a troop of horse lately raised by him, by authority of Parliament, for the security of that county ; and he would therewith endeavour to drive the enemy out of the country again. The which forces being conjoined on Sabbath evening to the number of 550, all of them newly raised men, and then understanding by a letter, received from Sir Henry Cholmley, that 600 Yorkshire horse with some dragoons were on the north side Trent about Gainsborough, who would interrupt their retreating over Trent to Pomfret again, or fight with them if they came over, Col. Rossiter marched on Monday morning towards Gainsborough. In the midway thither, there met and joined with him a troop of horse from Lynn, which the General had put under the command of Capt. Taylor, who together refreshed that night in and about Waddington fields, about three miles south of Lincoln. On Tuesday morning by three o'clock they marched through Lincoln towards Gainsborough, and understanding by a Lincoln man, who had been taken away prisoner by the Cavaliers and escaped that night, that the enemy were all drawn off from Gainsborough at ten of the clock on Monday evening, and were marched towards Newark, Col. Rossiter forthwith pursued eighteen miles that night, and refreshed his horse four or five hours in the night in a meadow, a mile from Newark, where he received intelligence that the enemy quartered about Bingham six miles before him. To this place came in to Rossiter's further assistance about 150 horse, the one half from Derby and Rutland, the other half were gentlemen and freeholders of Lincoln and Leicestershire, who voluntarily would adventure their lives for their country's freedom. On Wednesday morning Col. Rossiter commanded out a forlorn hope, 150 of the ablest horse under the command of Captain Champion of Nottinghamshire, to pursue at a fast rate, and so by falling on the enemy's rear to enforce them to a stand or halt, till he with the body of horse could come up to them. They after seven miles' advance overtook the rear of them, whom skirmishing with, they made their body of horse and foot, consisting of 700 or 800 at least, to draw up in a large bean-field belonging to Willoughby, seven miles from Nottingham, Of which Rossiter being informed from the commander of the forlorn, by marching at a full trot, having no dragoons on foot with him, within a short time brought his horse into the field, himself commanding the right wing wherewith he resolved to charge. But observing that the enemy's strength were placed in their body, consisting of a party of foot winged with horse, and those horse flanked with musketeers, and that with them the men of best quality, as appeared by their outward garbs seemed to be mounted, he resolved to charge the battle; assigning his right wing to be commanded by Col. White, and the left by Col. Hacker, placing two reserves of horse in the rear.

Being suddenly thus ordered, the enemy's word Jesus and Rossiter's Fairfax, he advanced to the charge, who was received with much resolution. The bodies and reserves through eagerness close in together; whereby the encounter proved very sharp, both sides falling presently to sword's point, and neither party giving ground for some space, till by the fierceness of each party both were put into disorder, being so intermixed, doing execution each on other; the dispute continued a while doubtful, at last it pleased God to give a full and absolute victory to Rossiter's forces, as may appear by the quality and number of prisoners taken, all their colours, arms, and carriages. About 200 that were best horsed, whereof divers Papists, got off in small parties, several of them wounded; but at least one hundred were that night and next morning taken in their flight by Leicester, Belvoir, Burleigh, and other honest countrymen, amongst whom was Sir Philip Monckton, their general, disarmed and brought into Nottingham by Mr. Boyer, a high constable of that county, who deservedly now wears his sword.

In the first charge Colonel Rossiter lost his head-piece, received a shot through the right thigh, and some other painful wounds with a musket bullet, notwithstanding which he kept the field fighting till he saw the battle wholly won, not discovering his wounding to any person for fear it might prove a discourage to the soldiers ; after which being ready to fall through loss of blood, he rode to Nottingham where he lieth capable of recovery, through the blessing of God upon the means used for that end.

In this service Colonel Hacker, commander of the Leicester horse, who is wounded, and Colonel White, commander of the Nottingham horse, having only his horse cut, merited much honour for their expressed valour."

The account, after mentioning the loss of Rossiter's force, 30 men slain, a cornet in Rossiter's troop killed, and Captain Greenwood, commander of the Derby troop, dangerously wounded, concludes thus:—

"By several letters taken in their general officer's pockets, it appears that men of high and low degree in several counties, before unsuspected, are deeply engaged in promoting and contributing towards a general rising in many parts ; some of the prisoners affirm, that their army resolved to have marched southward through Leicestershire and Northamptonshire, in whose march they doubted not but to have increased to many thousands, and to have joined with others rising about London, and to have raised Colchester siege."

Then follows a list of some 50 gentlemen taken prisoners, including Gilbert Biron, the major-general of the royalist army, and the statement that 500 of the common men were taken and about 100 slain. One item in the list of trophies is, "ten colours of horse and foot, whereof the greatest part in cloak-bags not delivered out."

IX.

The capture of Sir Marmaduke Langdale.

A letter from Sir Marmaduke Langdale, given in the Fair-fax Correspondence ("Memorials of the Civil War," vol. ii. p. 60), gives an account of his flight after Preston. "Sir," he begins, "this will give you an account of my employment, which is now ended, being a prisoner in Nottingham Castle, where I have civil usage." During the first portion of his flight he was accompanied by Lord Callendar and many others, but finally parted company. "I resolved to sever and shift every man for himself; but capitulate I could not with' a safe conscience. . . . I marched towards Nottingham where those few I had took several ways, and I got that night over Trent and came to a house six miles from Nottingham, where myself, Colonel Owen, Lieutenant-colonel Gallard, and Major Constable thought to have shrouded ourselves, and so made no resistance, but were discovered, and so are in Nottingham Castle." The letter is dated August 26, 1648.

A letter from Captain Poulton to Mr. William Pierrepont (Tanner MSS., lvii. 227) completes the story.

"Sir,—This day intelligence being given to me by a prisoner which was taken and brought to me, that Sir Marmaduke Langdale with some nine more were past over the Trent and intended southward, and immediately afterwards certain information being brought to me by a countryman, that there was a party at a place called the Lodge in the Oulds, pretending themselves to be Lieutenant-general Cromwell his men, which I knew could not be so, I speedily got what horse I could possible together, which was about twelve,

and gave orders for a party of foot to follow me. With
those horse I went to the said place and found Major
Widmerpoole and two men in the yard with the pretended
party of Lord Cromwell his men, which after proved Sir
Marmaduke Langdale, Colonel Owen, Colonel Constable,
one other gentleman and five servants, who were then ready
and absolutely intended had not we appeared, either to
have slain Major Widmerpoole with his two men, or taken
them some miles and then turned them up (?). Sir, I have
not only a great charge of the castle, but also of many considerable prisoners, having both Langhorn and his party,
Langdale and his, and some which was in the plot about
the castle, all prisoners remaining in it. My humble desire
is that you could be pleased to get an addition of foot for
this place and maintenance for them, that I may be enabled
to render an account of so great a charge committed to me.
I will not be uncivil to trouble you with many lines, but
shall humbly refer you to the bearer for further news. No
more at present from, Sir, your honour's most humble
servant,

T. POULTON.

NOTTINGHAM CASTLE, *August* 23, 1648.

P.S.—Sir, Colonel Hutchinson was pleased to go along
with us to the taking of Sir Marmaduke Langdale and the
rest."

" Mercurius Pragmaticus " (August 22–29) adds the following detail. Sir Marmaduke Langdale " being in an alehouse
and suspected by some saints of the town, they have to examine him and the gentlemen with him who they were ; they
answered, they were of the army ; being asked under whom,
they said Lord Cromwell ; with which answers they went
away satisfied. But meeting with three or four of their
servants without, and questioning them likewise, they

answered, those gentlemen within were their masters, and that they were under Lambert : so that this difference in the account wrought a jealousy."

A letter from the committee to Mr. Pierrepont gives a few further details (Tanner MSS., lvii. 233).

" HONOURABLE SIR,—We have sent up this gentleman, Captain-lieutenant Worthington, a known man for his constant and good affection to the Parliament, to attend you now to present this good news, of Sir Marmaduke Langdale being taken prisoner, with Colonel Owen, Lieutenant-colonel Gallard, Major Constable, Lieutenant Bellomye, and five more by Major Widmerpoole, a gentleman of constant affection and fidelity to the Parliament, and who hath also done much service in their cause. He had in the apprehension of the said prisoners to his assistance his own servant and the captain-lieutenant only. We conceive it will be grateful to the honourable House to be acquainted with this news, which we beseech you impart to them. We have no more to present to you but the humble service of your faithful servants,

FRANCIS PIERREPONT.
W. DRURY, *Mayor.*
NICHOLAS CHARLTON.
WILLIAM NIX."

NOTTINGHAM, *August* 24, 1648.

The committee at the same time sent up Major Widmerpoole to deliver the papers found on Langdale and represent the grievances of the county. These two letters were read in the House of Commons on August 26th, and Mr. Worthington received a reward of fifty pounds, while it was ordered that Widmerpoole should be indemnified for his losses out of the Earl of Newcastle's estates.

X.

> #### *Colonel Hutchinson to the Speaker.*

"On Thursday the twelfth instant at ten of the clock at night, I received two letters from you, directed to me as sheriff of Nottinghamshire—the one commanding me to publish the Parliament's declarations, which I have done : the other, to deliver your letters to the several members who serve for the county, which I have likewise performed, and received their answers. Mr. Pigott, who hath been of late in some distemper of his health, resolves with all speed, if God enable him, to give his attendance. Mr. Nevill, who at the present hath upon him a fit of the stone, so soon as he is able to ride, will do the same : and Mr. Millington is fitting himself with what speed his very urgent occasions will give him leave to make. As for myself, it hath pleased God to visit my whole family with great sickness, and of late my wife, watching with whom I have brought a distemper upon myself, which hath forced me into a course of physic, which I will break presently off, and, so soon as I am able to endure the air, which I hope will be within ten days, shall begin my journey, in order to my attendance upon my duty in the parliament ; blessing God for his great goodness, in restoring them to a freedom of sitting again, and praying that the results of their counsels may be as much to the glory of God, and good of this nation, as their reassembling gives joyful hopes thereof to, Sir, your most faithful and most humble servant,

JOHN HUTCHINSON."

OWTHORPE, IN NOTTINGHAMSHIRE,
   May the 14th, 1659.

—Tanner MSS. Bodleian, vol. li. p. 57.

In spite of this letter, Colonel Hutchinson did not appear in the House of Commons till five weeks later, probably detained by the illness mentioned in the letter. On June 20th it was ordered that Colonel Hutchinson should be dispensed with, as to his attendance on the office of sheriff in the county of Nottingham, and required to attend the service of the House. On the 22d of June he was present, and between that date and the 20th of August was appointed to serve on eight committees. On July 4th, for instance, he was nominated one of the members of the committee to inquire into "what is due for mourning for the late Lord-general Cromwell, and how the same may be paid without prejudice or charge to the Commonwealth."

After August 20th he seems to have ceased attending, and at a call of the House on September 30, he is fined twenty pounds for being absent.—Commons' Journals, vol. vii.

XI.

Letter from the Mayor and town of Nottingham to the Speaker.

" RIGHT HONOURABLE,—This morning the Lord Biron with Colonel Charles White, and divers other persons whose names are not yet discovered, rendezvoused themselves in the forest of Sherwood, near Sansom Wood, six miles distant from this town, where there appeared between sixty and eighty persons, some with swords and pistols, and other weapons, and from thence, intended to have seized on Captain Edward Cludd, and the militia troop under his command ; but divers of the prisoners taken by the inhabitants of our town of Nottingham, upon their examination taken before us, have confessed that they had intelligence that the country troop was gone to Newark, to join with two troops that came thither the last night, belonging to the army of this Commonwealth; and that thereupon the said Lord Biron and his company, receiving further intelligence that Captain Cludd and his soldiers were ready to engage to fight, they hasted in a disorderly and confused manner through our town of Nottingham, about eight o'clock this morning, where they met with Robert Pierpoint, Esq., son and heir of Francis Pierpoint, Esq., with six or eight of his men well armed, who are gone with the said Lord Biron and the rest of his company towards Leicestershire, and Captain Cludd in their pursuit, who hath taken one red colours of a troop, hath killed one of the enemy, and sorely wounded the cornet that carried the colours, and many prisoners are found in our town, who, as they are found, are secured in our common gaol; their pretence of raising arms was for a free parliament and religion. The prisoners taken are countrymen, that were engaged but the last night, and are not able to give any particular account of their intentions or actions.

Captain Lloyd, with a party of horse under his command, is joined with Captain Cludd in further pursuit of the enemy, who it is hoped will take divers of them.

This we have presumed to signify to your honours, that it may appear unto the nation how merciful and gracious the Lord hath been unto us in the discovery of this rising, which He also hath been pleased to disperse and bring to naught, before that they had any time to put the men they had raised in any command. Your honour may expect to hear a more full account from Captain Cludd at his return from the chase of the enemy. So as in duty we are bound, we subscribe ourselves, your honour's servants,

JOHN TILLINGHAM, *Mayor.*
W. DRURY, *Alderman.*"

NOTTINGHAM, 12*th August.*

The original of this letter is in the Tanner MSS., vol. li.
p. 144. It is printed in "Mercurius Politicus," No. 583, ·
August 11–18, 1659. It was read in the House of Commons
on August 15, 1659 (*vide* Com. Jour. vii. 758). The further
history of this insurrection may be gathered from Nos. 584
and 585 of "Mercurius Politicus." Some of the fugitives from
Nottingham joined the Earl of Stamford at his house near
Leicester, others made their way to Derby. Colonel White
and some few followers arrived at Derby about eleven
o'clock on the twelfth, whilst the militia commissioners were
busy there in raising and settling the militia, and openly
proclaimed Sir George Booth's declaration. The townsmen
shut their shops and shouted, some for "a king," others for a
free parliament. They even seized some of the militia
horses, and called on Colonel Saunders, the commander of
the militia, to put himself at their head. But, though
deserted by some of his officers, and threatened by the mob,
Saunders struggled to appease the tumult, and even arrested
Colonel White, though he could not keep him a prisoner.
In the end Saunders had to leave the town, but on the
following day he was joined by a detachment of Lambert's troops, and on the 14th, with these forces and the
Leicestershire and Nottinghamshire horse, the rising was
finally suppressed, and that without fighting ("Mercurius
Politicus," No. 584). Colonel White, who escaped, was
arrested a few days later: his confession was presented to
the Council of State on September 9th, and, with his examination, submitted to the House of Commons on the
24th September.' He was imprisoned until February 25,
1660.

XII.

Petition of Colonel Hutchinson to the House of Commons,
June 1660.

The Journal of the House of Commons records, under date June 5, 1660 :—

" Mr. Speaker communicates a letter, dated the 5th of June, 1660, directed to himself, and signed by Col. John Hutchinson, who was one of those who sat in judgment upon the late king's Majesty when sentence of death was pronounced against him, which was read.

" Resolved—That Colonel John Hutchinson be at liberty on his own parole to be given to Mr. Speaker."

The letter is as follows :—

" SIR,—Finding myself by his Majesty's late proclamation proceeded against as a fugitive, after I had so early claimed the benefit of that pardon the king's Majesty was graciously pleased to extend to all offenders, I fear what I spoke in so hasty a surprise as that I was in when I had last the honour to declare myself in the House, was not a sufficient expression of that deep and sorrowful sense which so heavily presses my soul, for the unfortunate guilt that lies upon it ; and, therefore, I beg leave, though my penitent sorrow be above utterance, to say something that may further declare it, and obtain your belief that I would not fly from that mercy which I have once made my sanctuary. They who yet remember the seeming sanctity and subtle arts of those men, who seduced not only me, but thousands more, in those unhappy days, cannot, if they have any Christian compassion, but join with me in bewailing my wretched misfortune, to have fallen into their pernicious snares, when neither my own malice, avarice, or ambition,

but an ill-guided judgment led me. As soon as ever my
eyes were opened to suspect my deceivers, no person with a
more perfect abhorrency detested both the heinous fact and
the authors of it, and I was as willing to hazard my life and
estate to redeem my crime as I had been unfortunate,
through a deplorable mistake, to forfeit them by it. For
this cause, even before Cromwell broke up the remaining
part of the House, when his ambition began to unveil itself,
jealous of those sins I did not sooner discern, I stopped and
left off acting with them. As his usurpations made it more
manifest, my repentance grew greater, and begot in me a
more earnest desire to repair, as much as was possible, the
misery I had undesigningly run myself and others into, and
to return to that loyal subjection to the right prince, from
which I had been so horridly misled. Thereupon I set
Cromwell's honours and all his friendship at that defiance
that I never could be drawn to accept anything from him,
to make or join in any address to him, or so much as to
give him one civil visit; for which I was watched with
jealous eyes, and designed to be secured as a person disaffected to him, and desirous to serve the king; which, how
really I was, both then and since, there are yet divers
honorable persons as the Lord Biron, Sir Robert Biron, Sir
Allen Apsley, Mr. Stanhope, Mr. Broderick and others can
testify, and the Earl of Rochester could say more if he were
now living; neither was I driven to this through fear, but
the conviction of my conscience that I ought so to act,
though I then ran great hazards in it, being a time when
not only those three kingdoms but all the neighbouring
nations courted that usurper, as a glorious and established
monarch; nor was it animosity against him for having
displaced me with the rest, but, when he ceased, the same
desires continued in me, when being summoned to return
among the members of the House, I had not sitten there,
but that I was advised I might thereby have a better oppor-

tunity to serve his Majesty than by refraining ; and, accordingly, I freely and openly acted, as far as the persons and
times would then bear.   Before Sir G. Booth was in arms,
I refused taking myself, and withstood the imposing upon
others, of that engagement to be constant to a Commonwealth ; and, whatever I acted as looking that way, was
but as much as was then possible to redeem the power out
of the soldiers' hands, at least into some face of civil authority ; but, that it never was my intentions to rest there, I
appeal to my after actings, when I hindered the oath of
renunciation, endeavoured the release of Sir G. Booth and
all his 'party from confiscation, and the restoring of the
secluded members, and the freeing of his Excellency, the
now Lord-General, from the yoke of fellow-commissioners ;
in all which I appeal to Sir Anthony Ashley Cooper, Sir
George Booth, and other worthy persons in this House, who
know how I have demeaned myself. Sir,—by all this I hope
my repentance will appear to have been long since, and not
of late expressed ; that it was real, rather declared by deeds
than words; that it was constant through several changes
of affairs ; that it was, through God's great mercy, a thorough
conviction of my former misled judgment and conscience,
and not a regard of my particular safety that drove me to
it ; all which, if you please to communicate to the House,
and they please to honour me with their patience to hear it,
I shall not despair, but, if mercy be to be mixed with justice,
I may become an object of it ; and therefore, as I did before,
I desire again to testify my resolution of abiding the commands of the honourable House, humbly begging, as an
earnest of greater favour, that I may be at liberty upon my
parole, till they determine of me, who, though I acknowledge
myself involved in so horrid a crime as merits no indulgence,
yet having a miserable family that must, though innocent,
share all my ruin, I cannot but beg the honourable House
would not exclude me from the refuge of the King's most

gracious pardon, and pluck me from the horns of that sacred altar to become his sacrifice ; and, if I thus escape being made a burnt-offering, I shall make all my life, all my children, and all my enjoyments, a perpetual dedication to his Majesty's service, bewailing much more my incapacity of rendering it, so as I might else have done, than any other wretchedness my most deplorable crime hath brought upon me, in whom life will but lengthen an insupportable affliction that to the grave will accompany your most obedient and most humble servant."

Endorsed by Colonel Hutchinson—"A copy of my letter to the House of Commons."

Printed by Mrs. Green in the *Athenæum*, March 3, 1860, from the original in the Record Office.

XIII.

July 23, 1660.—Petition of Colonel John Hutchinson.

To the Right Honourable the Lords assembled in Parliament.

" The humble petition of John Hutchinson, Esquire, most humbly showeth,—That whereas the honourable House of Commons, upon his humble petition, did extend their clemency and mercy to your lordships' petitioner, in not nominating him one of the seven exempted out of the act of general pardon and oblivion for life, and also passed a vote that your petitioner shall not be within that clause of exception in the act of general pardon and oblivion as to any fine or forfeiture of any part of his estate ; and were pleased to express in the said resolves that this favour was extended to your petitioner upon his signal repentance, which how early and real it was, his deportment for many

years past hath made clear ; and those actions being
attested by many honourable persons who have certified
the same under their hands.

Your petitioner therefore most humbly prays your lordships that he having been the first (when he had the
honour to sit in the House of Commons) that openly laid
claim to his Majesty's pardon, and freely gave up himself
to be disposed of by the Parliament, that, after he hath been
raised to such high hopes of preservation, both as to life
and fortunes, by the votes of the House of Commons, your
lordships would not now cast him down from them, but
confirm that favour and mercy they have been pleased to
show him, upon the humble and sorrowful acknowledgment
of those crimes whereinto seduced judgment, and not
malice, nor any other self-respect unfortunately betrayed
him ; and upon his serious profession of future loyalty
which he hopes will find as charitable a belief with your
lordships as it did in the House of Commons. And your
petitioner will ever pray, &c.,   J. HUTCHINSON."

Annexed :—
1. Certificate referred to in preceding :—

June 26th, 1660.

" These are to certify that about seven years ago, and from
time to time ever since, Colonel Hutchinson hath declared
his desire of the king's majesty's return to his kingdoms,
and his own resolutions to assist in bringing his majesty
back : and in order thereunto hath kept a correspondency
with some of us, when designs have been on foot for that
purpose ; and hath upon all occasions been ready to assist
and protect the king's friends in any of their troubles, and
to employ all his interests to serve them. He gave the
Earl of Rochester notice and opportunity to escape when
Cromwell's ministers had discovered him the last time he
was employed in his Majesty's service here in England.

He received into his house, and secured there, arms prepared for the king's service, well knowing to what intent
they were provided, and resolving to join with us when
there had been occasion to use them. For these, and other
things, Cromwell some time before his death had a very jealous
eye over him, and had intentions to secure him, which some
of us understanding gave him notice of ; that usurper being
the more exasperated against him, because he could never,
by all his allurements, win him to the least compliance
with or action under his authority. Nor were his resolutions of serving the king only in Cromwell's time, but when
the army invited the remainder of the House of Commons
to return to Westminster, whither he was summoned, he
declared to some of us before he went up, that he only went
among them to endeavour to settle the kingdom by the
king's return, and to improve all opportunities to bend
things that way ; and accordingly so acted there, openly
opposing the engagement, to be true and constant to the
Commonwealth, and endeavouring to bring the army under
a civil authority, and for that end highly standing against
Lambert's being put into employment against Sir George
Booth, and after his return, acting vigorously against him,
and the pretended Council of Safety, against whom he had
prepared considerable levies to assist the Lord-General if he
had had occasion ; then again at the last reassembling of
the House, openly, and highly opposing, and speaking
against the oath of renunciation, endeavouring to bring in
the secluded members, and moving that the army, which
was then governed by commissioners, might be put under
the sole command of his Excellency the now Lord-General,
and opposing the act for confiscation of Sir George Booth,
and his party, with endeavours to procure their liberties ;
opposing also in the House the commitment of these gentlemen who brought up the addresses for a free Parliament,
as also the destroying and pulling down of the city gates.

All or some of these particular actings and declarations of his, tending to his Majesty's service, every one of us who have here subscribed are able to attest,

ANNE ROCHESTER.	RICHARD BIRON.
AN : ASHLEY COOPER.	G. GRANDISON.
ROBERT BIRON.	A. BRODRICK.
ALLEN APSLEY.	JACK MARKHAM.
EDWARD VILLIERS.	A. BABINGTON."

XIV.

Letter of Mrs. Hutchinson on the sale of Owthorpe, 1671.

MR. BATEMAN,—I was last night at your Chamber after you went from Mr. Butler's, to have desired you that what notes you took of my affairs, wherein I dealt simply and clearly expecting to have found the like, might have been given up and burnt ; and that according to your engagement, as a gentleman, what I exposed to you might not at all be made public ; but in that particular now you have a little put it out of your power, by telling Mr. Clarke all particulars, which he again told Mr. Ward, and I perceive by himself hath been advising with every one he meets. I have desired my brother to show you two letters, upon confidence of which, I put by an offer of money that was made me, and is now disposed, and did not so much as send Sir William Jesson an answer to a letter he sent to me in order to a treaty ; and refused two others that were offered me for purchasers ; and whatever pretence is taken I cannot but discover, that this gentleman is young and continues no longer firm to his resolution than till the next designing person he consults, persuades him to a new one. I have nothing to accuse in this but my own ill choice, and rash confidence of

Mr. Ward's mistakes, who however it falls ill to me, I am confident meant well to both ; nor am I so much concerned in the loss of a purchaser (for that I cannot fear to want long) as in the failure of (what I thought so assured that I refused it elsewhere) money to take in my principal mortgages : and I confess too I have reason to be vexed, that I should be so sifted where there was no real intention to close with me. The least I can expect both from yourself and Mr. Clarke is a future silence to all persons of what I have too credulously opened to you, concerning my affairs, and thereby you will oblige, your servant,

L. HUTCHINSON."

Feb. 10*th*, 1670,

Endorsed, February 11th, 1671—"Madam Hutchinson's letter about Owthorpe."

· XV.

Dedication to Mrs. Hutchinson's translation of Lucretius.

Lucretius de Rerum Natura.

A note on the fly leaf—
. "Anglesey. Given me, June 11, 1675, by the worthy author, Mrs. Lucy Hutchinson."

To the right honourable Arthur, Earl of Anglesey, Lord Keeper of his Majesty's Privy Seal, and one of his Majesty's most honourable Privy Council.

"MY LORD,—When I present this unworthy translation to your lordship, I sacrifice my shame to my obedience ; for (though a masculine wit hath thought it worth printing his head in a laurel crown for the version of one of these books) I am so far from glorying in my six, that had they not by misfortune been gone out of my hands in one lost copy, even your lordship's command, which hath more authority with me, than any human thing I pay reverence to, should not have redeemed it from the fire. Had it been a work that had merited glory, or could my sex, (whose more becoming virtue is silence), derive honour from writing, my aspiring muse would not have sought any other patron than your lordship, the justly celebrated Macenas of our days, where learning and ingenuity finds its most honourable, I had almost said its only refuge, in this drolling, degenerate age, that hath hissed out all sober and serious studies ; which your lordship not only cherisheth in others, but are yourself so illustriously eminent in that most honourable acquisition of learning, that 'tis the noblest crown of any work to gain your lordship's approbation. And therefore, since I did attempt things out of my own sphere, I am sorry I had not the capacity of making a work, nor the good fortune of choosing a subject, worthy of being presented your lordship, whose dedication might gratefully have rendered some of the honour it receives in its acceptance. As your lordship's command will vindicate me from arrogance in offering so unworthy a piece to such a hand, so I beseech your lordship to reward my obedience, by indulging me the further honour to preserve, wherever your lordship shall dispose this book, this record with it, that I abhor the atheisms and impieties in it, and translated it only out of youthful curiosity to understand things I heard so much discourse of at second hand, but without the least inclination to propagate any of the wicked pernicious doctrines in it. Afterwards being convinced of the sin of amusing myself with such vain philosophy, (which even at the first I did not employ any serious study in, for I turned it into English in a room where my children practised the several qualities they were taught with their tutors, and I numbered the syllables of my translation by the threads of the canvas I wrought in, and set them down with a pen and ink that stood by me : how superficially it must needs be done in this manner, the thing itself will show) but I say, afterward, as my judgment grew riper, and my mind was fixed in more profitable contemplations, I thought this book not worthy either of review or correction, the whole work being one fault. But when I have thrown all the contempt that is due upon my author, who yet wants not admirers among those whose religion little exceeds his, I must say I am not much better satisfied with the other fardle of philosophers who in some pulpits are quoted with divine epithets. They that make the incorruptible God part of a corruptible world, and chain up his absolute freedom of will to a fatal necessity; that make nature, which is only the order God hath set in his works, to be God Himself, that feign a God liable to passion, impotence, and mutability, and not exempt from the vilest lusts; that believe a multiplicity of gods, adore the sun and moon and all the host of heaven, and bandy their several deities in faction one against another; all these, and all the other poor deluded instructors of the Gentiles, are guilty of no less impiety, ignorance, and folly than this lunatic, who not able to dive into the true original and cause of beings and accidents, admires them who devised this casual, irrational dance of atoms. So far yet we may usefully be permitted to consider the productions of degenerate nature, as they represent to us the deplorable wretchedness of all mankind, who are not translated from darkness to light by supernatural illumination, and teach us that their wisdom is folly, their most virtuous and pure morality foul defilement, their knowledge ignorance, their glory shame, their renown contemptible, their industry vain, all their attainments cheats and delusions, their felicities unsubstantial dreams and apparitions, and their lives only a varied scene of perpetual woe and misery. This is the best account I can give of the best of them, who toiled themselves in vain to search out truth, but wandered in a maze of error, and could never discover her by Nature's dim candle, which proved only an *ignis fatui* to lead them into quagmires and precipices, and to this day is no better to their admirers, who manifest they are still in their natural blindness, and never saw the sun, that can so extol corrupt glow-worms. I am persuaded that the encomiums given to these pagan poets and philosophers, wherewith tutors put them into the hands of their pupils, yet unsettled in principles of divine truth, is one great means of debauching the learned world, at least of confirming them in that debauchery of soul which their first sin led them into, and of hindering their recovery, while they puddle all the streams of truth, that flow down to them from divine grace, with this pagan mud ; for all the heresies that are sprung up in the Christian religion are but the several foolish and impious inventions of the old contemplative heathen revived and brought forth in new dresses, while men wreck their wits, striving to wrest and pervert the sacred Scriptures from their genuine meaning, to comply with the false and foolish opinions of men. Some of them indeed acknowledge Providence, a divine original and regiment of all things, an internal law, which obliges us to eternal punishment if we transgress it, and shall be rewarded with present peace of conscience, and future blessedness if we obey it ; but though they have general notions, wanting a revelation and guide to lead them into a true and distinct knowledge of the nature of God, of the original and remedy of sin, of the spring and nature of blessedness, they set up their vain imaginations in the room of God, and devise superstitious foolish services to avert His wrath and pro-pitiate His favour, suitable to their devised God ; inventing such fables of their Elizium and Hell, and the joys and tortures of those places, as made this author and others turn them into allegories, and think they treated more reverently of gods when they placed them above the cares and dis-turbances of human affairs, and set them in an unper-turbed rest and felicity, leaving all things here to accident and chance, denying that determinate wise counsel and order of things they could not dive into, and deriding heaven and hell, eternal rewards and punishments, as fictions in the whole, because the instances of them in particular were so ridiculous, as seemed rather stories invented to fright children than to persuade reasonable men ; therefore they fancied another kind of heaven and hell, in the internal peace or horror of the conscience, upon which account they urged the pursuit of virtue and the avoiding of vice, as the spring of joy or sorrow, and defined virtue to be all those things that are just, equal, and profitable to human society; wherein this poet makes true religion to consist, and not in superstitious ceremonies, which he makes to have had their original from the vain dread of men, imputing those events to the wrath of gods, which proceeded from natural causes whereof they were ignorant, and therefore sings high applause to his own wisdom, for having explored such deep mysteries of nature, though even these discoveries of his are so silly, foolish, and false, that nothing but his lunacy can extenuate the crime of his arrogant ignorance. But 'tis a lamentation and horror that in these days of the Gospel, men should be found so presumptuously wicked to study and adhere to his and his master's ridiculous, impious, execrable doctrines, reviving the foppish casual dance of atoms, and denying the sovereign wisdom of God in the great design of the whole universe and every creature in it, and His eternal omnipotence, exerting itself in the production of all things, according to His most wise and fixed purpose, and His most gracious, ever-active Providence, upholding, ordering and governing the whole creation, and conducting all that appears most casual to us and our narrow comprehensions to the accomplishment of those just ends for which they were made. As by the study of them I grew in light and love, the little glory I had among some few of my intimate friends, for understanding this crabbed poet, be-

came my shame, and I found I never understood him till I
learned to abhor him, and dread a wanton dalliance with
impious books. Then I reaped some profit by it, for it
showed me that senseless superstitions drive carnal reason
into atheism, which though policy restrains some from
avowing so impudently as this dog, yet vast is their number,
who make it a specious pretext within themselves, to think
religion is nothing at all but an invention to reduce the
ignorant vulgar into order and government. My philosophers taught me, by their own instance, that unregenerate,
unsanctified reason makes men more monstrous by their
learning, than the most sottish, brutish idiots, while they
employ the most excellent gifts of human understanding,
with all the other noble endowments of the soul, as weapons
against Him that gave them. This gave me a dreadful pro-
spect of the misery of lapsed nature, whereby I saw, with
sad compassion, the uncomfortable shadow of death wherein
they consume their lives, that are alienated from the knowledge of God. I saw the insufficiency of human reason
(how great an idol soever it is now become among the
gownmen) to arrive to any pure and simple truth, with all
its helps of art and study. I learnt to hate all unsanctified
excellence, if that impropriety of expression may be
admitted, and to run out of my monstrous self to seek
light, life, knowledge, tranquillity, rest, and whatever else
is requisite to make up a complete blessedness, and lasting felicity, in its only true and pure divine fountain.
As one that, walking in the dark, had miraculously
scaped a horrible precipice, by daylight coming back and
discovering his late danger, startles and reviews it with
affright, so did I, when I, in the mirror of opposed truth and
holiness, and blessedness, saw the ugly deformity and the
desperate tendency of corrupted nature in its greatest pretences, and having by rich grace scaped the shipwreck of
my soul among those vain philosophers, who by wisdom

knew not God, I could not but in charity set up this sea-mark, to warn uncautious travellers, and leave a testimony, that those walks of wit which poor vain-glorious scholars call the Muses' groves, are enchanted thickets, and while they tipple at their celebrated Helicon, they lose their lives, and fill themselves with poison, drowning their spirits in those puddled waters, and neglecting that healing spring of Truth, which only hath the virtue to restore and refresh sick human life. To conclude, let none, that aspire to eternal happiness, gaze too long or too fixedly on that monster, into which man by the sorcery of the devil is converted, lest he draw infection in at his eyes, and be himself either metamorphosed into the most ugly shape, or stupefied and hardened against all better impressions, as daily examples too sadly instance.

But I say not this to your lordship, though I leave it in your book, as an antidote against the poison of it, for any novice who by chance might pry into it. Your lordship hath skill to render that which in itself is poisonous, many ways useful and medicinal, and are not liable to danger by an ill book, which I beseech your lordship to conceal, as a shame I did never intend to boast, but now resign to your lordship's command, whose wisdom to make the defects and errors of my vainly curious youth pardonable, I rely on much more than my own skill in searching out an apology for them, and your lordship's benign favour to me I have so many ways experienced, that it would be great ingratitude to doubt your lordship's protection against all the censures a book might expose me to. And while I am assured of that I bid defiance to anything that can be said against, my lord, your lordship's most devoted, obedient, humble servant,

L. H.

INDEX.

———

A.

ALLSOP, Mr., i. 282.
Anglesey, Earl of, ii. 399.
Apsley, Edward, i. 12.
Apsley, family of, i. 11, 343.
Apsley, Lady Lucy, i. 15, 17, 21, 22; ii. 355.
Apsley, Lucy, *see* Hutchinson, Lucy.
Apsley, Sir Allen, i. 13, 14; made Lieutenant of the Tower, 18; character, 19.
Apsley, Sir Allen, son of the preceding, i. 18, 174; ii. 104; negotiations in 1647, 110, 179, 253, 258, 267, 302, 309, 313, 314, 316, 323, 330, 340, 342, 347, 398.
Arminians, i. 72, 94.
Army, new modelled, i. 336; hostility of Presbyterians to, ii. 97; falls out with city, 106, 108; breaks up Parliament, 148; remodelled by Cromwell, 163, 202; restores the Long Parliament, 216; breaks up the Long Parliament again, 227; insolence of, 229.
Ashby-de-la-Zouch, i. 257, 321, 385, 388; ii. 54.
Ash, Mr., ii. 174.
Atkinson, Mr., ii. 139, 140, 294, 295.
Ayscough, Mr., i. 249; ii. 13, 52.

B.

BABINGTON, Mr., ii. 398.
Ballard, Colonel, i. 205, 208, 209.
Barnstaple, ii. 104, 179, 180.
"Barondry," a, i. 18.
Barrett, Captain, ii. 34, 60.
Bateman, Mr., ii. 398.
Bee, Captain, ii. 381.
Bellomye, Lieutenant, ii. 387.
Bellasis, Lord, ii. 79, 93.

Hopton Heath, i. 354.
Hotham, Captain John, i. 215, 219, 220, 222, 363, 364, 365.
Hotham, Sir John, i. 154, 158, 215, 222.
Howard, Mrs, ii. 173, 175 ; Lord, 243.
Hubbard, Colonel, i. 218, 381.
Huet, Mr., ii. 9.
Hull, i. 154, 158, 212, 217, 222.
Humlack, Sir H., i. 297, 382, 387.
" Hurds," ii. 2.
Hutchinson, family of, i. 51, 52, 341 ; ii. 355.
Hutchinson, George—his birth, i. 58 ; suffers from the falling sickness, 67 ; cured by Dr. Plumptre, 188 ; arrested by mistake,
176 ; becomes major of Colonel Pierrepont's regiment, 198 ;
one of the committee of Nottingham, 208 ; becomes lieutenantcolonel in his brother's regiment, 278 ; letter to Colonel Dacre,
373 ; character, ii. 68 ; with his brother in Sandown Castle, 340,
344.
Hutchinson, John—description and character, i. 32 *seq.* ; birth, 57 ;
education, 66, 71, 74 ; enters at Lincoln's Inn, 77 ; hears of
Lucy Apsley, 82 ; meets her, 86 ; marriage, 92 ; comes to
Owthorpe, 137 ; made justice of the peace, 140 ; why called a
Puritan, 140 ; protects the powder magazine of the county, 142,
169, 347 ; wrongly termed a Roundhead, 169 ; attempted arrest,
173 ; flight, 174 ; accepts commission as lieutenant-colonel,
198 ; negotiations with the gentlemen of Newark, 201, 356 ;
appointed governor of Nottingham Castle, 224 ; government
of town added to that of the castle, 282 ; overtures made to
him to betray the castle by Mr. Ayscough, 249, by Mr. Wood,
276, by Colonel Dacre, 288, 369 ; quarrel with the committee,
307 *et seq.*; decision of the committee of both kingdoms
respecting the dispute, ii. 361, 366 ; decision of Parliament on
the question, ii. 72 ; end of this persecution, ii. 75 ; at the
siege of Shelford, ii. 81 ; at the siege of Newark, 91 ; elected
member for the county, 91 ; falls into ill health, 91 ; conduct
in Parliament—acts with the Independents, 94 ; supports the
army, 97 ; deceived by Dr. Frazer, 105 ; withdraws to the army,
107 ; resigns government of Nottingham Castle, 111 ; refuses
reappointment, 113 ; his friendship with the Levellers, 126 ;
frankness to Cromwell, 128 ; parting with Colonel Thornhagh,
129 ; offered command of Thornhagh's regiment, 134 ; makes
Langdale prisoner, 138, 186 ; how he obtains his arrears, case
of the Newark Commissioners, 140 ; protests against treating
with the king, 145 ; reasons for continuing to sit in Parliament
after Pride's Purge, 149 ; appointed one of the king's judges,
151 ; chosen one of the Council of State, 156 ; saves Sir John

Owen, 158 ; defends Overton, 162 ; offered government of
Jersey, 165 ; buys manor of Loseby, 167 ; protects Presbyterian
conspirators, 176 ; kindness to Sir Allen Apsley, 180 ; raises
three troops of horse, 181 ; share in opposing invasion of the
Scots, 183 ; conduct in the Council of State, 192, 198 ; conduct as justice of the peace, 192 ; quarrel with Cromwell, 185,
187 ; taste for art and music, 197, 199 ; conduct during the
Protectorate, 197, 200 ; informs Cromwell of a plot, 207 ; last
interview with Cromwell, 209 ; appointed sheriff of county of
Nottingham, 212 ; summoned to restored Long Parliament,
216 ; conduct in Parliament, 219 ; takes charge of Lord
Biron's arms, 222 ; opposes Lambert, 229 ; opposes oath of
renunciation, 236 ; saves Nottingham from plunder, 243 ;
chosen member for Nottingham, 244 ; speech on his share in
the king's death, 249 ; suspended from sitting in Parliament,
249 ; votes of Parliament respecting him, 251-2 ; action on
behalf of Sir G. Booth, 254 ; cleared by House of Lords, 259 ;
returns to Owthorpe, 261 ; not satisfied with his conduct, 261 ;
examined by the attorney-general, 264 ; obtains his pardon,
272 ; deprived of his arms and pictures, 274 ; marriage of his
son, 275 ; gives information of a Popish plot, 279 ; a remarkable dream, 280 ; arrested, 284 ; accused of betraying his
party, 287 ; released by the Marquis of Newcastle, 290 ; again
arrested, 291 ; examined by Secretary Bennett, 299, 302 ;
description of his prison, 303 ; refuses any pledge, 313 ; narrative written in the Tower, 315 ; dispute about fees with his
gaoler, 316, 317 ; articles against Sir John Robinson, 320 ;
removal to Sandown Castle, 328 ; description of his prison, 331 ;
diversions in prison, 333 ; conversation in prison, 334, 338 ;
illness, 343 ; death, 348 ; funeral, 352 ; epitaph, 354.
Letters of Colonel Hutchinson, ii. 374.
To the gentlemen of Newark, i. 358.
To Mr. Millington, i. 369, 376, 379, 383, 387, 388 ; ii. 373.
To Colonel Dacre, i. 374
To Lord Fairfax, ii. 372.
To the Speaker, ii. 388.
Petition to the House of Commons, ii. 392.
Petition to the House of Lords, ii. 395.
Certificate in favour of Colonel Hutchinson, ii. 396.
Regulations for the government of Nottingham, ii. 367.
Hutchinson, Lady Catherine, i. 57, 77, 242, 249, 352 ; ii. 87, 199.
Hutchinson, Lady Margaret, i. 55, 57, 58, 59, 62 ; ii. 354.
Hutchinson, Lucy—birth, 23 ; education, 24-26 ; meets Mr. Hut-
chinson, 87 ; courtship, 88 ; marriage, 92 ; birth of sons, Thomas
and Edward, 93 ; visited by Captain Welch, 175 ; birth of her

N.

O.

Wildman, Major, ii. 173.
Williamson, Sir T., i. 165, 200, 357, 360 ; ii. 139, 141.
Willis, Sir Richard, ii. 75, 373.
Willoughby Field, ii. 121, 381.
Willoughby, Lord, i. 165, 217, 223, 233 ; ii. 245.
Wilson, Dr., ii. 105.
Wingfield Manor, i. 382, 388 ; ii. 22, 27.
Wiverton House, i. 218, 219, 300, 363, 385, 388, 392 ; ii. 2, 22, 27, 81, 88, 112, 369, 377, 378.
Woollerton House, i. 266, 269.
Worcester, battle of, ii. 184.
Worcester, Marquis of, ii. 167.
" Worsted-stocking men," the, ii. 74.
Worthington, Captain-lieutenant, ii. 387.
Wray, Captain, ii. 83.
Wright, Captain, i. 278 ; ii. 58.
Wroth, Sir Henry, ii. 329.

Y.

YORK, i. 129, 141, 155, 343, 346 ; ii. 27.
York, Committee of the Northern Association at, ii. 80, 89.

PRINTED BY BALLANTYNE, HANSON AND CO.
EDINBURGH AND LONDON.

FEBRUARY 1885.

PUBLICATIONS

OF

JOHN C. NIMMO,

14 KING WILLIAM STREET, STRAND,

LONDON, W.C.

PROSPECTUS.

The Elizabethan Dramatists.

Post 8vo, cloth.   Published price, 7s. 6d. net per volume.

NOTE.—The type will be distributed after each work is printed, the impression of which will be four hundred copies, post 8vo, and one hundred and twenty large fine-paper copies, medium 8vo, which will be numbered.

To realise the supremacy of Shakespeare we must be acquainted with the writings of his contemporaries. Such masterpieces as *Dr. Faustus,* the *Duchess of Malfi,* and the *Maid's Tragedy* are of the highest value in preparing the student to appreciate the unique power of *Lear* and *Macbeth* and *Othello.*

But putting aside Shakespearean considerations, it may be justly said that there is no study more fascinating to thoughtful men than the study of the Elizabethan Dramatists. Their works were largely planned ; and there is the stamp of sincerity in every page.

That there is a great and growing interest in our Old Dramatists among educated men is undeniable ; but, strange to say, the works of some of the chief dramatists are unprocurable.

The noble contributions made to the English drama by Middleton and Shirley are known only to the few ; the books have long been out of print.

Library editions of Beaumont and Fletcher, Marlowe, Massinger, and others are greatly needed. The quartos of Ben Jonson's plays have never been carefully collated. It is barely a year ago since Mr. A. H. BULLEN discovered (and printed for private circulation) a tragic masterpiece by Fletcher and Massinger, and a sprightly comedy by Shirley, which were . lying, in MS., unnoticed in the British Museum.

This newly-edited Edition will begin with Shakespeare's greatest predecessor, *Christopher Marlowe,* in three volumes.

An edition of Middleton will follow ; and Middleton will be succeeded by Shirley.

For Beaumont and Fletcher much time and labour will be required : but the Editor has already commenced the arduous task, and will give the closest attention to the question, " How far was Massinger concerned in the authorship of plays attributed to *Beaumont and Fletcher ?* "

The remaining dramatists of this *Period* will follow in due order.

One of the chief features of this New Edition of the Elizabethan Dramatists, besides the handsome and handy size of the volumes, will be the fact that *each Work will be carefully edited, and new notes given throughout.*

The Elizabethan Dramatists.

The Works of Christopher Marlowe.

Edited by A. H. BULLEN, B.A.

IN THREE VOLUMES.

Post 8vo, cloth.   Published price, 7s. 6d. net per volume.

[*Ready.*

NOTE.—This is the first instalment towards a collective edition of the Dramatists who lived about the time of Shakespeare. The Edition is limited to Four Hundred copies, post 8vo, and One Hundred and Twenty large fine paper copies, medium 8vo.

SOME PRESS NOTICES.

Athenæum.

" Mr. Bullen's edition deserves warm recognition. It is intelligent, scholarly, adequate. His preface is judicious. The elegant edition of the dramatists of which these volumes are the first is likely to stand high in public estimation. . . . Middleton, who is to come next, might have been taken first, as he is quite out of reach. The completion of the series will be a boon to bibliographers and scholars alike."

Saturday Review.

" Mr. Bullen has discharged his task as editor in all important points satisfactorily. Marlowe needs no irrelevant partisanship, no 'zeal of the devil's house,' to support his greatness. . . . Mr. Bullen's introduction is well informed and well written, and his notes are well chosen and sufficient. . . . We hope it may be his good fortune to give and ours to receive every dramatist, from Peele to Shirley, in this handsome, convenient, and well-edited form."

The Academy.

" Mr. Bullen is known to all those interested in such things as an authority on most matters connected with old plays. His reading in them is extensive and peculiar. We are not surprised, therefore, to find these volumes well edited throughout. They are not over-burdened with notes. Where explanations are necessary, they are given in as terse a form as possible, without too much parade of parallel passages; and no difficulty, so far as we have seen, is passed over. . . . Mr. Bullen supplies an elaborate Introduction, extending over eighty pages, and we are glad to see he has printed in an appendix Hore's fine play of the ' Death of Marlowe.'"

Illustrated London News.

" It is, perhaps, a bold venture on the part of the publisher, or would be if he had chosen an editor less competent than Mr. A. H. Bullen. The series begins with the works of Marlowe, whose genius, considering when he worked and how, fills the reader with wonder. His power was felt by Shakespeare, and felt also by Goethe; and Mr. Bullen is not, perhaps, a rash prophet in saying that, ' so long as high tragedy continues to have interest for men, Time shall lay no hands on the works of Christopher Marlowe ! '"

PRESS NOTICES OF "MARLOWE"—*continued.*

Scotsman.

" Never in the history of the world has a period been marked by so much of literary power and excellence as the Elizabethan period ; and never have the difficulties in the way of literature seemed to be greater. The three volumes which Mr. Nimmo has issued now may be regarded as earnests of more to come, and as proofs of the excellence which will mark this edition of the Elizabethan Dramatists as essentially the best that has been published. Mr. Bullen is a competent editor in every respect."

Pall Mall Gazette.

"That Shakespeare learned from Marlowe a portion of the secret of his marvellous versification is now accepted, as is the fact that in his 'Edward II.' Marlowe came nearer Shakespeare than did any tragedian of later date, such as Webster, Chapman, or Ben Jonson. . . . Marlowe has indeed passed the age of simple eulogy, and has reached that of comment. The task set before him by Mr. Bullen is that of supplying a text which shall be as clear and intelligible as the conditions under which plays were printed in the sixteenth and early seventeenth centuries render possible. In this he has been successful. . . . If the series is continued as it is begun, by one of the most careful editors, this set of the English Dramatists will be a coveted literary possession."

The Elizabethan Dramatists.

The Works of Thomas Middleton.

Edited by A. H. BULLEN, B.A.

In Eight Volumes, post 8vo.

First Four Volumes ready in March.

Dyce's Edition of Middleton, published in 1840, has been out of print for many years, and is now difficult to procure. The need of a new edition has been keenly felt. Middleton had not the sustained tragic power of Webster or Ford; but in single scenes, when his work is at its highest, he is surpassed only by Shakespeare.

His romantic comedies display a freedom of fancy that belongs to the "brightest heaven of invention;" and his comedies of intrigue are always lively and attractive. No student of the English Drama can afford to neglect the works of Thomas Middleton.

NOTE.—*The above is uniform with the Works of Marlowe, both in price and number of copies printed of both small and large paper editions.*

"New Series of Historical Memoirs."

Memoirs of the Life of Colonel Hutchinson,

GOVERNOR OF NOTTINGHAM.

By his Widow, LUCY.

Edited from the Original Manuscript by the Rev. JULIUS HUTCHINSON.

To which are added the LETTERS OF COLONEL HUTCHINSON, and other Papers.

Revised, with Additional Notes, by C. H. FIRTH, M.A.

With Numerous Portraits, newly etched, of eminent personages.

In Two Volumes, fine paper, medium 8vo, and handsome binding, 42s.

NOTE.—Only 500 copies are being printed, 300 for England and 200 for America. Type distributed. [*Ready in March.*

To understand the history of any period, it must be studied not only in the records of public events, but also in the daily lives of individuals.

Of the many Memoirs and Autobiographies which illustrate the Civil Wars of the seventeenth century, none is more popular or entertaining than the "Life of Colonel Hutchinson." But though these Memoirs have passed through many editions, and their value universally admitted, they have not yet been edited with the care and labour they deserve.

In the earlier editions the irregular and unfamiliar spelling of the original renders the book difficult for the general reader to enjoy. In the later ones the text has been modernised with more freedom than fidelity. In the present edition the spelling alone will be modernised, whilst the phraseology and grammatical peculiarities of the original will be carefully preserved.

The most valuable of the annotations of the Rev. Julius Hutchinson will be retained, and a large number of new explanatory and illustrative notes will be added. Letters written by Colonel Hutchinson during his government of Nottingham, and other documents of interest, will be for the first time collected. A full and accurate index to the Memoirs will complete the work.

A number of etchings from the portraits of persons of whom mention is made in the text will help to render this a worthy edition of an English classic.

---

14 King William Street, Strand, London, W.C.

Old Times.

A Picture of Social Life at the end of the Eighteenth Century.

Collected and Illustrated from the Satirical and other Sketches of the Day.

By JOHN ASHTON,

Author of " Social Life in the Reign of Queen Anne."

One Volume, fine paper, medium 8vo, handsome binding, Eighty Illustrations, price 21s.

NOTE.—Sixty copies will be printed on fine laid imperial 8vo paper, with *an extra* 12 *plates*, not so suitable for the ordinary edition.

[*Ready in March.*

This book is a compendium of the Social Life in England at the end of the last century, corresponding with Mr. Ashton's " Social Life in the Reign of Queen Anne."

Avoiding history, except in so far as to make the work intelligible, it deals purely with the daily life of our great-grandfathers. Nothing is taken from diaries or lives of the upper classes ; it aims solely to give a fair account of the life of the majority of people then living, or, as we now term it, of the middle class. This could best be done by taking the daily notices in the press, which would, naturally, be a perfect record of each passing folly of fashion, or even of the markets; so that, by this means, we get a glimpse of the inner life of that time, unattainable by any other method.

"The Times," which commenced 1st January 1788, is taken by preference, but when that authority is unavailing, other contemporaneous newspapers have been consulted.

Profusely illustrated from the satirical and other sketches of the day, it forms a volume of reliable authority, such as, up to the present time, has been looked for in vain.

The work will contain some eighty full-page illustrations.

14 King William Street, Strand, London, W.C.

Uniform with " Characters of La Bruyère" and a " Handbook of Gastronomy."

Robin Hood.

A COLLECTION OF ALL THE ANCIENT POEMS, SONGS, AND BALLADS now extant, relative to that celebrated English Outlaw ;

To which are prefixed Historical Anecdotes of his Life,

By JOSEPH RITSON.

Illustrated with Seventy-Four Wood Engravings, by the celebrated
THOMAS BEWICK.

Also Six Original Drawings, painted by A. H. TOURRIER and etched by an eminent French Etcher.

8vo, half parchment, gilt top, 42s.

NOTE.—300 copies printed, and each numbered.   Type distributed. Also sixty copies on fine imperial paper, with etchings in two states. Each copy numbered.   [*Ready in March.*

This edition of "ROBIN HOOD" is printed from that published in 1832, which was carefully edited and printed from Mr. RITSON's own annotated edition of 1795.

The Original Wood Engravings by the celebrated THOMAS BEWICK have been again used, and, from being printed on China paper, will be found superior in clearness and beauty to the first impressions.

The Six Etchings now given are from newly-painted drawings by A. H. TOURRIER.

14 King William Street, Strand, London, W.C.

Romances of Fantasy and Humour.

(Uniform with the Old Spanish and English Romances.)

To be completed in Twelve Volumes crown 8vo, cloth or parchment,
7s. 6d. per volume,
And Illustrated with Etchings by Eminent Artists.

The Tales and Poems of Edgar Allan Poe,

With *Biographical Essay* by JOHN H. INGRAM; and *Fourteen Original Etchings, Three Photogravures*, and a *Portrait* newly etched from a life-like Daguerreotype of the Author. In Four Volumes, crown 8vo.

Weird Tales, by E. T. W. Hoffmann,

A NEW TRANSLATION FROM THE GERMAN.

With Biographical Memoir, by J. T. BEALBY, formerly Scholar of Corpus Christi College, Cambridge.

With Portrait and Ten Original Etchings, by AD. LALAUZE, in Two Volumes, crown 8vo.

NOTE.—The type is distributed as the edition is printed, the impression of which is one thousand copies crown 8vo, and one hundred and fifty each large fine paper copies, with Etchings on Japanese and Whatman paper.

SOME OPINIONS OF THE PRESS.

Saturday Review.

"A very handsome edition, in four volumes, of the Tales and Poems of Edgar Allan Poe. The edition is remarkable for containing the fragment called 'The Journal of Julius Rodman,' hitherto unpublished in any collection. Furthermore, it should be stated that in the new edition the works are, for the first time, intelligibly classified."

Athenæum.

"Mr. Ingram is so well known for his great knowledge of Poe, and the services he has rendered to the poet's fame, that there is little need to dwell at length on this handsome and convenient edition which he has edited for Mr. Nimmo. The tales have been classified; the poems have been chronologically arranged as they should be; the text has been corrected and revised. Both publisher and editor may be congratulated on this edition."

Notes and Queries.

"This new edition puts forward strong claims upon recognition. It is, in the first place, the most attractive collection that has yet appeared, the etchings with which it is accompanied giving it precedence over any other edition. Mr. Ingram's biographical essay is remarkable in the respect that it gives a concise, a readable, and an animated account of Poe's career."

---

14 King William Street, Strand, London, W.C.

OPINIONS OF THE PRESS—continued.

Daily Telegraph.

"The volumes before us are unquestionably the fullest and best arranged edition of Poe's writings as yet given to the world; in fact, it is the only one in which any serious attempt is made to classify the prose tales, those of Imagination being assigned to one volume and those of Humour to another, the Miscellaneous Stories and the Poems filling the third and fourth."

Pall Mall Gazette.

"Mr. John H. Ingram is well known to be a specialist on the subject of Edgar Allan Poe, himself the most insoluble of the many problems with which he mystified the world. The etchings and photogravures are most appropriate. There is something entirely harmonious with the manner of Poe in the weird Rembrandtesque effects attainable by these processes, and the artists have entered thoroughly into the spirit of their task."

Whitehall Review.

"In the empire of fantasy Hoffmann is undisputed autocrat. Indeed, that empire is itself strangely limited, and contains not only few possible rivals and peers, but very few subjects. We can easily count on the fingers of our two hands all the names that can with any show of reason be mentioned in connection with that of Hoffmann's in the part of the continent of romance where he has built his kingdom. Next and nearest to Hoffmann comes his wild American brother, Edgar Allan Poe, kinsman in mind, kinsman in riot, kinsman in melancholy death. What Mr. Bealby has done he has done well, and as his book is beautifully printed and illustrated with some delightful etchings by Lalauze, it will be a welcome friend on the shelves of the few who have long known and loved Hoffmann, and of the many who must love him if they will give themselves the pleasure of reading these ten intoxicatingly attractive stories."

British Medical Journal.

"A new translation from the German, in two volumes, with ten original etchings by Ad. Lalauze. These tales, to many to whom they will now become known for the first time, will have a charm which they largely possess in the original, and of which they have lost little by being translated into another tongue."

Bookseller.

"An acceptable service has been rendered to students of German literature by presenting, in a handsome and compact form, the volume of the stories by Ernst Theodor Wilhelm Hoffmann, a striking figure in the most attractive period of German imaginative literature. The stories are in themselves very attractive, and would have made a reputation for a less gifted author; but Hoffmann always appeared to be capable of greater achievements, which he never realised. Carlyle said of him, 'There are the materials of a glorious poet, but no poet has been fashioned out of them.' Imagination he unquestionably possessed, fancy was still more conspicuous, and he possessed a strange, weird faculty of relating incidents which appear to have been conceived in dreams, exercising an influence over the reader which it is difficult to account for on ordinary principles of criticism. Mr. Bealby's biographical memoir is well written, and his estimate of Hoffmann's powers appear to be able and impartial. Eleven stories are included in this collection, and, besides a portrait of the author, eleven exquisite etchings by Lalauze—little gems of art."

The Characters of Jean de La Bruyère.
NEWLY RENDERED INTO ENGLISH.
With an Introduction, Biographical Memoir, and Copious Notes,
By HENRI VAN LAUN.
With Seven Etched Portraits by B. DAMMAN, and Seventeen Vignettes etched by V. FOULQUIER, and printed on China paper.

8vo, half-parchment, gilt top, 42s.

NOTE.—Three hundred copies printed, and each numbered. Type distributed.

Athenæum.
"If either the living M. Van Laun or the dead M. de La Bruyère is dissatisfied with the care and expense which the publisher has apparently devoted to the equipping of the *Characters of Jean de La Bruyère*, translated by Henri Van Laun, all we can say is that there is a very unreasonable translator in this world or a very unreasonable author in the other. Almost all the details of the book's production deserve praise."

Saturday Review.
"M. Van Laun's translation of the immortal *Caractères* deserves one recommendation at least, which may be given heartily and without stint or qualification. It is one of the handsomest books that have recently been issued from any English press or publishing house, tastefully bound, portly without being unwieldy, excellently printed, with well proportioned margins, and on paper of good colour, texture, and substance."

Daily Telegraph.
"This English rendering of La Bruyère should be welcome to all who study style. As M. Van Laun aptly remarks, 'perhaps no author is oftener quoted in Littré's "Dictionnaire de la Langue Française" than is La Bruyère.' The present edition is adorned with many etched portraits and vignettes."

Scotsman.
"La Bruyère was one of those men who have risen from time to time in France, and who, in the midst of comparatively frivolous surroundings, wrote down high and useful thoughts. The book is a repertory of wit and wisdom. It has furnished many an orator with suggestions; it is a mine from which many of the philosophers of these later days have drawn what seem to have been some of their happiest inspirations, and in its present form it will do much to foster thought and enlarge the sphere of the reader's knowledge."

Notes and Queries.
"To see M. Van Laun's English at its best, the chapter on opinions should be read. The short, crisp, epigrammatic sentences of this are reproduced in English with singular spirit and fidelity. To say that this is the best translation of La Bruyère is little. . . . He has, besides, enriched his edition with a series of admirable notes. A chief attraction of the volume has yet to be mentioned. Six portraits specially etched by M. Damman, a series of lovely headpieces etched by M. Foulquier, and a portrait of La Bruyère by the same artist, render the book one of the most sumptuous issued from the English press."

Pall Mall Gazette.
"Handsome even among the handsome books which the last few years have seen issuing in much greater numbers from the English press than at any time during the present century. The merit of this version and the remarkable beauty of the book ought pretty speedily to exhaust the limited edition which has, we understand, been printed, and which, according to a practice agreeable to collectors, if not to lovers of literature, the publisher binds himself not to reprint."

Carols and Poems

FROM THE FIFTEENTH CENTURY TO THE PRESENT TIME.

Edited by A. H. BULLEN.

With Seven Illustrations newly designed by HENRY G. WELLS.

Post 8vo, full parchment, gilt top, price 10s. 6d.

NOTE.—One hundred and twenty copies printed on fine medium 8vo paper, with the illustrations on Japanese paper. Each copy numbered.

Saturday Review.

"Since the publication of Mr. Sandys's collection there have been many books issued on carols; but the most complete by far that we have met with is Mr. Bullen's new volume, 'Carols and Poems from the Fifteenth Century to the Present Time.' The preface contains an interesting account of Christmas festivities and the use of carols. Mr. Bullen has exercised great care in verifying and correcting the collections of his predecessors, and he has joined to them two modern poems by Hawker, two by Mr. William Morris, and others by Mr. Swinburne, Mr. Symonds, and Miss Rossetti. No one has been more successful than Mr. Morris in imitating the ancient carol:—

> 'Outlanders, whence come ye last?
> The snow in the street and the wind on the door.
> Through what green sea and great have ye past?
> Minstrels and maids stand forth on the floor.'

Altogether this is one of the most welcome books of the season."

Spectator.

"Mr. Bullen divides his 'Carols and Poems from the Fifteenth Century to the Present Time' into three parts, 'Christmas Chants and Carols,' 'Carmina Sacra,' and 'Christmas Customs and Christmas Cheer.' These make up together between seventy and eighty poems of one kind and another. The selection has been carefully made from a wide range of authors. Indeed, it is curious to see the very mixed company which the subject of Christmas has brought together—as, indeed, it is quite right that it should. Altogether, the result is a very interesting book."

Morning Post.

"Good Christian people all, and more especially those of artistic or poetic inclinations, will feel indebted to the editor and publisher of this fascinating volume, which, bound as it is in white parchment vellum, ornamented with sprigs of holly, may fairly claim to be considered *par excellence* the gift book of the season. 'Carols and Poems' are supplemented by voluminous and interesting notes by the editor, who also contributes some very graceful dedicatory verses."

Notes and Queries.

"Mr. Bullen does not indeed pretend to cater for those who regard carols from a purely antiquarian point of view. His book is intended to be popular rather than scholarly. Scholarly none the less it is, and representative also, including as it does every form of Christmas strain, from early mysteries down to poems so modern as not previously to have seen the light."

14 King William Street, Strand, London, W.C.

Egyptian Obelisks.

By HENRY H. GORRINGE.

With Fifty full-page Illustrations, Thirty-one Artotypes, Eighteen Engravings, and One Chromo-lithograph.

Royal 4to, cloth elegant, price 42s.

NOTE.—This work is devoted to what may be termed the recent records of those striking monuments of history, minute particulars of the difficulties which have been experienced in the transportation of many across the high seas, and the engineering operations by which these have been overcome.

The Times.

"There is really more stirring incident in the book than in many a popular sensational novel, though much of the technical matter may be only of value to experts and engineers. But every one ought to be interested in the ingenious speculations as to the means by which the ancient Egyptians manipulated and moved the ponderous masses of stone, which may endure while the world remains as colossal monuments of their achievements."

Building and Engineering Times.

"The American engineer, pardonably enough, gives the foremost place to his own work, and we have illustrations of the mode in which he cased the obelisk after possession was given to him, how he lowered and finally conveyed it and its pedestal to New York, and there re-erected it. On taking it down it was found by an inscription on the 'crabs' which supported it that it was erected by Pontius, an architect, in the reign of Augustus Cæsar (circa 22 B.C.), and its size and weight are about the same as the obelisk on the Thames Embankment, weighing about 448,000 lbs., 69 ft. high, and 7 ft. 9 in. square at base. The greatest known obelisk erected is that of the Lateran, which weighs 1,020,000 lbs., and is as 104 to 64 in height to the obelisk on the Thames Embankment. In the quarry at Syene there is one less in height but greater in bulk, whose estimated weight is no less than 1,540,000 lbs. The smallest recorded is one at Lepsius, which only weighs some 200 lbs. Thus we have them of all sizes and weights. . . . Of the inscriptions and their purport we need here say nothing, but refer the curious to the valuable contribution to our knowledge on the subject which we owe to Lieut.-Commander Gorringe, whose handsome volume is profusely and elegantly illustrated."

Daily Telegraph.

"Lieutenant-Commander Henry Gorringe has contrived to make a volume which holds some curious matter likely to amuse the general reader, besides carrying out the primal and technical objects of the work. There is a chapter on Egyptian obelisks in general, and notes on the ancient methods of quarrying, transporting, &c., while forty full-page illustrations and numerous 'artotypes' add to the usefulness of the book."

NEW WORK by **GEORGE W. CABLE,** Author of "Old Creole Days,"
"The Grandissimes," &c.

The Creoles of Louisiana.

With Fifty Full-page Illustrations.

Square 8vo, cloth, gilt top, price 10s. 6d.

Daily News.

"Mr. Cable's account of the Creoles and history of Louisiana are curious in
themselves and full of picturesque interest. Necessarily the story centres in
the capital of the province, which, together with its environs, furnishes a
considerable proportion of the subjects of Mr. Pennell's charming pictures.
The story of the battle of New Orleans, when the British forces were so dis-
astrously, though not ingloriously, defeated under the Duke of Wellington's
brother-in-law, Pakenham, by General Jackson, is told with spirit in a narrative
which the reader will find it interesting to compare with the accounts by
English authorities."

Daily Telegraph.

"Written with a purity which is itself indicative of ancestral or patriotic
pride, this book is full of interest, and its many illustrations of the picturesque
old city, which looks as though it had been transported bodily from Southern
Europe, increase the value of the text."

St. James's Gazette.

"This book recalls the period when France bid fair to be a greater colonial
power than England, when her settlements in America were apparently more
flourishing than ours, and when in India her influence was greater. No man
is more competent than Mr. Cable for the work he has here undertaken. He
knows his subject thoroughly—the land and the people alike; while as a
writer he belongs to the elect, who are 'born, not made.' His work is one of
great interest and lasting value."

Scotsman.

"Mr. Cable is the poet of the Creole and of New Orleans. He has written
for the delectation, not merely of the American public, but of the whole world,
a series of stories of Creole life in New Orleans, which for tenderness and
beauty are nowhere surpassed. . . . It is a book in which there is much of
historical value told by one who loves his subject, and who has always some
touch of tenderness with which to light up the dark passages. . . . . There is
lucidity in every sentence."

Manchester Examiner.

"Mr. Cable is now an authority about Creoles, and he provides us with a
definition which effectually shuts out all idea of negro blood; he calls them
"the French-speaking native portion of the ruling class" in Louisiana, and
they do not extend much beyond the city of New Orleans. The very beautiful
volume before us is really a history of the short but chequered life of this city,
from its French foundation to the present time. History does much to make
a city picturesque, and the picturesque look which New Orleans has more than
any other American city is not a little owing to the time when French and
Spanish banners waved over her. The book contains some charming illustrations."

A Wonder Book for Girls and Boys.

By NATHANIEL HAWTHORNE.

With Thirty-six New and Original Illustrations by the eminent American Artist, FREDERIC S. CHURCH.

Royal 8vo, cloth elegant, price 10s. 6d.

Extract from the Author's Preface.

" In performing this pleasant task—for it has been really a task fit for hot weather, and one of the most agreeable, of a literary kind, which he ever undertook—the author has not always thought it necessary to write downward in order to meet the comprehension of children. He has generally suffered the theme to soar, whenever such was its tendency, and when he himself was buoyant enough to follow without an effort. Children possess an unestimated sensibility to whatever is deep or high in imagination or feeling, so long as it is simple likewise. It is only the artificial and the complex that bewilder them."

Magazine of Art.

" The new edition of Hawthorne's delightful ' Wonder Book,' which has just been issued by Mr. Nimmo, should be one of the books of the season. Hawthorne retold the old stories—' King Midas,' the ' Quest of the Golden Apples,' the ' Slaying of the Gorgon,' and all the rest of them—so beautifully and well, that his work is even now as full of life and charm as it was when it was first given to the world."

The Graphic.

" Perhaps English boys and girls are not over-familiar with Nathaniel Hawthorne's delightful rendering of classic myths, so that the present handsome edition of a ' Wonder Book ' will form an acceptable gift. Mr. Church's engravings are cleverly drawn, and as imaginative as the legends they illustrate."

Daily Telegraph.

" It is now almost thirty-five years since the author of ' The Scarlet Letter ' and ' The House with the Seven Gables ' offered his re-readings of classical myths to a rising generation which has since risen, and is giving place to younger comers. By the very indestructibility of these immortal fables, they are legitimate subjects, as the author pleads, ' for every age to clothe with its own garniture of manners and sentiment, and to imbue with its own morality.' "

Literary World.

" The present edition of the ' Wonder Book ' is probably the handsomest form in which it has ever appeared. It is beautifully illustrated with thirty-six new original drawings by an eminent artist, and has further the attractions of fine paper and printing and handsome binding. In its new dress it ought to find many new friends, and revisit many of the old ones too."

Illustrated London News.

" Nathaniel Hawthorne, prince of American story-tellers, wrote a ' Wonder Book for Girls and Boys,' consisting of six fine old legends of classical origin, or of still remoter antiquity, which he interfused with Gothic or German sentiment, and made them attractive to modern youthful minds, and not yet worn out by two or three thousand years' popularity among different nations."

14 King William Street, Strand, London, W.C.

A VERY FUNNY ILLUSTRATED HUMOROUS BOOK.

Stuff and Nonsense.

By A. B. FROST,

The Illustrator of Carroll's " Rhyme and Reason."

Small 4to, illustrated boards, price 6s.

Mr. Frost has made a wonderfully amusing and clever book. There are in all more than one hundred pictures, many with droll verses and ludicrous jingles. Others are unaccompanied by any text, for no one knows better than Mr. Frost how to tell a funny story, in the funniest way, with his artist's pencil.

Standard.

"This is a book which will please equally people of all ages. The illustrations are not only extremely funny, but they are drawn with wonderful artistic ability, and are full of life and action.
"It is far and away the best book of 'Stuff and Nonsense' which has appeared for a long time."

Times.

" It is a most grotesque medley of mad ideas, carried out nevertheless with a certain regard to consistency, if not to probability."

Figaro.

"The verses and jingles which accompany some of the illustrations are excellent fooling, but Mr. Frost is also able to tell a ludicrous story with his pencil only."

Press.

"The most facetious bit of wit that has been penned for many a day, both in design and text, is Mr. A. B. Frost's 'Stuff and Nonsense.' 'A Tale of a Cat' is funny, 'The Balloonists' is perhaps rather extravagant, but nothing can outdo the wit of 'The Powers of the Human Eye,' whilst 'Ye Æsthete, ye Boy, and ye Bullfrog' may be described as a 'roarer.' Mr. Frost's pen and pencil know how to chronicle fun, and their outcomes should not be overlooked."

Graphic.

"Grotesque in the extreme. His jokes will rouse many a laugh."

Daily News.

"There is really a marvellous abundance of fun in this volume of a harmless kind."

Athenæum.

" Clever sketches of grotesque incidents."

Literary World.

"A hundred and twenty excruciatingly funny sketches."

14 King William Street, Strand, London, W.C.

The History of England,

FROM THE FIRST INVASION BY THE ROMANS TO THE ACCESSION OF WILLIAM AND MARY IN 1688.

By JOHN LINGARD, D.D.

Copyright Edition, with Ten Etched Portraits. In Ten Vols. demy 8vo, cloth, £5, 5s.

This New Copyright Library Edition of "Lingard's History of England," besides containing all the latest notes and emendations of the Author, with Memoir, is enriched with Ten Portraits, newly etched by Damman, of the following personages, viz. : — Dr. Lingard, Edward I., Edward III., Cardinal Wolsey, Cardinal Pole, Elizabeth, James I., Cromwell, Charles II., James II.

The Times.

" No greater service can be rendered to literature than the republication, in a handsome and attractive form, of works which time and the continued approbation of the world have made classical. . . . The accuracy of Lingard's statements on many points of controversy, as well as the genial sobriety of his view, is now recognised."

The Tablet.

" It is with the greatest satisfaction that we welcome this new edition of Dr. Lingard's ' History of England.' It has long been a desideratum. . . . No general history of England has appeared which can at all supply the place of Lingard, whose painstaking industry and careful research have dispelled many a popular delusion, whose candour always carries his reader with him, and whose clear and even style is never fatiguing."

The Spectator.

" We are glad to see that the demand for Dr. Lingard's *England* still continues. Few histories give the reader the same impression of exhaustive study. This new edition is excellently printed, and illustrated with ten portraits of the greatest personages in our history."

Dublin Review.

" It is pleasant to notice that the demand for Lingard continues to be such that publishers venture on a well got-up library edition like the one before us. More than sixty years have gone since the first volume of the first edition was published ; many equally pretentious histories have appeared during that space, and have more or less disappeared since, yet Lingard lives—is still a recognised and respected authority."

The Scotsman.

" There is no need, at this time of day, to say anything in vindication of the importance, as a standard work, of Dr. Lingard's ' History of England.' . . . Its intrinsic merits are very great. The style is lucid, pointed, and puts no strain upon the reader ; and the printer and publisher have neglected nothing that could make this—what it is likely long to remain—the standard edition of a work of great historical and literary value."

Daily Telegraph.

" True learning, untiring research, a philosophic temper, and the possession of a graphic, pleasing style, were the qualities which the author brought to his task, and they are displayed in every chapter of his history."

Weekly Register.

" In the full force of the word a scholarly book. Lingard's History is destined to bear a part of growing importance in English education."

Manchester Examiner.

" He stands alone in his own school ; he is the only representative of his own phase of thought. The critical reader will do well to compare him with those who went before and those who came after him."

Imaginary Conversations.

By WALTER SAVAGE LANDOR.

In Five Vols. crown 8vo, cloth, 30s.

FIRST SERIES—CLASSICAL DIALOGUES, GREEK AND ROMAN.
SECOND SERIES—DIALOGUES OF SOVEREIGNS AND STATESMEN.
THIRD SERIES—DIALOGUES OF LITERARY MEN.
FOURTH SERIES—DIALOGUES OF FAMOUS WOMEN.
FIFTH SERIES—MISCELLANEOUS DIALOGUES.

NOTE.—*This New Edition is printed from the last Edition of his Works, revised and edited by John Forster, and is published by arrangement with the Proprietors of the Copyright of Walter Savage Landor's Works.*

The Times.

"The abiding character of the interest excited by the writings of Walter Savage Landor, and the existence of a numerous band of votaries at the shrine of his refined genius, have been lately evidenced by the appearance of the most remarkable of Landor's productions, his 'Imaginary Conversations,' taken from the last edition of his works. To have them in a separate publication will be convenient to a great number of readers."

The Athenæum.

"The appearance of this tasteful reprint would seem to indicate that the present generation is at last waking up to the fact that it has neglected a great writer, and if so, it is well to begin with Landor's most adequate work. It is difficult to overpraise the 'Imaginary Conversations.' The eulogiums bestowed on the 'Conversations' by Emerson will, it is to be hoped, lead many to buy this book."

Scotsman.

"An excellent service has been done to the reading public by presenting to it, in five compact volumes, these 'Conversations.' Admirably printed on good paper, the volumes are handy in shape, and indeed the edition is all that could be desired. When this has been said, it will be understood what a boon has been conferred on the reading public; and it should enable many comparatively poor men to enrich their libraries with a work that will have an enduring interest."

Literary World.

"That the 'Imaginary Conversations' of Walter Savage Landor are not better known is no doubt largely due to their inaccessibility to most readers, by reason of their cost. This new issue, while handsome enough to find a place in the best of libraries, is not beyond the reach of the ordinary bookbuyer."

Edinburgh Review.

"How rich in scholarship! how correct, concise, and pure in style! how full of imagination, wit, and humour! how well informed, how bold in speculation, how various in interest, how universal in sympathy! In these dialogues —making allowance for every shortcoming or excess—the most familiar and the most august shapes of the past are reanimated with vigour, grace, and beauty. We are in the high and goodly company of wits and men of letters; of churchmen, lawyers, and statesmen; of party-men, soldiers, and kings; of the most tender, delicate, and noble women; and of figures that seem this instant to have left for us the Agora or the Schools of Athens, the Forum or the Senate of Rome."

The Fables of La Fontaine.

A REVISED TRANSLATION FROM THE FRENCH.

With 24 original full-page Etchings and Portrait by A. DELIERRE.

Super royal 8vo, half parchment elegant, gilt top, 31s. 6d.

NOTE.—*500 copies printed. Type distributed.*

Athenæum.

" Mr. Nimmo has issued ' The Fables of La Fontaine,' with etchings by A. Delierre, who has designed and drawn them in a manner which is curiously in keeping with the date, and even with the taste, of La Fontaine. They are neatly delineated and prettily composed."

Bookseller.

" We are tempted to linger over these beautiful etchings ; and how gratified will be the fortunate recipients of such a book, elegant as it is in style and workmanship, and embellished with drawings of the highest merit."

Spectator.

" This translation has the recommendation of being sufficiently easy and readable. The merits of the etchings with which it is illustrated are evident."

Art Journal.

" An admirable translation, founded on that of Robert Thompson ; and the etchings which lighten this present edition are very good."

Daily News.

" The force and breadth of M. Delierre's etchings contrast favourably with the pretty feebleness which is apt to characterise the efforts of the etcher's needle when employed on book illustrations. The elegant simplicity of the vellum back and grey-green covers, with their decorative ornaments, is very pleasing to the eye."

Harper's Monthly.

" The happy rendering of the quaint and piquant fables, and the perfection with which the printer and binder have done their work, make the volume everything that could be desired."

Daily Telegraph.

" This beautiful edition of ' The Fables of La Fontaine,' which now appears in a form that is highly creditable to the publisher as well as to the printer, is enriched with etchings by Delierre, which are admirable alike for quality and appropriateness."

Westminster Review.

" A splendid edition of ' The Fables of La Fontaine,' with twenty-five original etchings by Delierre. Of these we cannot speak too highly, and select for special commendation the portrait of La Fontaine, the Heron, the Peacock, and the Ducks and Tortoise."

14 King William Street, Strand, London, W.C.

The Fan.
By OCTAVE UZANNE.
ILLUSTRATIONS BY PAUL AVRIL.
Royal 8vo, cloth, gilt top, 31s. 6d.

The Sunshade, Muff, and Glove.
By OCTAVE UZANNE.
ILLUSTRATIONS BY PAUL AVRIL.
Royal 8vo, cloth, gilt top, 31s. 6d.

NOTE.—*The above are English Editions of the unique and artistic works " L'Eventail" and " L'Ombrelle," recently published in Paris, and now difficult to be procured, as no new Edition is to be produced. 500 copies only are printed.*

Saturday Review.
"An English counterpart of the well-known French books by Octave Uzanne, with Paul Avril's charming illustrations."

Standard.
"It gives a complete history of fans of all ages and places ; the illustrations are dainty in the extreme. Those who wish to make a pretty and appropriate present to a young lady cannot do better than purchase ' The Fan.'"

Athenæum.
"The letterpress comprises much amusing 'chit-chat,' and is more solid than it pretends to be. This *brochure* is worth reading ; nay, it is worth keeping."

Art Journal.
"At first sight it would seem that material could never be found to fill even a volume; but the author, in dealing with his first subject alone, 'The Sunshade,' says he could easily have filled a dozen volumes of this emblem of sovereignty. The work is delightfully illustrated in a novel manner by Paul Avril, the pictures which meander about the work being printed in varied colours."

Daily News.
"The pretty adornments of the margin of these artistic volumes, the numerous ornamental designs, and the pleasant vein of the author's running commentary, render these the most attractive monographs ever published on a theme which interests so many enthusiastic collectors."

Glasgow Herald.
"' I have but collected a heap of foreign flowers, and brought of my own only the string which binds them together,' is the fitting quotation with which M. Uzanne closes the preface to his volume on woman's ornaments. The monograph on the sunshade, called by the author 'a little tumbled fantasy,' occupies fully one-half of the volume. It begins with a pleasant invented mythology of the parasol; glances at the sunshade in all countries and times ; mentions many famous umbrellas ; quotes a number of clever sayings. . . . To these remarks on the spirit of the book it is necessary to add that the body of it is a dainty marvel of paper, type, and binding ; and that what meaning it has looks out on the reader through a hundred argus-eyes of many-tinted photogravures, exquisitely designed by M. Paul Avril."

Westminster Review.
"The most striking merit of the book is the entire appropriateness both of the letterpress and illustrations to the subject treated. M. Uzanne's style has all the airy grace and sparkling brilliancy of the *petit instrument* whose praise he celebrates ; and M. Avril's drawings seem to conduct us into an enchanted world where everything but fans are forgotten."

A Handbook of Gastronomy

(BRILLAT-SAVARIN's " Physiologie du Goût").

New and Complete Translation, with 52 original Etchings by
A. LALAUZE.

Printed on China Paper.

8vo, half parchment, gilt top, 42s.

NOTE.—*300 copies printed, and each numbered.   Type distributed.*
(*Out of print.*)

The Times.

"The translator's notes are interesting and scholarly ; and M. Lalauze's
etchings are so prettily executed, that they form quite an attractive gallery of
bijou pictures."

The Athenæum.

"A *new* and *complete* translation of Brillat-Savarin's 'Physiologie du Goût,'
former editions of this piquant work being more or less incomplete.   The translation is lively, clear, and practically exact.   No man who likes his dinner ought
to dine without having read this book at least once.   The vignettes and *culs-
de-lampe* are charming, and the only cause for regret is that fifty-two is not half
so many as we could have welcomed."

Daily Telegraph.

"A numbered edition of the 'Physiologie du Goût,' translated afresh into
English, and illustrated with upwards of fifty Etchings by Lalauze.   It is a
volume for connoisseurs."

The Saturday Review.

"The translation is a decidedly good one.   The paper is splendid, and
taken as a whole the work has been well done.   Therefore we would say, read
'A Handbook of Gastronomy,' and as Brillat-Savarin himself would put it,
'You will see something wonderful.'"

Scotsman.

"The excellence of this volume depends not only upon the goodness of the
translation of Savarin's book—it is all that could be desired—but upon the
general beauty of its get up, and its illustrations by Lalauze."

Illustrated London News.

"One of the most sumptuous books of the season is the 'Handbook of
Gastronomy,' being a new translation of Brillat-Savarin's 'Physiologie du
Goût.'   The English translation has been executed with the minutest care and
the most thorough appreciativeness.   Among its charms, with its handsome
paper, uncut edges, and 'river of type running through a meadow of margin,'
are the fifty-two exquisite illustrative etchings by A. Lalauze, printed on China
paper in the text."

Glasgow Herald.

"In every respect a dainty volume, and replete with excellent matter
throughout."

14 King William Street, Strand, London, W.C.

Imperial 8vo, fine paper.

The Complete Angler;

OR, THE CONTEMPLATIVE MAN'S RECREATION OF IZAAK WALTON AND CHARLES COTTON.

Edited by JOHN MAJOR.

This Extra-illustrated Edition of THE COMPLETE ANGLER is specially designed for Collectors of this famous work ; and in order to enable them either to take from or add to the Illustrations, it will simply be issued unbound, but folded and collated.

The Illustrations consist of **Fifty Steel Plates**, designed by T. STOT-HARD, R.A., JAMES INSKIP, EDWARD HASSELL, DELAMOTTE, BINKEN-BOOM, W. HIXON, SIR FRANCIS SYKES, Bart., PINE, &c. &c., and engraved by well-known Engravers. Also **Six Original Etchings and Two Portraits**, as well as **Seventy-four Engravings on Wood** by various Eminent Artists.

To this is added a PRACTICAL TREATISE on FLIES and FLY HOOKS, by the late JOHN JACKSON, of Tanfield Mill, with **Ten Steel Plates**, coloured, representing 120 Flies, natural and artificial.

One Hundred and Twenty copies only are printed, each of which is numbered.

A HANDSOME LARGE FINE PAPER EDITION OF

The Works of William Hickling Prescott.

In 15 Volumes 8vo, cloth (not sold separately), 25s. per vol.

With 30 Portraits printed on India paper.

Athenæum.

"In point of style Prescott ranks with the ablest English historians, and paragraphs may be found in his volumes in which the grace and elegance of Addison are combined with Robertson's majestic cadence and Gibbon's brilliancy."

J. Lothrop Motley.

"Wherever the English language is spoken over the whole earth his name is perfectly familiar. We all of us know what his place was in America. But I can also say that in eight years (1851-59) passed abroad I never met a single educated person of whatever nation that was not acquainted with his fame, and hardly one who had not read his works. No living American name is so widely spread over the whole world."

Types from Spanish Story;

OR,

THE OLD MANNERS AND CUSTOMS OF CASTILE.

By JAMES MEW.

With 36 Proof Etchings on Japanese paper by R. DE LOS RIOS.

Super royal 8vo, elegant and *recherché* Binding after the
18th Century, 31s. 6d.

The Times.

" It was a happy thought that of illustrating the most famous Spanish or Franco-Spanish romances with this blending of the real, the quaint, and the fantastic. The volume is a worthy key and companion to the most entertaining books of the witty authors who sprinkled their pages with the ' Spanish salt ' that Richard Ford appreciated so thoroughly."

Daily Telegraph.

" Mr. James Mew displays both scholarship and geniality in his critical analyses of romances, and has invested them collectively with an additional interest. The etchings of Senor de los Rios enrich the book in such a manner as to make it a picture-gallery in boards. Indeed the cover itself is like the exterior of a graceful edifice, designed as a storehouse of art."

Athenæum.

" The etchings have considerable spirit, richness of handling, tone, and other picturesque qualities."

Glasgow Herald.

" The illustrative story essays have been selected chiefly from books which may be taken to represent the classic literature of romance in Spain. The idea is a good one, and has been industriously worked out, the result being the present handsome volume."

Standard.

" The etchings are charming alike in drawing and execution, and afford an admirable illustration of manners and customs in Spain in the days of Don Quixote. The printing and get up are worthy of the illustrations."

Scotsman.

" It is a volume which ought to be greatly prized because of its illustrations. It is in all respects handsome."

Publishers' Circular.

" A right grateful book to take up from a drawing-room table for half an hour. Its chapters equal in number its illustrations, each of which is a genuine piece of art work. The binding is a choice and appropriate bit of colouring."

Old English Romances.

Illustrated with Etchings.

In 12 Vols. crown 8vo, parchment boards or cloth, 7s. 6d. per vol.

NOTE.—A few copies printed on large fine white paper, with etchings on Japanese and Whatman paper. (*Out of print.*)

THE LIFE AND OPINIONS OF TRISTRAM SHANDY,
GENTLEMAN. By LAURENCE STERNE. In Two Vols. With Eight Etchings by DAMMAN from Original Drawings by HARRY FURNISS.

THE OLD ENGLISH BARON : A GOTHIC STORY. By CLARA REEVE.

ALSO

THE CASTLE OF OTRANTO : A GOTHIC STORY. By HORACE WALPOLE. In One Vol. With Two Portraits and Four Original Drawings by A. H. TOURRIER, Etched by DAMMAN.

THE ARABIAN NIGHTS ENTERTAINMENTS. In Four Vols. Carefully Revised and Corrected from the Arabic by JONATHAN SCOTT, I.L.D., Oxford. With Nineteen Original Etchings by AD. LALAUZE.

THE HISTORY OF THE CALIPH VATHEK. By WM. BECKFORD. With Notes, Critical and Explanatory.

ALSO

RASSELAS, PRINCE OF ABYSSINIA. By SAMUEL JOHNSON. In One Vol. With Portrait of BECKFORD, and Four Original Etchings, designed by A. H. TOURRIER, and Etched by DAMMAN.

ROBINSON CRUSOE. By DANIEL DEFOE. In Two Vols. With Biographical Memoir, Illustrative Notes, and Eight Etchings by M. MOUILLERON, and Portrait by L. FLAMENG.

GULLIVER'S TRAVELS. By JONATHAN SWIFT. With Five Etchings and Portrait by AD. LALAUZE.

A SENTIMENTAL JOURNEY. By LAURENCE STERNE.

ALSO

A TALE OF A TUB. By JONATHAN SWIFT. In One Vol. With Five Etchings and Portrait by ED. HEDOUIN.

The Times.

"Among the numerous handsome reprints which the publishers of the day vie with each other in producing, we have seen nothing of greater merit than this series of twelve volumes. Those who have read these masterpieces of the last century in the homely garb of the old editions may be gratified with the opportunity of perusing them with the advantages of large clear print and illustrations of a quality which is rarely bestowed on such re-issues. The series deserves every commendation."

Athenæum.

"A well-printed and tasteful issue of the 'Thousand and One Nights. The volumes are convenient in size, and illustrated with Lalauze's well-known etchings."

Magazine of Art.

"The text of the new four-volume edition of the 'Thousand and One Nights' just issued by Mr. Nimmo is that revised by Jonathan Scott, from the French of Galland ; it presents the essentials of these wonderful stories with irresistible authority and directness, and, as mere reading, it is as satisfactory as ever. The edition, which is limited to a thousand copies, is beautifully printed and remarkably well produced. It is illustrated with twenty etchings by Lalauze. . . . In another volume of this series Beckford's wild and gloomy 'Vathek' appears side by side with Johnson's admirable 'Rasselas.'"

Glasgow Herald.

"The merits of this new issue lie in exquisite clearness of type ; completeness: notes and biographical notices, short and pithy ; and a number of very fine etchings and portraits. In the 'Robinson Crusoe,' besides the well-known portrait of Defoe by Flameng, there are eight exceedingly beautiful etchings by Mouilleron . . . . In fine keeping with the other volumes of the series, uniform in style and illustrations, and as one of the volumes of his famous Old English Romances, Mr. Nimmo has also issued the 'Rasselas' of Johnson and the 'Vathek' of Beckford."

Westminster Review.

"Mr. Nimmo has added to his excellent series of 'Old English Romances three new volumes, of which two are devoted to 'Tristram Shandy,' while the third contains 'The Old English Baron' and 'The Castle of Otranto.' Take them as they stand, and without attributing to them any qualities but what they really possess, the whole series was well worth reprinting in the elegant and attractive form in which they are now presented to us."

Essays from the "North American Review."

Edited by ALLEN THORNDIKE RICE.

Demy 8vo, cloth, 7s. 6d.

Saturday Review.

"A collection of interesting essays from the *North American Review*, beginning with a criticism on the works of Walter Scott, and ending with papers written by Mr. Lowell and Mr. O. W. Holmes. The variety of the essays is noteworthy."

♱ld Spanish Romances.

Illustrated with Etchings.

In 12 Vols. crown 8vo, parchment boards or cloth, 7s. 6d. per vol.

NOTE.—A few copies printed on large fine paper with etchings
on Japanese and Whatman paper. (*Out of print.*)

THE HISTORY OF DON QUIXOTE DE LA MANCHA.
Translated from the Spanish of MIGUEL DE CERVANTES SAAVEDRA
by MOTTEUX. With copious Notes (including the Spanish Ballads),
and an Essay on the Life and Writings of CERVANTES by JOHN G.
LOCKHART. Preceded by a Short Notice of the Life and Works of
PETER ANTHONY MOTTEUX by HENRI VAN LAUN. Illustrated
with Sixteen Original Etchings by R. DE LOS RIOS. Four Volumes.

LAZARILLO DE TORMES. By Don DIEGO MENDOZA. Trans-
lated by THOMAS ROSCOE. And GUZMAN D'ALFARACHE.
By MATEO ALEMAN. Translated by BRADY. Illustrated with Eight
Original Etchings by R. DE LOS RIOS. Two Volumes.

ASMODEUS. By LE SAGE. Translated from the French. Illus-
trated with Four Original Etchings by R. DE LOS RIOS.

THE BACHELOR OF SALAMANCA. By LE SAGE. Trans-
lated from the French by JAMES TOWNSEND. Illustrated with Four
Original Etchings by R. DE LOS RIOS.

VANILLO GONZALES; or, The Merry Bachelor. By LE SAGE.
Translated from the French. Illustrated with Four Original Etchings
by R. DE LOS RIOS.

THE ADVENTURES OF GIL BLAS OF SANTILLANE.
Translated from the French of LE SAGE by TOBIAS SMOLLETT.
With Biographical and Critical Notice of LE SAGE by GEORGE
SAINTSBURY. New Edition, carefully revised. Illustrated with
Twelve Original Etchings by R. DE LOS RIOS. Three Volumes.

The Times.
"This prettily printed and prettily illustrated collection of Spanish Romances
deserve their welcome from all students of seventeenth century literature."

Daily Telegraph.
"A handy and beautiful edition of the works of the Spanish masters of
romance. . . . We may say of this edition of the immortal work of Cervantes
that it is most tastefully and admirably executed, and that it is embellished
with a series of striking etchings from the pen of the Spanish artist De los
Rios."

Scotsman.
"Handy in form, they are well printed from clear type, and are got up with
much elegance; the etchings are full of humour and force. The reading
public have reason to congratulate themselves that so neat, compact, and well
arranged an edition of romances that can never die is put within their reach.
The publisher has spared no pains with them."

Saturday Review.
"Mr. Nimmo has just brought out a series of Spanish prose works in
twelve finely got-up volumes."

A Cursory History of Swearing.

By JULIAN SHARMAN.

Post 8vo, cloth, gilt top, price 7s. 6d.

" Ha ! this fellow is worse than me ; what, does he swear with pen and ink !"
THE TATLER.

Notes and Queries.

"A difficult task is accomplished with as much delicacy and taste as could well be expected. The 'History of Swearing' is, indeed, both philosophical and scholarly."

St. James' Gazette.

"Mr. Sharman has written a very interesting book on an ancient custom which is now falling into decline."

Scotsman.

"The book is one of great interest. Some curious facts are brought to light in it, and a good deal of industry on the part of Mr. Sharman is proved. The volume is admirably got up, and it is likely to take its place as one of those curious monographs which attain a high value in the book market."

The World.

"The account of 'The Scufflers' Club' is amusing, and there is much quaint lore and there are some good stories in Mr. Sharman's volume, which is, moreover, very well bound and printed—no slight advantage in a book of this class."

Bookseller.

"Throughout it is uniformly interesting and genial. There is a certain dash of kindly Bohemianism, and a broad, humanising feeling which gives a fine flavour to the book. Altogether it is both a curious and a pleasant production."

Glasgow Herald.

"To any one who cares to go into the matter, Mr. Sharman's book promises some reward, as he has there brought forward some very curious and interesting information."

Publishers' Circular.

"This quaintly but appropriately-titled volume takes us into a bypath of literary history, and from the early oath-taking, half pagan, half barbaric, down to all the modern varieties of the curse, he traces the growth and progress of the habit of using expressions which are so often sacred in their origin, although in modern parlance they have reached a secular if not a vicious platform. The appendix to the book contains some interesting documentary evidence on the matters dealt with in the preceding pages."

14 King William Street, Strand, London, W.C.

The Imitation of Christ.

FOUR BOOKS.

Translated from the Latin by Rev. W. BENHAM, B.D.,

Rector of St. Edmund, King and Martyr, Lombard Street.

With Ten Illustrations by J. P. LAURENS, etched by LEOPOLD FLAMENG.

Crown 8vo, cloth or parchment boards, 10s. 6d.

Scotsman.

"We have not seen a more beautiful edition of 'The Imitation of Christ' than this one for many a day."

Magazine of Art.

"This new edition of the 'Imitation' may fairly be regarded as a work of art. It is well and clearly printed; the paper is excellent; each page has its peculiar border, and it is illustrated with ten etchings. Further than that the translation is Mr. Benham's, we need say nothing more."

BOOK-CORNER PROTECTORS.

Metal Tips carefully prepared for placing on the Corners of Books to preserve them from injury while passing through the Post Office or being sent by Carrier.

Extract from "The Times," April 18th.

"That the publishers and booksellers second the efforts of the Post Office authorities in endeavouring to convey books without damage happening to them is evident from the tips which they use to protect the corners from injury during transit."

1s. 6d. per Gross, nett.

The American Patent Portable Book-Case.

For Students, Barristers, Home Libraries, &c.

THIS Book-case will be found to be made of very solid and durable material, and of a neat and elegant design. The shelves may be adjusted for books of any size, and will hold from 150 to 300 volumes. As it requires neither nails, screws, or glue, it may be taken to pieces in a few minutes, and reset up in another room or house, where it would be inconvenient to carry a large frame.

Full Height, 5 ft. 11½ in.; Width, 3 ft. 8 in.; Depth of Shelf, 10½ in.

Black Walnut, price £6, 6s. nett.

"The accompanying sketch illustrates a handy portable book-case of American manufacture, which Mr. NIMMO has provided. It is quite different from an ordinary article of furniture, such as upholsterers inflict upon the public, as it is designed expressly for holding the largest possible number of books in the smallest possible amount of space. One of the chief advantages which these book-cases possess is the ease with which they may be taken apart and put together again. No nails or metal screws are employed, nothing but the hand is required to dismantle or reconstruct the case. The parts fit together with mathematical precision; and, from a package of boards of very moderate dimensions, a firm and substantial book-case can be erected in the space of a few minutes. Appearances have by no means been overlooked; the panelled sides, bevelled edges, and other simple ornaments, give to the cases a very neat and tasteful look. For students, or others whose occupation may involve frequent change of residence, these book-cases will be found most handy and desirable, while, at the same time, they are so substantial, well-made, and convenient, that they will be found equally suitable for the library at home."

www.ingramcontent.com/pod-product-compliance
Lightning Source LLC
Chambersburg PA
CBHW022011110726
47901CB00006B/1479